CARNELIAN

JULES DEVITO

Inked
in gray

This book is dedicated to my son, my Coconut Prince Callum, and to my mom Judy. I love you! Thank you for always cheering me on. And to Dad, Gram, and Gramp; I miss you!

JESSE
OCTOBER 13TH

Six crows sat on a wire cawing at the sky, silhouetted by late afternoon sun. What did six crows foreshadow? It didn't matter, did it? One day soon, Jesse Westchurch would get into a bed and never leave it again, as his father had.

Dogs barked and caught tennis balls thrown by their owners, all of whom would probably still be alive by the time winter rolled around. He should have waited until he was home to check his Patient Health Record account. Any of his clients could see him here, on a bench in a dog park of all places, crying over his phone.

Tears blurred the images, and Jesse wiped his eyes on his sleeve. He was a doctor, he knew what he was looking at. With results like this, he would be looking at his patient — or rather, his patient's owner — with sympathy, and they would ask him if there were any options, or if euthanasia was the right choice. He would tell them that euthanasia wasn't the wrong choice if only suffering lay ahead.

Jesse had no such option and wouldn't take it if he did. Some fool was bound to tell him to stay hopeful, that a cure might be right around the corner, that there were clinical trials. He would stay hopeful, too. He would seek out the trials in whatever time he had left.

Trials would drain away his family's savings, all the money he and Stella had been saving to buy the practice. Stella took her role as big sister to heart; she would tell him to do it anyway, and when he was gone, she'd take care of their mom and Finn on her own. Finn at twenty-five was harder to deal with than teenage Finn, he had become so distant lately. How would Stella even begin to deal with that, on top of her grief? These questions were no longer hypothetical.

Jesse couldn't fathom being separated from his family. He couldn't be separated from the shapes the sun was making on the grass as it danced through the leaves, from the scent of the bay on the autumn breeze, or the smell of the earth. He was only 33.

His phone pinged and a notification popped up, obscuring the images of his quick-time march into the void. It was from STELLA FIVESTAR.

STELLA FIVESTAR

> Mom wants to know if you'll be home for dinner. Also Shep asked if you'll work tomorrow cause he wants to go golfing and for you to do his surgeries for him, he says it's just cats he's being a dick

He pretended for a minute that he was going home for dinner, and everything would reset. They would talk about Doctor Shepherd and how they couldn't wait until he retired, and what they would do with the practice once he was gone, how they wanted to update it. Mom would come downstairs for dinner. Finn would probably skulk out and they'd talk in serious tones about setting him down and making him tell them what was going on. These things had seemed overwhelming even yesterday.

Maybe he would ignore it all and not tell them, let it play out until it was obvious. A few more weeks of normalcy — what could it hurt? Stella's bullshit meter was set pretty low; she'd know that something was going on, but this time the truth was worse than any dark path her mind would wander.

He texted her back: *I think I'm going to stay at Jared's tonight.* Then he added the *:)* so she wouldn't think something was up. Jesse never said no when Shep asked him to work.

STELLA FIVESTAR:

> K Jessebess have a good night. Too bad, I'm gonna grab some greek I don't wanna cook long day LOL. I'll save some for u

Jesse swiped tears from his eyes.

Maybe they would name the dog park after him.

"Doctor Jesse!" A woman jogged up to him, her pug trotting beside her, unleashed. She was small, with long, brown hair in a bun, fair skin, and she wore a coat a little too warm for autumn.

Jesse scrubbed a hand over his face and strained for a smile. It took a few seconds to place her: one of Stella's clients, Marcie . . . something?

"Doctor Jesse, how are you?" she asked.

"I'm great!" *Too cheerful, too forced. Scale it back.* The pug came up to the bench and put its little paws on his legs. He scratched it behind the ears.

"Barney, get down," she said. Barney did not get down. "This dog just cost me hundreds of bucks. He will be the death of me, I swear."

"What happened?" He genuinely didn't care, but after he was gone, Stella would drag around his reputation forever.

"First thing," she said, "he starts coughin'."

I'll have to tell Mom not to waste money on a coffin. Maybe put me in one of those pods so I can become a tree. People can sit under me. I can drop my nuts on their heads.

"Turns out he'd been eating rocks," she went on. "Can you believe it?"

Or they can turn my ashes into a diamond and take turns wearing my pressurized corpse.

"That's not uncommon," he finally managed. "We've done

loads of obstruction surgeries." He would probably never do another one.

The bells from the church down the street rang out five times.

"Oh, crap," Marcie Something said, checking her phone. "I had no idea it was so late. For whom the bell tolls, right? Will you pass on our regards to Doctor Stella?"

He searched her face for any indication that she was messing with him: eyes a little too tight, smile a little too rigid? His social programming was offline; he couldn't read her, he could only stare.

He stood, startling Barney. "Yes, sorry. I'm late for a thing . . . dinner. I will send your regards to Doctor Stella, of course."

She smiled a little too long.

His heart battered at his ribs as he left the park and made his way toward his car. When he looked back, the woman and the pug were gone.

He should call Jared. They'd been seeing each other for eight months; it was probably fair to share this with him. Besides, Jesse wanted to hear another human voice. He would keep this from Stella and Mom for as long as he could, but his boyfriend should know. He dialed him, but it went to voicemail.

"Hey, Jared." He put a stop to the quivering in his voice. "Um . . . give me a call when you get a second. Are you free tonight for dinner? Okay, give me a call."

As soon as he hung up, a deeper, older urge filled him. He scrolled through his texts until he found one from three months back. He clicked it, and typed:

JESSE

Hey Lucy. I always thought there'd be time for us to bang, but I'll be dead soon so if you don't want to miss the window of opportunity, call me. I'm at the dog park that they're going to name after me.

He deleted it unsent. He couldn't do that to Jared, nor could he put Lucy on the spot like that. Immediately, another notification popped up.

> LUCY<3:
>
> Jesse, where are you?

Okay, that wasn't too strange: they did have that 'I had a feeling you were about to call' thing between them, and a way of living in each other's heads. God, could he even tell Lucy? Sixteen years of friendship. Lucy would mourn, maybe even freak out, and Jesse wasn't sure he could deal with that. Or maybe instead they'd make a terrified attempt at humor together: Lucy would say that being alive was so mainstream anyway, they'd call each other hipsters, and laugh through their tears.

> LUCY<3:
>
> Jesse text me. Please.

When he didn't answer, the phone started ringing: "*Peace up, A-town down!*" and the opening notes to Usher's "Yeah!" — Lucy's ringtone.

Not yet. He couldn't deal with Lucy's grief on top of his own. The phone stopped ringing.

> LUCY<3:
>
> Please, it's important.

He waited another ten minutes for Jared to call him back, but his phone didn't ring again.

> LUCY<3:
>
> I'm in town. I came home last night.

He could drive around town until the rest of the family was in bed.

> LUCY<3:
>
> Turn on your location, we need to talk
>
> Jesse!

The crows leapt off the wire and flew over him. Their black wings reminded him of Lucy's hair.

Jared didn't call back, so Jesse got in his car.

LUCIAN

L ucy and his sister walked silently on the dirt path between the headstones, with their heads down. It was 10:45 PM. An owl called from one of the towering pines, because of course it did. A cold wind whipped a plastic flag away from a shoulder-height arched monument. A few steps down, someone had placed little painted gourds around a fresh grave. The headstone hadn't even been placed yet, just one of those little markers. Next to it was a headstone covered in moss, the top and sides crumbling.

Cemeteries were awful; even after all this time, they still freaked Lucy out. Death was such bullshit.

"This way," Ciceline said with a tug on his sleeve. A fitted black cap covered her ice-blond hair, and her tight black coat blended in with the night.

The caretaker had swept the fallen leaves into the corner of the chain-link fence, and the sweet smell of leaf-rot reached them. Past the groundskeeper's shed with shattered windows stood a private mausoleum, its flimsy doors held together by a rusted padlock. A plastic Madonna lay toppled on the first step, her arms out in front of her, palms up, as if to say, "Can you believe this shit?"

Exasperated Mary had a point: he could not, personally, believe this shit.

The family name on the mausoleum: BENNING.

Ciceline pulled wire cutters out of her bag and nudged him aside to break the lock. "Lucy, for real, I can go in there for you."

"No, this is my thing. Just stay in the shadows."

"Duh," she said. "They want the oldest one, okay? And you better hurry, because it's the time of year when goths like to hang out in cemeteries at night. Get in, get out."

"Got it," Lucy replied, taking the bag from her gloved hands. He tied his hair back, pulled out a headlamp, and strapped it on. A mask went on next, fastened so firmly it bit into his skin.

He yanked the door open, cringing when it squealed on rusty hinges. His hair stood on end when he stepped inside. Why this, of all things? Why a dark, small place, crawling with bugs, with bacteria, with mold that was definitely going to get his lungs started?

Bodies lasted longer in mausoleums — *gross*. It would be even more work — and more obvious — to dig up a grave.

Inside, Lucy flicked on his headlamp and checked the dates on the crypts: 2006, 1997, 1988, 1964, 1903, 1887. The time-worn inscription on the 1887 one read "Charles A. Benning - FATHER." Dark stains crept out from the 2006 vault in a finger pattern. Bad crypt-keeping, but it wasn't like anyone was in here visiting.

He swore he could feel mold spores seeping through a gap in his mask, sparking a faint, familiar pressure in his lungs. His only light sources were the chintzy headlamp and a glint of moonlight through a circular stained-glass window with an image of a dove.

"Ciceline, are you still out there?"

"Of course I'm out here," she said. "Did you think the East End killer got me? Hurry up."

Hilarious.

He pulled a small, battery-powered drill out of his bag and bored a hole in the cement that held the coffin. The face mask should prevent the smell from getting in, the goggles should protect his eyes from flying bits of debris and—

"Fuck!"

Ciceline peeked her head inside the mausoleum. "Are you okay?"

"Coffin flies. In my hair." He couldn't take his hands off the drill to swat them away. "I hate them," Lucy groaned, and he didn't mean the flies.

"I know you do, hon. I hope he's worth it."

"He is," he gritted out.

He pushed the drill through until it splintered the wood of the coffin within. Next came the tissue sampler, which he snaked through the hole until it pushed against something that gave under the pressure. He triggered it three times — *snick! snick! snick!* — and pulled it back. His hands were steady, as they always were, when he deposited the samples of decomposed whatever-bit-it-was into a glass vial and capped it.

He shoved all his equipment back into the bag and fled the mausoleum.

Ciceline was waiting outside, closing the doors behind him as he staggered down the steps, nearly tripping over Exasperated Mary. He heard Ciceline click another lock on the door — equally rusted so as not to raise suspicion — as he bent over with his hands on his knees and ripped off the mask, trying to suck in fresh air. He wanted to shower for weeks. He leaned down and righted Exasperated Mary; a small 'thanks and sorry for robbing your grave' to the Benning family.

"Come on, let's get out of here." Ciceline took his hand and pulled him, speed-walking through the graves. They got sparser and more spread out until they came to the gap in the cemetery fence. She lifted the jagged chain-link and together they slipped out. She had parked a block away and that was fine: Lucy preferred to walk in the open air for a few minutes, on concrete sidewalks instead of graveyard dirt, under sodium lights instead of moonlight. His scalp tingled, like bugs were still walking on it. The cold ground numbed his toes through his shoes.

As they neared the car, Ciceline pulled out her phone and dialed. "Ciceline Taran, 10301877."

A man's voice answered, something about 'blah blah speak directly to Yvette?'

"I'd rather stick my head in a bucket of leeches," Ciceline said. "We got your DNA." She turned to him. "What year?"

"1887."

"1887," she repeated into the phone. "Good?"

The man answered, but the wind picked up and Lucy couldn't make out the words.

"Okay, great." Then— "Wait, six weeks? No, that's . . ."

Panic pooled below his ribs. Naturally something had to go wrong; had he dared to think this would be a simple operation? Did Carnelian ever let anything run smoothly?

Ciceline held up a hand as Lucy reached for the phone. "Six weeks is too long. He'll be dead by then." A pause. "No. Not good enough."

The man on other end came through again, this time agitated: "I don't know what to tell you . . . best we can do . . ."

"This is bullshit." Ciceline paced to the front of the car and back. "This is why everyone hates Carnelian and you're constantly having to mop up other factions. I'll be there tomorrow night with the paperwork to cut two years off Lucian's contract."

"No—" Lucy began, because how would stirring the pot even begin to help now?

Again, she held her hand up in his face and projected her entire Lawyer Voice into the phone. "If you can't get us in at least this week, we'll be renegotiating Lucian's contract."

Hurried, panicked babbling came from the phone. Lucy caught the phrases "Advise against this," and "unforeseen circumstance—"

"Are in his contract," Ciceline said. "Which I have with me; I can read it to you if you want."

"I can't make it happen!" said the poor bastard.

Lucy's heart plummeted. It had to be now.

"In that case, you'd better rush the paperwork through," she said. "We will be renegotiating terms."

Lucy almost pitied him. It mustn't feel nice to be on the receiving end of Ciceline's battering ram.

"We're doing it this week," Ciceline said, her temper igniting. "I don't care! Lucian robbed a grave and stole human DNA from a corpse for their lousy cover-up! Tell her to get those papers to me tonight and at least get us some decent painkillers." Another pause. "Then figure it out."

She hung up and shoved the phone into her purse, sagging back against the car.

"I'm sorry," she said.

"I hate them."

"I know. They're getting ridiculous with these missions. They sent me all the way to Germany with Archer last month, identity heist."

"Archer? He's back in?"

"For now. He said they needed the extra money for the business. Hey, after what you did tonight? I mean it, Lucian. I will get you those two years."

It was what he wanted after all — a legal opportunity to walk away from Carnelian.

For that to happen, Jesse had to suffer, if he even lived through the procedure.

STELLA
OCTOBER 14TH

T he creak and click of the front door downstairs woke Stella at 3:47 AM. It was Finn skulking in again.

She turned over in her bed and ran her finger along the tattoo Finn had done when he'd first started out: five stars on the inside of her forearm. Once, in college, Jesse had come home from seeing Streetcar Named Desire on Broadway calling her "Stella for Star" and she'd told him, "Bitch, I am five stars." She and Finn had laughed together at her cringing as he'd tattooed her. That brief period after his stormy teen years and before Dad had passed had been so pleasant.

Finn crept up the stairs and into his room, probably to grab some clothes for his shower. At least he was home. Jesse was out somewhere with Jared.

Thoughts of Jesse riled up her anxiety. He'd had some tests a few days ago. What if he'd found out something terrible? What if he'd gotten the disease their father had? She reined in her thoughts: it was around this time five years ago that their dad had died. Autumn always sent her into a spiral, making her dwell on the worst outcomes.

Her legs twitched under the heavy blanket. It irritated her, like her legs were on strings someone else kept jerking on. The sensation had intensified in the last few days as she waited on Jesse's results. There was no reason to worry until there was something to worry about — or so said her therapist — yet Stella already knew there was. It gnawed at her heart, prickled up her spine. This was anxiety talking, sure, but sometimes anxiety was right.

Stella threw the weighted blanket off, swung her feet directly into her slippers, and headed down the hall.

Finn's bedroom door opened as she passed by, and Finn nearly ran into her on his way out. He had his robe and sleep pants in his hands and was on his way to shower; why did he look so guilty? Also—

"Why do you smell like a Renaissance Faire?" Stella asked.

He scowled at her. "My boss smokes."

"Smokes what?"

Instead of answering, Finn rolled his eyes and edged past, carefully not touching her.

So much for trying to connect with him. Stella made her way downstairs.

Mom sat in the kitchen stirring tea in her mug, one hand knotted around the spoon like dark, knobby oak branches, the other absently scrolling on her phone. Her braided, coiled hair and pink robe were a comforting sight. The cane she'd taken out of the closet, less so. Mom was having a flare.

"They found a body by the river," Mom said. "That little abandoned fishing place. It's all over the news, the East End Killer."

"Gross," Stella said. "Finn wake you?"

"Yup." Mom's voice was slow with fatigue. "You too?"

"Yeah. Figured I'd do quick rounds while I'm up. You need anything?"

Mom didn't look up from her phone. "No, honey."

The door to the hospital was through the kitchen. Noise from the surgical ward and kennels often woke the whole household, but Shep shaved another fifty dollars off their rent to have her or Jesse do rounds after midnight.

Stella shuffled into the lab and hit the switch. Fluorescent lights glared unnaturally in the middle of the night, the whining hum eerie with no human sounds to drown it out — a liminal space. The groggy animals sounded out of place, with their confused whines and questioning meows for food and attention. Her slippers whispered against the linoleum floors. Stella acted casual, as if she were watching herself move through the lab, like her nonchalance would fool her brain. Sometimes it even worked.

Her surgeries were recovering in the middle ward past the lab, a dark little room between rooms. As she made her way toward it, she passed the drug cabinet.

Shep stood behind it.

It took Stella a full second to scream — the sound was too big for her throat. She knew that it was just Shep, not a spirit or a zombie or the thousand other things her mind filled in, but the scream came out anyway because *what the hell?* Her legs buzzed, her fingers itched for a weapon to hit him with.

"Shit!" Doctor Shepherd scolded. "You scared the life out of me!"

"I scared you?" Her voice trembled with anger, but then a sudden urge to laugh tickled in her throat. She had damn near peed herself. Her boss was lurking there in the dark, his gangly ass looking like Nosferatu in the shadows. "What are you doing here?" Stella put her hand over her chest as if she could stop her heart from clawing its way out.

"What are you doing here?" he countered.

"My rounds! Like you hired me to!"

"You usually come in around midnight."

"You said rounds could be between ten PM and five AM."

He laughed, dipping his bald head in embarrassment. "Yeah. Right, of course."

"Now you!" She couldn't drive the hysteria out of her voice.

His narrowed eyes searched the lab. "I need to set up cameras."

"What for?"

He leaned in like he was about to impart some great secret. "The other day, one of my dogs didn't go down right away with anesthesia. We finally had to mask him."

"Okay?"

"Someone is diluting the ketamine."

"The cabinet is locked, though. Who has a key aside from us, Jesse, and the techs?"

"Well, that's what I don't know. I ordered a security system; I just need to install it."

"That's a great idea," she said. "In the meantime, you drove all the way here to wait and see if anyone came in? How long have you been doing this?"

"A few weeks."

"I didn't see you. All the times I came to do my rounds, I was alone."

"No," Doctor Shepard said. "I was in the back wards, checking in through the window."

"You were standing there in the dark watching me? Shep, that's creepy as hell. My skin crawls just thinking about it."

They stared at each other uncomfortably until Stella said, "Install the cameras. Don't be lurking around here at night watching me."

"I'll still be watching you," he said.

"But you won't be lurking, scaring the life out of me when I come to check my surgeries."

"They're fine."

Stella rolled her eyes. "Good night, Shep." She edged past him into the middle ward. The dogs thumped their tails at her, tired and sore, but otherwise normal.

"Jesse said no?" Shep called after her. "About covering tomorrow?"

"Jesse is out tonight," she said. "Text him yourself."

"Can you come in?"

Jeez, the nerve. Living attached to your workplace was decent if you liked sleeping in a little later and no traffic, but it also made it easy for your boss to call you in to work at any given time, and you couldn't use the 'I'm not at home' excuse. "I'm not working a solid week."

"Well, damn," he fussed. His keys jingled from the next room, footsteps shuffling on the tiles.

She marked the charts on the kennels, wrote the time, and went back to the lab.

"Is Jesse okay?" Shep asked.

Anxiety surged like a tide and her mind whispered the word: *Erythrocalcinosis.* Jesse's red blood cells would crystalize until he was dead, just like their father. "Why?"

"I don't know, he seems off lately. A little tired. He's never once told me no."

Yes. He does seem tired, doesn't he? It's not just me. At the same time, she needed it to not be true. Having someone else acknowledge it threw her into a spiral of panic. "Maybe he is," she answered. "Best to let him have his day off. Sorry, Shep."

"I'll give you overtime."

"No." She crossed the lab and over to the door that led to her kitchen.

"The next three days off after, and I won't even text you."

She already had two days off in a row and he was offering just one lousy day on top of it? She had plans with her girlfriends tomorrow night; they were going to a haunted corn maze. "Good night, Shep."

He sighed, defeated. "Good night, Stella. Sorry for scaring you."

She waved over her shoulder.

"I'm sure Jesse is fine," he said, right before the door clicked shut.

Stella leaned against the door, cold sweat pricking at her skin. Mom had gone back to bed. The shower was off, and Finn was probably in his room by now.

It was just her, alone in the kitchen with her racing thoughts.

JESSE

So much for his plan not to tell his family; he cracked first thing in the morning, the moment he saw them in the kitchen.

"Erythrocalcinosis." It hurt his throat to say the word, just as it had hurt when he'd had to say it about his father.

Mom broke the silence by slamming her cane on the tiles. "No."

What could Jesse say to that? When Mom said "no," she meant it, although he had no idea how she planned to fight this one.

Stella just stood there, leaning against the counter like it was the only thing holding her up, her hands pressed together in front of her mouth. Finn slouched against the sink, hands in his pockets, eyes cast down at a patch of morning sunlight on the bland linoleum.

"There's a clinical trial in Norway, or Germany or something," Stella said, her voice breathy with tears.

"We can't afford a thing like that," Jesse said. Also, it wouldn't work. It might, maybe even for a few months, until it didn't, and they would be left with nothing. Mom worked part-time, Finn's pay varied weekly, and if Stella couldn't buy the clinic, someone else would. The three of them would have to move, which they wouldn't be able to afford after his travel expenses and missed work bled them dry and he wasn't around to contribute.

Finn remained silent. He had always been quiet, even as a baby. Jesse and Stella were only three years apart, but Finn was eight years younger than him. Maybe Jesse hadn't bonded with him enough or whatever, but he could at least say something. He could at least look up, like he gave a damn.

"We'll find a way to get the money." Mom's eyes gleamed with pointless determination. "We can use that crowd-funding thing."

"We could," Jesse said. "But . . ."

"No buts," Mom snapped. "I'm not going to watch this happen again, and I won't lose you. You're younger than your father was. You can and will go anywhere you have a chance, because you'll take every chance there is. Promise me."

He longed to hang onto the hope in her voice, to let it excavate something aside from dread in him. "I promise," he whispered.

He would, too. He would try to live until he exhausted every option and fell down dead anyway. They would be broke, but they would at least know that he'd done everything in his power to stay with them.

Jesse's phone pinged, offering a much-needed distraction. Jared, finally?

But no: Lucy again.

LUCY<3:

Jesse, talk to me.

'Talk to me' sounded like the kind of thing you said when you knew something was up. Lucy was like that, though, able to guess around corners and read his silences.

"Is that the doctor?" Stella asked.

"No, it's Lucy."

Finn jerked his head up. "Aren't you going to answer?"

"Uhh, not right now." Maybe he could handle telling Lucy later. For now, he shoved the phone into his back pocket.

Finn pushed himself off the sink, stalked to the back door, and rushed out, letting the screen door slam behind him. Well, at least he had feelings about this, whatever they were.

Stella stared after him, shaking her head. "How do we start?"

God, how was he supposed to know?

"We keep moving forward," Mom said. "We work, we live, we pool our money, we find those clinical trials online, and get you into one."

He allowed her this denial. He wanted it, too.

"Unless something better comes along," she added.

A few more days of this relentless hope and he'd start to resent it. He forced his annoyance down, struggling for a mild tone. "Yeah, Mom. I'll do whatever it takes."

Mom threw her frail arms around his neck and squeezed, laying the entire weight of her love across his shoulders. What could he do but accept it? Jesse leaned into the hug, savoring the moment before she let go.

"That's it, then," Mom said, tapping her cane on the floor again, like a judge banging the gavel, decision final. "We're not going to lose you, Jesse."

They were. His blood would crystallize in his veins, and he would suffocate slowly — if he didn't throw a clot first — and they would watch it happen, just as they had with Dad.

"Okay," Stella said. "Let's get to work."

STELLA
OCTOBER 15TH

S tella zoned out, focusing on the white tiles in the X ray room, trying to imagine life without Jesse, and found that she couldn't. More than that, it didn't feel like he would actually die. He was alive now. How could that change? She wasn't ready to say he was dying. Saying it aloud, or even thinking the words, would put the notion out into the universe and bring it into being.

Jesse had called out of work for his doctor appointment. She couldn't recall him ever calling out before; Jesse's boundaries sucked, he didn't seem to have "no" in his vocabulary. Soon Shep would start pestering for answers. It would all come out once they started crowd-sourcing the travel funds for his treatment, if he even got accepted into a trial.

Stella dragged her feet through the empty lab to get her scrub coat from the hook by the door. Outside, the autumn sun shone cheerfully. How dare it. Also outside was the food truck, the delivery man packing pallets of dog food onto his dolly to bring into storage. It distracted her from her dread for a moment — a new brand? She turned her head to the side to read the label: Tritious, which everyone agreed was junk. Shep had promised he'd never sell it.

The practice employed three technicians, all named Jenn, all with blond hair in varying shades, so they had given the Jenns different designations: Very Blond Jenn, Ash Blond Jenn, and Bottle Blond Jenn.

Bottle Jenn came into the back room. "We missed you at the corn maze last night," she said. "What happened?"

The words refused to come out. "Hey, Bottle," Stella managed, still peeking out the door because looking anyone in the eye was too much to consider. "What's with the new food?"

When Bottle Jenn didn't answer, Stella turned. Bottle had this cornered look, like she wasn't supposed to say anything, but she was about to tattle anyway. The Jenns always told Stella everything.

"It's not a bad thing, I guess?" Bottle said. "There's a new vet, Doctor Treece. She put in the order."

Stella's words stuck in her chest. She and Jesse were supposed to hire new vets once Shep retired, but Jesse might not even be here by then, and oh, there they were, those traitorous tears. How could she function like this?

"Oh, no!" Bottle Jenn cried out, putting one clumsy arm around Stella's shoulders and patting her back. "It's okay, she seems really nice, and she'll be there to help out when you guys take over. It's just to cover for Jesse until he's better."

Now the ugly sobbing started.

Bottle Jenn backed away, searching out Stella's eyes.

"Jesse's gonna be okay, right?"

"It's going to come out soon anyway," Stella said. "He is very ill. He's looking at different treatments."

"Oh shit," Bottle Jenn said. She flailed her hands helplessly before grabbing a paper towel from the dispenser and shoving it at her. "Is there anything I can do to help? I can definitely bring you some dinners. Clean the house? I mean it, anything. You and Jesse are gonna be my new bosses soon, so I better suck up to you."

Stella wiped her eyes and nose, laughing through her tears.

"Let's get you cleaned up," Bottle said. She wet another paper towel with water from the eye-cleaning station and handed it over. "You have to make a good first impression to your new future employee."

"My new future employee needs to realize that we don't sell this junk here." She waved her hand toward the food truck outside.

"We do now," came Shep's voice from down the hall.

Why was he so sneaky, lurking like that? Stella wanted to punch him. He rounded the corner and frowned when he saw the state of her..

"It's just food," he said.

"Shut up," Bottle Jenn scolded. "Jesse's sick. It's a stressful time."

Shep held up both hands. "Okay, no need to be irrational, ladies. I know Jesse's been sick, that's why I hired a new vet — to cover for him until he feels well enough to keep a steady schedule."

"Why this crappy food?" Stella asked. She patted under her eyes, blotting the runny mascara. She better get her act together before her first appointment.

Ah, and here was the new vet, coming into the room and catching her like this. Terrific first impression. Well, too bad. Let her judge all she wanted, with her perfect blond curls and unsmeared make up.

"Doctor Treece," Shep said. "This is Doctor Stella Westchurch."

"She's gotten some bad news," Bottle said. "Can we do introductions later?"

"I'm alright," Stella said. She wiped her hands dry and reached out to Doctor Treece.

"Hi, you can call me Jenny."

Stella burst out laughing.

"I know, I know," Treece said, rolling her eyes. "I can be Doctor Jenny. Or just Jenny is fine. I'm terribly sorry you got bad news. I hope everything will be alright?"

"Yeah," Stella said. "Thank you."

"What's the bad news?" Shep asked, because he never knew when to quit. "Is Jesse going to be okay?"

If she cried harder, that would obviously mean 'no,' so she sucked back her tears. "His treatments are going to be a lot harder than we thought. I'll have to let him tell you anything else, since it's really his business."

"Alright, well . . ." Shep shifted from one foot to the other, eyes darting to the door. "I'll shoot him a text later, see how he's doing and if he needs anything. I'm here for you two." He patted Stella on the shoulder and hustled out of the room like a big awkward bird.

Treece turned to Bottle Jenn. "Can I have a moment with Doctor Westchurch, please?"

"Sure," Bottle said. After another brief half-hug, she left the back room.

Treece leaned against a treatment table and looked Stella up and down. "I'm not here to take your job."

"Okay."

"I mean it. Shep explained that you guys plan to buy the place from him. Would I love to own my own practice? Sure, one day, but it's impossible right now, and I'm not that kind of person. I'm sorry you don't like the food I'm bringing in, but it was part of my deal. Tritious gave me every scholarship I got, so I have to peddle them."

Wow, must be nice to have no student loans. Her emotions were out of control; she'd better keep her mouth shut.

"I know this is hard for you," Treece said. "And even though we just met, I'll be there for you. I'll cover for Jesse whenever he needs it. If he's got a crowdfunding thing going, I'll donate to it, too. I want to get off to a good start."

"Yes. Of course," Stella said. Could everyone leave her alone now? She had to get cleaned up for her first appointment. Wasn't that going to be fun?

"Here." Treece reached into her purse and handed Stella some makeup wipes. "We have to straighten each other's crowns, right? I'm here to help."

"Thank you," Stella said, turning to the small, streaky mirror over the eye-wash station to clear off what was left of her mascara. Now her eye-circles were out in full force.

"You would do the same for me, I'm sure," Treece said. "If the need arose."

Treece stood behind her, smiling her placid smile: affluent, self-assured, presumably without the impending loss of a loved one hanging over her shoulder.

Stella hated her. She forced a smile.

"Of course I would."

JESSE
OCTOBER 16TH

After a dismal follow-up with his doctor, Jesse came home exhausted and ready to give up. He couldn't eat. He couldn't look at his mother. Stella was still at work, and Finn was wherever, so Jesse trudged to the shower, and then to his room. His bedroom was on the second floor with western-facing windows. He turned on the television, muted it, and watched the sun dip behind the trees. *Goodbye, sun.*

He was to start some useless treatment tomorrow morning. Once that was over, he would add his name to a waiting list for a highly experimental protocol in Germany. Tomorrow was the last day to sign up this quarter. Next quarter, he would not be here to try. His dad had only gotten five months from his diagnosis.

He took a breath — *one more try* — and dialed Jared. This time he got an answer.

"Jesse, hi!"

Jared sounded so excited, Jesse's resolve to tell him wavered. "Hey babe."

"How are you?"

"Hanging in there." *Ugh.* "You?"

"I got called to shoot in France. It was supposed to be a one-day deal, but my model never showed up. It's madness, not like her at all. I'm so stressed I could die. There's so much going on right now, I can't even tell you. Sorry, darling. I wish you were here."

"I do, too. I've been wanting to see you."

"I'll be in New York next week if all goes well."

"Great." Jesse would be dying in Germany by then, if they accepted him. If not, then he'd be hanging around town, dying. "I'm looking forward to it."

"I'll bet you are." Jared's voice was sly and foxy. Jesse managed an awkward laugh. This was the least horny he'd ever felt.

"I love that little chuckle of yours," Jared said. "But I can't do this right now. I'll tell you everything as soon as I'm able. You sound tired. Take care of yourself, alright? I miss you."

"I miss you, too," Jesse said.

"Okay. Mwah, see you soon."

There was no way Jesse was going to make a kiss noise, so he said, "Definitely. Bye," and hung up.

The front door opened and then swung shut. The stairs groaned with heavy, thumping footsteps. These days, Finn only made that much noise when he wanted to. The floor outside Jesse's door creaked, like Finn was shifting his weight, indecisive. Jesse got out of bed before Finn could change his mind about whatever he wanted to say and opened the door.

Finn stood there, his hand raised as if he'd been about to knock. "Sorry, I—"

"It's okay," Jesse said. He stepped back, pulling the door open so Finn could come in.

Finn shook his head, refusing to meet Jesse's eyes. "No, I just wanted to ask you something."

"Shoot."

"I wanted to . . ." Finn shifted again, swallowing like his throat ached. "If you want me to finish your tattoo before you . . . before you leave for the trial thing."

"Yes," Jesse said, the word springing out of his mouth before he even considered the logistics of it. He'd honestly forgotten about it: the uncolored outline of a crow on his shoulder. One of the first things he'd done as a vet was to set the broken wing of a crow, and the image of it — its black eyes, how it had gone still when he'd held it — had never left his head. Finn had started the tattoo a year ago, but had been too busy to work on it since. Jesse doubted they'd be able to finish it now, but how could he say no, with Finn standing outside his door, asking him for a little more time? "I could come by the parlor tomorrow afternoon or . . ." No, tomorrow he had to make a million phone calls. "After dinner, even. Or the day after."

"Yeah," Finn said. "Any of those times would work. This way, before you go, you know, to Germany or wherever the trial thing is . . . you'd have that."

Jesse wanted to hug him, but he had a feeling that would be unwelcome, or would end with both of them in tears. Finally, Finn raised his eyes. The tears were already threatening.

"Jesse," he said. "Jesse, if . . . I don't know, actually. If something happens."

If I die? No, he couldn't say those words to Finn. Besides, it wasn't much of an "if."

"You'll do whatever it takes, right?" Finn said.

"Yeah," Jesse said. "Of course." Why did everyone seem to doubt him on that? He would do whatever gave him a chance to live longer. That was a short, hopeless list, but he'd still do it, because at least in Germany, his family wouldn't have to watch it happen.

"Okay." Finn looked down the hall, longingly eyeing his bedroom door, apparently having had enough of this *feelings* shit already. "So just text me tomorrow when you're done with whatever."

"I will, Finn. Thank you."

"Sure." With his head bowed, Finn hustled back to his room.

Jesse closed the door and climbed back into bed, his chest a giant sore ache of longing. The tattoo would never get finished, and they both knew that.

His phone pinged with a notification. He swiped over to see a new app icon on a third screen: a red dollar sign within a circle and beneath it the words "GREAT DEALS GO!" When he tried to delete it, it popped back up. He went into his apps to uninstall it, but only found the loading bar stuck at zero.

Jesse gave up and opened Instagram, eyes unfocused as he scrolled until he found Lucy's latest picture posted two weeks ago, a view of city lights from a third-story hotel room. He knew this profile by heart: *Lucian Grey Callahan, principal cello, son of immigrants, Pisces, eerie pale brunet.*

Pictures whizzed by, taking him backwards in time: a street musician cellist, sheet music, a cat in an alley, a cocktail, and finally, the one he was looking for. He and Lucy were seated on a log, squished together, the ocean at dusk behind them. Jesse was in summertime short sleeves and swim shorts, Lucy in sweatpants and a terrycloth sweater with "Ponquogue Beach" embroidered on the front. Lucy got cold at night, even in summer. The caption read: 'My person <3 :)'

Jesse stared at it until his eyes burned and he had to close them. Fatigue swept him out to sea, and for a few moments he swam in that limbo between asleep and awake. Vaguely, from far away, he felt his phone fall onto his chest as he thought of that last picture and tried to focus his dreams on Lucy. The past was a safer place than the present.

He had been home from grad school on break. It had always felt like a dream to him, too weird to be real, a recollection that occurred to him once in a while, forgotten with the next distraction.

It's high summer, the Beethoven festival in the park. The concert-master calls Jesse from Lucy's phone. *He can't go on, get him to the hospital.*

It's not the first time he's witnessed Lucy hacking up what sounded like an entire lung, but it is the worst one yet, and the inhaler doesn't even make a dent. Jesse doesn't bother trying to convince Lucy to go to the ER anymore, but he stays with him in his rental apartment close to the school. A few hours pass, with Lucy making him promise to never call an ambulance. If anything happens, call the emergency contact instead, it's number 1. Lucy's rambling turns to delirium with the onset of a fever that registers at 105.6, a number that stays with Jesse forever. Adults don't run fevers that high unless they're dying. He dials the number 1 and Lucy's sister answers, but she's out of town and it will take her two hours to get there.

The night is a blur of bone-shaking coughs and a rattling wheeze that comes and goes. Then just a rattle. Then silence. Crystal clear: hurrying out of his makeshift bed on the sofa, into the bedroom, and pressing his hand to Lucy's forehead in the middle of the night. Cool, damp skin, like a broken fever. His own voice, too loud in the quiet room, asking "Lucy?"

In waking hours, Jesse thinks he must have made up this part in his confusion, but in dreams, he absolutely knows it happened: shaking Lucy and getting no response, pressing his fingers to a neck with no pulse, then panic, gut-twisting terror, breaking his promise, reaching for his phone—

Then Lucy's eyes open, gemstone blue, a fixed stare into the middle distance. Lucy is dead. Jesse had sat there and done nothing while it happened, so why are Lucy's cheeks still so flushed, mouth still so red, fever-red, like an open pomegranate—

It's then that he hears Lucy's voice in his mind:

Jesse, don't be afraid.

He woke to Lucy's ringtone.

He had dreamed of that night again. Imagined, or recalled? He snatched his phone and swiped down, couldn't even consider speaking to anyone right now, could not deal with lying or telling the truth.

The sun had set, the television screensaver was on, and the clock on his bedside table told him it was midnight.

His phone pinged, this time with a message.

LUCY<3:

Don't be afraid

The text jolted him, a current zinged from the base of his spine to his neck.

Something rattled outside his window. After the rattle came a distinct *tap-tap-tap*.

Jesse threw his robe on over his pajama pants and went to the window. He parted the drapes and started back, tripping over his own feet and landing on his butt on the cold hardwood floor. There was a face out there, features all wrong and out of place, with some kind of menacing, black mass beneath them. A white hand descended from the top of the window and tapped again.

"Jesse!"

"Lucy?" Hanging upside down outside his window? The black mass below his inverted features was his hair. "Lucy, what the hell?"

"Can I come in? It's important."

Jesse laughed; a short, terrified sound. He got to his feet, his heart beating so hard it ached. How funny would it be to die of fright before his sickness could kill him? He unlatched the window and pushed it up.

Lucy slithered into his room in a way that didn't seem possible, hands gripping the frame, supporting his entire weight. "It's too easy to get onto your roof," he said.

Jesse tried to form words, but only a pathetic croak came out.

"I didn't mean to scare you," Lucy said, "I just didn't want to wake your family. I'm sorry to cross your boundaries, but I need you to come with me." He held up both hands, placating. "If you want. But it's important, so I'm willing to beg."

Lucy creeping in through his bedroom window at night instead of texting that he was coming over and knocking at the front door . . . it didn't make sense. Unless—

Heat rushed to his face. "Did you get a text from me?"

"Tonight?" Lucy asked.

"No, a few days ago."

"The last one was three months ago," Lucy said. "'I miss you, heart emoji.'"

Thank god. He hadn't accidentally sent his pathetic "I'm dying, let's bang" message.

Lucy flipped his palms up, staring at Jesse with his ridiculous eyes that stopped him dead every time. Jesse took his hands. The moment was so surreal, his mouth went dry and his head buzzed. Anything he could have said died in his throat.

Lucy looked terrible. Not sick, (*lungs rattling, radiating heat, pomegranate lips*), just pale and tired, dark curls unwashed and oily, as if he'd been running his hands through them.

Jesse bit the inside of his cheek to see if it would wake him up. Lucy arched one sharp eyebrow.

It was time to tell him. "Lucy, I'm—"

"No, don't say it." He pulled his hands away and pressed them over Jesse's lips. "I know. I just can't hear it, please. Come with me?"

Jesse pushed Lucy's hands away, sick of being silenced. No, Lucy did not know. He couldn't. Alright, yes, he totally could. Lucy had always had "the gift," as he called it. Their mental connection ran particularly deep, and they were always in each other's heads in that weird way, but this? He'd kept his diagnosis to himself, he had tried so hard to block it from Lucy's reach.

Lucy sighed. "Jesse, I know."

So he'd broadcasted this, too. Now Lucy was here, in his bedroom.

"Should I get changed or . . ?" Because what in the world was this? "If this is about sex, because you feel sorry for me, or . . ."

"What?" Lucy jerked away from him, rubbing at his eyes like a headache was building up behind them. "Jesse, shut up and put a shirt on. Oh my god, I wouldn't — well, not like this."

Jesse was far beyond embarrassment. He whipped his robe off and grabbed the first shirt he could find out of his clean laundry pile — a maroon thermal — and pulled it on.

"That's fine, you're perfect," Lucy said. "Come on, and be quiet." He took Jesse's hand and led him out of the bedroom. They left the door open; it always creaked when he closed it.

Still, Stella's door opened and she peeked out. "Jesse? What's going on?"

Jesse turned back, halfway down the stairs. *So much for not waking everyone.* "I'm going to Lucy's house?"

Pressing a finger to his lips, Lucy whispered, "Hey, Stella."

She didn't bother lowering her voice. "Right now?"

"Yes?" Jesse said.

Mom's bedroom door opened next.

"I'm — we're — going out," Jesse said.

Mom didn't say anything. She wasn't even looking at Jesse; she was staring over his shoulder at Lucy, her face unreadable.

"Michaela," Lucy said, with a strange, courtly little bow of his head.

Jesse had never heard Lucy refer to their mom by her first name before. She nodded and retreated into her room, closing the door.

"Good night, Stella Fivestar," Lucy said, tugging on Jesse's arm. "Good seeing you." He hustled Jesse to the front door so fast Jesse barely had time to slip into his shoes before they were outside.

He stopped on the porch, yanking Lucy back. "I need answers."

"There's a car parked at the corner; I'm going to walk to it. It's up to you if you decide to walk with me." He made his way down the gravel driveway.

Jesse followed.

Cottages lined the street tucked behind hedges, some of them decked out for Halloween. Plastic skulls on spikes grinned as they passed, lawns littered with Styrofoam tombstones, "RIP" painted on them to look like dripping blood. All these cute little images of death: *very funny, universe.*

At the corner, a streetlight cast an orange pyramid on a silver hybrid car idling beneath it. Lucy stopped walking. The window rolled down to reveal a woman with olive skin, bleach-blond hair, and dark eyes: Ciceline, Lucy's sister. Jesse hadn't seen her in a few years.

"Ready to go?" she asked.

When Lucy began to steer him toward the door, the blood rushed from his brain into his legs. His head throbbed, and the silver lines of the car turned wavy and gray.

"I've got you," Lucy said, both hands on Jesse's back as he stumbled. "Try to stay calm."

"Sure." Jesse got into the car because it was the closest place to sit. Lucy slid into the backseat with him.

"Seriously?" Jesse said. "What is this, The Godfather with a hipster car?"

"I'm trying to do my small part to help the environment," Ciceline said.

Jesse put his head in his hands. "Me too. Sorry. The car is nice." He peered at them through his fingers.

Ciceline turned around and shared a glance with Lucy. There was so much eye contact and vague nodding between them that it made Jesse laugh through the queasiness.

"I have everything printed up at your house," Ciceline said as she pulled away from the curb.

Whatever that meant, but — "Why are we going to your house? Guys, this could not get any weirder."

Lucy laughed, a frantic sound that Jesse had never heard from him before.

The first time he'd laid eyes on Lucy, in their soon-to-be shared dorm room, Jesse had thought, *Whose little brother is this?* No way was this child going into college. As they'd unpacked, Lucy had brought out his cello and asked, "Mind if I practice?" and Jesse had thought, *Weird. He's too old for college.* Then Lucy played "Yeah" by Usher, grinning up at him until Jesse started singing along.

Jesse had always accepted Lucy's little mysteries: he was "old money," his mother was French, his father had grown up in Romania and was Romani; Lucy was fluent in all three languages; and he was ill with some chronic, unnamed thing. Jesse had never asked where the money came from, or what his illness was. Ciceline was adopted, and had never spoken of her past.

They headed towards Lucy's cottage in the woods, twenty minutes east, which he'd had since before Jesse moved to Long Island. Lucy was rarely there, with all his traveling orchestra business.

"I brought extra towels," Ciceline said.

"What the hell?" Jesse snapped. Maybe Lucy knew of another experimental treatment, but that didn't explain the fucking towels. "One of you better start talking."

Lucy turned to face him, tucking one leg under and leaning forward. Again, he took Jesse's hands. "I've seen a lot of death. I know when it's hanging around someone."

Anger, despair, and a weird sense of betrayal knotted up like a ball of thorns in his chest. "I tried to keep that from you. Anyway, there's this new trial—"

"It won't work. But you can hear what we have to offer, which will leave you with two choices. Your first will be to go home to your family and struggle for the rest of your life. And though I would mourn for you, deeply and forever, I will respect your decision and never mention this again. The second choice is a really difficult option, but one that might save you."

"You're sick, too," Jesse said. His dream — his memory — from that night rushed back.

"Sometimes I get flares," Lucy said. "You've seen them."

Yes, not only the flares, but the pills that Lucy took, knocking them back by the handful, and waking up the next day as if nothing had happened.

"If you have some off-market treatment, you need to explain it to me. Or get me a doctor who can, in detail, with peer-reviewed studies, and it has to be before I sign up for the trial tomorrow."

"I can," Lucy said. "But not before tomorrow. I wish I could give you more time."

"Our diseases are different."

"You can unlock my entire tragic backstory once we're done."

"What's in the pills?"

Ciceline glanced up at the rear-view mirror, and the knowledge of what Lucy was going to say, suspended above Jesse since the day they'd met, descended on him.

"There's a transferrable mutation," Lucy said, "in some human blood."

"Stop the car."

"Cice, pull over," Lucy said.

Ciceline darted her eyes up again to the rearview as she pulled over to the tree-lined side of the street.

Jesse scrubbed his hands over his face, bracing himself to accept the truth. His best friend, a full-grown man, believed in vampires. And worse, he thought he actually *was* one. "God, Lucian. Are you in a cult? Holy shit. Did you leave that body by the river?" It was a joke, one that he hadn't meant to blurt out, but the words filled him with dread.

"No," Lucy said. "Not my style."

"You have a style?" Jesse opened the door and stumbled out into the night.

The smell of the water hit him as he breathed in the murky, low-tide scent. It mingled with wet leaves and smoke from someone's chimney, irritating his lungs.

Lucy sat in the backseat, still turned toward him, hands in his lap, looking miserable and afraid — not frightening, just frightened.

Which will happen first? Jesse wondered. *Will I die starving for oxygen? Or will a clot take me out tomorrow?* He took an unsteady step towards the car and got back in. Lucy let out a breath in a trembling rush. Jesus, he was crying.

"Okay," Jesse said. "Why the hell not. Are we going to go all the way with this and say the word? Can you say it?" His voice sounded pathetic, pleading.

"I say it every day," Ciceline said. "Vampires."

"It's not what you're thinking," Lucy said.

"Kind of is," Ciceline mumbled. Lucy shot her a look.

"How old are you?" Jesse blurted out.

Lucy attempted a smile but it fell short. "Old as balls."

"Please," Ciceline said, "I've drunk wines older than you."

"Shut up. Don't complicate things. I am old as balls."

"Whose balls?" Jesse said.

Lucy thought for a second. "My own?"

"And how old are they?"

"I promise you," Lucy said, "my tragic backstory will be revealed. Let's get to my house first. We have lots of papers to sign."

"Papers?" Jesse asked.

Ciceline piped up from the front, raising a hand as she pulled onto the road. "Lawyer."

Twenty minutes later, Jesse stood outside Lucy's house, taking in every detail by the moonlight as if it was the first time: the lawn, barren in fall; an unused fire pit; decorative stones arranged around mulberry trees. The house was in good shape, painted forest green, the front porch illuminated by a soft amber light. The deck overlooked a steep slope down to the creek, and a mess of shrubs and bittersweet bordered a pebbled path that led to a battered wooden dock and a boathouse with one small rowboat.

His fingertips buzzed and his ears rang. Crickets sang their slow autumn trill, and a dog barked from inside. When had Lucy gotten a dog? Jesse breathed in the smell of the creek with his eyes closed and let the desire to remain overwhelm him; to be awake for more midnights; to see the spring.

Lucy pulled him around to look in his eyes. "The more your symptoms advance, the harder the rest of your life will be. Come on." He opened the door and ushered Jesse inside.

Moonlight streamed in through the half-circle window in the loft. Ciceline came in behind them, hit the lights, then hurried to the kitchen. There came the unmistakable sound of a dog crate opening, nails skittering on the tiles, followed by a dog bounding into the small room, twenty pounds of silky black fur, blue eyes, and a sense of entitlement. A Shetland-Keeshond mix, looked like. It bounced around Jesse's ankles and pawed at his pants.

"Is this your Hell Hound?" Jesse asked.

"Hilarious," Lucy said. "And no, it's hers."

"He's a good boy," Ciceline said. "I would donate my liver to him."

Jesse kneeled to pet him, his hands evaluating automatically: palpable ribs, good weight, normal lymph nodes, relaxed posture. The dog jumped up and licked him. Nice teeth; about two years old.

"Alright, Lucy, off," Ciceline said.

Jesse looked up at Lucy, who was doing nothing, then back to Ciceline. "You named the dog Lucy?"

Ciceline waved her hand. "I mean, look at him."

"Fair enough," Jesse said.

Lucy hung his jacket on a peg by the door. "If you two are done?"

His chest clenched. For a minute, Jesse had pretended that none of this was happening. Ciceline swept a stack of unopened mail from Lucy's reclaimed wood dining table, opened her briefcase, and took out a stack of papers whose purpose Jesse could not even begin to guess at.

Dog Lucy jumped onto her lap — he was too big, but she didn't seem to care — and turned in precarious little circles until he settled down. She petted him with one hand, flipping through the papers with the other. "Okay, can we continue to use the word 'vampire,' going forward? Is everyone okay with that?"

Jesse sat back on his heels, no more pretending that this was some obscure medical trial. "Sure, why not."

"Good. Let's get your papers signed and get this done."

Jesse stood up too fast and almost toppled over trying to back away. "Woah woah woah, slow your roll, you're not doing anything before I know what this entails."

"Of course," Lucy said. "We'll answer your questions before we change you."

"Change?" Jesse asked. "We're going with that, too?"

Lucy had the good grace to look embarrassed. "I know how it sounds. Most people have more time to decide if they even believe it. That was my plan, Jesse. I was going to tell you next year. I had you booked for the week after your 35th birthday."

"Booked? You make it sound like a spa day."

"It's more of a clinic, where we could have done this the right way. Sometimes you can move a person up in an emergency, but there's a lot going on. Things out of my control. So, we're stuck here, doing it the godawful, old way. I wish it was different."

Jesse stared at him, stunned into silence. The only words he had were pointless and tedious. "You don't even have fangs!"

"No fangs. No bursting into flames in the sun. Crosses, mirrors, that's all nonsense."

"Wooden stake?"

Lucian looked away, eyes lowered, a slow blink. "Hurts like hell and will land you in the clinic if you're lucky. In the interest of informed consent: you can still die pretty easily. Getting stabbed in the heart with anything might do the trick, but you'd have a longer time to get help. You can be shot, you can drown, get hit by a bus and die. Prions will still kill you. They haven't worked that one out yet."

"Rabies, too," Ciceline added.

"Really?" Lucy said.

"Mia knew a vampire once who died from rabies."

"Mia knows everyone who died from everything," Lucy said.

Jesse sat on the faux-suede sofa — no leather in Lucy's house, he didn't want to contribute to harm to animals — *haha, hilarious* — and folded his legs. "Well, I've had my rabies shot, so."

"Right," Lucy said. "There you go, then." He took a seat

beside Jesse. "You'll still age, but slowly. There's no such thing as immortality. You will have, like me, a chronic, but manageable condition. But the down sides?" He glanced at Ciceline. She was busy reading. "The whole blood thing, for a start."

"Drinking blood. You've . . . done that."

"You don't have to drink it anymore, though some people do. You'll need a lot at first, since you're already . . ."

"Dying?"

Lucy looked away.

"How did you know?"

"I just knew," Lucy said, tapping his head. "And then Finn called and gave me the details."

"Finn called you? What the hell?"

Lucy gave him a mystified little shrug. "Yeah, it was weird. He said he knew how close we were and thought I should know. But I mean, I already had a feeling before he called."

"How dare — *Ugh*. Never mind. So have you . . ." God, how could he ask Lucy a question like this? "Have you killed anyone?"

Lucy looked at the sofa, fingers plucking at imaginary lint. "Times have changed; you don't have to kill anymore. It's very antiseptic. There are pills now, which are a godsend to people like us. Because, fresh blood? It's unbearable. It never gets any easier. That's where Carnelian comes in."

"Carnelian?"

Lucy waved toward Ciceline and the stack of papers. "The syndicate that keeps this business under wraps and under control. You work for Carnelian and they work for you."

"Work for them?" Jesse really was sitting here and listening to all of this, asking questions as if they might chat about it in a diner over coffee. *Yes, tell me about life as bloodsucking vampires, I totally believe you.* His best friend wanted to bite him on the neck and . . . oh wait, hang on, Lucy didn't have fangs, fangs were too mainstream! Lucy wanted to do something to him to make him live for a few hundred years, because he and his sister were vampires working for a vampire syndicate. Jesse laughed, clutching the fabric of the sofa.

Maybe he was dreaming. Maybe he had even dreamed the last few months, and he would wake to a beautiful spring day without this sickness, and his best friend would not be this stranger who had dragged him into his home to be creepy at him.

Yet he halfway — maybe almost — believed them.

"Would I mess with you?" Lucy asked. "Over something this dire? I can't prove any of it. This is all I have." He reached toward the end table next to the sofa and opened a small drawer. Inside was a compartment hidden beneath a middle layer. He pried it open and took out a slim stack of pictures, placing them gently into Jesse's hand. The scent of old chemicals wafted up, mixed with mold and smoke.

The top picture was sepia-toned, the edges split, brown with age. A group of musicians stood on a stage behind footlights, before a circular backdrop. The men were in tuxes, the singer in a sequined gown, holding a big, square microphone. In the far back, a man sat on a bench holding a guitar, his hair short and gelled into tidy waves. There was no mistaking the angle of his cheekbones or the familiar sharp arch of his eyebrows. Jesse held his breath and shuffled the photo to the back of the pile. The next was in color and showed Lucy at the beach — *their* beach — standing knee-deep in the surf. A red-haired woman stood beside him, kicking water towards a man with the same shade of red hair. At the bottom, someone had written "PUNK ROCK BEACH 1993!"

He came to a photo with Lucy and another man on the boardwalk along the East River. The Manhattan skyline towered behind them, the World Trade Center clearly visible. Jesse's heart stuttered; Lucy should have been eleven when the Towers fell. The man beside him was tall, with dark, slicked hair, a wolfish grin, and a 1980s business suit. His arm was around Lucy's waist, pulling him a little too close, his hand on Lucy's hip tight enough to crease his pants. Jesse recoiled in spite of himself.

"Not that one," Lucy said, snatching it from him.

That left the last one, a newspaper clipping of an outdoor music festival: a chaotic crowd, Lucy among them, coated in mud, recognizable only by his eyes and the shape of his smile. A man and a woman, the same two from the beach photo, both muddied, stood on either side of him. The man had his arm around Lucy's neck; the woman was throwing mud at the sky and howling with laughter. On the stage behind them, a singer hunched over a microphone, screaming his guts out. It took Jesse a second to place him: Trent Reznor, Woodstock II.

Jesse let his hand drop onto his lap, limply holding the photos. "You could have edited these," he said, but the words sounded ridiculous even to him.

Lucy looked him dead in the eyes. "Did I?"

Ciceline turned her attention to Jesse. "I don't blame you for not believing us. We could still do this tonight, because what would you lose if we were lying? A few weeks? Consider what you would do if you believed us. It's not immortality. It's not coffins and garlic, bats flying out of your ass, or stopping to count grains of rice."

"That would be a deal-breaker for me," Lucy said. "I'm terrible at math."

Jesse leaned back on the sofa, closing his eyes. He could convince himself to leave and sign up for the trial. He might not make it in, but if he did, and if he lived that long, he'd live out his last days in Germany, away from his family.

"Is it dangerous?" Jesse asked.

"Very," Lucy said. "You could die."

Dad had suffered so much that the relief they'd felt when it was over still haunted him five years later. Mom would probably not make it if she had to watch him go through the same thing.

"What happens if I die here, tonight? What happens to my . . . body? To the two of you?"

Ciceline folded her hands on the table. "You're already sick.

You came to spend time with your friends and took a bad turn. Carnelian Inc. covers it up."

"Unacceptable," Jesse said. "I mean, do what you have to do with your syndicate or whatever, but Stella needs to know the truth. Promise me."

"We can't," Ciceline said.

Jesse gripped Lucy's hands tight and pulled him so they were face to face. "Promise me."

"Yes," Lucy said. "Anything you need."

Jesse dug his phone out of his pocket and typed.

JESSEBESS

Stella? Are you up?

Text sent, he tucked his phone away. Ciceline looked pale and solemn. Lucy looked plain miserable.

"Before I say one more word," Jesse said, "what, exactly, do you guys want to do to me?"

STELLA

15 MINUTES PRIOR

Stella sat at the top of the stairs, her mind looping on Jesse, churning out horror after horror: ways that Jesse would die, the last words they would say to each other, her first day without him. Catastrophizing, her therapist had called it. But the catastrophe had come true. Now she was just planning.

Some other feeling meddled around beneath her grief, a strange excitement that she didn't dare label "hope." Hope was a fairy tale. She couldn't land on exactly what she was feeling, but it buzzed all over her skin, tempting her to fantasize about miracles. She didn't entertain it. It was probably one of the stages of grief — denial, maybe.

She hadn't heard Lucy come through the front door or go up the creaky stairs, and yes, he was a slight person, but the stairs groaned when someone so much as looked at them.

Fifteen minutes ticked by before her senses came back online, and it all clicked at once: the smell. Stella knew the scent of old, dried blood. She had smelled it drying on surgical instruments and crusted onto drapes and gowns. She couldn't mistake it for anything else, but why was it coming from behind Finn's closed door?

That disconcerting iron tang lingered beneath something

stronger, something that reminded her uneasily of undergrad school, and took her a second to place. It was incense.

Finn was not an incense kind of guy, never had been, and he hadn't had any guests in his room either, as far as she knew.

Judging by the last few months, Stella had at least another two hours before Finn came stomping up the stairs again. She got up and crept down the hall, as much as this old house allowed for creeping. A little night-light cast a shadow on the ceiling. It was supposed to look like latticework, but instead resembled a giant spider. Finn's door was locked, with a sliver of light slicing across the wooden floor from beneath it. Locking doors in this house was ridiculous, just ceremony; an interior door key hung on a hook in the bathroom, it worked on every lock. She took it to Finn's door.

He would know, but so what? What was he going to do about it, confront her? Good, let him. She had some confronting to do, too. His door creaked when she opened it. She cringed.

Nothing sprang out at her. The walls weren't dripping with blood. Instead, as always, they were covered in Finn's art: bright landscapes, dark alleys, intricate scrolling letters, stylized faces. His sketchpad lay on the center of his messy bed, an unfinished drawing of an unfamiliar woman peering out from the top page: dark eyes and skin shaded in charcoal, her hair in long black twists. Stella stepped into the room for a closer look. Beneath the image, someone had scrawled a phone number.

Her phone pinged and she gasped in a high-pitched breath, backing out of the room like she'd been caught. She locked the door from the inside before closing it again and took her phone from the pocket of her robe.

JESSEBESS:

Stella? Are you up?

If she talked to him up here, she'd wake Mom, so she rushed downstairs to the kitchen. The digital clock on the microwave said 1:17. She dialed Jesse's number. It rang once before he answered.

Before he could say hello, she blurted out, "What's wrong?" When all he said was "Um," she sank down on the chair.

"I'm alright," Jesse hurried to assure her.

"What's going on?" Stella glanced around on the counter behind her for her car keys, knocking over a used paper plate that Finn hadn't bothered to throw away, and the saltshaker. "Are you with Lucy?"

"Yes, and here's the thing." His voice was too bright, on edge. "Lucy has, I guess you could call them, connections. You know he has money, right? He's got a way into this one clinical trial and I don't have to leave the country. Or even home. It's pretty deep underground, and it's risky, but I think I have to take it. It's had some success."

Her heart wanted to jump out of her chest. Her entire cardiovascular system wanted to, but suspicion, that ugly traitor, squirmed under her skin, making her hair stand up. Nothing this good could be true. "We would have heard about it."

"Not this one."

"Put Lucy on!" She tried to take deep, easy breaths to dispel the hysteria in her voice.

"Yes," Jesse said. "Okay."

There were muffled voices from the background, and then Lucian saying, "Stella Fivestar."

"You're a cellist," she said. "How do you know anything at all about underground medical trials?"

"Because I've been sick since childhood, and I should have been dead before I graduated high school, but my parents had connections, and now I have them."

That much was true. Jesse had gone running to help him more than once over the years. Still, Stella knew Lucian was lying through some basic truth. "How risky is it?"

"Extremely. Jesse could die."

Wasn't 'could' a step up from 'will?' "When does it start?"

"Since it's best to start as soon as possible, right now."

"Put Jesse back on."

"Yes. Of course."

Stella stifled her tears. This bizarre, exhilarated grief wasn't helping anyone. "What is the procedure?" she asked when Jesse had the phone again.

"An implant, and then pills."

"What's in them?"

"There's a nondisclosure agreement. I'm sorry."

"This is ridiculous," she said. "How are you going to take an implant and some pills you just found out about today, without even knowing what they do, or what the long-term side effects are?"

"Right now, I'd give anything to have a long-term side-effect. Also, I've . . . read some literature on the subject?"

"Literature." He was bullshitting her about some part of this, but she was too frantic to figure out what. "Where is this supposed to happen?"

"There's a specialist in the city."

Wow, the lies flowed from him so smoothly now it was dizzying. "So, what, you're just going to head over there in your pajamas? And don't tell me you're going to borrow Lucy's clothes. You've got six inches and thirty pounds on him."

"I have clothes here."

God, he didn't. She would know if he'd ever spent the night at Lucy's house, he would have been ridiculous about it. "Jesse—"

"I need you to trust me."

His harsh tone made her back off; she was pressing a boundary. "Okay. But I will be calling you every half hour. If you don't pick up, if I don't hear your voice, or if I lose track of you, I'm coming over."

"That's fair," Jesse said. "Lucy's sister is here, too. Ciceline Taran; she's a lawyer."

"I know who she is." Lucian had a lot of followers on social media and Stella was one of them. From his socmed she had followed his sister's (*Ciceline, lawyer, do not try me*), and seen pictures of her over the years, a blonde with olive skin and dark eyes. When Jesse had first met her, he'd offered to introduce them. 'She's very smart, you'd like her,' *wink wink, nudge nudge.* They'd never gotten around to it.

"I need to sign some more papers. Anything I say to you, or send you, now or in the future, and anything I hand you for safe-keeping, has to stay between us. Not even Mom. After the first . . . trial, I'm going back to the doctor to see if there's any difference. I'll text you in half an hour, okay?"

"Love you, Jessebess. Don't die."

"I'm trying not to. Love you too, Stella Fivestar."

He hung up, and Stella sat there clutching the phone. Her body wanted to get up and do something, even something as trivial as turning on the radio or going for a drive, but anything she did right now would forever remind her of this moment. Even sitting here in the kitchen would never be the same, with the analogue clock ticking away the hours until sunrise, the click of the radiator, the moon shining through the window above the sink.

Jesse was doing something proactive. She wanted to hope, but logic, driven by experience, told her that hope was pointless.

He had thirty minutes. After that, she would call again and hear Jesse's voice, alive and well. If not, she'd be paying a visit.

JESSE

J esse forced his hands to stop fidgeting and asked, "What now?"

Ciceline went back to the table, beckoning him to follow. "Legal shit."

"Right. Obviously, I need a lawyer to be undead."

"You won't be undead," Lucy said.

"Yes, Lucy, I got that part."

"I'll be your notary public for today," Ciceline said, "because you're not my client yet and I have no vested interest. Later you can get someone else to represent you, if you ever have a complaint. Or you could stick with me."

"What kind of complaint? 'This blood tastes like shit, send it back'?"

Ciceline turned to Lucy. "He's funny."

"I've been telling you," Lucy said.

"More like if you're being treated unfairly by Carnelian or someone in it. Which is ridiculous, because Carnelian supplies the representatives. If you ever decide to turn someone else, your representative helps you with that, gets your papers and everything together. Everything still requires hard copies and physical signatures. There's some extra stuff to go through because you're sick, and we rushed this through, so you have to sign waivers on your one-year decision period, the form that says we explained this to you, and a release of liability. It's kind of like having an operation. And of course, the NDA."

"Gimme those," Jesse said, snatching the papers. They looked like real, legal documents, with embossed seals of the Carnelian insignia. "Are those crossed stakes?"

"Swords," Ciceline said. "Carnelian goes back to the day of swords and stuff."

"And the moon?" Jesse asked.

"Ah, the moon thing," Lucy said. "Back when the syndicate started, the founders were at the age where they only had to drink blood once a month, which they did at the first quarter phase."

Jesse looked up at him. The words "drink blood" brought it home, hard. He was sitting here getting ready to sign papers, a fucking terms of service to be a vampire. "Guys," he said, "I think I'm gonna throw up."

Ciceline pushed his head over the edge of the table. "Don't get any on the papers. They were really hard to get on such short notice."

Jesse shoved her hand away and took some deep breaths until the feeling passed, then straightened up. When he got his bearings, he flipped through a few forms, wishing he had his glasses. Lucy turned on the light over the table.

"What's all this shit written in legalese?" Jesse asked

"Lemme see." Ciceline scanned the first paper. "The NDA. Pretty straightforward. It's about not divulging this to any other parties until you offer to change them, and that if you do, you have to clear it with Carnelian first."

"That's such bullshit," Jesse said.

"I don't entirely disagree," Ciceline said. "But they don't want every shithead vampire turning their shithead friends into more shithead vampires, changing their girlfriends or boyfriends or the random guy they met at 7-11 last week. It's pointless, because there are groups outside of Carnelian who don't follow the rules and make up their own little vampire populations, and people still turn their shithead friends into shithead vampires."

Jesse glanced up at Ciceline. "I could choose who I wanted? Stella, Finn, my mom, Jared? My kids if I decide to have any?"

She looked down at the papers. "Carnelian is strict about who you choose, and you only get one per generation, not including any children you might have; as of last century, kids are a given. Whoever Jared is, maybe? Stella, possibly, since she's a professional. Finn, a harder sell. Your mom, even less likely: Carnelian advises against it because you only get one person every time you change identities, and it's assumed that your parents were naturally going to die before you anyway. But if she's got a job in the sciences, they might take her."

The horrific weight of deciding who lived and who died lurked in the distant future. Stella? Finn? Jesse would have to choose between his siblings. He buried that thought immediately. They wouldn't accept his mother as a candidate; she was a retired model. As kids they'd taken such pride in telling their friends to look up the video "Fantastic Beach Bash" on YouTube. Mom was Bikini Girl #3, Dad was Dancing Guy #6. He would have to watch her die, too.

"That's cold," Jesse said. "Is that why I don't know your parents?"

Lucy looked away, cornered.

"Sorry," Jesse said.

Lucy shrugged it off. "My parents are both still alive."

"Then they must be—"

Ciceline took the papers out of Jesse's hands and flipped a few of them. "Here's the paper stating that if you kill people, Carnelian doesn't clean up after you. You're on your own. That policy came into effect about fifteen years ago."

"I'm not going to kill anyone. Hard pass on that."

"Thought so," Ciceline said. "You'll need to sign it anyway."

Jesse stared at the stack of papers, frozen. If this was happening and if it was, in fact, not bullshit, then it didn't matter what he signed. If he was to trust these two, then he had to trust them to not mess this up.

"Just show me where to sign," he said in a small, broken voice.

Lucy's eyes softened and he put a hand on Jesse's shoulder. "We already explained the important bits to you, so I guess . . ." He looked towards Ciceline, who nodded. "We can get this out of the way and get started."

Jesse snapped his fingers for a pen.

"Here." Ciceline pointed to the bottom of the first. "The NDA. It's the longest—"

Jesse signed it before Ciceline had finished talking and threw it aside.

"This," Lucy said, "is the one . . ."

Signed and thrown aside. "Next?"

Ciceline handed over another paper. "Disclaimer. Carnelian is not responsible for your death, or any disabilities or side-effects incurred during the procedure, now or in the future."

Again, Jesse scrawled an impression of his name.

"This last one," Lucy said, pulling the paper away before Jesse could grab it from him, "states that you understand and agree that even though you won't be getting my blood, you're still my choice of this generation."

"Why don't I get your blood?"

"Because of my illness; my blood is weak. Hear me out. If you ever change anyone, you can't use your blood either; you'll have to pick a surrogate. Though this will save you, the sickness still exists."

"What you're doing to me . . . for me. Someone did for you."

"Yes. I was dying tragically before it was cool."

Sixteen years, he'd known Lucian — a boy who had looked too young for college, a man who looked too old. He took more care signing the last form.

"Lucian Callahan can't possibly be your real name."

"Later, yes?" Lucy said.

If I'm alive, that doubtful voice whispered to him.

"Later, then," Jesse said. "You promised me a tragic backstory."

Lucy took his hand. "Come into the bathroom."

Jesse followed him in a daze, with Ciceline pulling the black suitcase behind them. In the bathroom, Lucy lowered the lid on the toilet and sat Jesse down. Lucy had a clawfoot bathtub, because naturally he did. Jesse had peed in this toilet, he'd checked his teeth for food in the mirror above the rustic blue vanity, he'd washed his hands with soap from the teal glass dispenser, and now he was sitting here waiting to . . . he had no idea.

"So, what do we do?" Jesse asked. The lights glared in his eyes. He felt dizzy with nerves, over-exposed, and a little awkward.

"It's like a transfusion done on the fly," Lucy said, kneeling in front of him. "It's not biting and sucking blood and all that nonsense. It used to be more primitive. That's where the myths come from. These days it's very scientific. Vein catheters, surgical instruments, things of that sort."

"Okay," Jesse said. He could deal with those.

Except Ciceline started pulling shiny, stainless steel instruments out of the suitcase, and this rig sure as hell didn't look like a butterfly cath — oh hey, that sharp, stainless steel thing was a surgical trocar, the hollow sleeve around it was a cannula — and there was nothing romantic or mythical or legendary about it. It looked clinical, real, and for the first time since they had said the word "vampire" to him, he believed them.

"Catch him," Ciceline said without looking up from her instruments.

Jesse hadn't even realized that the light was fading and the world was tilting until he felt Lucy's arms around his back, steadying him and then pushing his head down to rest on his knees.

"Jesus," Ciceline's voice came through the buzzing in his ears. "Do you want him to bash his skull on the tub and get killed before we even do this?"

"Shut up," Lucy told her. His hand rubbed over Jesse's back.

"Hey, are you okay? You're still doing better than I did. If I can do it, you definitely can. But it will hurt. Fair to warn you."

Jesse nodded, too numb to do anything else. Fear, dark and dreadful, settled into his bones.

"Up you go," Ciceline said in a practical tone, pushing him back so that he leaned against the tank.

When the black spots faded and his vision cleared, Ciceline was uncoiling a plastic tube, which she attached to the cannula and ran into the tub.

"Aren't you going to . . ." Jesse gestured uselessly.

"What, drink it?" she asked. "You're too sick; I'd feel like shit for hours." She glanced up at him. "No offense."

"No, of course not." His blood was going to run into Lucy's spotless, fancy tub, where Lucy would likely bathe again someday. How much did he have to lose? Enough to die, probably.

In any of his few musings about vampires, he had never imagined becoming one up against the back of a toilet. He laughed a little. Then Ciceline came at him with the trocar, making a motion towards his neck. "I need to stick you with this."

Lucy shook his head and took it from her. "My hands are steadier."

Jesse grabbed Lucy's wrist and pulled him close, pressing their foreheads together. "Lucian, please. Please don't kill me."

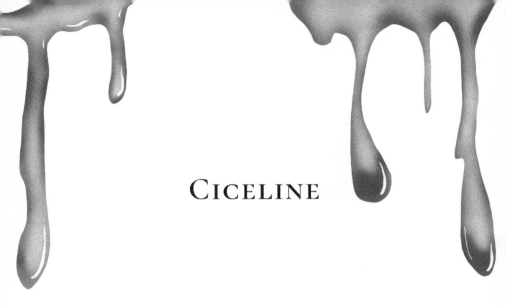

CICELINE

Ciceline had only done this once before, over a century ago, and under vastly different circumstances. She'd been present with some of her clients for their change, in the comfort of the clinic. How hard could it be? It couldn't be worse than her adoptive father changing her behind his wife's back when she was barely a teen. It couldn't be worse than when she'd had to change Lucian. She could totally do this.

Once Lucy was done sticking Jesse with the trocar, he left the rest to her. How odd, seeing him use it for something other than murder.

She drained Jesse's blood into the tub. In the clinic, they measured this out according to body weight and knew exactly when to stop. The best they could do was eyeball it; if Jesse got too weak to drink her blood, he would die. Another reason Carnelian didn't want people doing this themselves.

Jesse's pulse went wild, trying to get blood to his head, and then it slowed, as his lips faded gray. He was barely conscious when Lucy eased him off the toilet seat and kneeled on the floor, cradling him while she removed the catheter from his neck. Lucy had his eyes squeezed shut and face turned away, and she couldn't even tease him about it.

Ciceline tugged fresh gloves on and grabbed the occlusive dressing from the kit. Carnelian hadn't supplied them with much, and again her anger rose. She took a breath, let it out, and pulled the catheter out of Jesse's neck, pressing the dressing over it. But now she needed her hands free because she had to cut herself.

"Lucy? You need to hold this down."

"Of course." His lips were a thin white line, forehead a worried scowl that might have aged him if he wasn't eternally youthful — or close enough, anyway. Still, he did as she asked and his hands didn't shake. Did they ever?

Ciceline took the scalpel in her right hand and nicked her left wrist. It hurt more than she'd expected, and she hissed in a breath. She pressed her wrist to Jesse's slack lips, pulling his mouth open and letting her blood trickle in. He was conscious enough to choke when it hit the back of his throat, and conscious enough to swallow when the first few drops made it down the right way. Good; she hadn't killed him yet.

Then came this terrible suction, a drawing out. She'd been alive for a long time, she'd had people drink her blood before, but in this context, it was purely unpleasant.

Next, he had to die. Lucy knew this, but Ciceline wasn't sure how prepared he was to sit here and watch.

Jesse's pulse slowed to nothing and he went limp in Lucy's arms. What if he hadn't gotten enough blood? Or if he was too weak for his body to take up the slack and reboot? In the clinic, it usually took about two minutes for the heart to restart; breathing a few seconds later. She didn't have her phone to time it, so she counted the seconds off in her head.

One hundred. One-fifty. Two hundred.

"Jesse," Lucy whispered.

She checked his wrist, then the undamaged side of his neck. Nothing.

Fuck, fuck, fuck. She was going to sit here and watch a good kid die and watch her brother finally snap. If Jesse died because Carnelian had dropped the ball and forced them to do this in a bathroom, they wouldn't have to worry about whatever new vampire faction was rising up against them. Lucy would nuke the entire regime, and at that point, she'd probably let him.

"Jesse, please," Lucy said. He folded himself over Jesse, pressing his face against his chest, eyes closed. She hoped he was calling out to him in the way they shared, urging him back to life.

Lucy jerked upwards to look at Jesse's face. Ciceline didn't see any changes in his condition, but Lucy looked relieved.

"Alright?" Ciceline asked.

"Yes," Lucy said.

Color came back into Jesse's cheeks, a hectic flush. Lucy ran his hand over Jesse's short hair, tears gathering at the corners of his eyes.

Exhaustion hit Ciceline like a truck. It wouldn't be long before she lost her ability to remain upright, and she needed a few handfuls of pills. She stood, shaky on her legs, and took a red velvet scrunchy out of the vanity drawer. She gathered Lucy's hair and tied it back. No one liked cleaning blood out of hair, and it was bound to get everywhere when Jesse woke up; so much flailing. She was glad they'd decided to do this in his house and not hers.

She shook about ten pills into her palm, knocked them back, and took a swig of water from the faucet. Before she left, she took Lucy's inhaler out of the cabinet and put it next to the sink, just in case.

"Call me if you need me, I'll be right downstairs. He'll need a lot of pills once he's able to swallow them. There's water in your room and I turned your bed heat on."

He didn't look away from Jesse as he answered, "Okay. Thank you, Cice."

There was more work to do, papers she had to email, and a meeting to set up, but those could wait. Ciceline stumbled out of the bathroom and down the stairs. She crashed onto Lucy's sofa and waited for the screaming to start.

LUCIAN

Lucy let Jesse clutch his hand almost hard enough to crack
the bones. When Jesse said, "Kill me," Lucy had to look
away. No one had ever begged him to end their life; he
wanted to crawl away and die himself. Jesse's other hand gripped
the rim of the tub as he dry-heaved.

The transition had begun peacefully as he held Jesse across his
lap. His skin, such a lovely warm brown, smooth as a river stone,
had gone mottled and ashy. Lucy had looked away as he died, not
because he hadn't looked Death in the face hundreds of times, but
because it hurt when it was someone you loved. If ever anyone
didn't deserve to die screaming in agony, or to die at all, it was
Jesse.

Then Lucy felt him come back to life, felt the spark reignite
before his heart started beating again. The color of returning life
suffused his cheeks, a blush across the constellation of freckles on
the bridge of his nose. That brief, teasing moment of quiet before
Jesse's eyes flew open, amber and blank. His eyes focused on Lucy,
and the life, the personality, and everything that was Jesse, came
back into them. For a second he looked confused, sleepy. Then he
went rigid as the pain hit.

Lucy held Jesse's hands back as Jesse tried to claw out his own aching bones. Lucy remembered that part from his own change. Time and trauma had erased most of it aside from hazy images — the darkness, the rot of the dungeon — but it had not dulled the memory of the pain.

This was the transfusion reaction as Jesse's system tried to reject the blood, but it didn't take weeks or days. The entire organ rejection process happened all at once, over a few hours, the intensity making up for lost time.

Lucy had only seen it a few times like this. Any other time he'd witnessed someone being changed, it had been through parted curtains in a stainless room, with the patient anesthetized. Jesse should have been sleeping through this in a private suite with a soft bed. He hated Carnelian for this, more than he had ever hated them, more than he had hated them in the dungeon.

Lucy shook his head free of that thought.

"Make it stop," Jesse cried.

Lucy rubbed his back. "Soon."

"I hate you."

"I'm sorry. It's almost over." A terrible, but necessary lie.

"I'm dying. You poisoned me." Jesse flailed around for his phone in the pocket of his pajama pants. "I trusted you."

"You're welcome, jeez. You're not dying; you did that bit already." Lucy wet a washcloth and did his best to wipe away the tears and the blood as Jesse glared at him. Christ, all he'd wanted to do this week was power-wash his deck.

"How many times have you done this?" Jesse asked.

"Never. You're my first."

"How old are you?"

Lucy didn't answer. Jesse was right on the edge, spilling the truth all at once would knock him for a loop.

Jesse stared at him, defiant. "I think I've unlocked your tragic backstory."

"Yes, I suppose you have."

"Help me up."

"'Help you up,'" Lucy scoffed, lifting him easily.

Jesse threw his arms around his neck, startled. "You're strong. I never noticed before."

"Most people don't."

"It's hot," Jesse said.

"You're running a fever."

Jesse laughed against his shoulder. "You're so dense."

Lucy settled him on the bed in the loft and drew the curtains; the sun would cause Jesse a headache. A lot of the myths came from the first week or so. Jesse turned onto his side and shivered. The chill was coming; bitter ice that would settle into his bones, as if the new blood wasn't enough to keep him warm. Lucy pulled the duvet over him and climbed into the bed. Dog Lucy hopped up, circling a few times before settling down at their feet.

"Come on, man," he scolded Dog Lucy. "Really?"

"Don't be precious," Jesse said. "Whatever I'm getting on your sheets is probably worse."

Downstairs, Ciceline shuffled around on the sofa. Lucy envied the sleep she was about to get; he was on his fiftieth hour awake.

"It's not over yet," he told Jesse. "The pain comes and goes for a few hours. You should give Stella a call while it's bearable. Tell her you're alive."

"You're right." He still had his phone in his hand. He tapped it and said, "Call Stella."

Stella picked up before the end of the first ring; Lucy heard her frantic voice: "Jesse?"

"Who else?"

"Shut up," she said, and the rest was muffled.

"I know," Jesse said. "I thought I'd call you first, so you didn't have to spend another minute sitting there going nuts. Here I am. Alive and well, though a little woozy."

She asked what they'd done so far.

"Signed the papers, took the implant and some pills," Jesse told her.

'Implant,' what a novel way of putting it, Lucy thought.

She said something about making an appointment.

"We can make one tomorrow," he said.

"What if you're dead by then?" she asked, her voice too loud, shrill with panic.

"Then I won't make one. But I feel really good, actually." He flicked his eyes to Lucy: what a fabulous lie.

Lucy caught the word "cocaine."

"God, Stella, it's Lucy, he's never even smoked a joint." Jesse rolled his eyes — *can you believe this?*

Oh boy. He had to tell Jesse the truth about everything now.

"I'm calling in another thirty minutes," Lucy heard her say.

"I'll be here," Jesse said. "Love you."

Stella replied in kind, and Jesse ended the call.

"She thinks we're over here tripping balls, doesn't she?" Lucy asked.

"I think she does, but I also think she doesn't. Speaking of balls, you were about to tell me how old yours are."

"One hundred and forty-one years old."

"Shut up."

"Ask me," Lucy said, taking his hands. "I'll tell you everything."

Well, almost everything.

JESSE

Now that he had the opportunity, Jesse didn't want to push him too hard. "Are you comfortable telling me the name you were born with?"

"Of course. Alexandru."

"Aha," Jesse said. "I knew you chose the name Lucian Callahan."

"I was going through a phase."

"It literally means 'Light Bright.'"

"Is that really all you're taking away from this?"

Jesse grinned. The pain had gone, and the resulting peace was euphoric. He felt safe, cocooned, better. The bed warmed him, the sky outside Lucy's loft window was the darkest pre-dawn blue. Dog Lucy lay curled up at their feet, sleeping.

"You should be able to keep down some good drugs soon," Lucy said. "I couldn't get ketamine, sorry."

"I don't want ketamine," Jesse said. "Honestly, I think the worst is over. I feel better than I have in months. Years, maybe."

"That sounds wrong, but okay."

No, it had to be right. Jesse floated away on his senses: the warm softness of the sheets, Dog Lucy's soft breathing at the foot of the bed, and the scents of—

"Flowers? And pepper or something? Why do I smell peppery roses?"

"Oh, that's my new deodorant," Lucy said. "Isn't it nice? I forgot to mention the senses thing. Your sinuses clear up faster, your hearing and eyesight, all of that gets sharper. Until you take a downswing, and then you're back where you started. Less blood means relapses. No blood, you die from your illness."

Whatever. Jesse had only been stoned a few times and it had made him paranoid and antsy. This was what being stoned should have felt like.

"How old were you when you were . . . changed, since we're calling it that?" Saying it aloud made him feel like a dork.

Lucy let out a long breath and squeezed his hands, and Jesse knew he wasn't going to like the answer.

"Eleven."

"Excuse me, what?"

"I was very sick."

"So, your parents . . ."

"No."

Jesse raised his eyebrows, unsure of what to say. Maybe now was not the right time to press what was starting to seem like a boundary.

"Sorry," Lucy said. "No, not my parents. It was a point of contention between them because of my age. Ciceline did it. It happened in a very unsavory place. I ran away from home, and that's when it happened."

Jesse reached up and twirled a lock of Lucy's hair around his finger. "That sounds awful."

"I've had a very long time to get over the trauma. It's okay."

"Did you still age at a normal rate?" Jesse asked.

"No; that's one reason it's considered immoral to change children. I didn't pass as a teen until round the early 1900s, maybe 1910? And by then I was in my thirties. By the 1920s, I passed for an adult if I acted like it. That's when I came to America. So at least I was able to get work and get into some parties, which, the twenties? You can't beat that."

"That's why you weren't into partying in college," Jesse said. "You got spoiled." "You and I went out a few times, dancing and things like that."

The memory stood out like a recording, every second pristine in his mind: 2008, Lucy in a club under strobe lights, in a torn purple party dress, mascara smeared around his eyes, both of them covered in glitter, dancing to "Yeah!" and Jesse shouting, "It's our song!"

"I was in college to make connections, so that I wouldn't appear out of nowhere," Lucy said. "I wasn't looking to be a kid again; I wanted a job."

"Who else have you changed?"

"I meant it, Jesse, just you."

"You picked me even before I was dying. Over a century, and just me? Why?"

"You had empathy before it was cool."

"A real reason."

Lucy pursed his lips, thinking. "We need scientists to live longer. Since the forties it's been mostly actors and musicians, because people get obsessed. We don't have many doctors, scientists, nurses, therapists, clinicians, technicians."

"I'm a vet," Jesse said.

"Yes, but I knew you in undergrad, when you first started getting into all the pre-med classes. You're a scientist."

"So why not change someone doing medical research? Come on, Lucy. A real answer."

Lucy was quiet for a while, looking toward the bottom of the bed, petting Dog Lucy absently with his foot. Jesse kept silent, letting him think over whatever he was trying to say.

"You saved my life so many times," Lucy said.

"When?"

"Twice in college. You went to a pharmacy in the middle of the night and picked up my pills for me. Another time, post-grad,

I called you, and you made a two-and-a-half-hour drive to pick me up and take me back to my apartment. I think you thought that someone had roofied me. The pills were new and not as effective, and I got blood-addled. It's like if you're diabetic and you get low blood sugar, except with blood."

"Low blood blood?"

"Something like that."

"I remember finding you dead once and being scarred for life. That was real, wasn't it?"

"Maybe. Your body can shut down for a while and restart, if it's not for too long a time, and if whatever is killing you is removed or repaired, so to speak. A pathogen, an obstruction or something. I don't remember that, but I'm sure it happened. You always took care of me."

"Anyone we knew in undergrad would have given a kidney to nurse your tragic poet-looking ass back to health. So much about you makes sense now, by the way."

"Stop it." Lucy grinned.

"I love that you think I'm kidding. Everyone wanted to be your friend."

"I wasn't there to make friends," Lucy said.

"Well, you made one anyway."

Lucy moved closer and pressed their foreheads together. "I did."

"So now what? Do I get a vampire certificate, a cape, sunscreen?"

"You get an app on your phone. It should be there already."

"A lousy app? My phone got jacked last night with some spammy thing. Was that it?"

"It's really intrusive, but it will keep you alive. You'll pay for your pills and all of Carnelian's services through it. It's like paying taxes, but to a shadow economy."

"The blood for the pills," Jesse asked. "Who does it come from?" Even if he didn't have to kill anyone himself, having it done on his behalf would be just as bad.

"Reserves," Lucy said. "People who are scheduled to become vampires. That waiting period you didn't get? Carnelian requires those people to make donations. The blood is processed in secret factories or something. Not everyone uses the pills, though. Some people just—" He made a throat-stabbing gesture.

"Big yikes."

"It's usually consensual; lots of fetishists out there, and clubs that cater to them. I know it's a lot to take in."

It is a lot, but I get to live.

Jesse was about to say so, but his throat closed up. When he tried to suck in a breath, his diaphragm seized with sudden pain.

"Ah, there it is, see?" Lucy said. "I told you it would come back."

"Shut up," Jesse gritted out.

"I think you're cleared for painkillers. Hang on." He swung his legs over the edge and scooped Dog Lucy up in his arms as he left.

The ringing of his phone startled Jesse so much that his arm snapped out reflexively to grab it. It had to be Stella, and he'd just have to bear the pain so she wouldn't freak out.

He swiped up and tried to say "hello" but the next spasm hit, and he couldn't say anything at all.

"Jesse?"

Shit, Jared. Of all the times for him to call back. Jesse struggled to answer but could only sob into the phone.

"Are you there, Jesse?"

"Fuck!" Jesse hissed, gripping the phone because it was the only thing he had in his hand to squeeze, trying to twist his body away from the pain.

"Jesse, what's going on? Oh my god, are you . . .?"

"Oh god," Jesse panted, biting back a scream.

There was a moment of silence from Jared and then, "Oh, did I interrupt you? You really did want to see me last night, didn't you? I'm sorry, baby. Tell me what you want."

I want to die. The words didn't make it past his teeth.

"Don't be shy," Jared said. "Hang on, I'm in public. Let me find a bathroom."

Gross. Jesse bit his knuckles, but his bones were on actual fire and his muscles were crushing his organs, and there was no way to stifle the low moan.

"You sound so sweet," Jared said.

Was he really going to have to go with this?

The door opened again, and Lucy came in, announcing, "Time for hard drugs, my love."

Jesse caught the beginning of Jared's shocked voice asking "Who's with you?" before his arm spasmed and the phone flew out of his grip. Lucy caught it before it hit him in the face.

"Stop throwing phones at me," he whispered, before putting it to his ear. "Hello, Miss Stella Fivestar." Silence. "Oh. No, I'm sorry, I meant drugs as in medicine. Hello?"

"FUCK," Jesse wailed.

Lucy sat beside him and placed the phone on the bedside table. "I can fix at least some of this," he said, shaking a handful of pills. "Can you tell whoever that was that I'm really sorry?"

Jesse snatched the pills and knocked them back with water that was too cold and almost made him choke. "Don't worry about it," he said, once they were down. "I'm single now." He pulled the pillow over his head. "So you can introduce me to Keanu Reeves."

"Sure, I'll get right on that."

Jesse pushed the pillow aside to check Lucy's face for any indication that he was joking. Lucy smiled serenely and got under the covers with him.

It took a few minutes, but the pain receded. In its wake came the sensation of the new blood slithering through his veins and arteries, repairing his damaged red blood cells: Ciceline's blood, scrubbing out what had been killing him. Lucy climbed into the bed beside him and closed his eyes. Jesse drifted off, too.

"There were creatures in the corner," Lucy said.

"Huh?" Jesse cracked his eyes open. "Lucy?"
Lucy's eyes remained closed. He didn't answer.

CICELINE
OCTOBER 20TH

Ciceline had turned her brother's best friend into a vampire a grand total of four days ago, and now she had to deal with this bullshit from Carnelian Inc. as she sat in the office she had come to despise.

Two crossed broadswords hung on a board above an oak desk, live blades layered in dust. On either side of them were stained glass windows, art nouveau. Carnelian was not subtle. Ciceline could not imagine how they'd gotten away with it for more than half a millennium.

The cluster of free-standing, colonial-style buildings clung to the shadows of the woods off Montauk Highway. The one they were in now masqueraded as a law firm that was always too busy to take on more clients. They even had a waiting room and receptionist when you walked in the door. The surrounding buildings were owned by Carnelian as well, functioning as front companies, most of them actual businesses — a real estate firm, a bank, a liquor store — all too boring for most non-vampires to bother with.

On the desk in the office past reception was a cheesy hourglass with actual red sand glued to the top half because of course, a desk-lamp from the forties, and a computer tablet.

Behind the desk sat a woman as old as the hills — six-hundred-year-old hills, give or take — which showed in the fine lines around her eyes and mouth. Yvette, the leader of Carnelian, who refused to retire from her position.

Lucian sat beside Ciceline on a red two-seater. Ciceline had copies of their contracts in her briefcase, and a tablet of her own in her hand. Yvette studied them in that amused way she had. Ciceline glared back, unwilling to look away. Lucian stared at the wall, refusing to meet anyone's eyes.

"You seem in fine fettle," Yvette said.

"The state of my fettle is none of your business," Ciceline said.

Yvette's smile didn't waver. "Two years is a lot to cut for a lousy six-week holdup." She turned to Lucy. "It didn't prevent you from going through with changing your reserve anyway. You're lucky I let you have him at all. Do you know how many people we turned down this month alone? I should be adding more services punitively."

"With that bullshit, Yvette," Ciceline said, "you can fuck right off. Jesse would have died on the waiting list. Lucian's never even asked for a reserve before."

Yvette spread her hands out on the desk. She was missing the last two fingers of her left hand. Vampires had taken their shots at her over the years, but sheer luck, and those who were loyal to her, had managed to keep her alive. "It costs millions to turn blood into pills," she said, "and we've nowhere near enough to go around. With the younger generations of vampires eschewing the old techniques, and outright refusing to . . ."

"Yeah," Ciceline said, "millennials killed the killing industry. You should be grateful. Those pills keep you in business."

"We still need people like the two of you," Yvette said. "What else can you do, Lucian Callahan? Ciceline is a lawyer, but you have no other skills."

Lucian refused to take the bait.

"Now, this Jesse Westlake," Yvette went on.

"Westchurch," Lucian said. "And don't expect him to do your dirty work."

"He has a pre-existing condition as well, yes?" Yvette said. "A bad one, at that; there's a good chance he'll need extra pills, and probably extra care now and then just to stay alive. He didn't sign anything saying he won't be needing extra care, and I don't see any forms saying he refuses to do the, as you call it, dirty work. Did he sign those, Ms. Taran?"

"Somehow, we didn't get that paper," Ciceline said. She snapped her fingers. "Ah, that's right. Carnelian didn't send it."

"He won't do it," Lucian said.

"Is there someone willing to cover his fair share, should that need arise?" Yvette asked.

Ciceline gripped Lucian's wrist: *Don't*. The option to click "agree" appeared on her tablet; she swiped it away.

"I will," Lucian said.

"He will not," Ciceline said. Damn it, could he not just listen to his lawyer for once?

Yvette slammed her palms on the table, making them both jump, and stood, towering over them, sneering to show her teeth. She did have fangs, old ones, that had been carved out of her incisors, from the days when they still did that sort of thing. "Vampire business is dirty work," she said, sitting back into the chair, her smile once again serene. "Maybe it won't even come to that. What does this boy do?"

"He's an adult, and a veterinarian," Ciceline said.

"How nice. He can look after kitties. Damn it, Alexandru, we need doctors. Scientists."

"Do you not know what a veterinarian is?" Lucian said.

"Well there, see?" Yvette said. "Perhaps he'll never see a drop of blood outside of a laboratory or a surgical theater. We can have him work the machines, or do extractions, or even distill evidence."

Also bullshit. Vampires who 'worked the machines' spent hours a day in underground factories, often in addition to their regular jobs.

"How about this," Ciceline said, "cut the two years from both our contracts for breaking the unforeseen circumstances clause. You should have gotten Jesse into a clinic that night. I don't care if they were all full, that's not Lucian's fault. But give us a few of the tougher jobs and stack them closer together. Instead of every two or three months, we'll work once or twice every month for the next two years."

Ciceline typed in the new phrases and sent them over.

Yvette eyed them both and twirled the stylus. "Any job?"

"No more hits," Ciceline said.

"Oh, one more. On a very bad person. And then no more, for . . . let's say a year."

"How bad is the mark?" Ciceline asked.

"Terrible; you'd want to do it even without being asked. And Mr. Westhouse?"

Oh, she was doing it on purpose. Neither of them bothered to acknowledge her.

"I'll pay for his pills in cash," Lucian said.

Yvette rolled her eyes. "Carnelian doesn't need your money, Alexandru. We need your service."

"You said yourself the pills cost millions to make," Lucy shot back. "Even though you have them made in sweatshops."

She laughed, a merry tinkling sound. "There you go, trying to discuss business again. Why don't you stick with what you're good at? Your boy will get his pills for as long as you work, and so will you. Or you can leave Carnelian? The option is always available, you know. If you don't need our services or protection for yourself and your friends, and you'd prefer to go back to sucking blood from strangers in a filthy club and getting ill every few weeks, you're free to go. I wonder how you'll keep your music hobby if you can't get out of bed. And what will Jesse do? He seems like the kind of vampire who won't even make it out of his thirties without all the extra help he can get. But you're so clever, Alexandru, I'm sure you can find some other company to provide it for him."

Lucy said nothing.

"Good," Yvette said. "Once your contract is up—"

"Then we'll renegotiate," Ciceline said. "Two years, Yvette."

"Let's worry about it then," Lucian said. He looked to Ciceline to confirm. She kept her mouth shut.

"Extra missions for two more years," Yvette said, tapping her stylus against her bottom lip. "Any job."

Ciceline's skin crawled. "No. I want to check them first and reserve the right to decline if I deem it too dangerous or immoral."

"If you decline a job," Yvette said, "you'll accept two extras."

"Of lesser value and danger," Ciceline said.

"The body beside the Peconic. He worked for Carnelian, did you know? Your future missions will likely be tied in with that mess."

Lucian frowned. "Was it the new faction? The ones who call themselves Via Nova — The New Way. Who else hates Carnelian that much, aside from literally everyone? What do they want?"

"Access to the pill technology, no doubt," Yvette said.

"So give it to them," Ciceline said.

"You just said yourself that the pills saved Carnelian."

"Hang on a sec." Ciceline shifted to dig around in her pockets, before turning them out, empty. "Oh no. Completely out of fucks."

"Vulgar child," Yvette huffed. "Via Nova hasn't taken credit for the murder. No one has, so just do your missions, get your pills, and let me handle the business." She swiped around with her stylus and typed a few quick words. "Ready to sign?"

She shoved the tablet toward Lucian. He signed with a fingerprint, then handed it to Ciceline, who did the same.

"Print," Ciceline commanded. "I want an e-file and paper."

"You're supposed to be the eco-conscious ones."

"I one hundred percent would not put it past you to alter the contract's language after our signatures."

Yvette shook her head, with a 'not mad, just disappointed' look. "It will be a shame to lose you both. You're so good at what you do." She reached across the desk, gentle this time, and wrapped her three fingers around Lucian's wrist. "Especially you, Alexandru. You're a decent vampire when you make an effort; I'm glad I didn't throw you into the lake like they told me to."

Lucy snatched his hand back.

"Troublesome since the day they cut you out of me," Yvette said.

"One of these days, I'm going to get tired of you." Lucian's voice was soft, venomous.

"Oh, threats?" Yvette asked. "From the baby vampire?"

"Are we done?" Lucian asked.

"We're done." Ciceline got up, grabbed the papers from the printer, and flipped through them before slipping them into her briefcase. She'd gotten good at speed-reading for potential bullshit in the last few decades. It all looked legit.

Lucian was already waiting by the door for her.

"Alexandru," Yvette said.

Lucian stopped, but didn't turn.

"Good luck, son."

Ciceline shot Yvette her best "whatever" look before closing the door.

Another dangerous mission, another few years of servitude to the woman who had thrown her out of their home, starving for blood that she didn't even know she needed; who had locked their father away to stop him from saving Lucian as he lay dying. A hundred and thirty years later, Ciceline was not over it.

Fucking Yvette. How did she end up like this? She had always been cold, from the moment she and her husband had stolen Ciceline out of a prison to ask her for blood donations for their ailing son. But Yvette had once been on the side of freedom. She had wrestled control of Carnelian from its heavy-handed predecessors. She had gone to war for it; they all had. And here she sat, handing down sentences and denying people the right to change their loved-ones.

Ciceline could run things so much more smoothly, if she had the chance. The thought had started to worm its way into her head, how much easier their lives would be if their mother was out of the picture.

STELLA

S tella shifted the laundry basket to her other hip as she climbed the steps from the cellar. On the second floor, Jesse's bedroom door closed. It made a distinctive noise — *squeee-kee!* — whenever it closed, no matter how much coconut oil Jesse slathered on the hinges. It also made a ka-klunk when pulled all the way shut, because the frame had warped with age and the door didn't completely fit anymore.

Stella hurried up the stairs. If Jesse was home, something was wrong; maybe he was getting sick and had to go lie down, or he'd gotten a call from his doctor and his bloodwork had crashed again. Maybe there was an unknown side effect to this new drug and he'd had a heart attack or stroke. *Or, or, or.* The thoughts pounded into her head in time with her footsteps.

"Jesse?" she called, when she reached the main floor.

Instead of Jesse, Finn came down from the second floor, gaze fixed at his feet.

"Is Jesse up there?" Stella asked.

He glanced at her as he got to the last step and started toward the front door. "I don't think so."

Their dad had taught her how to change Finn's diapers. That had been twenty-three years ago and she recalled it as if it happened yesterday, his wiggly little baby legs kicking. She and Jesse looked more like their mom, but Finn looked like their father: broader, more muscular, dimpled — although she hadn't seen him smile in ages. Once, when she was studying for her SATs, he had asked her to play with him. She'd snapped at him to let her be, and made him cry. The regret of it now, the guilt, still choked her up.

She hooked his arm before he pushed past her. "Hey."

He jerked away.

"Finn, for goodness sake," Stella said.

He sighed, shirty and eye-rolly, but avoided her eyes as he leaned against the wall by the front door, hands jammed into the extra large pockets of his coat.

Stella set the laundry basket down. "This isn't easy for any of us, Finn. Why don't you just talk to us?"

"It's nothing," he said. "I'm just tired from working nights all the time."

"I'm tired too," she said. "We're all tired. I don't see anyone else shutting people out. I'm worried, Finn."

He shook his head. "I'm fine. I just have to get to work. They keep changing my hours. That's all."

"Are you depressed?" she asked.

The way he kept staring downward, shuffling his feet, his mouth a tight line, scared her more than she liked to admit. He didn't answer. She took a step back and rallied her fear into anger. "Fine. Just go."

Finn turned and fled through the front door, yanking it closed behind him. A few seconds later, she heard his car start in the driveway.

Jesse's door. She'd almost forgotten her panic about why he was home.

She picked up the laundry — not in a rush, nothing was wrong, totally casual. This was another little trick she had picked up: rushing to find out what was wrong wouldn't change the outcome, it only made her panic more.

Once upstairs, she placed the basket in her own bedroom before going to Jesse's room at the end of the hall.

All was quiet. She knocked on the door. "Jesse? You home?"

Her mind loved to fill in the blanks: Jesse was unconscious or possibly dead in there. She would open the door and find his lifeless body on his bed.

When she opened the door, his room was empty.

She pulled her phone from her pocket and texted, *Jesse? Did I hear you come in?*

Texting casually was her way of checking up on people without seeming to check up, though by now everyone knew this. It always embarrassed her a little, like she was getting caught worrying when she wasn't supposed to be.

It took a few minutes, but Jesse texted back, *No Why did you hear a ghost come in or smthg*

Lol yeh I guess so, she replied.

How was she supposed to tell him via text message that Finn had been snooping around in his room?

JESSE
OCTOBER 21ST

O f all the circumstances in which to realize he needed his meds that very second, performing surgery had to be in the top five. Especially when "meds" was "blood pills" and the guy who turned you into a vampire was 2800 miles away. And the surgery wouldn't be something quick and simple like a neuter or even a mast cell tumor with good margins. No, this would have to be a vascular tumor with just . . . wow, tons of blood. More than he'd ever seen during any surgery, though it was possible that he was imagining some of it.

"Jesse?" one of the three Jenn-techs said.

He looked up to see which of them had called his name, but their hair — and everything else — now looked red, and their faces blurred. Bottle Jenn wore glasses though, and Very Blond Jenn loved patterned scrubs, blue-footed boobies, this time; he could discern the dots that were the boobies.

He laughed a little.

"Oh, shit," said Very Blond Jenn. "Jesse, are you having a seizure or something?"

"No," Jesse said. "But I should probably go sit down. Can you get Shep, please?"

Wow, how calm and professional his voice sounded, which

was odd, as there was no oxygen getting to his brain. He still managed to pull off a pretty good forceps clamp.

Very Blond Jenn left the room calling for Shep, while Ash Blond kept monitoring the anesthesia. Bottle peered up into his face. "You're sweating."

That was nothing new; surgery was always hot, all those big lights.

"And shaking," she said. "I'm calling an ambulance."

"No." His voice sounded completely normal. He was doing great. "I'm in a clinical trial, and I'll lose my rights to the trial if I break the NDA."

"So, you're just gonna die?" Bottle Jenn asked. "You shouldn't even have come in today!"

"Shep asked me to." Why weren't the pills working? He'd taken the right amount: four at night, and four in the morning.

"Jesse, you know, you don't have to do everything everyone asks of you," she said.

"It's fine."

He did another excellent clamp, but everything still looked so red in there, like paint.

Shep hustled in, already scrubbed and gowned up. "Damn, Jesse," he said. "You're about to keel over. Get out of here. Thank god for Treece, at least she can cover a few of my appointments. The rest I'll have to cancel."

Jesse took a few lurching steps away from the operating table as Shep bitched under his breath.

Sorry my terminal disease is inconveniencing you, Jesse thought, and he might have said it if his lips hadn't been buzzing.

Various shades of Jenns hovered around him, plucking his bloody gloves off, tugging at the sleeves of the surgery gown, pulling the mask away from his face — air, how nice — oh wait, the smell of blood, a sudden cramping that nearly doubled him over.

He opened the Carnelian Inc. app, its red dollar sign thumb-

nail proclaiming "Great Deals Go!", and clicked the "Help" icon.
A text popped up:

> Are you in need of immediate help? Type or
> say Yes or No.

> Yes

Another text, this one from CAR244:

> I can pick you up on Ballard and Goose
> Creek.

That was walking distance.

Bottle helped him out the back door to sit on the steps. How
he wished he could take those few steps back to the clinic,
through the lab, into his kitchen, and up the stairs to his bed.

Did he wish that? Sort of, but a different part of his brain
urged him to roam the streets . . . looking for something?

God, he was such a vampire.

He closed the app ("Thank You for Shopping Great Deals
Go!") and turned to Bottle.

"Take this," she said, pulling a wrapped bagel out of the
pocket of her scrubs. "Get some blood sugar."

"Thank you."

She threw her arms around his neck, almost knocking him
backwards. "Jesse. Are you going to be okay?"

"If I can stay on the meds."

"Because that's pretty miraculous." Her pulse throbbed too
close to his face.

"Yes. Science," he said, pulling away from her grip.

He left Bottle on the back steps and made his way toward
Ballard. He could manage this.

The sky faded to pink, and the sidewalk had a reddish tinge to
it. Cars dragged by in slow motion but left a blur. There was no
pain, just a weird, colorful detachment. Sounds came across

hollow, as if he was in a metal tube. His fingertips buzzed and itched with lack of blood flow.

As he gazed up at the pink sky, he walked into a street sign and knocked himself backwards a few feet.

"Whoa!" a voice said behind him. "Watch where you're going."

"Wow, yeah," Jesse agreed. He turned to see an old man in a stained camo jacket, sweatpants, and a fitted black hat. He replayed the sound his head had made when it collided with the metal pole, and if that wasn't the funniest shit he'd ever heard, then what was?

This guy looked like he could use some coffee, or a donut or something. Jesse handed him the bagel.

"Well sure son," he said. "If you don't mind." He grinned his toothless grin, his mouth a black hole, and his eyes seemed to grow large, twice the normal size. When he took a bite, jelly from the donut stuck to his tongue. Except Jesse hadn't given him a donut, and the bagel didn't have jelly. The man took another bite and blood ran down his chin onto his chest. It surged out of his mouth, lots more, gallons more.

Jesse gestured towards his coat. "Uhh, you have a little something . . ."

The guy swiped at himself, confused, like he couldn't see it flowing from his mouth — rivers of it, until it soaked his clothes and washed along the street, seeping into their shoes.

A sudden trill made Jesse stumble backwards, confused.

"That's your phone," the man said.

Jesse struggled to find his pocket, then struggled to pull the phone out. Finally, he got his shit together and swiped to answer. "Hello?"

"Jesse, you called for help?"

"Lucy? Why didn't I hear your ringtone?"

"Different phone. What happened?"

"Pills stopped working."

"Okay, that's not right," Lucy said. "Someone is coming to

help you; they'll have extras and get you somewhere safe. I'll be there tomorrow, dragul meu."

Oh, so now it was 'my darling.' That rolled *r* always made him weak, and combined with the lack of blood, nearly buckled his already lax knees. His heart slammed against his ribs, working overtime to push around blood that couldn't bring oxygen along. "I love you, Lucian," he blurted out.

"I love you too, darling."

"Hey Lucy, question: Can vampires suck each other?"

"Do you mean recreationally?" Lucy asked. "Or like, for . . ."

"For food, survival."

"It can keep you upright in a pinch," Lucy said. "But not for long."

"Oh well," Jesse said.

"Do you want me to stay on the line?"

"No, I'm alright. Are you killing people? Is that what you're doing out there?"

"Wow, rude. Get in the car, okay? You'll be fine."

"I will." He hung up, realized he hadn't meant to hang up without saying goodbye, and tried to call back, but the number was blocked.

A little black car zipped around the corner.

"Hey, this is my ride," he said to the old man, but his bloody friend had disappeared. It gave him a moment of panic until he spotted him retreating in the distance.

The window rolled down and the driver said, "Jesse Westchurch?"

"That's me."

The driver gave a nod and Jesse climbed into the back.

"Where to?"

"Huh? I have no idea."

"Open your app," the driver said with forced patience. "Go to the three dots on the bottom right, click 'map,' and find the place you need to go."

Those instructions were ridiculously detailed and hard to

follow, but finally Jesse got to the map, and a few dots showed up. There was one just under two hours away, in Brooklyn, that said "BLOOD" in all caps. A closer one, way out east on the island, said "Clinic," but did not mention the word "blood." Unthinkable.

"Blood," he said. "I guess."

"You sure?" the driver asked.

"Yes. I'm sure."

"Whew, okay." He pulled onto the road. "It's gonna be one of those nights."

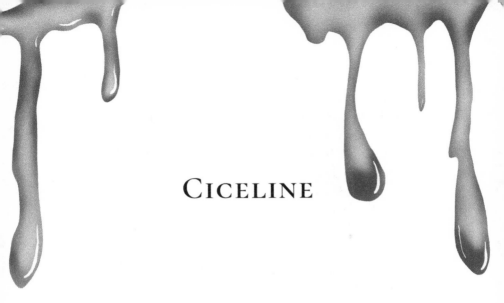

CICELINE

Tacky buildings blurred by as Ciceline drove the car deeper into Los Angeles. Lucy sat in the passenger seat, glaring out the window, chewing his nails, and spreading his sullenness like a virus. Ciceline let him fret. When this business was going on, Lucy needed to go to his dark place.

He stopped chewing his nails long enough to pick up his phone and fidget with it again.

"They're gonna charge Jesse an arm and an asshole for picking him up and getting him extra pills," she said.

"It's already paid for," Lucy snapped.

Ciceline still felt in her heart of hearts that most of their throwdowns were due to her brother's ability to be such a little punk bitch. Ciceline had run off with his girlfriend that one time — okay, that was on her. Another time, Lucy had stolen and crashed Ciceline's automobile, one of the first ones ever sold. All families had their moments. Families that lived for centuries tended to have more of them.

She'd abandoned him entirely in the early 1900s over the blasted cough medicine. Who had come up with the brilliant idea to put morphine in cough medicine for god's sake? Yes, the miserable hacking had disappeared, but so had he. They'd fought about it on and off for over a decade, but when he nodded off during a debriefing about a mission, that was it. He was impossible to work with, she'd told Yvette. Thinking about it still stung.

She saw now how this stuff was peddled to people who needed medicine. It still happened today. Nothing had changed except a few ingredients, but the basics were still the same.

Lucy scrolled and swiped on his phone. The clicking and pinging set her on edge. She was long since done with trying to get him to be in his feelings and confront his anger. One day he'd snap, and when he did, it would be volcanic.

"Stop thinking about me," Lucy muttered. "I'm fine."

Ciceline's hands clenched the steering wheel, not because of what he said, but because that breathy croak of his was back, the one that always came before a crash.

Yeah, he was fine alright.

"You're really going to pay all the medical bills he's going to rack up?" she asked.

"I have money coming out of my ass; what do I need it for?"

Ciceline drove on, grinding her teeth. He'd had one business in the 80s and had sold it for a few hundred bucks when he got bored with trying to run it. He was Carnelian's legal heir, he should have been socking his money away so that he could change things when he took his turn at the helm, only he wouldn't want that business, either. Lucy would let her run it. Not that it did any good thinking about it. As long as Yvette was alive, they were both good and stuck. More than almost anything in the world, it galled Ciceline to be dependent on such a shoddy, archaic bureaucracy when she knew she could run it better. An irritating voice of self-doubt scraped at her nerves: hadn't Yvette thought the same way, over a century ago? Yvette had sacrificed so many people in her war for control, because she said she wanted to make things better. Meet the new boss blah blah blah.

Ciceline parked in an abandoned lot. They had a lot of walking ahead of them. "It'll be over in a few hours and we'll be on a plane by midnight. You can take some time at home, huh? Help Jesse get adjusted."

"Sure."

She turned to Lucy, the boy in the dungeon, the baby vampire. Yvette had thrown Ciceline out for trying to help their dad change Lucy before he died. Lucy had run away, trying to follow her, a dying little boy chasing after his big sister, ten years old and too small for his age. But Carnelian — old Carnelian, before Yvette's war — had caught him. They had both ended up in the dungeon with the rest of the Outcasts, other kids from vampire families who had been denied by Carnelian, some already changed by their parents, others snatched up and discarded before their grieving parents had the chance. Lucy, not yet changed, hadn't even seemed like a tasty morsel to the starving vampires down there, he was so sick.

After their escape, they had gone back to the dungeon, but it was too late. Only a few of the other vampire children had survived.

Ciceline had cried for them, had raged at Yvette and Carnelian, but Lucian had not. He'd cried for his mother, begged her to take them home, and she had. She'd taken both of them back, as well as the few surviving dungeon children, but not for the reasons any of them of them had hoped.

"Are you alright?" Lucy asked.

Ciceline snapped back to the present. "Of course," she said. "Showtime."

Lucy pulled on tattered black gloves, stuffed his hair under a dirty, gray baseball cap, and put on an oversized parka despite the 80° heat. He became someone else in that costume, shuffling along with his head down, shoulders scrunched, his hands in his pockets. Ciceline threw on a dark wig and wraparound sunglasses before they made their way into the high-toned LA neighborhood. She wasn't as good at playing characters as Lucy was. Ciceline hated the character that Lucy became, but she hated her own character more. While Lucy played the desperate fuckup, she was the sleazy hardcase who had brought him here.

Iron gates loomed up around them and security cameras swiveled to track their movements. The mark's mansion rose above the others on the street, wings jutting toward the fences like it was trying to elbow the neighbors away. Ciceline pressed the buzzer on the security gate. It swung open, and they made their way up a long, gravel driveway that sparkled with crystals in the sun. The cameras around the porch were off, as promised. Mr. McMansion here — Russel, the file said, no last name listed — didn't want witnesses any more than they did. At the door, Ciceline rang the bell. When no one answered, she banged on it.

"Fuck, I'm coming, fuck off!" A bolt clicked, the door cracked open, the mark squinted at them. "About fucking time."

He was smooth-shaven, his teeth bleach-white, his skin tanned and toned. A black satin robe, tied too loosely, skimmed his knees.

Shit, she knew him. This was Russel Busquet, he was running for office out here. They'd passed a billboard on the way with a picture of him giving the thumbs-up, his slogan across the top demanding, 'GET ON THE RUSS BUS!'

Fucking Yvette. This was a big deal.

"You know how it is," Ciceline said, nodding over her shoulder at Lucy.

Behind her, Lucy shuffled his feet and coughed a few times. "We were told you could pay cash," he mumbled in that hideous rasp.

"Well shit." Busquet closed the door, unlocked it, and held it open, allowing them to enter his immaculate home. Ciceline touched nothing, keeping her hands folded in front of her. Her heels clicked on the parquet floor, echoing up to the arched ceiling. There was a loft, like in Lucy's house in the woods, only about three times the size, and marble instead of oak. Straight on through, you could see to the backyard, where a pool gleamed in the sunlight.

Busquet led them through an open-floor plan kitchen — a child's drawing stuck to the massive fridge — to a back room filled with craft supplies. They followed him out that back door, past the sparkling pool, and into the pool-house. Chlorine lingered in the air, but it masked another, similar scent: straight up bleach. *Amateur.*

Busquet put his hand on Lucy's back and shoved him into the shed. Ciceline followed. He ignored her to focus on Lucy, inspecting the goods. "What are you? A girl or a boy?"

"I'm whatever you want me to be," Lucy said.

"Well, it doesn't matter, I'm not a fucking pervert, okay? Anyway, aren't you a dismal sight." Busquet opened a small safe on the table and pulled out a gun. "Take that disgusting coat off," he sneered. "Let's take a closer look before I get my camera out."

Lucy did, looking down at the floor, turning this way and that like he didn't know where to set the coat down. Busquet took it from him, threw it down, and wiped his shoes on it.

"Pool house speakers," he called, "Play Sono Andati, La Boheme, Puccini."

Lucy glanced at Ciceline and flashed a delighted smile while Busquet wasn't looking — *It's my jam!*

Busquet snatched Lucy's sunglasses, knocked his hat off, and grabbed him by the hair, dragging him up to his face.

Lucy didn't flinch, didn't look away.

Busquet leaned closer, taking a long look into Lucy's eyes. "You're no junkie."

He didn't even twitch when Lucy slid the trocar into his carotid and pulled back, leaving the catheter in. Poor bastard didn't even realize what happened until he looked down and saw the tube jutting out of his neck, pouring blood. That happened often: Lucian was so quick about it, people didn't notice that they'd been murdered. He even tried to swat it away, reaching for his gun with his other hand, but dropping it before he could fire. Lucy skittered out of the way as the gun clattered onto the floor. He kicked it away in disgust.

Busquet sank to his knees and Ciceline put her latex gloves on.

"Lucy, take some blood," she said.

"Gross."

"You won't make it back home otherwise. You look like you're at least 30."

"I'm just tired."

"Lucy."

"I'm not going to eat a shit sandwich just because I'm hungry."

Ciceline grabbed Busquet's short hair, removed the tube, and leaned over to drink. One time, she had tried leaving the catheter in like a little straw, but it moved around too much. It was easier and cleaner to seal your lips over the wound. Some vampires loved this. She wasn't one of them. Evil blood somehow always tasted worse.

"Come on, you have to hurry," she said, when she was done. The maid was coming, and plus, this asshole was dying. His blood trickled now, and dead blood was no good. How Carnelian managed to preserve it was their jackpot.

Lucy bent over and drank. He barely got an ounce before pulling away and doubling over until he was on the floor, gagging.

"Don't throw up at the crime scene," Ciceline said. It would not be the first time by far. The pills were a literal lifesaver for people like Lucian, but the un-distilled, fresh stuff worked faster. He had a little more color in his cheeks already, apart from the blood all over them.

The music from the speakers played on.

Ciceline grabbed wet wipes from her purse, handed a few to Lucy, and wiped herself down. She used the rest to scrub their spit off Busquet's neck. She didn't have any descendants, and neither did Lucy, but you still had to be careful. Vampires left their DNA all over the world; even if they weren't in any databases under original names, they could still be traced. Even fingerprints. She'd been printed after passing the bar exam and for her passport.

"You okay?" she asked.

He gasped. "Yeah."

He wasn't, but his fingers were steady and quick as he pulled a glass vial out of his pocket and unsealed it, good old *BENNING - FATHER*. The stolen tissue from the corpse was liquid now, distilled and merged with inorganic plasma, recognizable as human DNA, but untraceable. Lucy lifted Busquet's hand and used the swab in the top of the vial to smear it around his fingernails.

Ciceline took out her phone, hit speed dial. "Ciceline Taran, 10301877. We're done."

"Okay, good work." How the hell did he know what kind of work they'd done? She'd talked to this guy before, recognized his peppy cheer and his accent, Pacific Northwest. "He's got a maid coming around at one. Can you get clear by then?"

"Obviously," she said, and disconnected.

She took Lucy's bloody coat and folded it in her arms. Busquet's blood seeped into the floorboards and disappeared. *Weird.* There should be cement underneath. Ciceline squatted down and tapped a knuckle against the wood. It sounded hollow. She ran her finger along a seam, pulled her pocket knife out, and wedged it in. The slat lifted and she yanked it away, revealing a handful of mini-VHS tapes with dates on them. Like recording on VHS rather than digital and hiding them under the pool-house floor would save him, the dipshit. How many kids were on those tapes? Jesus Breakdancing Christ. The mission had been to kill him, but exposing him on top of that felt like a nice little extra.

Damp, crumpled papers jutted out between the tapes. She pulled them out, unfolded them, and read them over.

"Shit."

"What?" Lucy asked.

"These are Via Nova papers. He was a reserve. This is going to start a war."

He looked up at her, jaw tense, grinding his teeth. "Fucking

Yvette. Can she really be that incompetent, or is she trying to get us killed now?"

"Well, it's done. Come on, out the back way."

She led and he followed, past the tennis court, through the tall hedges in the back, to another spiked fence. She took off her heels and threw them over before she climbed. They pushed through a dense patch of underbrush, then out onto the next street. Her shoes dangled from her fingers by the straps; too much walking to put them back on.

What was Carnelian thinking, sending them to kill a Via Nova reserve? Russel Busquet had to be vital to something Via Nova was planning; changing a big-name politician was pretty huge. When Via Nova found out, it would blow up. Fake DNA would fool the authorities, but not another syndicate who probably used the same techniques.

Not telling her and Lucy the details was shitty and went against the contract. She burned with helpless rage, and the desire to make Yvette pay. Over a century with their lives on the line and every time the end was in sight, Carnelian came up with some other reason to pull them back in: You don't work, you don't get health care. No work, no pills. No work, we let your friends die.

They got back to the car. Lucy stood staring at the door. Ciceline went past him and opened it for him. "Lucy?" He continued to stare, so she touched his arm.

He jumped. "Sorry. Glitched for a second."

"Okay? You should have taken more blood."

He shrugged. "What are we going to do about this mess? God, I am so done with this."

Yeah. They were done with Carnelian every few years, weren't they? "We'll figure it out," she said. "Get in. We have to catch our flight."

JESSE

T he sun had gone down, and the streetlights glowed a hazy, reddish orange. Headlights streaked into long, pink lines, and taillights bled down the road. The driver, who had introduced himself as Rupert, had given Jesse four spare pills, barely enough to keep him upright and something akin to functional.

After about two hours of driving west into the city, they stopped outside a club. The sign above the door proclaimed "BLOOD" in a silly font that looked like dripping blood. The neon lights surrounding the sign were lurid pink. Guards blocked the entrance behind a velvet rope, where a crowd of goths stood in line, pretending to be chill and unbothered by the wait. Bassy music pulsed from beyond the doors.

Not exactly the funky little "family pharmacy" he remembered from when he'd gone to pick up Lucy's pills for him ages ago.

"Here you go," Rupert said. "You have an hour, then I need to drive you home."

Jesse hesitated with his hand on the door handle. "There are pills in there?"

"Those pills are hard to make. If you blow through your

supply before the end of the month, they don't send you more. You have to do it the old-fashioned way. Sorry."

"Maybe it'll be in a cup?" Getting close to strangers, watching them as he drank their blood? He couldn't imagine doing that.

Rupert shrugged. "Maybe? Just follow the rules. I won't run off if you take a while."

"Thanks," Jesse said.

"Whatever. I know who not to fuck with."

His brain felt foggy; he didn't know what Rupert was getting at or how to respond, so he just nodded and stepped outside. The chill was harsh, made worse by his new physiology that seemed to demand more heat. More food. More water. More life. More anything.

"Have your app open before you go in," Rupert said out the window. "They'll scan you at the door. Tell you apart from the rest."

"Right." Jesse opened the Carnelian app and punched in his ten-digit code. He got a few curious stares and a few resentful side-eyes when the bouncer waved him in.

The bass almost knocked him off his feet, and the strobe lights were not doing him any favors. This was a terrible place to be when you were feeling like this; hadn't they thought of that? The desperation, the confusion, the lack of equilibrium? Jesse was literally passing away; he didn't want to grind all over the dance floor.

A DJ up on high was spinning throbbing music, and people were, in fact, grinding all over the dance floor. There were definitely hands under tight skirts and shoved into black pants, and he was fairly certain that some people were having straight up sex.

The smell of blood dragged him in. He stood at the back of the room, close to the entrance. What was he supposed to do, just ask someone? He shouldered past a group of goths crowding the short, metal staircase that led down to the main floor. Two of them swayed on the steps, locked in an embrace, the taller person's face tucked under their partner's chin, and, oh, that's where the blood-scent was coming from. The actual sucking of actual blood.

"Aww, first time."

Her shout in his ear made him start back. A gentle hand landed on the small of his back and he tried to squirm away from it without looking like he was squirming. He ducked his head guiltily, and turned to see a small, pale-skinned, red-haired girl.

By the flashing strobes he saw her teeth, stained red. "I'm Mia. You look like a taker, am I right?"

"Uhh, I guess," he said as low as he could, unable to look at her.

"Then come with me. Unless you want to try out there?" She gestured to the dance floor.

Jesse couldn't fathom the idea of going up to some random person and . . . what? Cutting them? Ciceline and Lucy had their fancy little surgical instruments; he didn't see anything like that here. The thought of sinking his teeth into someone's jugular almost sent him off into hysterics, and not the funny kind. "It looks a little intimate out there."

"Yeah, I can see where it would be weird if you're not into that kind of thing."

"I guess I came to the wrong place."

"Looks like you didn't have a choice." Jesse thought he heard sympathy in Mia's voice. "We have another option, the Black Room. It's probably not what you're used to, but at least you won't have to look anyone in the eye. Or even know who they are."

"Sounds a bit ominous?"

"Don't worry," she said. "It can get hedonistic here, but we do have some hard and fast rules. Everyone who gives gets tested. Blood from a sick person will make you sick, too. You know as well as I that people can falsify records, but that's a chance you take at any fetish club. If you tell someone to stop whatever they're doing, they stop. There are guards everywhere. Total anonymity by honor system and absolutely no photographs or videos. If you tattle outside the club, you get blacklisted. Via Nova aren't banned, but they usually don't bother. The Black Room is soundproof, so the music won't distract you too much. Come on."

Mia took his arm and led him away from the dance floor and through a side-door. Florescent lights flickered on when they entered the small room with beige walls and an elevator at the back. The floor indicator at the top was the old kind, with the numbers listed on a brass arch. Mia pressed the button and the doors slid open.

Under the harsh lights, his nail-beds were grayish-purple.

"Gosh," she said, pursing her lips in a look of sympathy. "You were really sick."

"Yeah. That's why it was rushed."

"That's rough," she said.

The elevator lurched as it descended. Jesse had to hold the rail to stay upright.

Mia lifted the hem of her fitted, red velvet shirt, showing a vague, pink scar from her hip to her ribs. Below it, just peeking out from the top of her pants, was a faded tattoo that he couldn't make out. "I was changed on the fly, too. It's really hard when you don't have time to make a decision. After my change, I was left alone to figure out how to take care of myself. A kind old vampire helped me out." She winked at him. "So, I like to pass that kindness on."

"Thank you," Jesse said.

The elevator gave one last shudder as it came to a stop and the doors opened. The bass from the music upstairs still thudded at the ceiling, but muffled now. He followed Mia down a corridor lined with wrought iron light fixtures with lightbulbs that flickered like flames, the kind you could get at the dollar store this time of year. The walls were red — or at least he thought they were red. Maybe they were black? He trailed his hand along the wall to see if it was wet, but his fingers glided along dry satin paint.

"Let's get you in there before you get any more blood-addled," Mia said.

They came to another door, this one also either red or black. Mia took a key out of her cleavage and unlocked the door to reveal one of the most over-the-top rooms he'd ever been in. The wallpaper was definitely red and looked like velvet. High-backed chairs lined the walls behind long, shiny, black tables, and black chandeliers hung from a barrel-vaulted ceiling. The smell of incense curled into his lungs and his clothes, jasmine or something. As for the patrons, he had never seen so much lace in one room. Everyone's eyeliner was perfectly winged. Jesse was still in surgery scrubs. None of the few people who looked his way seemed to mind; maybe they thought it was part of his thing, his persona or whatever. Anyway, most of their attention was on a person with long, purple-streaked black hair, who stood on a slightly-elevated platform at the far end of the room, under a blue spotlight, reading from a paper held in her pale hand:

> "Now I strap my device onto my hips,
> As embalming fluid shoots from between the
> sutures of your lips."

Mia snorted quietly. "That's our dear Helen Back," she said. "Always alarming, strangely charming. Come on, keep moving."

She led Jesse to a black curtain by the side of the stage. Behind it was a staircase of only three steps. Helen Back must have finished her poem, because there came a smattering of applause from behind them.

"Here are the rules," Mia said. "When the person you're sucking on says 'Midnight,' it means they're done, and you have to move on. You have to, or you could kill someone. As with any scene, the person giving is always in control."

Jesse swallowed hard and nodded.

Midnight.

"If you get in trouble or start to bug out, the safe word is

'Nevermore.' When you're ready to leave, say 'December'. Either way, one of the guards will find you and lead you out the back door, so you don't have to go upstairs again. Okay?"

"Safe word. Okay."

"Repeat what I said."

Jesse took a second to think about. "'Midnight' means I have to stop . . . drinking. If I get in trouble," — he stopped to consider what trouble he might find in there, and came up short — "I say 'Nevermore.' When I want to leave, 'December.'"

She smiled again. "Good. Don't tell anyone your name. Don't say any names out loud, we enforce anonymity in the Black Room. If you want to meet someone and get to know them, that's what the upstairs floor is for, and there are private rooms if you want to hook up, but you probably don't. Oh, and turn your phone off." She stepped aside. "You'll be fine."

Jesse didn't believe her about being fine, but he stepped into the room anyway, finding it completely dark. For the brief second that the light from outside illuminated the tiny space, it looked like he was about to walk into a wall. Then she closed the curtain and plunged him into darkness so deep it almost suffocated him.

Then he did indeed walk into a wall. It reminded him of the darkroom in college, the time Lucy had taken a photography class: maze-like hallways painted black so that no light came in when someone opened the door. His fingertips skimmed along the walls until he found a sharp corner and went around it, then another. Then a third one, where whispered voices came through the darkness. Not only voices: gasps, panting, the shuffling of bodies, and wet, sucking sounds.

Jesse plastered himself against the nearest wall, wondering how big the room was, and mentally listing OSHA violations. Wasn't there supposed to be a properly lit exit sign? He tried to take deep breaths, but the smell of blood was overwhelming. *December, December, December*, he wanted to call out, but he needed this.

A hand brushed across the front of his scrubs and shrank further into the wall.

"Taker?" a voice whispered.

Jesse nodded, before remembering that they couldn't see him. "Yeah," he whispered.

Then something hot, wet, and sticky was being pressed against his lips: someone's wrist. He tried to turn away, but it was impossible; his mouth wanted this more than water in the desert. This was new. The pills didn't arouse this urge. He didn't know what the etiquette was. Did he just suck on their wrist? Did he lick it?

"Go ahead." Their wrist smelled like cheap perfume underneath the blood.

As gently as possible, closing his eyes even though the place was dark as hell, Jesse tentatively drew the blood from them. He didn't want to consider the repercussions of throwing up in here. Then he thought of how many people maybe did throw up in here, which almost made him want to throw up, but the blood instantly revived him, more than the pills ever had. His body grew hot. He had fire in his veins and warmth in his cheeks. His muscles thrummed and burned to life, tissues healing so fast they almost cramped.

"Midnight," she whispered, pulling her wrist from his mouth. Then she quietly moved on.

More. Jesse peeled himself away from the wall, took a few tentative steps, and collided with two bodies, clinging together. He murmured an apology, then felt awkward when they seemed too involved to answer him.

Someone nudged him in the shoulder and whispered the word "Giver."

"Taker," he answered, too quickly, and a hand groped for his and found it. He lifted it to his mouth. That burning feeling came again, threading out from his stomach.

"Midnight," this one said, and moved on.

The next one had a thick wrist covered in hair, and smelled of car grease beneath the blood. Jesse's face had to be a mess by now. He hoped they had some paper towels to use for clean-up before he left.

It might soon be enough. Weird feeling, this satiety, when only a few minutes ago he'd been starving, like he could drink up everyone in here and still want more. One more, maybe, and then he would be the one whispering "December" and exiting. He dreaded having to face his family after this — hell, anyone — but the desire to be out of this dark, sticky, hot room was starting to override the urge to keep drinking.

"Giver," whispered a voice in his ear from behind him.

"Taker," he whispered back, and turned. This time when he groped for the other person's hand, they pulled away. Instead, cool fingers slid around the back of his neck and tilted his head down. He was too shocked to say 'no.' The safe word disappeared from his brain. The hand pulled him downward, toward the stranger's neck, and that was way too intimate, possibly against the rules, and probably dangerous. They tucked his face under their jaw, and he went with it. It was weird, but then, he was a vampire, so what wasn't weird?

"Go on," the voice whispered, gentle.

He searched around until a thin, warm trickle touched his tongue. Thank god he didn't have to bite him.

Time to go for it. It was just food.

The other man exhaled softly into his hair once he fastened his lips to the tiny cut and started sucking. He smelled like Jared, and Jesse had never felt so alone. When the man's arm curled around his back, he accepted it. He would be disgusted with himself later. He wrapped his arm around the other man's waist in return.

The man breathed out shakily. Jesse slid his other hand up and gently touched the other person's hair. It was the same length and texture as Jared's. It could have been blond for all he knew; hell, it could have been green.

They stayed like that, and after a while the awkwardness of having a stranger's arms around him faded.

"Midnight," the man whispered in a spent voice.

Jesse caught his breath, clinging to the stranger in the dark. There was no reason for this to go on any longer. He could say "December" and run away, but that felt cheap. Whoever this was, he had given him something precious, had bled to keep him alive. He'd never see the guy's face, but he didn't want to be a dick to him anyway.

The man ran shaking fingers over Jesse's short hair.

"Hey, are you alright?" Jesse asked.

The other man gasped. "J—"

Then he squirmed against Jesse, nudging him away, panicking, pressing his hands against Jesse's chest. The contact between them broke, but Jesse caught his wrist. He almost blurted out his name, but then he remembered the damn rules. Instead, he turned the man's hand over and started to spell into his palm. He got as far as making the J and A before the hand pulled out of his grasp again and then . . .

"December, December, December!" the man whispered into the dark.

There was shuffling and footsteps, someone brushing past him.

"December!" Jesse repeated. "December!"

"Alright," said a calm voice, as a hand grabbed his arm.

They turned a few corners and a new door creaked open. Jesse stepped into a dimly lit room and waited for his eyes to adjust. It was a bathroom, with private stalls and towels. A few people milled around, dabbing their faces dry.

"You okay, hon?" Mia asked him. She still had his arm.

He nodded, looking for the way out of the bathroom. There was a door at the opposite side, and Jesse bypassed the sinks and towels as he ran for it.

"Hey, you're all bloody," Mia called after him, her hurried steps echoing behind him.

Jesse ignored her. He crashed through the door and sprinted down a deserted alley, which opened to a full parking lot behind the club. He scanned for Jared's car, but it wasn't there. He couldn't even hear retreating footsteps.

"Jared!" he called into the night. "Jared!"

Jesse's phone pinged and he scrambled to get it out of his pocket; it had to be Jared.

But no, it was a notification:

'Did you enjoy your experience at BLOOD? Please rate BLOOD before you go!'

LUCIAN

Lucy always felt gross post-kill, and being on a plane made it worse. He shook some antacids out of a bottle and popped five. The small amount of Russel Busquet's blood was through his system already, but the thought of it made him want to heave. He wanted off the Russ Bus. The turbulence wasn't helping; he couldn't get comfortable even in the spacious seat of Carnelian's private jet. The drone of the engines usually lulled him, but not tonight.

Something was off. The whole situation was a mess; the last month jumbled around in his head, a tangle of anxiety. He was angry at Yvette, but when wasn't he?

Because of the new faction rising up against Carnelian, he had been paying for security for the Westchurch family. He had even grudgingly fronted some cash to have someone look after Jesse's boyfriend. Jesse didn't need to know any of that, though. All Carnelian had to do was what he had paid them for, and not drop the ball. If Jesse or anyone he loved was harmed because of Carnelian's recklessness, well then, Lucy would be the one starting his own faction, wouldn't he?

Anger emanated off of Ciceline in waves. She was too quiet. He didn't like quiet Ciceline.

"Everything okay?" he asked.

"Yeah." She nudged his arm. "Still worrying about Jesse?"

"He should be done at the clinic by now. I wonder why his pills stopped working. That hasn't happened in years." Jesse's illness was so severe, his risk of relapse was high.

"It is weird," Ciceline said.

They had four more hours in the air. He wanted to call Jesse again, as if constant checking up gave him more control over the situation.

Ciceline stayed quiet for a few minutes, texting her pet sitter. She'd left Dog Lucy at Lucy's house and hired someone local. Finally, she said, "Via Nova is going to hit Carnelian back for this."

The knot in his stomach tightened. "I don't know what Yvette was thinking."

"Oh, I get the idea behind it. Busquet was going to loosen up some laws, get Via Nova some connections. Cover their asses. Vampires in high places are never a bad thing if they're on your side."

"He was too big of a hit," Lucy said. "The body by the river, the one from Carnelian? That feels personal. I bet if you look into anyone Carnelian hurt, you'd find a lot of people in Via Nova."

"Who hasn't Yvette hurt, though?" Ciceline asked.

"Yes," Lucy said. "She could be in danger."

"Meh," Ciceline said.

"She always has a way of making every problem worse."

"And yet we keep following her orders."

"You have other options, Cice; you're better than this. I'm the one who needs the pills; you can get by without them better than I can." Lucy was really bad at being a vampire; wanting to claw his guts out after drinking blood was such an inconvenience. Ciceline didn't like it either, but always seemed to tolerate it better. "I just wish you would walk away from these missions. You could change the system. Get people out of the underground blood factories, make things better."

"Unfortunately," she said, "I'm not the one in control."

"I'd cede control to you if Yvette was gone. If anyone could do it—"

"Yeah. If Yvette was gone." She looked back down at her phone, lips pressed together, locking something up behind them.

"Ciceline, what—"

Her phone pinged. She swiped it and frowned at the screen. "They gave me another mission already. Tomorrow night, Long Island. This is bullshit; I'm going straight to my apartment once we land. I'll have to sleep all day."

"The island?" Why drag her down from the city when he was right there? Why hadn't he been asked to accompany her? They were probably lining up something else for him already. Fucking Yvette. At this rate, it seemed like he would never get around to power-washing his deck. "What's the mission?"

"I have to listen in on a meeting and get some intel. Damn it, I need to get back to taking actual clients."

"What do they want to know?"

She texted, waited a minute, and got another text back. Raised her eyebrows. "They suspect that someone in Via Nova is trying to get their hands on Carnelian tech, seeing if they can replicate the pill form."

"How bad would that be?" Lucy asked. "Making it more accessible."

"You're not wrong, hon."

Her mission sounded simple enough. Still, something was twisting up in his gut.

"War is coming," Cice murmured. "Christ, I need a nap, first."

"And a shower," Lucy said.

Ciceline rolled up her sweater and pushed it against the window, leaning her head against it. "Guess I'd better try to get to sleep, since I have to do some bullshit tomorrow night."

Lucy folded his legs under him and scrunched up in the seat, leaning against her side, and went back to fidgeting with his phone.

There was no way he was getting any sleep on this plane.

CICELINE
OCTOBER 23RD

T wo days and not nearly enough sleep after killing Russel
Busquet, Ciceline's assignment found her waiting in the
brush under a bridge like a troll. Critters scuttled in the
swamp behind her, but she'd long since gotten over any fear of
noises in the woods at night. She'd slept under a bridge for a few
months in the seventies, made friends with the wildlife. That had
been her Athanasia Disorder. The Century Snap, some called it,
but it all came down to the same thing: vampires turned bonkers
usually sometime after the first hundred years. Their brains
couldn't handle the unnaturalness of the lifespan. Lucian had
found her when she had hers, and got her into a sanctuary. Her
Snap lasted fifteen months.

The creek was quiet tonight, barely a trickle, not a lot of
traffic going by overhead until headlights swung around on top of
the overpass. The car pulled off to the side and parked. The driver
killed the engine, got out, and made his way down the
embankment.

Ciceline planted the device onto the concrete of the bridge
and crept around to the other side, deeper into the woods and out
of sight. Crouching behind some low brush, she tugged her
phone free, dimmed the screen, and started the app to transcribe

the voices. As she was doing this, a notification popped up: incoming call from Carnelian.

"Okay," she hissed, "what seems to be the fuck?"

"Oh, hi Ciceline."

It was the west coast guy, the one she usually dealt with. "Hi, Seattle. What is it? I'm busy."

"I'm just here to make sure all goes according to plan, and to read the transcriptions real-time. Would you mind sharing the screen?"

"You're going to distract me."

"I'm sorry. Carnelian's orders."

Fucking Yvette. "Whatever." She clicked him through. "Just be quiet."

"Yes Ma'am."

So far, she'd heard nothing but the first guy's echoing foot-steps as he paced beneath the bridge.

Come on, other person. Get here. I'm tired.

After about fifteen minutes, someone else showed up on foot and took the same path down the embankment. The first guy said, "Do you have them?" There came a muffled answer that her phone translated as "Just a handful, I'm sorry I [inaudible]."

Then a third person came, this one behind her, higher up on the hill, noisy as hell. Whoever they were, they were going to wreck this entire operation, and probably get themselves killed.

The voices from under the bridge kept chatting away and her phone kept transcribing: *a week's worth but we wanted [inaudible] sorry I don't care I don't care I need proof of life I can't give you [inaudible] going back on your deal man can't help you anymore please can't you let her [inaudible] innocent—*

"There's someone else here," Ciceline whispered into her phone.

"Oh wow," Seattle said. "Do we know who or why? Maybe they're just walking by?"

"No, they're in the woods." She aimed her night-vision binoculars up the hill.

The other person was about twenty feet away from her. The person closed in, what could only charitably be categorized as "sneaking," as they managed to step on every twig in the vicinity. Finally, the figure came into focus: a tall, willowy woman with long braids. "Oh, shit," Ciceline muttered.

"What is it?" Seattle asked.

She might be five stars, but her stealth skills were like negative one or two.

"I deem the mission too dangerous to continue," Ciceline said. "Stella Westchurch is out here. She's going to blow my cover."

"Hang on," Seattle said. "Hold your position."

"Fuck off, I'm going to take her home."

The voices stopped; her app showed nothing but a reloading ellipsis. A raccoon or something scurried by and burst out of the clearing, running along the bank of the creek. Thank god. The two men began talking again, and Stella stopped walking, and had the sense to at least crouch down a little.

Seattle came back on the line. "Yvette wants you to proceed."

"Yvette can eat my entire ass!"

"What am I supposed to tell her?" Seattle hissed.

"Tell her I know it's important but consider this: fuck you." Stella started down the hill again. Christ, they would kill her. "Stella Westchurch is my reserve," Ciceline blurted out.

"You can't just . . . you have to have known her for five years, this isn't—"

"Of course I've known her for five years," she whispered. "She's my brother's boyfriend's sister, we're practically in-laws. Get this in writing for me, Seattle. I'll transfer the down payment for her fees tonight."

Silence from the other end. The transcript kept going, with more [inaudible] readings. They were whispering now, probably coming to investigate.

"Damn it," Seattle said. "To be clear, this is definitely a mistake."

"I'll handle it."

Ciceline disconnected, pocketed her phone, and pushed back up through the brush. There was still time to get Stella out of this situation and away from the Via Nova creeps if they could make a quiet enough escape.

JESSE

Jesse sat in the silent kitchen, in his pajamas, with a cup of coffee in one hand, and the pill bottle in the other. The clock read 12:40 AM when his phone pinged.

LUCY<3:

I'm on my way over, fragile menu <3

LOL *dragul meu

JESSE:

LOL I'm ok, you don't have to but I wouldn't say no to seeing ur face.

Sleep wouldn't come anyway. He couldn't shake the feelings from the club: that desire to fill all of his cells with more blood, the cloying scent of incense, the sticky floors.

Jared.

He'd texted him earlier, but had not gotten a reply.

"That you, Jesse?" Mom called from upstairs.

"Yeah. Sorry if I woke you."

"You didn't. Hang on, I'm coming down."

It would take her a minute with her cane, but she did not

accept help; she said it only made it harder, getting two people down the narrow stairs. When they bought the house, maybe he'd put in a chairlift, or a room downstairs for her, for her flares. That he was even planning for the future gave him a little thrill. He was here to worry about his mom, to fret over whatever was going on with Jared, to have his human problems back. The void before him had closed.

Mom came into the kitchen in her pink robe and slippers. "Tell me again what the doctor said. Just repeat it for me, because I need to hear those words again so I can sleep."

She'd asked him to do this three times since yesterday. "He said he's cautiously optimistic, but he's never seen anything like this. He said he's honestly wondering if he and at least three other doctors made a series of mistakes. I should follow up in a week to see if this trend continues."

"That's right," she said, grabbing the bottle of pills. She gave it a shake. "I don't care what's in these pills. If these keep you on this Earth, then nothing else matters. You don't go before me."

"Yes." Jesse choked on the words. "Whatever it takes."

She handed the bottle back, turned to the counter, and started making tea. "Your sister is out chasing your brother to see what he's up to."

"Huh?" It took him a minute to catch the change in subject. "Really?"

"Yes. I think worrying about him takes her mind off worrying about you."

"Still," he said. "Whatever Finn is involved in, she should steer clear. I'll talk to him."

"You can try all you want," Mom said. "He just shuts down."

A contradictory emotion, this relief at focusing on something as ordinary as his kid brother getting into trouble.

"I'll still try."

He toyed with the bottle. The label didn't show a name or ingredients; just directions on how many to take and when, the words "Carnelian Inc." in script, and beneath it, "By Our Grace."

Carnelian sure was pleased with themselves, but they weren't wrong. Jesse was alive right now because of Lucy, and Carnelian's pills.

Why had the pills failed him? What if they did again? Or if they stopped working altogether and he had to drink raw blood all the time? He'd ask Lucy what to do.

"Hey Mom," Jesse said, "Lucy might stop by. It's late, so you can head up. I'm gonna do rounds."

"Grab Stella's phone if you see it," she said. "I think she left it in the lab again. I texted her and she didn't answer."

"I will." Stella not answering because she had misplaced her phone was a weekly thing, so it shouldn't worry him, but out there in the middle of the night, following Finn into the dark? He liked that a lot less. "Get some sleep, Mom."

He kissed her cheek, then took his bottle and went into the lab.

The lights hummed on, and Jesse hurried through his rounds in the middle ward. The surgery dog he'd had to abandon was still in there, doing as well as he could expect. There was another one on a drip. He checked the rate of the drip, marked the charts, and left the ward.

He passed the supplies closet, unlocked it, and grabbed a fecal occult testing kit.

Rolling a chair over, he took a seat at the lab counter next to the sink, fished his glasses out of his pocket, and opened the kit. The glasses only made things blurry, so he ditched them. He shook a pill out — it really did look like a smooth, oval carnelian stone — and pried it open with his fingernail, studying the contents. They looked and smelled like Chinese herbal medicine, the kind you got at an acupuncture clinic. He touched his finger to it and dabbed it onto his tongue. It didn't have that coppery, salty flavor, but then, there were probably all sorts of substrates in it, so no definitive results from a taste test.

He sprinkled some of the dust onto the card and dropped the hydrogen peroxide onto it.

"Jesse?"

His entire stomach jumped into his throat, and he backed his chair away from the counter so fast he almost toppled it.

"Whoa!" Doctor Treece said, holding up her hands as she came out of the back ward. "Sorry. Didn't mean to startle you."

"No worries," Jesse said, pulling his chair back in.

She looked around the lab, trying to peer past his shoulder at what he was doing. "I'm on rounds tonight," she said. "Why are you here?"

"You are? Oh, sorry. I wanted to test my pills to see if some of them were placebos. Considering how sick I got the other day."

"With a fecal occult test?"

"Well, you know, copper, reducing agents . . . I just want to know what else is in there."

"Okay?"

"So, how are you settling in?"

"I love it," she said. "Thinking about renting a place a little closer."

"That's a great idea," Jesse said. "The east end is beautiful."

"It is." She peeked over his shoulder again. "Well, hey, at least it looks like your pills are free of any blood contamination."

Jesse spun the stool around. His blood pills were indeed negative for blood. "Huh."

"I almost forgot," Treece said. "Stella left this." She took Stella's phone out of her pocket and handed it to him.

"I'll give it to her. Thanks. Oh, I did the rounds already." He swept the test, the pill, and the rest of the kit into the garbage.

"Good night, Jesse," Treece said. "Get some rest."

"You, too," he said. "Get home safe."

He left her in the lab, locking the door behind him. Mom's cup was in the sink and she'd left the lights on for him. He turned the bottle over in his hand, wishing he had more pills for a control group. They couldn't all be fake; his improvement was real and documented. If only a few of them were fake, that would make sense, but how could that happen? They had been sealed when he'd gotten them. He'd left them in his bedside drawer, and the only people who had access were in his house.

He needed to tell Lucy. The clock now read 1:05 AM. Lucy should have been here by now if he'd left when he had texted, but maybe he had to take Dog Lucy out of his crate to let him pee or something. Maybe he'd wanted to change clothes.

No, it couldn't be any of that. Jesse wasn't prone to dark imaginings the way Stella was, but he felt it, right down to his guts: Lucy was in trouble.

He took out his phone and sent a text:

Hey Lucy, you there?

He waited five minutes for a reply.

"Call Lucy," he told his phone.

It dialed and went straight to voicemail.

STELLA

Stella had followed Finn in her car until they reached the bridge — *seriously, Finn, under a bridge?* — then she'd parked around the corner and crouched behind some bushes to get a closer look. Finn went down the embankment, not bothering to hide where he was headed.

Stella sidled off to the edge of the hill for a better look. The streetlight above illuminated a little patch where she spotted the two of them. The person Finn was meeting looked like a man about Finn's height, but she could discern no other details.

Finn took something out of his pocket. Stella tried to focus her binoculars on the object he held in his palm, but she couldn't make it out. She widened the focus. Finn turned. He seemed to look directly at her, and Stella startled back, dropping the binoculars to her chest. He couldn't have seen her. When she looked again, both men were gone. She lowered the binoculars and scanned the area below.

There they were, climbing the hill to where she crouched behind the weeds. Finn trailed behind, striding to catch up to the first guy like he meant to slow him down or stop him. They were heading right towards her. If she stood up and ran now, she'd be an easy target. Could she crawl away? Could she keep her cover as she escaped?

An arm wrapped around her from behind and a hand clasped over her mouth. She screamed through it, scrambled to her feet, kicked backwards into their shins. They didn't let go.

"Shh!" someone hissed into her ear. "Jesus Christ, Stella, calm down, I'm helping you. Oh shit, okay. Time to run."

The man who'd met with Finn took off in their direction. He held a cylindrical object, indiscernible in the dark but menacing. Finn reached out as if to catch him, scraping the collar of his coat before falling behind.

The person behind her grabbed her hand. Long nails, smooth skin; a scarf obscured her face. Stella didn't have much choice but to run with her. Together they clambered up the hill.

Heavy footsteps thudded through the brush, too close. Her breath came ragged and loud. A yank on her arm pulled her the rest of the way up the embankment and onto the road. Her feet slammed on the pavement so hard it hurt through her sneakers, her lungs ached from the cold air. They reached the top, where a silver car stood parked behind a patch of tall grass.

A different figure burst out of the woods behind the silver car, leaping over the hood.

"Shit!" the woman yelped, swiveling her head, searching up and down the street as if nothing was familiar.

"This way," Stella said, tugging her hand as the two men closed in on both sides. *Where was Finn?*

Stella pulled the woman off the road, over a split-rail fence across from the road she'd taken to get here, and through a thicket of Christmas trees. Beyond the tree farm, a corn maze overlooked a steep slope.

"Seriously?" the woman said. She didn't sound out of breath, not like Stella felt, and far too calm, maybe even a little annoyed.

They crashed through the corn stalks. Thick leaves snagged on her sweater and scratched her face. Her eyes bulged out of her skull, with tears pushing at the back of them. Her nose was dripping, legs about to buckle. She could die tonight. The sudden realization hit Stella so hard that she almost stopped running.

They whipped past a life-sized stuffed clown in the corner. The woman huffed out a startled "fuck!" and damn if that wasn't just a little bit funny, in spite of it all. If she lived, this would make a hell of a story.

They cleared the maze and came out on the other side. At the top of a hill before them stood a cavernous barn, set up for the Halloween dance. A dirt path wound around the farm, and a tractor with a trailer hooked behind it stood parked in the center, filled with bales of hay.

The woman gripped her arm. "Stop."

"We can't!" The muscles in Stella's legs jumped like they were being electrocuted.

The corn rustled in the breeze, and through the rustling came those footfalls again.

"God damn it," the woman said, before throwing her arms behind Stella's shoulders and under her legs and lifting her off the ground. Stella shrieked, not like it mattered now, with the hulking figure bursting out of the maze. She saw his face: gaunt, pale, angry. The object in his hand was a gun.

Then Stella was airborne. The woman had tossed her. She cleared the back of the trailer and landed hard on a bale of hay, rolled off of it, and thudded onto the floor. Her lungs emptied of air and her head smacked against the wood.

Strong, strong, too strong! Stella thought wildly.

She tried to roll over and lift herself up, but her arms were useless, and her chest burned from lack of oxygen.

The pop of a gun resounded just outside of the trailer. She flattened herself back down. A softer crack followed, and then a thud.

"Jesus Inconsolable Christ," the woman huffed.

A head peeked over the edge of the trailer. Her eyes were visible — dark brown — and a lock of bone-white hair had come free, falling over her forehead.

"Ciceline Taran?" Stella asked. Her voice was shot, hoarse with gasping.

"Yeah. Looks like the bastard who jumped over my car fell behind, but he might still be out there, so we have to move. Come on." She held out her hand.

Stella took it, getting her throbbing legs under her. Ciceline helped her from the trailer with one arm around her waist. The man who had chased them this far sprawled face-down in the dirt. A rivulet of blood pooled from beneath his cheek.

"Is he dead?"

Ciceline shrugged. "He was going to kill us, so hopefully yes. I hit him with a hoe."

"You need to explain so much to me right now."

"So do you!" Ciceline said. "What in god's name were you doing out here tonight?" She took a furtive look around and started walking along the dirt path at a decent pace, leaving the fallen body in the middle of the farm.

"What were you doing?" Stella asked. "Aren't you the one who got my brother into a medical trial? Why were you following my — my other brother?"

Ciceline stopped and turned to her. "Your other brother? Fucking hell, are you serious? The other guy was Finn? He's stealing pills, Stella. Probably Jesse's."

That stopped her in her tracks. Damn it, she had been right. Jesse's pills stopped working yesterday. He could have died. Where was Finn, anyway?

"I need to get home. I need to tell Jesse. Cops."

"Let me handle that," Ciceline said. "I'm a lawyer."

Her brain was offline. Yes. A lawyer should handle this.

"Not far to your house, right?" Ciceline said.

"No." Tears clogged up her voice; she sounded pathetic. "But my car is all the way back there."

"That's alright," Ciceline said. "We'll walk together."

CICELINE

C iceline followed Stella and pulled out her phone. She wanted to dial Lucy first, but if she didn't give Carnelian something, they'd be so far up her ass she'd start tasting them. It would be hard to call with Stella standing beside her. She was a reserve now, so she'd find out soon enough, but if Ciceline hit her with the real business right now, she'd freak out.

Ciceline dialed Carnelian, expecting her usual handler, Seattle, but some other guy answered.

"Ciceline Taran, 10301877," she recited.

"Go ahead."

Wow, no greeting, nothing. She wanted Seattle back. "So, not a total bust," she said. "Someone is stealing the pills, but I don't have the details. Check the transcript. For what it's worth, this guy sounded innocent, probably doesn't know what they are, or is being coerced." Not that it mattered: Carnelian handled everything the same way and would just off Finn Westchurch if they knew. "Also, we were pursued, and I left one of them in a farmfield, so you need to send someone to identify him and clean up."

"Okay. And?"

"I didn't get any names."

Stella turned and gripped her arm, mouthing the words, 'Thank you.' Ciceline nodded.

"I need protection for the Westchurches. Send a patrol."

"Why was your . . . your reserve out there?" the guy said. "And the Westchurches already have protection as per Lucian."

"Clearly it's not enough."

"It'll cost—"

"The fuck it will," Ciceline said. "The price has already been paid, out the ass, I might add, and obviously they're not doing their job since we almost got killed tonight."

"Why was Stella Westchurch there?" he pressed.

"Trying to hook up with me, obviously," Ciceline said. "Send more people, every hour."

"I can't make any guarantees, especially since you broke protocol."

"Aww, that's too bad, since I have more information. You'll get it when they get more protection," she said, and hung up.

Stella glanced back at Ciceline. "Thank you for that."

"It's mostly the truth."

"Who do you work for?"

"A private company."

"The company doing the trial?"

"Yup. The NDA that Jesse signed was a big deal, and stealing those pills is pretty huge. Do you know why Finn might have gotten caught up in that? Or how?"

"I don't know," Stella said. "He's been shutting us out for months now."

Months would be before Jesse was changed — maybe before anyone even knew he was sick? "I'll talk to him," Ciceline said. "Alone. Maybe without his family around, he'll tell me something, and we can help."

Her phone rang again. It wasn't Lucy, so Ciceline didn't answer. She couldn't resolve this yet, and she had to ignore them for a few hours to make a point. She'd get Lucy to pick her up at the Westchurch house, so he could hear the whole story. Maybe he had some intel on Finn, having known Jesse for so long.

She dialed his phone, but it went straight to voicemail.

Stella's feet were starting to drag as they crossed under a towering pine and turned onto a narrow, unlit road lined with quaint little homes. They soon came to a wider road, and passed through the business district, and beyond it, a two-story white colonial, with a widow's walk around the roof. Withered honeysuckle vines and overgrown shrubs obscured the bottom half of the house. A lighted sign outside the yard proclaimed it the office of Doctor Dylan Shepherd, veterinarian. Two more placards hung beneath his: Doctor Jesse Westchurch and Doctor Stella Westchurch. Next to it, written in chalk on a standing board: "Please welcome the newest addition to our veterinary family, Doctor Jenny Treece!"

"Around the back," Stella muttered, leading Ciceline through an archway draped with barren wisterias to a wooden back porch. She unlocked the door.

The lights were already on in the kitchen, where Jesse and their mom sat at the table. Ciceline glanced at the clock: 1:20. Entire families awake at that hour didn't bode well. Jesse had his head in his hands, but he looked up when they came in, surprised to see Ciceline there.

"Oh my god, what?" Stella asked. "Jesse?"

"I'm okay," he said. "Finn left."

"I know," Stella said. "He's mixed up in something bad. They had guns. Ciceline was following the people he was meeting. Jesse, Finn has been stealing your pills."

Their mother handed a phone to Stella. There was a text on the screen. Stella held it so Ciceline could read it too.

FINN:

> I'm okay. It's better for all of you if I stay away for a while. I'm sorry. I'll explain everything when I come home. Please don't look for me, I'll come back when the air clears but I am totally fine so don't worry.

Below it, another text:

MOM:

> Whatever happened, we'll fix it together. Come home.

And then, from JesseBess:

JESSEBESS

> Just come home and let us help you.

"It's a group text," Jesse said. "We all got one."

"Finn didn't write that," Stella said. "Call the cops."

"No." Ciceline held her hand up. Jesse and their mom looked up at her, their mom's eyes sharp with suspicion, Jesse's with the dawn of understanding. "Sorry," she said, holding her hand out to their mother. "Mrs. Westchurch, I'm Ciceline Taran. I'm a lawyer."

"Michaela," she said, taking Ciceline's hand. "And I know who you are. I follow social media like anyone else. What has any of this got to do with you?"

"I have a bead on what he's involved in; cops won't do any good. We get him to safety first, then maybe we can work it out." She gave Michaela a quelling look. "I handle this kind of thing all the time."

"Oh!" Jesse lurched to his feet up so fast he almost knocked his chair over, startling everyone. "What time . . ? Oh my god, Lucy."

Ciceline's heart stuttered. "What?"

"He said he was coming over. That was more than an hour ago. I tried calling him . . ."

"So did I," Ciceline said. She got her phone and tried again. Again, it went to voicemail.

"This has to do with Finn, doesn't it?" Stella said. "Lucy got the pills for Jesse. Whoever chased us tonight . . ."

"Chased you?" Michaela asked.

"I think it does," Ciceline said. "I have to go."

"I'm going with you," Jesse said.

"No."

"Yes. It's Lucy."

"Me too," Stella said.

These Westchurches and their obstinance were going to kill her. "Let me handle it."

"How are you gonna get there?" Stella asked. "We left our cars on the road."

Ciceline growled. "Jesse, just let me borrow your car. This is dangerous."

"We should hurry," Jesse said, grabbing the keys and his jacket off their hooks.

"Come on," Stella said. "The work van will fit everyone."

Stella and Jesse each gave their mom a kiss on the cheek, and they hustled out the door. Ciceline got in the driver's seat; she knew the way to Lucy's house better than anyone. They were three minutes into their drive when the alarm on Ciceline's phone went off; a blaring "BEEP BEEP" that she had never heard before, but understood right away: Lucy's distress call.

LUCIAN

Lucy pulled into his driveway with a fresh bottle of pills in the well between the seats. It was not the first time he had paid someone shady a shit-ton of money to fetch him more pills, though this time they were for Jesse. It could probably wait until morning — the fresh blood Jesse had gotten the day before would hold him over — but Lucy wouldn't get a moment's sleep if he didn't at least look at Jesse's face tonight and assure himself that he was okay. He would take Dog Lucy out, then make the trip to Jesse's house. He left the ignition on and reached for the car door.

A tickle started at the base of his neck. Everything looked normal, as he'd left it: lights off, doors closed.

He cracked the window, letting in the scents of dry autumn leaves, the creek at low tide, and woodsmoke. Dog Lucy was barking from inside the house. That's what his ears had picked up on before. Dog Lucy wasn't much of a barker. He yipped and panted a lot when he was excited, but this was an actual bark.

He should go, just up and leave, call for help, let Carnelian take care of it . . . but then he'd have to leave Dog Lucy alone with whatever was about to go down. Anyway, whoever was in his house already knew he was in the driveway. The smoke smelled too acrid to be from wood, not unusual this time of year, people burned all sorts of things. But it was close, and getting stronger.

He grabbed his phone from the passenger seat, clicked on his home security app, and called up the feed from the cameras in his house. The alarm hadn't been triggered, so if someone was in there, they must have hacked his security. Small night-lights lit the corners of the house, mostly for Dog Lucy, when Ciceline was visiting. The kitchen camera was aimed toward his crate, but he was barking in the opposite direction, toward the pantry.

Lucy swiped the screen to move the camera, caught the quick motion of a shadow across the floor, and stopped swiping. The shadow stilled, too. It could have come from anything. Maybe the pantry door had swung open in a draft. He moved the camera again. The pantry door was closed. Back again. The shadow was gone.

He opened the Carnelian app ("DAIRY FREE WORLD-WIDE!") and hit the red button on the top right of the screen: the distress signal.

Ciceline would be notified. Hopefully her mission would keep her busy and give Carnelian time to arrive before she did. If this was Via Nova, there was a good chance they were waiting for her, too.

His phone pinged with an automated response: *ETA 60 minutes*

"Damn it," Lucy muttered.

Dog Lucy's barking got more frantic.

A car pulled up on the side of the road and idled there. Lucy had enough room to gun it, to just back out of the driveway, but not by much. He'd be run off the road, trapped in his car, and executed. There was, however, a small bunker that locked from the inside, under his pantry floor. If he could get to it.

Oh well. It hadn't felt right to leave Dog Lucy to die anyway.

He opened his glove compartment and retrieved a switch-blade, which he stuck in his pocket, and a box cutter, which went into his sock. He left the car running and got out.

Maybe he was being paranoid. He wasn't, but it was nice to think that for a second.

Flood lights came on when he approached his front door, illuminating a footprint on the doormat, way bigger than his own. He opened the door to smoke crawling across the ceiling. Where in the world? Nothing seemed immediately on fire, but there was no way he could lock himself in a bunker under his burning house.

A few quick strides took him across the living room and into the kitchen, where Dog Lucy was scratching at the bottom of the crate, frantic to get out. Lucy opened the latch and swept him into his arms. If he got the dog out of the way, he could run into the woods and take cover or something because now, yes, that was definitely the creak of a floorboard. He must have passed right by them. No way to get to the bunker now.

Back door it was, then. The floorboard squeaked again, and Lucy bolted toward the back deck, the dog wiggling in his arms like a complete asshole.

Lucy pulled the door open. A gunshot shattered the glass, sending shards flying back into his face. He leapt back, gripping Dog Lucy tighter. The dog bit and clawed, desperate to get down as Lucy lurched out onto the deck and threw him over the railing.

Blood from the cuts on his face obscured his vision. He pivoted and lunged, crashing into his attacker, trying to grapple him to the floor. The guy was bigger than him in every way, breadth, width, and height; a mountain of a man. But the deck was slippery with mold and the man lost his footing, wheeling his arms for balance. Lucy was just tall enough to get his teeth under the guy's jaw, and he bit him, for shock value. The surprise of it toppled the man backwards. Lucy fell with him. *Underestimate me now.* He let go before the blood started spurting, and wrenched the gun away.

The man flipped them, pinning him to the ground with a knee on his chest. He'd never be able to use the gun before the guy got it back, so he flung it over the railing. He no longer heard Dog Lucy barking; maybe he'd run off.

The man stood up with Lucy's neck in his hand, threw him back against the railing of the deck, and followed through with a straight kick, like he was trying to knock down a wall. The railing splintered — so did his ribs — and he flew over backwards.

This had to be a retaliatory hit for Russel Busquet, but it felt personal, and he couldn't concentrate long enough to get a vibe for why. Busquet had been pure business and not even his decision. He got to his feet, but his attacker was already on the ground coming after him, trying for another kick to the chest. This time Lucy caught it with both arms and threw him. The guy cried out as his knee popped.

By the time the man got up, Lucy had freed his switchblade. The guy took a hard swing at his face, hands knotted into meaty fists. Lucy ducked back, and the swing went wild.

Three things that he had learned a hundred years ago in America: One, the cough medicine he'd always taken was opium and he was addicted to it. Two, orgies were dull, especially when you were addicted to opium. Three, boxing was a gold mine if you were a long shot, but also secretly a vampire. *A champion is someone who gets up when he can't.* Jack Dempsey, King of the Ring, had said that.

Lucy threw his hips into the next punch and popped the blade out as he made contact. It glanced off the cheekbone, slicing upwards and laying it open, blood pooling in the man's eye . . . in his eye socket, rather. The man bellowed, but still kept coming at him, backing him up toward the boathouse by the creek. He took swing after swing; Lucy ducked under, back, to the right. He saw an opening, smashed the man's cheek, and felt it cave.

Time to run.

Flames from his house lit up the night, and the smoke poured out, gagging him, closing his throat. Lucy froze.

Burning oil. The flames of the pit. Bodies on fire.

The man reached for him. Lucy tried to dodge, but the

distraction cost him. A giant fist snagged his jacket, whipping him back.

Smoke almost obscured another figure approaching. The guy from the car, probably. He could deal with one at a time, not both.

Lucy jammed the blade under the first guy's ribs, but it didn't get far; something blocked the blade, a vest, maybe? He threw Lucy down into the icy creek.

"Move!" the guy from the car shouted. "I have a shot!"

The man didn't move. He pinned Lucy, straddling him, hands wrapped around his throat, and pushed him under the water. Strangling was about as personal as it got — slow, intimate, painful.

Lucy kicked, clawed, sliced with the blade. His pulse throbbed in his head; sounds from above faded. The strength of the grip made him panic; soon those hands would crush his windpipe and possibly his bones, too.

Boxing wasn't the only way to win: Get your heel in a man's cock and balls and the fight was over. He twisted, pulled his knees up, kicked, and missed.

Red lights flashed in his eyes in time with his pulse. His arms and legs were free, the box-cutter in his sock within reach. He grabbed it, pushed the blade up, and jammed it where he thought the guy's neck might be.

He heard a muffled shout as the hand on his throat slackened. He lifted his head out of water and dragged in one terrible, sweet breath.

The world swam back to life: the weight of the body still pinning him, closer now, smothering. The other guy shouted, "Move! Move!"

The guy from the car had to be within reach; some part of him anyway. Lucy snaked his hand out from under the body on top of him, found a denim-covered leg, and stuck the blade in the soft webbing behind the Achilles tendon, judging by the scream.

With what little strength he had left, he pushed the blade back, like cutting through tough meat.

Something fell next to his head. Whatever it was, it didn't matter, he fumbled for it.

The gun, the *gun*. Lucy aimed what he hoped was the barrel toward what he hoped was one of them and pulled the trigger. The kick jerked his hand back and the gun fell into the creek.

The body lolled on top of him. He'd wiggled his way out from under bigger guys. He managed to turn himself over, but that only put him face-down into the water, so he had to turn his head to breathe. Breathing hurt like hell and he choked on ice water.

His throat swelled, his lungs sloshed with water that his fractured ribs couldn't cough up. The smoke was extra helpful. The option of up and dying was now on the table and not looking so bad.

There was only one way for a champion to finish, after all.

STELLA

S tella gripped the "Oh shit" handle as Ciceline whipped the van around tight, dark turns. Jesse sat in the back, dialing Lucy over and over again.

Why did Lucy even have a distress signal? She'd asked that question as they'd piled into the van, but no one had answered. Exhaustion enveloped her body like a cold blanket, and she shivered. Her nerves were shot. She wished she'd gone to sleep instead of following Finn, but then she never would have confirmed that Finn had stolen Jesse's meds. Ciceline might have caught him, and not known who he was. What would have happened to him had she not intervened?

There were no streetlights on this road. An orange light glowed from up ahead, the kind you'd see from a distant town on a foggy night. It seemed to move with the wind, and the smell of smoke seeped into the vents, even with the filter on.

"Shit," Ciceline muttered, slapping her palm against the steering wheel, and gunning it until they careened down the twisting road at seventy-five. They were going to die.

At a distance, you could write off the smoke as someone's chimney, at a distance. No one would have called it in yet if it was a house-fire, which, naturally, it was.

Ciceline lurched out the door, leaving the keys in the ignition. It took Stella's eyes a few minutes to adjust: they had parked far from the driveway, nothing but bushes, underbrush, and trees, lit by the flicker of flames. She couldn't see the way in, and the smoke invaded her lungs, already choking her.

Jesse pitched out of the van after Ciceline. Stella followed his lead until they came to the gravel drive, where Lucy's car sat with the ignition running, the door open.

Flames licked out of the shattered windows of the house, and smoke poured from the open front door. Stella caught sight of Ciceline's blond hair as she sprinted toward the porch and disappeared into the smoke.

Jesse stood in the driveway, running his hands over his head. Stella took out her phone and dialed 911. When they asked what her emergency was, she shouted "House fire!" before realizing that she didn't know Lucy's address.

She looked to Jesse, but he was gone, running toward the back of the house. Stella called out to him and followed, still clutching her phone. As she got near the house, the whooshing of the flames bursting through the windows drowned out her voice. She caught up to him by the porch. Jesse stood in the yard, covering his ears like he couldn't bear the noise. She gripped his arm, but he shook her off.

"I can't hear him. I can't hear him. He's not answering."

Stella wrapped herself in calm. Years of imagining every disaster had given her an edge in actual ones. "Jesse, address," she said, holding her phone up to him.

He opened his eyes and rattled off Lucy's address in a shaky voice, and the 911 operator squawked something in reply.

She couldn't see much through the haze, so she pulled her sweater up over her nose and mouth, lit the flashlight on her phone, and cast it around.

The railing of Lucy's back porch was broken. Below it, the bushes were crushed. Okay, good sign, someone — hopefully

Lucy himself — had jumped out. Why he'd jumped through the railing and not over it was a mystery.

Now that she was looking for it, an actual trail ran through the fallen leaves. Jesse must have seen it too; he hooked her by the arm and dragged her toward the water, behind the boathouse.

Something was floating close to the bank. It looked like a body. No, bodies, plural. Neither of them was moving, neither of their shapes was familiar to her, neither of them was Lucy. Jesse hooked his fingers around the arm of the bigger one and pulled. Stella pulled with him, and together they rolled the body over.

"Fuck!" Jesse yelped, as they both stumbled back.

A wide, dark slit gaped where the man's eye should have been. The man's throat was torn, jagged and brutal, like a piece of his jaw had been ripped off.

Do enough surgeries and few things shock you anymore, but still, there was something about seeing a ripped up human face that rattled a person. She shook it off to check the other body, and laid her eyes on Lucy, face-down in the creek.

Her hands flew to her mouth. Stella knew dead when she saw it. Even in the dark, there was a sense for respiration, minute movements present in unconsciousness that weren't there when someone was gone. She reached for him, but Jesse got to him first, leaping over the other body and dragging Lucy away. He was waterlogged, a sponge. Jesse turned him over and sat there looking terrified, with Lucy across his legs.

She clambered over the first body — he was so large, she had to use her hands and legs — and grabbed Lucy's arm.

Jesse snapped out of his daze and pulled Lucy back. "No!"

"Jesse, stop." For Jesse to beat his disease, only to lose his love? He would lose his mind, especially when he realized that he hadn't let Stella try to save him.

"No," Jesse said. "Just . . ."

He pulled Lucy back against his chest and wrapped his arms around him, like the Heimlich maneuver, which was not drowning protocol—

Yet that's exactly what he did, and Lucy coughed up a massive amount of water. He reached up to grip Jesse's arm.

Stella scooted back, nudged up against the body, shrieked, and moved away.

Okay? That made no sense, but okay. Maybe Lucy hadn't been under for long. Or maybe she'd seen it wrong. Panic played tricks with perception.

"Lucy!" Ciceline's voice screamed out from the house, hoarse and thin.

"Out here!" Jesse yelled. "Ciceline! Out here!"

In the distance, a firetruck wailed, startling them both. Jesse sat back on his heels, his eyes wide and shocked, holding Lucy's hair from his forehead.

Ciceline came barreling down the hill, paying no heed to either Stella or the two bodies. She vaulted over the big guy like it was nothing and took Lucy out of Jesse's arms.

"He got me some pills," Jesse said. "They're probably in his car."

"No time," Ciceline said. Then, to Lucy, "Sorry, hon. I know you hate this." She hauled the stranger's body out of the way. His mouth slackened for a moment, a silent protest. She drew a blade out of her coat pocket, shoved the man's sleeve up, and sliced his wrist. Then she hooked Lucy by the back of the neck and pressed the man's bloody wrist to his lips.

What—?

No, that couldn't be right. It wasn't logical. She was seeing this wrong. Her eyes-to-brain function was offline, tonight was a lot; this was irrational.

"Isn't that guy a —— I mean, will this save him?" Jesse asked. His voice was a high, trembly thing.

"Quick-fix in emergencies," Ciceline said. "Like drinking vodka when you're dying of thirst. It'll give you a little lift, but you can't live on it. He'll need fresh blood soon, or he'll crash." She put a hand on his arm and gave him a firm shake. "We need to move."

Lucy coughed again, and gagged. Jesse gripped him tighter. "You're okay, you're okay," more to himself than to Lucy.

Stella's legs were stiff and frozen to the ground, swampy water wicking into her pants. Her brain informed her that she was freezing, but she didn't feel the cold. The shaking was outside of her. Reality had flipped. She really saw what she saw. There was no other logical explanation.

Of course Lucy was a vampire.

Hadn't she known it all along? From his overarching weirdness, to how modern colloquialisms sometimes didn't seem to fit in his mouth? One time he had said "watch me yeet this bottle into the trash bin" and she'd laughed until she nearly peed and had no idea why. Their mom had told Lucy once, "You're not kidding anyone with that baby face, I see those eyes."

Had Jesse known all along? No, not until recently. The pills, his miraculous recovery. Finn made sense now. Was everyone a vampire except her?

A laugh burst out of her mouth, one that could equally be categorized as a scream. Ciceline and Jesse turned to her.

"Oh," Ciceline said.

Yeah, 'oh.'

"Are you going to kill me?" Stella asked.

"What? No. Why would I? Go ahead, tell all your friends. They'll believe you and you'll be so popular."

The sirens grew louder.

"We have to go," Jesse said.

Ciceline stood up with Lucy in her arms, stepped over the giant guy, and stormed passed Stella toward the car.

Jesse gave Stella a hand up. It was weird touching his cold, wet fingers; she almost drew back from him, but he let go before she could react. He didn't look at her as he walked past, head down.

Ciceline handed Lucy off to Jesse, who took him, staggering a little in surprise. When she leaned into Lucy's car, she hissed a swear. "I don't have time to look for his fucking keys!" She slapped the steering wheel in frustration.

"Grab the pills," Jesse reminded her. "We'll take the van."

"Where are you going?" Stella asked.

"A hospital," Ciceline said. "You should both go home; I've got it from here."

"You don't have a car," Jesse said. "Get in the van."

If Stella let them go now, she'd find a way to convince herself that none of this had happened. She would un-know it by the time she got home, make up some other explanation for what she'd seen. She couldn't let that happen. A hospital with actual doctors would either confirm that everyone was a vampire except her, or that she was having a nervous breakdown.

Jesse hurried past without a word, clutching Lucy tight.

"I'm coming, too," Stella said.

Ciceline gaped at her as the sirens wailed closer.

"We're not leaving my sister here with all the dead bodies," Jesse said. "I was going to tell her anyway."

"Shit." Ciceline stomped passed Stella and helped Jesse get Lucy into the backseat. "I have to drive. This hospital has no real address to put into GPS."

Stella handed the keys to Ciceline and got into the middle seat. The clock read 2:10 AM. Her mind was a haze of smoke and flames and questions she couldn't ask until she wrote them out in a nice, bullet-pointed list. Ciceline peeled away down the street as the fire trucks came screaming up behind them. They'd find the bodies, what then?

Lucy coughed, dripping water and probably blood all over the back seat. It would have to be the work van, wouldn't it? Jesse murmured to him, "Hey, it's okay."

It was not okay. How was Stella supposed to square with the knowledge that her brother's ride or die was the undead?

CICELINE

OCTOBER 24TH

iceline stood before the mirror in the clinic's bathroom, trying to wipe the soot from her hair with a wet paper towel. She only succeeded in creating sticky streaks across her equally sooty face.

Lucy was safe. That was the main thing. She hated every instance she had to be at this clinic, but Lucy would live.

Her lungs ached and her throat burned, though not as much as Lucy's probably did. At least he got to sleep it off, even if it was on a crappy cot in what barely passed for a hospital room. The clinic was a renovated old motel just before Montauk, over an hour from Lucy's home. Or what used to be his home, but which by now was probably a blackened skeleton. Lucy was lucky he wasn't in the same condition. This was a close one; it had been a long time since he'd been this badly harmed. These times were supposed to be over. Hadn't Carnelian said these retaliations were done ten years ago, and they would be protected? Twenty years ago? Hadn't they promised them over a century ago that the dead children from the dungeon were going to be the end of it? *Fucking Yvette.*

She sucked the tears back. The time for crying was over; it was time to do something. As long as she and Lucy were under

Carnelian's rule, this would keep happening until both of them were killed. She had to tell Lucy what was on her mind. He would know anyway — hell, maybe he already knew. She had never kept anything important from him, no matter how dark. How would she tell him? 'I think I need to depose our mother to save our lives, and if she refuses to leave, we have to take further action against her. By the way, I've considered murder.'

The rest of the Carnelian higher-ups were firmly behind Yvette — no democracy among the old-timers — but Ciceline wondered if she could find support among the workers.

The bathroom door opened. Stella came in, looking almost as bad as Ciceline felt.

"It was a long ride," Stella said. "I need to pee."

Ciceline didn't trust her burning throat to answer, so she nodded. Stella went into a stall while Ciceline continued trying to rinse her hair. When Stella was done, she joined Ciceline at the sinks to wash her hands and face. She made a kind of "ugh!" noise as she rubbed her face dry with the scratchy paper towel.

They turned to each other.

"You have a little something . . ." Stella said, pointing to Ciceline's face.

Ciceline wiped at her mouth. It was way more than a little something: soot caked on her nose and lips.

"Hang on." Stella wet more paper towels under the faucet and wadded them up, beckoning Ciceline closer.

Ciceline went, her lips pressed shut, sealing everything up behind her tongue. When Stella started scrubbing the ash from her skin, her other hand cupping Ciceline's cheek, the ache in her lungs grew until it came out in a sob.

"Hey," Stella said. "It's okay. Lucy's gonna be okay. Right?" She put her arms around Ciceline, pulling her against her chest. "I mean, he's . . . you guys all are . . . so, he'll be fine, won't he?"

Ciceline let herself go on for a minute. No one aside from Lucy got to see her cry, or got to see her do much of anything, really; she wasn't a fan of people getting close. She pulled away, turned the faucet on, and stuck her entire head under it, letting the cold water shock her skin as it trickled down her ruined blouse. Stella stood silent, waiting for her to finish.

There was a shower in the basement, though not a good one. She longed to stand under the water and scrub herself clean. Not until they came out to tell her Lucy's condition.

"It's not that," Ciceline said, straightening up to dry off. The tears kept coming anyway. "I mean it is, of course it is, Lucy being . . . being hurt. But my dog was in that house."

Stella's face crumpled. "Oh no. I'm so sorry. Did you find anything?"

Ciceline shook her head. "I think I saw the crate, but I couldn't tell if the door was open. If Lucy got into the house first, he probably opened it, so I don't know."

"I think he did."

Ciceline side-eyed her. Was this like one of Lucy's intuitions?

"The back railing was broken, and I saw a trail going from there to where we found him. I think Lucy went inside first."

Hope and anger mingled in her chest. Lucy had probably been trying to get to his safe room, but he had stopped to rescue her dog on the way.

"Your dog might be out there somewhere. Hang on, let me send a text out, okay?"

Right: local vet. It was a long shot, and hope was usually a waste of time — oh what the hell, she was being cynical. A long shot beat no shot at all.

Stella typed, her thumbs flying across her screen. "Send me a pic?"

They traded phones; Ciceline entered her number. Only Lucian and Carnelian had her personal number. When they traded back, Ciceline had to go through photos of Dog Lucy to find a full-body one. Seeing them, and thinking of his little body in the house, of his fear when strange men had come in, got her choked up again. She found one and sent it.

"Thanks," Stella said. "Microchipped?"

"Yes."

"What does he answer to?"

"Lucy."

Stella looked up, concerned. "I mean your dog."

"Yes, his name is Lucy."

She chuckled and continued to text. "Okay. We have three really great techs there. Two are on tomorrow . . . well, today, I guess, and one is off so maybe she'll take a ride around town. Oh, I better call my boss and tell him we won't be in. If Lucy is out there, he'll turn up."

Sure, unless he'd gotten picked up by a coyote or hit by a car.

How Stella could stand there caring about her and her dog after what she'd just seen spoke to a strength that Ciceline couldn't access for herself right now. "Hey," she said, "are you doing okay with all of this?"

Stella's laugh was too loud, echoing off the walls. She clapped both hands over her mouth. "Sorry, no," she said, quieter, through her fingers. "I need answers."

"You'll get them," Ciceline assured her. "I just have to get my mind right first."

"Fair enough," Stella said, then turned and left the bathroom before Ciceline had a chance to say anything more.

Ciceline smoothed her hair down — useless — and followed Stella out into the hall. The walls were a blueish gray, the lighting a dreary florescent despite the clinic being a privately owned, refurbished art deco hotel. The building was angular, with peaked windows, most of which had been fitted with blinds. As far as anyone knew, it was a re-opened spa, always too expensive or too booked to get into. It wasn't refurbished very well. Carnelian Inc. had the money, but they hoarded it.

Doctors, nurses, and orderlies hurried by, sleepless and hungry, the same as any emergency room on a bad night. Some of them were probably a little blood-addled, too, which dangerous and cruel: Carnelian kept closets stocked with pills right downstairs, but they had to be earned through labor. There was nowhere else for vampires to go, so anytime someone got hit by a car, or in a fight, or any of the chronic-illness ones relapsed, they ended up here, if they were lucky.

Ciceline went around the curve of the hall to the vending machine. She opened her app, swiped the reader, and chose four waters.

Across from a nurses' station, a couple stood in the hallway, locked in a tight embrace. The woman murmured to her partner, "Don't worry, okay? You won't even feel it; you'll just wake up starving. They'll give you the pills right away. Then your new life starts. I'll be by your side the whole time."

"Forever?" he asked her.

She stood on her toes and kissed him. "And ever."

How nice for them. Ciceline had been changed by her father on the roof of their manor. He had done it through iron bars that had imprisoned him in the attic, their last-ditch effort to go behind Yvette's back and save Lucian as he was dying. She had climbed to the roof on her last night in their home, lit only by the moon, promising Tata that if he changed her, she would change Lucy. He had used bedsheets to tie her to the bars so she didn't convulse herself off the roof. Fun times. And yet, Tata had married Yvette. He'd loved her, in the beginning. Over a century they had been together, Tata said. How could anyone change so drastically? Could Ciceline? This was exactly why it wasn't wise to get involved with people.

She left the two lovebirds to their life-changing moment, carried out with the safety and comfort that Carnelian had not extended to Jesse. Never again would Ciceline allow someone to be changed like that.

Back around the corner, she found Jesse seated in a plastic chair outside Lucy's room, leaning his head against the wall and just about nodding off. His shirt was still damp, streaks of blood standing out stark against the light gray.

Jesse stirred. Ciceline handed him a water. "Thank you. If you say, 'for what' I'll sue you."

Before he could answer, the door beside his chair opened, and a nurse came out.

"He's resting comfortably," she said. "We'll do everything we can to speed up the process, but we didn't have many donors this month."

"He'll be okay?" Jesse asked.

The nurse frowned at him.

"He's new," Ciceline said. Then, to Jesse, "Yes, he'll be okay; it's just a matter of how long, and how bad it will be in the meantime."

"I can donate," Stella said, looking up from her phone. "I'm already here, and I'm not a . . . one of you. That's what you need, right?"

The nurse looked to Ciceline. She nodded, but stopped Stella with a hand on her arm. "It's not too different from a regular blood drive. Make sure you drink some orange juice, okay?"

"Sure," Stella said. She followed the nurse down the hall.

"Since we can't go in now," Jesse said, plucking delicately at his filthy clothes, "I'm going to wash up in the bathroom."

"There's a shower downstairs," Ciceline said, "and scrubs in the locker next to it, if you want to change."

Jesse didn't need to be told twice. When he was done with his shower, she went next, and by the time she finished, it was 4:10 AM. She dragged herself back upstairs. It had quieted down, doctors and nurses doing their exhausted hallway walk, most of the patients settled for the night.

Ciceline pushed open the door to Lucy's room. It was dark, but he looked, yeah, as she had thought: really bad. That godawful sound bubbled in his lungs again, and no matter how many times she heard it, even knowing that he'd be sitting up and talking sometime tomorrow, she hated it. It was a death rattle, and her feeling was primal. She had failed him as a child; for all her and Tata's effort, he had been changed in a filthy dungeon, seconds before death. She had resolved then to never fail him again.

Jesse slept in a chair next to the bed, while Stella curled up on another chair, scrolling on her phone, not even attempting to sleep. A wad of cotton was taped to the soft crook of her arm. Someone had thought to put a third chair in the cramped room. It had arms and a cushioned seat. She sank into it, the entire last week pulling her down.

With her imagination filling her head with the cries of her dog, she thought that sleep would never come. It did, though, at least for a few hours.

When Ciceline woke next, it was to a shrill ring, and Stella's voice saying, "Hello?"

She opened her eyes to see everyone awake, dazed, looking like shit, and surprised they had survived the night. She glanced at her own phone. It was 8:17 AM.

"Oh my god," Stella said, and then, bizarrely: "Bottle! That's so great. Thank you."

Bottle? It sounded like good news, at least?

Jesse shook his head and scooted his chair closer to Lucy's bed, looking him over, his mouth pursed, not pleased that he wasn't up yet. Those cuts on Lucy's face looked worse by the thin sunlight that streamed in through the slatted blinds.

"We'll be there," Stella said, and ended the call. "Ciceline, someone dropped your dog off at the hospital. He's fine."

Oh, and here came the waterworks. She felt ridiculous, but it couldn't be helped. Jesse handed her a wad of scratchy tissues.

Stella said, "They can hold him for a while, if you need to stay here, but I can drive you back of you want. I want to see how Mom is doing, so I was going to head home." She looked over to Jesse. He gave her a small nod.

"I'll be back in a few hours," Ciceline said. "I'll get a ride back here later; Stella can stay home. Call me if anything changes, okay?"

She got up and stretched, twisting her back to pop it. There was still all this shit with Yvette and Via Nova to deal with, but Jesse would take care of Lucy, and her dog would be in her arms again soon.

She bent over Lucy's makeshift bed and kissed his forehead, before awkwardly patting Jesse on the back.

Outside, it had grown even colder; the sky was the color of wet cement, threatening rain. They got into the van, Stella behind the wheel this time, and Ciceline wondered how they would fill the silence for an hour.

Then Stella pulled out of the hidden drive and said, "So! Vampires, huh?"

JESSE

When the door closed behind Stella and Ciceline, leaving Jesse alone in the room with Lucy, the rest of the world evaporated, sealed away outside. Doctors and nurses shuffled past, sometimes speaking, sometimes urgently, muffled by the door. A few keening cries came from the other rooms; Jesse hadn't heard them before.

An open trash bin stood in the corner, with Lucy's wet, bloody clothes at the top, shirt hanging over the edge, cut in two. Even the animal hospital was cleaner and more efficient. Lucy hadn't exaggerated about the lack of doctors and hospital staff.

If Jesse stared long enough without blinking, he could watch the cuts on Lucy's face seam together, and the ring of bruises around his neck fade. How often had this speed-healing hidden something from him? They read each other's minds so easily, yet he had overlooked so much.

More pressing: who had done this? Why? Would they be back to finish the job?

He grabbed handful of scratchy, brown paper towels, wet them in the sink, and wiped the dried blood and soot from Lucy's face and hands. It passed the time.

He felt a stirring of awareness, and Lucy's anxiety — *I know how bad it looks* — something about his eyes? Oh, of course. Someone had strangled him.

Jesse tossed the paper towels into the bin. "I'm a doctor, I know what petechiae looks like."

But when Lucy blinked his eyes open, they were more than bloodshot; it looked straight out of a horror movie, burst blood vessels everywhere. Jesse's hands tightened into fists.

You're angry.

"Yeah."

"At me." Lucy's voice was sandpaper on glass.

"No," he said, but that was bullshit. "Yes, but it's irrational." He reached behind him for the bottle that Ciceline had given him and held it out. "Water? Or have you already had enough?"

"Hilarious."

"You have to stay hydrated."

". . . Worst person . . . entire planet."

"Correct."

Lucy croaked out a mangled word. He coughed weakly, took a few sips, and tried again. "I'm guessing you found me not breathing again. I'm sorry."

Jesse shrugged. "Breathing is so mainstream."

Lucy took more water and swallowed it hard. "Maybe saving each other's lives is our love language."

"I thought it was song lyrics and hipster jokes."

"Both."

"I hate how calm you are about this."

Lucy handed the bottle back and gestured for Jesse to lean closer. He cupped his cheek, scratching over unshaven scruff with short nails and calloused fingers. "You're getting beardy."

"My hair grows faster now."

"That does happen. You should leave it; it's hot." Lucy didn't move his hand right away. Something between them shifted.

"Seriously?" Jesse said, when he found his voice. "After all these years, this is you shooting your shot? On your death bed?"

"You know as well as I do that my death bed would have four posts and a canopy, and *Lacrimosa* playing in the background."

"You're literally bleeding from your eyes. What just changed?"

"Not 'just.'"

"Leave." Jesse moved Lucy's hand away from his face.

"I called you eighteen months ago and asked you to come to Paris with me. But you had a lot going on at work."

"I figured you meant as friends," Jesse said.

Lucy folded his hands and stared down at them. "Did it escape your notice that I couldn't live without you?"

"But at any time over the years, you could have . . . *oh*." Jesse covered his burning cheeks with his palms, because wow, how humiliating. Dragging Lucy out to dance with him, his ridiculous teenage pining that had stretched out into his adulthood. "I was a kid to you. I must have made you so uncomfortable."

Lucy rolled his eyes, revealing more bright red below the lids. "It's alright, I can handle it. You thought I was your age."

"Are you telling me we could have been having sex for the last eighteen months but we both almost died horny about it? I should have left you in the creek."

"But we have time now. Maybe one day, dragul meu."

"Maybe now," Jesse said.

"Your boyfriend?" Lucy reminded him.

Right, Jared. They hadn't officially ended it. But — "Shit. Jared. I saw him at BLOOD. It's a club where you can get blood from volunteers. I was in a tight spot with my . . . oh, I haven't even told you about Finn." God, the words still jammed up the back of his throat in a tight knot. "Well, Finn actually stole some of my pills and then disappeared." It sounded just as bad coming out of his mouth as it had in his head.

"Sorry, he what?" Lucy tried to sit up in the bed, and Jesse gently pushed him back down.

"It sounded like he was coerced. We haven't heard from him since. But Ciceline is on it, so." He didn't dare tell Lucy how hard he had crashed without those pills, that Finn's actions might have killed him. He didn't want to think about it. "So anyway, I ended up at this club."

"Okay," Lucy said, unconvinced. "Go on. You ended up at the sexy fetish club."

"There was definitely copulating, and really bad poetry."

"I am, uh, familiar with it. Jared?"

"Yeah, he was there," Jesse said. "I went into the Black Room, and I recognized him. He was a giver. He ran off before I could say anything."

"I'm sorry," Lucy said. "He could be a fetishist?"

Jesse shrugged, trying to care way more than he did. It seemed like ages ago.

They sat in awkward silence, a thing that had never happened to them before. Maybe Lucy was trying to save his voice. Jesse opened his mouth to ask if Lucy needed anything, but Lucy spoke up.

"This was a retaliatory hit. I killed Russel Busquet."

Jesse blinked a few times, forcing the words to make sense.

"I did it because it was my job," Lucy said. "But I'm not sorry. He was torturing and killing unsheltered people."

Jesse's mouth formed the word 'what' but nothing came out.

Lucian rubbed his temples and squeezed his eyes shut like he was fending off a headache. "She's here."

"Who?"

"Fucking Yvette. Okay, you need to know this. After Ciceline and I were changed, my mother took us both back in, as well as the other survivors who were locked up in the dungeon with us. What I didn't tell you was who locked us up in the first place."

"Oh my god," Jesse said.

"If you guessed Carnelian Inc., you are correct. They didn't want me to be changed because I was too sick. My father wanted to go against their rules. My mother — that's Yvette — didn't think I would survive. I ran away from home, and they caught me. My mother made a power grab right after our escape, and ultimately became the head of the syndicate. But we had to fight for it."

"We?" Jesse asked. "Weren't you, what, eleven?"

"Ciceline and I were the only ones who survived the battles. Turned out we excelled at killing. No one saw us coming."

"When you were eleven?" Jesse sputtered on the words.

Before Lucy could answer, the door opened without so much as a knock.

"Ah," said the woman who entered. "Sleeping Beauty is up. And he's got a Disney Prince, how nice. You must be Jesse West."

"Westchurch." He did not offer his hand to Lucian's mother. He hated her on sight. This was the leader of Carnelian, a thief of innocence, the architect of this pain.

Lucy didn't look up at her.

"I came in to see how you were faring, and to congratulate you on a job well done." She smiled at Jesse. "At least he's an accomplished killer."

"I do try," Lucy said.

"Baby vampire, when are you going to Snap?" Her smile was gentle but did not reach her eyes.

"In about thirty seconds if you don't leave."

"Has he told you yet?" she asked Jesse. "What he does for a living?"

"He told me enough," Jesse said.

Her laughter was the clinking of crystal wine glasses. "Oh, Alexandru, he's adorable. He thinks you're brainwashed."

"I think anyone who was forced to start killing at eleven years old didn't have much of a choice," Jesse shot back. That much was true, but the rest of it still left him reeling.

Yvette rubbed her temples, the same gesture Lucy had made moments ago. "How long is this infatuation going to last?"

"What do you care?" Jesse asked.

Her shoulders dropped and she huffed out an annoyed breath through her nose. "The next time your beloved 'Lucy' has to kill to save his own skin, he'll think of your disapproval, and he'll hesitate. Then he'll be the one in the incinerator, instead of the clinic. Picture that very vividly."

Jesse's throat closed up; words sealed behind his tongue.

She put her manicured hand over Lucy's. She was missing the last two fingers. "Alexandru, I am happy that you're alive; I'm not that much of a bitch. But killing Russel Busquet was the right call."

"I'm not saying it wasn't," Lucy said. "I'm saying that I'm done with high-risk jobs, especially when you don't give us the details, as specified in our contract. It's sabotage, and it puts everyone in danger."

"Let me handle it."

"You'd better. Make it clear that if they come after anyone I know, I'll go off-leash. They won't survive."

Lucy — his Lucy, in a torn dress on the dance floor, playing Yeah! on his cello, helping him practice Romanian, laughing with him, and mourning with him when his father died — Lucy had killed people since the age of eleven, and would kill more if he had to.

"Why can't you always be like this?" Yvette asked. "Dangerous and brave, a proper vampire?"

"Get out," Lucy hissed.

"For what it's worth, I'm sorry you got harmed; it was not my intent. You're to stay here for at least a week and stay out of trouble."

"Send protection to Jesse's house," Lucy said.

"I can't possibly afford—"

Lucy glared up at her.

She rolled her eyes. "Fine. Your Disney prince and his family will have protection. Your new orders are to remain here until I say so."

"Sure."

Yvette swept out of the room and didn't bother to close the door.

"Is that our cue to blow this joint?" Jesse asked. "I kind of hate everything about this."

"It sure is." Lucy sighed so hard it turned into a cough. "Help me up? I need a shower."

Jesse held his arm out so Lucy could grab it and pull himself up. They had dressed him in a gown and hospital pants, daisy yellow. Jesse checked the hallway before leading Lucy out of the room.

In the hall, a few nurses or orderlies, or whatever they were called in a vampire hospital, glared at them. One even opened her mouth to say something before shaking her head and going about her business. When they passed a nurses' station, Lucy shot them an "I dare you" look, and no one said a word.

In the elevator, Lucy leaned against the wall to stay upright. The doors slid open to the basement, darker and colder than upstairs. They went down the hall to a locker room with damp walls and damper air, and the scent of mold creeping up from beneath the floral, fruity smells of the shampoo and soap that Jesse had just used a few hours before.

Jesse opened the metal locker with a rusty squeal, where starchy, overly bleached scrubs hung from plastic hangers, mismatched. He rifled through them, looking for medium-sized ones of any color. He found a matching set, purple ones, and handed them to Lucy.

"I'm alright," Lucy said, holding the scrubs against his chest.

"Oh, yeah, of course," Jesse said. "I'll wait outside the door."

Lucy gave him a smile, and a small, gracious nod. "I won't be long. There's a vending machine if you want some water or something to eat." He reached behind himself as if to grab his wallet. "Damn it," he muttered.

"It's okay," Jesse said. "I have a few dollars in my pocket."

He left Lucy to his shower and went back out to the hallway. Under the dim, dusty overhead lights, in a grimy alcove, he found the vending machine. His options were pretty limited. The bottled water was probably a few years old.

Down the hall, the elevator rattled again and Jesse's skin prickled with a little shiver. Was he even allowed down here? He leaned out of the alcove to peer down the hallway. He'd just have to explain to whoever it was—

A figure drifted past the far end of the hall and disappeared around the corner, and Jesse glimpsed dark, curly hair, and Lucy's familiar silhouette. Had Lucy forgotten something, and maybe there was another exit? If so, how had Lucy gotten here so quickly?

He'd seen enough horror movies that he didn't call out Lucy's name or ask who was there, but . . . it was probably a better idea to go back to the locker room and see what Lucy was up to. He turned, and the figure came around the corner again, this time facing him, about fifty feet away. Jesse stared, torn between going towards him and running away. It looked just like Lucy. It wasn't. The person took a step toward him, and Jesse backed away.

Ridiculous. This was a hospital, there were guards everywhere. He'd seen them on the way in. Jesse raised his hand in a small wave.

The man who wasn't Lucy narrowed his eyes. "Are you security?" he asked. "I'll go where I damn please."

Jesse held up his hands. "No, just visiting."

"Really?" His voice was low and dignified, but there was something crafty in it when he asked, "Then why are you in the basement? Hmm?"

The man came closer, moving so quickly Jesse didn't even have time to think. His nerves jumped, muscles urging him to turn and flee. The man's curls were frizzy and unkempt, his forehead was slightly creased, and there were fine lines around his mouth. He looked to be in his early fifties.

"My friend is here," Jesse said. "Sorry, I thought you were him for a second."

"Oh, did you? And who might . . ." He smiled, and that shrewd look disappeared. "Wait. Are you Jesse?"

"Yes?" He hoped that was the right answer. "Do you know—"

The man lunged and grabbed his hand. Jesse started backwards, ready to call for help. "Ah, Jesse, what a pleasure to finally meet you in person. I've heard so much about you, my dear. What a shame we have to meet here, of all places. I can't even offer you a place to sit, or a cup of coffee."

It hit Jesse all at once. "You're Lucy's Dad?"

"Yes, yes!"

He must have heard that Lucy was here, then. "He's alright," Jesse said. "Actually, he's taking a shower, I'm just waiting for him."

"My son speaks of you often," Lucy's father said. He still held Jesse's hand.

Jesse gave a pleased, awkward little laugh. "We've been friends a long time."

Lucy's father nodded. "He's made you into a vampire. It's about time. You're his first." He flashed a smile, showing teeth that had been filed to points, but were now rounded at the tips. "It's not fair, you know."

Jesse rewound the conversation, but couldn't make the connection. His brain refused to kick in. "Sorry?"

"They won't give me blood." He looked into Jesse's eyes from about a million miles away, still smiling politely. "Just those blasted, useless pills. So dry. I need blood. Fresh, hot, filling my veins, fattening up my skin and muscles, making me warm all over. I need to drink it, damn this place."

Jesse took another involuntary step back, but Lucy's father jerked on his hand and pulled him forward.

"Get me fresh blood," Lucy's father said. "Bring it to me, and I'll pay you. I'll give you some. You want it, too, don't you? The pills just don't cut it. They're shit, aren't they, Jesse?"

Jesse yanked his hand away and stumbled backwards, directly into someone else. He yelped and leaped away.

Lucy steadied him with a hand on his shoulder. His hair was dripping water on the floor, and the purple scrubs stuck to him in dark patches, as if he hadn't completely dried himself before running out. "Tata," he said, "what are you doing down here?"

"Looking for you." There was something sly in the man's eyes, and Lucy must have seen it, too, because he shook his head and took his father's hands.

"Tata, you can't leave yet. Can't we go back to your room?" He took his father's arm and motioned for Jesse to follow them back to the elevator. "Jesse, in case you haven't guessed, this is my father, Doctor Alexandru Latari."

What could Jesse possibly say to that? It hadn't exactly been a pleasure to meet him this way. He settled for a small nod as the doors closed, and the elevator rose.

Doctor Latari looked back at him with narrowed eyes. "Ah, Lucian. He doesn't know, does he? Why did you not tell him?"

Jesse's chest clenched tight. "Tell me what?"

"I didn't get a chance to," Lucy said. "We were kind of in a rush."

"Dying, were you?" he asked Jesse. "That's fair. Lucian was dying, too. Lucian, tell him."

Lucy stared down at the floor of the elevator. "I was going to tell you . . . god, the night we changed you, the next day, last night, tonight. Things just kept happening. When Yvette asked when I was going to Snap, she wasn't just trying to wind me up."

"My goodness," Lucy's father said. "Did she really say that to you?"

Lucy went on, "The human mind didn't evolve to live much longer than a century. Maybe one-twenty, tops. So what happens is, most vampires go into a kind of dreamlike state at around a hundred years. And then again, and again, for however long you live; although I'm told they get fewer and farther between the older you get, like you're getting used to the idea after about five hundred or so. It's called Athanasia Disorder. 'The Century Snap,' as some people call it. It doesn't happen to everyone; I think the statistic is something like ninety-eight percent."

Jesse's mind whirled. What must it be like to be alive for that long? To live to a certain point expecting death, and then to not get it, with the world changing around you? Hundreds of years in a body, with all of its annoyances and inconveniences. He had an errant curl behind his ear that always grew the wrong way; he'd be cutting it every few weeks for centuries.

"For a few generations," Lucy said, "they tried sedating the ones going through it, putting them into a coma for the duration, but the drugs made it more severe. It just doubled when they woke up. The brain has to purge it. It's similar to dreaming, they say: if you can't lose touch with reality for a few hours a night, you'll do it awake. Like that, only times a thousand."

"And that," Doctor Latari said, "is where I am now. So you'll forgive me if I slip into that state now and then."

"How long does it last?" Jesse asked.

"A few months to up to two years at a time," Lucy said. "Two years would be a lot."

"It's been a year for me," Doctor Latari said.

"Some vampires never come back," Lucy said.

"What?" Jesse asked.

Lucy gave him a wan smile. "It's rare. I don't know a single person that's happened to."

"You're over a hundred," Jesse said. "So . . ."

"No. That's why she was needling me. I've been lucky."

"Lucky? You were floating face-down in a river as your house burned."

"Lucian," Doctor Latari snapped, "is this true?"

Lucy rolled his eyes and made a placating gesture. "I was lying face-down in a creek. I wasn't in the main stream." He gave Jesse an expectant look and a little nod, waiting for acknowledgment. When Jesse ignored him, he continued. "I've been through worse. Maybe I'm in the two percent."

"How special of you."

"Oh, Lucian," Doctor Latari said, "you've found someone who doesn't take your shit. I like him very much."

LUCIAN

Walking was hard, though Lucy tried to hide his struggle from Jesse and Tata. His ribs ached all the way around to his spine. He forced down the need to cough; cartilage took longer to heal than bones. His vision pulsed light and dark in time with his heartbeat. He'd make it — he always did — but he had to get out of this wretched place before he ran into Yvette again.

The elevator doors opened to the top floor and Jesse reached for his hand. Jesse was dragging his feet, drawn and hunched over, his eyes dazed. He hadn't slept in over twenty-four hours and Lucy sensed the dark thoughts that played on his exhausted mind, things outside of this mess. Maybe the boyfriend? Finn, more likely. Whatever it was, Jesse didn't want to talk about it. A well-known feeling of protection swelled in Lucian, as old as the day he'd met Jesse. His threat to Yvette had not been idle, and he hoped she realized she was on the list, too.

There were no windows up here, just private rooms in a circular hall, and no doctors, only a few nurses and orderlies taking laundry and bringing food. He took Jesse and Tata to room nineteen. The door squealed as he opened it, like a bad bow on a violin.

"My humble dwelling," Tata said. "At least for now."

The small room was tidy, with a few of his father's belongings placed on the bedside table; an open notebook with pages of his doctor-scrawl; framed photographs on the wall, mostly landscapes, but one of Ciceline in Romania, and one of Lucy on stage; and a neat little stack of antique books on a compact bookshelf.

"Wow," Jesse said, looking over the books.

"Ah, do you admire them?" Tata said. "I can give you one, if you want. Do you like Shakespeare? He's a fine man."

Jesse turned his head so fast he almost stumbled. Tata gave him a small smile. Lucy was never sure if Tata was joking or not, and he'd given up on asking.

"We can't stay very long," Lucy said. "I'm on my way to steal some pills and make a break for it. So, Dad, can I borrow your car?"

Tata went still, staring at the old books, silent as a tomb.

The last time he'd been like this, Lucy had been a child, and he was dying. *His grief for you broke him*, Yvette had told him, before locking Lucy away in his bedroom and Tata in the attic. Lucy would hear him walking at night, rattling the bars of his window, and crying for him. Lucy had not known his parents were vampires. To his mind, his father was a scientist, toiling in the cellar laboratory of their home in Romania, the red tinctures in glass vials nothing more sinister than attempts at medicine.

Lucy turned to Jesse, to see if he was ready to leave; there was no telling how long his father would remain in this state. He owed Jesse more of an explanation. But Jesse wasn't looking at him; he was staring at the open notebook on Tata's table.

Lucy touched his arm. *Let's go.*

"The pills don't work well for you, do they?" Tata asked, turning around to face them. "Fresh is best."

The thought alone made Lucy want to gag, but Tata was looking at Jesse, eyes narrow and shrewd. "Your young man here understands, Sandu. He's a true vampire. Don't try to make him into something he isn't."

Jesse's pupils were a little too wide, lips a little too red. Lucy put a hand on his arm.

"Hungry, aren't you?" his father taunted.

"That's enough of that," Lucy said. "Come on, Jesse." Forgetfulness, having no filter, saying things out of character: all part of the Snap. You said things in dreams that you would never utter in real life.

Tata gripped his arm. "I'm sorry. Please, Sandu, I didn't mean it. I've been trapped here for a year. I already let you down once."

"Don't worry about it," Lucy said, leaning down to kiss his father on the cheek.

"Of course you can take my car. It's parked in the garage; the keys are probably in the locker behind the front desk. Goodness knows I'm not allowed to use it."

"Thank you," Lucy said.

"Wait a sec," Jesse said, still staring at the notebook. "Is this what I think it is?"

Tata followed his eyes, and smiled. He ripped a sheet out of the notebook and held it up proudly. It was some kind of chart with points, too many numbers, parenthetical mathematical formulae, and words like "sublimation" and "recovery of cells," words Lucy understood, but could not contextualize.

"I've been meaning to show you this, Lucian," he said.

An ancient, shameful anxiety filled him. "Tata, you know I can't read this."

His father's face softened. "Darling, I know you never try."

"Can I see that for a sec?" Jesse asked.

Pleased, Tata handed it to Jesse. "You're a doctor?"

"Well, I'm a vet," Jesse said as he scrutinized the paper. "But this is . . . lyophilization?"

"Yes, of course," Tata said.

Ah, now that word he knew: freeze-drying. So it must have been his notes for the blood pills, the one formula that had worked. Carnelian's ace.

"That's the secret?" Jesse asked. "Anyone could be doing this with enough money. That's literally all Carnelian has? Money?"

"Well, you could be a bit more impressed," Tata said. "I invented it."

"Of course," Jesse stammered. "I mean, yes, it's wild that you came up with a system that works, but—"

"But this is a better formula," Tata said. "Do you see? It will make the pills more effective, for a longer time. Fresher."

"What do you want us to do with it, Tata?" Lucy asked. "Do you think we should make it available? Because I agree, but it is Carnelian's last claim to power. Without that . . ."

"Carnelian will likely fall over the next few decades, yes," Tata said.

Something inside him, coiled tight since childhood, unwound at the thought of life without Carnelian. He wanted it more than anything. Yet somehow, fear crept in to fill the void. What would he even do?

"We'll get it to Ciceline," Lucy said. "She handles these things better than I do. If this is what you think is best."

"I do," Tata said. "Seeing you hurt like this once again is the sign I needed that it's time for all of us to be free."

Lucy took his hands. "Thank you, Tata. I'll see you again soon."

"I hope so." He nodded to Jesse. "Get some real blood, because all the pills in the world will never measure up to it." He gave Lucy's hands a squeeze and let go.

Lucy took Jesse's hand and led him out of the room. In the glare of the hallway lights, Jesse looked ready to drop dead. "Let's get some pills before we escape."

"How?" Jesse asked.

"Shouldn't be too hard in a hospital."

They went down the hallway, back into the elevator, and to the main floor. Around the first curve, a nurse's cart stood outside an open door. There was the bottle, visible through one of the plastic drawers. The nurse was standing beside the cart, organizing the supplies.

He pulled Jesse back around the corner, out of the nurse's sight. "I'm going to create a distraction, and you swipe a bottle."

"What kind of distraction?"

He considered pulling the fire alarm, but that would put the patients in danger. "This is going to be a bit crass," he said. "Stand by."

He left Jesse in the hall while he stole into one of the rooms. There were two patients in here — not everyone was *the heir* and got their own private room — and one of them was being monitored by ICU machines. The patient was covered in stitches and bandages, face bruised to hell. Car accident, maybe. A feeding tube was wired through his nose and stitched on, with a blood-bag attached to an IV pole beside the bed. He was drugged into a deep sleep, but seemed stable enough. A little extra attention would probably do him some good.

Lucy crept closer, pulled the heart monitor leads free, and yanked the pulse-ox monitor from his finger. Then he ducked out of the room and back to Jesse.

He and Jesse stood aside, polite and helpful, backs to the wall as three nurses filed past. No one rushed, like they did in the movies. Lucy had been in hospitals often enough to know that alarm fatigue was a thing, and the most likely cause for an alarm was a loose lead, but still urgent enough to leave a cart unattended long enough for Jesse to swipe two bottles.

They hurried to the elevator, where Jesse popped the bottle open and gave Lucy a handful of pills. They hadn't brought any water and had to dry-swallow them.

"By Our Grace," Jesse said, grimacing as he swallowed. "Carnelian sucks."

"One day I'll tell you about the time they tried to ban all jokes and puns referencing 'sucking,' and how badly that backfired. Good story."

Downstairs at the front desk, a security guard sat behind the check-in counter, across from the elevator.

"Hello," Lucy said. "My father wants someone to get a book out of his trunk."

The guard scowled. "I have specific orders from Yvette not to let you leave the building."

"I can get it," Jesse said. "Right? I'm allowed to leave." He gave a casual little shrug and Lucy's heart almost burst with pride at Jesse's ability to roll with his plan without even knowing what it was.

The man sighed. "I guess."

"Great," Jesse said. "I'll go to the garage with you? You can guard me." He smiled, cute and a little flirty.

"Sure." He went to the next room for the keys, jerking his chin for Jesse to follow him to the stairs leading to the garage.

"Hey," Jesse said, looking back over his shoulder to Lucy. "I'll bring the book to your dad and then head out, okay?"

"Thank you," Lucy said. "I'll see you in a few days, then."

Lucy went back to the elevator. Once inside, he pressed the button for the garage.

When he got out, Jesse and the guard were a few paces ahead of them. The guard turned when he heard Lucy's footsteps. "Shit," he muttered.

Lucy held out his hand. "Just hand the key to me. This doesn't have to be difficult." He practically felt the guy contemplating different ways to stop him, wondering if he should call Yvette and tattle. Lucy turned to Jesse. "What is it you millennials say?"

"Uhh," Jesse said, "fuck around and find out?"

"Yes, that's the one," Lucy said. "The key?"

"Yvette's going to kill me," the guard said.

Lucy gave him a sympathetic smile. "I'll kill you worse."

"Can you at least punch me to make it look good for the cameras? But not too hard."

Lucy groaned. His ribs really hurt.

"Can I do it?" Jesse asked.

"Yeah," the guy said, "let him do it."

Lucy held his arm out and stepped aside, and Jesse let fly a haymaker to the guard's jaw, sending him toppling backwards over the car. The keys flew out of his hand and skittered across the cement.

Lucy took a moment to find his voice. "Why was that hot?"

Jesse unlocked the car doors. "Îți place."

"Unfair, using it against me," Lucy said. "Are you alright to drive? Everything hurts and I want to die."

"The pills are kicking in; I'm good."

Once they were in the car, a handful of security guards appeared in the garage.

"Just drive through the pylons and the boom barriers," Lucy said. "I'll pay for them later."

Jesse gunned it, his knuckles white as they crashed through the barriers.

"Wow, Jesse," Lucy said. "I didn't know you had it in you."

"I don't," Jesse said through clenched teeth. "I've never even run a stop sign before."

"They won't bother to follow once we get on Sunrise Highway; my mother won't punish them too harshly. It's hard to find help."

"Hey, Lucy, about what your dad said . . . about the blood. About it being fresh. I was just thinking, maybe there's a place . . . I'm not saying I want to go back there specifically, to the sexy club, but . . ."

"Hey," Lucy said, placing hand on Jesse's knee. "First of all, no shame in needing fresh blood, so put that thought out of your mind. Second, I love the sexy club, that's literally where we're going."

Jesse turned his head so quickly Lucy heard his neck crack. He was so much fun to tease, sometimes. BLOOD offered him a high level of security, as well; it only made sense.

And, more: it was an opportunity for Jesse to finally meet his actual family.

STELLA

S tella drove in awkward silence, with Ciceline beside her. Ciceline had chosen not to answer her initial ice-breaker about vampirism, so Stella kept her mouth shut, the rest of her questions too big to fit between her teeth.

Thirty minutes into the ride, Ciceline asked, "Do we know why Finn would be stealing pills for Via Nova?"

Stella swallowed past the tightness in her throat. "Via Nova? A few hours ago, my entire world was a different reality; you'll have to explain."

Ciceline heaved a resigned sigh. "Okay, we're doing this. Yes, vampires. What do you want to know?"

Stella's heart sped up; her body flashed hot and her palms grew slick against the steering wheel. It was real. They were having this conversation. What did she want to know? Everything.

"Start with Via Nova, I guess?" she asked. "Is that some kind of vampire clan?"

"Not a clan," Ciceline said. "There are governments — syndicates, more like — and Via Nova is yet another rebel faction in a long line trying to knock Carnelian Inc. out of the King Shit slot. Carnelian is who we work for, and yes, they are shit. But they're also the ones who get people like Jesse their pills, so we're stuck with them."

"So, Via Nova. That's who you think it is blackmailing Finn?" Stella asked.

Ciceline didn't answer.

"He wouldn't do anything like that unless someone forced him," Stella said. "No matter what, he loves Jesse. He doesn't want him to die."

Ciceline tapped her fingers against her thigh as she stared out the window. Silence reigned in the car for a full twenty seconds before she answered, "I believe you."

Stella didn't press. "Are you stronger than non-vampires?" It didn't feel right to refer to herself as "human," and imply that Ciceline wasn't. Ciceline, Lucian, her brother, possibly Finn? Who aside from her wasn't a vampire? "The way you picked Lucy up. The way you picked me up and tossed me into that truck."

"Thick thighs, it turns out," Ciceline said, "do save lives."

Stella couldn't tell if she was joking, so she said nothing.

"Yes," Ciceline said. "We are stronger. Muscles get more oxygen, bones grow harder, and everything heals faster."

"Can I ask how old you are? Is that rude?"

"I'm a hundred and fifty-one," Ciceline said. "My birthday is next week. I guess, anyway. I never had an actual birth certificate, so who knows. Lucy's a hundred and forty. We've changed identities four times now, because lifespans used to be shorter, and it wasn't unheard of for people to disappear; it was easier back then. These days it's challenging to create a whole new identity, so vampires tend to stick around longer. You can look older by not taking as much blood. That will be harder for people like Lucian and Jesse, because they'll start manifesting their original illnesses again. You've seen it with some famous vampires, suddenly getting old and haggard and dying out of nowhere."

Stella went through a list of some of her favorite celebrities who had died, wondering who among them might still be alive. It wasn't as important as she'd thought it would be.

"So who . . ." Stella took one hand off the wheel and flailed it awkwardly, trying to come up with the right way to ask. "Who made you a vampire?"

"My father did," Ciceline said. "Or, Lucian's father technically, but he's like a father to me. Our mother had locked him up to stop him from changing Lucy. I was supposed to get back into the house to change him, because he was dying, but Lucy's mother put a stop to it. Neither of us had been chosen. Lucy's mom didn't think he would survive the change. And I was just there as a servant, basically."

"That sounds traumatic," Stella said. "I'm sorry."

Ciceline didn't answer.

"Chosen," Stella said. "Who decides?"

"Carnelian has the final say," Ciceline said. "If you're angling to see if you're on the list, you are. I had to put you down as my reserve two nights ago. You were in Carnelian's way and they would have let Via Nova kill you."

Stella was a 'reserve' now? Without even saying yes yet? It irked her a little. "Can people decline?"

"Of course. You usually get six months to a year to think it over, and it's usually done at the clinic. Jesse didn't get that luxury."

"Does it hurt?"

"Like the dickens."

The idea of pain didn't frighten her, and the blood obviously came in pill-form now, but even if they weren't killing people and drinking blood, was it fair that only a select few had this opportunity? Was it moral that you had to know the right people? The disease that took hold of Jesse was genetic; the chance that she or Finn would get it too was not insignificant. Though she was thankful that Jesse had said yes, she wasn't sure she could do the same.

The sky was overcast and colorless as they pulled onto the farm-lined road to her street. It was too early in the year for snow, but a few flakes fluttered down and stuck to the windshield. A harsh winter was on the way.

But what relief she felt now when she thought of a future with her brother still in it. She was closer to owning the home she loved, to being her own boss. Finn would come back; of course, he would. Driving the tree-lined streets of Hampton Bays, away from the vampire hospital she hadn't known existed until last night, eased her spirit.

Ten minutes later they pulled up to the house. Stella's elation deflated when she thought of Mom in there, alone, waiting for her kids to come back. How could she keep this from her? Vampires existed and she had to choose to either become one, or to accept whatever life she was allowed. How would she even get through a conversation without yelling it out? How did Jesse? Stella cast her gaze down as she walked, willing her face to remain neutral, wondering how she usually looked when she didn't have a secret this big. What was her face supposed to do?

The front yard hadn't been raked. Shep cut fifty a month from their rent so he wouldn't have to hire someone to do maintenance, but this month, with everything going on with Finn and Jesse, it just hadn't happened. Stella's sneakers crunched over the fallen leaves; Ciceline's footsteps were weirdly silent behind her.

She opened the door to the mingled smells of coffee, an apple cider scented candle, and, faintly, bathroom cleaner.

Act casual.

Mom appeared in the doorway of the kitchen, phone to her ear, holding her finger up for 'one minute.' "Jesse," Mom said into the phone, "Stella and Ciceline just walked in. Alright baby, I'll let you know. Love you too."

She hung up, and Stella hugged her — a quick way to hide her eyes. She felt the tremor in Mom's shoulders; stress always brought on relapses.

"You smell like smoke," Mom said. "It's all in your hair."

"I know. Lucian's house burned down."

"Yes. How does a thing like that happen?" She looked at Ciceline as she asked. Stella kept her face stony.

"We don't know yet," Ciceline said. "I'm just glad my brother and my dog both made it out alive."

"Let's go get him, okay?" Stella said. "You can stay a while to rest if you'd like. Or if you have to get back—"

"I do," Ciceline said, "but I'll gladly accept a cup of tea before I head back out, if you don't mind Lucy in the house."

"Shep doesn't allow pets," Stella said. "But he doesn't have to know"

"A vet who doesn't allow pets in the house he owns, and rents to other vets? He sounds like a dick."

"He is a dick," Mom said.

"Come on," Stella said. "Let's get your baby."

There was no mistaking the tears in Ciceline's eyes again as they entered the lab.

"Stella!" Bottle Jenn said through her mask. She was doing a dental on a cat, its jaw cranked open while she planed its teeth. "Holy shit! I heard about the fire at your brother's friend's house. It's all over the news! Is he okay?"

"He's doing okay," Stella said. "Jesse is staying with him for a while. This is Ciceline; she's Lucian's sister. And the dog?"

"In the middle room," Bottle said. "Marcie Skeltin brought him in first thing this morning; you know, Barney's Mom? You did the foreign body surgery a few weeks ago. She was waiting outside the front door for us to show up."

"I'll send her a reward," Ciceline said.

From the middle room, a small dog barked. When Stella led Ciceline into the ward, they found Dog Lucy bounding around a second-tier cage, pawing like mad at the bottom to get to her. Ciceline's hands came up to cover her mouth as if to stop a cry bursting out.

"My muppet!" she said, struggling with the latch on the cage.

Stella lifted the latch and Ciceline lifted Lucy out, burying her face in his curls like he hadn't spent most of the night in the woods and didn't smell like a swamp.

Doctor Treece barged in, almost plowing into them. "Oh!"

she said, looking up. "Sorry, I — Hi, Stella, I didn't realize you were coming in today." Her hands fluttered at her sides before she clenched them into weird little fists. "I guess this dog is . . . I'm glad someone came for him."

"Yeah," Stella said. "You okay?"

"Yes." More little hand flutters. "Just so busy, we're getting killed. I'm super late for my surgeries."

"Oh," Stella said. "Don't let me keep you."

Treece scurried off. Ciceline gave Stella a look over Dog Lucy's head as she pressed her face into his fur. *That was weird.*

Stella shrugged.

In the lab, Bottle was gently rubbing the intubated cat while running water into the dental table. Shep stood at the counter, his back to them, looking into the microscope.

"Hey Shep," Stella said.

He waved to her without turning around.

"Okay then. Bottle, thanks so much."

Bottle air-kissed her as she passed by. "See you tomorrow."

Shep glanced at them as they passed by, then darted his eyes away.

"I'm going to drive them home," Stella called over her shoulder.

He didn't answer.

Once in the kitchen, with the lab door closed behind her, Ciceline said, "Wow, he really is a dick. But I owe the whole practice a tremendous thanks."

"Don't worry about it. I'm just happy you got your baby back."

Mom came over and pet the dog, who was still in Ciceline's arms. "Better not keep him here long," she said. "You know how Shep is."

"We won't," Stella said, giving Ciceline an apologetic look for having to rush her out. "I'll make some tea while we wait for your ride."

"Thank you," Ciceline said. "For everything."

Once Ciceline and Dog Lucy were on their way, Stella would take a real shower and nap the rest of the day away. And when Finn came home, everything would be fine.

She leaned against the door and laughed a little sigh of relief.

JESSE

Lucy had told him to drive to Brooklyn. The cars had only tailed them for about thirty minutes before backing off, and then Lucy had fallen asleep in the passenger seat. Jesse drove on in silence and let him rest.

They got to Brooklyn just before one o'clock. Lucy woke up, popped open the pills, and handed some to Jesse before taking a few himself. The pills scraped the edge off Jesse's hunger, but Lucy's father had drawn that gnawing ache up to the surface.

"There's a place close to BLOOD," Lucy said, and groggily gave him directions.

When they got there, Jesse couldn't help noticing that they weren't close to BLOOD; they were right behind it.

They got out of the car and Lucy straightened his spine gingerly, his upright posture forced and stiff. Jesse reached out to put a hand on his back but second-guessed himself and quickly withdrew. He'd never felt weird about touching Lucy before.

"Are we going in?" Jesse asked.

"Yes, but you don't have to stay if you don't want to."

His heart rate quickened. He was disgusted with himself for how much he wanted to get back in the Black Room. Lucy wasn't like that. He was normal, he hated blood, gagged on it.

Jesse walked toward the front of the building, but Lucy linked their arms and pulled him back, to cement steps that descended to a metal door.

"Rock star entrance?" Jesse asked.

"That's pretty apt, actually."

At the bottom of the stairs there was a buzzer, an intercom, and a camera. Lucy pressed the button and waved.

The intercom blared to life with the static of old technology. A woman's voice called out, "Holy shit."

The door clicked open and Lucy led him into a cavernous, empty room with black walls: the Black Room with the lights on. This was where he'd realized what an absolute vampire he was; where he'd recognized Jared, drank from him. He shuddered with revulsion and the desire to do it again. A man came around the corner, pulling a bucket on wheels with a mop. Jesse didn't want to think about what he had to clean up.

They left the Black Room, and in the corridor with the elevator, a small, burgundy-haired woman rounded the corner. His memories of that night were wonky and vague, but he recalled an image of her with a face full of makeup, her teeth stained red. Now her hair was piled in a messy bun, and she wore only lipstick, winged eyeliner, and a floor-length purple cardigan over plain black jeans and a t-shirt with the club's logo on it. Under that shirt would be a long, thin scar across her abdomen, and a faded tattoo.

Mia.

"Oh my god," she said, and threw herself at Lucy. "Lucifer Motherfucking Morningstar. As I die and asphyxiate. It's been almost a year, you asshole."

Her accent hinted deep south, which he'd either missed that first night, or she had hidden. Lucy hugged her with one arm, still hanging onto Jesse with the other.

She pushed Lucy back and raised an eyebrow. "My poor Buttercup. You look like run-over dog shit."

"Wow," Lucy said.

"Carnelian still have you doing their dirty work?"

"Yup," Lucy said. "Mia, this is Jesse."

Her eyes sparked with recognition, but she held out her hand. "A pleasure to finally meet you."

Jesse took her smooth, chilly hand. "It's okay. He knows I was here."

"It's policy to keep quiet," she said. "Anyway, I knew you the second I saw you, from Lucy's Insta. Come on. Let's get you both some real blood."

As Jesse followed her, he asked, "Wait, so 'Lucifer Morningstar . . ?'"

She giggled over her shoulder. "It was his stage name. We were in a band in the nineties. Now he just plays a boring cello."

"Excuse you," Lucy said, "but if orchestra was a movie, cello would be the sex scene. Literally everybody knows that."

"It's the porn section," Jesse said.

Lucy laughed, a dry, pained sound that turned into a cough.

"Huh, maybe," Mia said. "But now that you're home, there's no need to pretend to be anything other than the classless dick we all know you are."

"Thanks, Mia," Lucy said. "That means a lot."

"Oh, honey, I'm gonna show your boyfriend some pictures."

Lucy groaned. Jesse couldn't help smiling. Today was shaping up.

"Upstairs?" Lucy asked.

"No, not yet. I have something for you. You'll love it, and it will help. And we have to catch up!"

She led them outside into the gray, damp day, across the busy street, and to a corner coffee shop with cheery, yellow benches outside. A standing chalk-board advertised avocado chicken wraps, today's soup — "broccoli cheddar, YUM!" — and "specialty drinks." A hand-painted sign above the door proclaimed it:

Espres*So Extra*

A bell tinged as Mia opened the door. Inside was exposed brick, with bold red accent walls. A blue and teal sofa sat nestled in the corner by the window, behind a reclaimed-wood table. Barstools stood along the counter, where warm muffins steamed under glass domes. The chairs around the tables were plush and mismatched.

A list of those "specialty drinks" was scrawled in chalk over the counter. "Ruby Soho — dark berries and warm spices! Disco Lemonade — just what it sounds like! A Little Bitter — orange juice with zest!"

"Nineties much?" Jesse said.

"I'm Gen X, hon," Mia replied.

She patted the sofa, and they took a seat while she ordered "Pumpkin Spice Marys" from a young man behind the counter. Then she grabbed three muffins and brought them over to the table. Jesse's stomach growled when he saw them; he was hungry for real food, but the hole in his insides could only be filled by fresh blood.

Mia plopped herself down next to Jesse and scrutinized both of them.

Jesse cleared his throat. "So, how did you two meet?"

Mia giggled. "Lucy, I love him. Please keep him."

"I intend to," Lucy said, and Jesse felt a flush creep up his neck that did not come from the smell of blood wafting from behind the counter.

"My brother and I were hit by a drunk driver," Mia said. The smirk never left her face. "Some rando changed me on the side of the road and left me there."

"Wow," Jesse said. "That must have been so traumatic."

She shrugged and took a bite of her muffin. "I wandered into a club and found help."

Lucy stared down at the table and fidgeted with a spoon.

"A kind old vampire helped you?" Jesse asked.

Lucy rolled his eyes. "Really, Mia?"

"Well, it's not a lie. So anyway," she said to Jesse, around a mouthful of muffin, "how'd you manage to bag this prude?"

Jesse froze as he was about to take a bite.

"Here we go," Lucy muttered.

"Seriously," Mia went on. "People tried to climb that ivory tower every night and no one ever made it inside. Now, you? Yeah, you're hot. I see the appeal. But lots of people are hot. What's the secret to getting Ye Olde D?"

Lucy scoffed. "I'm not that old."

"Okay Victorian."

Jesse took a minute to wrap his head around that. "There's been no climbing."

"Aww. So you're not banging? Because from your social media, it really looks like you are, and honestly? Lucy hasn't had a lover since the ice age. Get his clothes off and see if moths don't fly out."

"You try telling someone your dark secret," Lucy said, "and get stabbed in the chest with a pointy stick for your troubles, then see if you feel comfortable putting yourself out there again."

"Seriously," Mia said. "I hated that fucking guy. You should have let me kill him when I offered."

"Oh my god," Jesse said. "I would never stab you."

"That is so sweet," Mia said. "So you want to bang, but you're not. Go upstairs and do it, what's stopping you? You only live once, for a really long time."

"I have a boyfriend," Jesse said. A boyfriend who was ghosting him, sure, but they hadn't formally ended it yet.

"And I have morals," Lucy added.

Mia snorted, reaching across the table to pat his cheek. "Goody-two-shoes."

"That's what we called him in college," Jesse said.

"Hey, check this out." Mia took her phone, entered a search into her photo app, found what she was looking for, then turned it to Jesse. Lucy leaned over to see, too.

It was a picture of a printed photograph of a band on BLOOD's main stage. Mia was clearly recognizable in a plaid mini-skirt over tight shorts and a bustier top, as she leaned on a propped-up bass guitar. He saw the tattoo on her hip, darker in this picture and the same one he'd seen his first night at BLOOD, but he still couldn't make out what it said. She had her arm around a man who could only be her brother. Jesse had seen them both before, in the pictures that Lucy had shown him, 'Punk Rock Beach' and Woodstock II. A slim, blond man leaned up against Mia's other side, twirling a drumstick. Sitting on the edge of the stage, with Mia's thick-soled platform boot on his shoulder, was Lucy, with short, bleach-blond hair. He wore a skirt identical to Mia's, and an open, loose-fitting flannel shirt over a black top with "ROCK & ROLL" emblazoned across the front in silver glitter. Behind them, a backdrop proclaimed, in gothic lettering: "THE ZEROES."

"This is the most blessed image I've ever seen," Jesse said.

Mia ran her red, pointed nail over the screen. "Good times."

"Have you heard from him?" Lucy asked.

"Raven? Nah, not since last year. We fell out pretty hard. Family, right?"

Jesse knew all too well, though he couldn't imagine a future where he and Stella wouldn't still be close. He supposed that was unfair to Finn. Maybe that was why things had turned out the way they had. If he had paid more attention to Finn, maybe he'd be home right now.

The young man brought over their drinks . . . although Jesse was starting to second guess every "young man" and "young woman" he met through Lucy. This guy could be a thousand years old for all he knew. He was slight, with pale blond hair. Ah, the drummer in the photograph.

"Buttercup," the man said, leaning over the table to kiss Lucy's cheek.

"Hey, Bubbles," Lucy said.

Mia nudged Jesse with her elbow. "We went as the Powerpuff Girls for Halloween once."

"It wasn't Halloween, it was just a Saturday," the man said. "I'm Archer." He reached out and shook Jesse's hand daintily before turning his attention back to Lucy and placing their drinks down. "Gosh, you look awful. Drink these. Is this your boyfriend? How is Cice? I worked with her last month. They sent us all the way to Germany for pete's sake. And then she went off-grid."

"She's good," Lucy said.

An unfamiliar feeling squirmed around in Jesse's chest. It took him a few seconds to figure it out: an uncomfortable combination of jealousy and fear. Lucy had an entire past that Jesse had never known about — a family — and now they were casual old friends living completely different lives. That happened even when you didn't live for hundreds of years. Would he ever meet up with Lucy in a café a few decades from now to talk about old times before going their separate ways again?

Jesse took a sip. The permeating flavor of pumpkin spice was the first to touch his tongue. Not bad. The next sip brought the deeper, darker taste of hot blood. It was immediately gross and wrong, until he swallowed it. It swelled in his chest, shot down his arms, filled his cells. His muscles burned with returning life. It made the pills seem like dust and ash; nothing compared to this. It was better than the first time he'd had it, in the Black Room. He felt them watching as he downed the rest, but couldn't bring himself to stop. The lights in the café burned his eyes.

He placed the mug down and wiped his face with a napkin. Beside him, Lucy struggled to choke down his own drink.

"Pumpkin spice blood," Lucy said, after one small sip. "That's such a great idea." His lips were pale, pressed together like he was struggling to hold it down. He looked nothing like how Jesse felt.

Mia cackled and clapped her hands. "You're such a loser. Now, your boyfriend here." She patted Jesse's hand.

Jesse pulled away.

"Oh, don't be upset," Mia said. "I love it, too; most of us do, except for this dork. You're supposed to love it. It's survival." When he finally looked up at her, she was a different person: flushed, glowing skin, a sheen to her eyes. She did look like how Jesse felt. "Hey," she said. "This is a no-shame zone. I don't allow it, especially when it comes to something that literally keeps you alive."

Some of the weight of this entire past few weeks lifted away from him, and what he had been trying to convince himself finally began to sink in: it was just medicine. How different was it from needing a blood transfusion?

"How much blood was in that?" he asked.

"Two shots," Archer said. "It's usually one, but I gave you extra."

"That's it?"

"That's it, honey," Mia said. "It doesn't come cheap. Does the trick though, doesn't it?"

"So." Lucy's voice sounded a little stronger, less hoarse. "Business is good?"

"Most of the money we make comes from here now," Mia said. "EspresSo Extra keeps BLOOD's doors open. Fucking Carnelian with their insane business tax. They hate that we make blood available. They still make me do deliveries for them; I tell them I give them half, but honestly, we keep most of whatever we can get our hands on. The club is almost a charity at this point. We mostly get vamps who are desperate because their pills didn't come in or whatever, so we haven't jacked up our entrance fee. Honestly? It's the non-vampires who pay the rent. We have excellent food."

"You always were good at business, Mia," Lucy said. "I'll need the upstairs for a while, if it's free."

"Wow, that bad, huh?" Mia said. "Going to the mattresses?"

"Russel Busquet."

Mia's eyes widened. "Shit, that was you? I saw it on the news. Nice work. What a creep, right? Killing all those kids? 'Get on the Russ Bus,' for goodness' sake. Was he a vamp?"

"He wasn't, actually," Lucy said. "He was a Via Nova reserve."

Mia drummed her fingers on the table. "Remember that drained body by the Peconic? Did he do that?"

Lucy shrugged. "That victim was from Carnelian."

"Holy shit, really? Someone must have beef with them." She tapped her bottom lip with her fingernail. "Though that doesn't narrow the list of suspects, does it? I hope they catch them. It's terrible for our business, all this bloodless body stuff. Pretty soon the FBI is going to come sniffing around fetish clubs. People are gonna start staying away."

"Also," Jesse added, "people have died."

Mia flicked her hand. "Yes. That, too. So, what do you say, Lucy's cute boyfriend? Gonna stay for a bit?"

Jesse had to get home. He had to get to searching for Finn. He had to get back to work before he lost his job. But Stella was home right now, and he could probably spare at least a few hours, while Lucy got settled in.

"Sure," he said. "I can stay for a while."

LUCIAN

Lucy led Jesse through BLOOD, past the DJ booth, and up two flights of rickety, metal stairs, to the loft door. Light wove through the slats in the floor from the fluorescents that illuminated the room below. Lucy's eyes still weren't one hundred percent and he had to squint to see the keypad next to the door. He keyed in his code, disabled the alarm, and the door squealed open.

Lucy flicked the switch. A compact laptop on the table hummed to life, its split screens showing a live feed of the stairs, outside the window, and the street below. A half-circle fan window illuminated the motes that floated down.

The loveseat and bed had been unwrapped of their dustcovers; the sheets on the bed were goddamn black silk. A television hung on the wall, attached to a DVD player, next to a shelf stacked with DVDs that had been new about fifteen years ago.

Jesse took a few steps into the room. "Wow. Are all vampires this extra?"

"The ones I know are." Lucy replied.

In the top drawer beside the mini fridge was Archer's thermal camera and spectrum analyzer, which would reveal any tech surveillance. Archer had done this already, but Lucy always did a physical sweep of his own. Never rely on technology or other people, that was the first rule. Look with your eyes. He wrapped himself in calm; security was the easy part.

Jesse started browsing the DVDs but stopped to watch Lucy. "What are you looking for?"

"Just doing a technical surveillance countermeasure sweep." Behind the fridge, in the closets, above the microwave. Bathroom next. "By the way," he called, as he pulled the mirror off its hook to check behind it. "I want to send someone to your apartment to do a TSCM there, and install security measures, too. Cameras, an emergency button, things like that." Via Nova striking back at him by trying to take out his closest friend wasn't out of the question, but the threat he'd told Yvette to send around would carry weight. Soon, word would get out that he was staying with Mia. That should make anyone think twice. "I hope you don't mind being followed by burly vampires in black cars," Lucy added, to offset the horror of the situation.

Jesse didn't acknowledge that, which stung a little, but was understandable.

Lucy moved on: Clothing closet. Sofa, under the cushions. Bed, drapes, closet. So far everything looked clean — of course it did, Mia wouldn't stand for anything else — but he kept moving, inching through the space. The closet. It was very dark. He checked again.

"Did you find something?" Jesse asked.

"Hmm?" Lucy turned away and closed the door.

"In the closet. You've been staring into it for a while."

Had he? He closed the door. "No, all is well." He went back to the sweep: behind the television, the stack of DVDs, and in the corners. There could be something in the corners, there always was, things that came out—

"Hey, check it out," Jesse said, holding a photo album.

God damn it, Mia. "Gimme that," Lucy said, and tried to snatch it away.

"Hell no. It's here for a reason." Jesse grinned at him, vaulting over the back of the loveseat and plopping down. He flipped the album open as Lucy looked over his shoulder.

The first page held a grainy picture of Mia and her brother as pre-teens, dated 1978. They were on a beach, arms around each other, the shadow of the person holding the camera cast over them.

Lucy sat down beside him. "Wow. I've never seen this one before."

"Is that Raven?" Jesse asked. "What happened between them?"

"As far as Mia told me, Raven got involved with some dangerous people, and she confronted him about it. I don't know who the people were, and I don't know exactly what she said. When she gets angry, well . . . it's pretty volcanic. It's like she said, families are rough. If it's Finn you're worried about, I don't think it will ever get that bad in your family. You're a talker, Jesse. You'll work it out because you communicate." Finn had been a child when Lucy met him. He was shy, but not withdrawn, and he'd seemed fairly happy. He had changed when his father died, but didn't everyone? Grief had changed Jesse and Stella as well.

Jesse let go of a breath and his shoulders dropped a little. He flipped the page to a photo of Archer, with white, teased-up hair. "Where does Archer fit into this?" he asked.

"Mia changed him in the mid 90s. She needed a drummer."

Jesse laughed.

"Hell of a decade," Lucy said.

"What was your name back then?"

"I was between names, so Mia started calling me Lucifer, and 'Lucy' stuck. She was having a Milton phase." There was always something a little shaming about people finding this out, but Jesse deserved to know everything now. "BLOOD belonged to me in the eighties. I was terrible at running it, and Ciceline was in school so she couldn't help. I was going to take the loss and close it. When Mia came along with her idea of turning it into a vampire refuge, I sold it to her really cheap. She's the one who made it what it is, but she still thinks of me as a business partner, even though I do literally nothing to help."

No reason to mention that 'really cheap' amounted to what Mia had in her pocket that day, which was 130 dollars. He'd been slightly afraid that she would kill him if he let the business close.

The next page had a photo of him and Raven. He was wearing a black, sequined gown, sitting on Raven's lap on a bench in front of a stand-up piano.

"He played beautifully," Lucy said.

Below that was another one, which just about knocked Lucy back in his seat. The band was performing on stage. All of them were seated, with Mia at the mic, a look of pain on her face. Lucy sat stage left, playing his cello, with another mic tilted close to his face. Ciceline stood in the crowd beside the stage, her head down, black curls obscuring her eyes.

"Wow," Jesse said. "What was this?"

Lucy pointed to the date: 4/9/94, in Mia's loose scrawl.

"Kurt Cobain?" Jesse asked. "Sorry. I was four."

Four? How could that be right? Then Lucy must have been — no, not four. How could he be the same age as Jesse? He was sitting here looking at an adult photo of himself from that year. What in the world? He was over a hundred. For a moment, the numbers didn't make sense.

"Lucy?"

"Hmm? Yes, the night after. A Saturday. The club was packed, we wanted to do a tribute. Ciceline requested 'Something In The Way.'" That first, piercing bow stroke. It still hurt. How had so much time passed?

"You've been a part of my life since practically the last few seconds of my childhood," Jesse said, "but there's so much more to you than I ever knew. I can never catch up."

"You don't have to catch up."

"What will we be like, thirty years from now?"

Lucy turned to face him, to have this discussion, but the pain in his ribs flared up. "I should get horizontal," he said instead. He left the sofa and climbed onto the bed.

Jesse closed the book and flopped sideways the loveseat, his long legs dangling over the arm. "I think I'll stay here until Ciceline comes back, in case you die again. Also, I need to sleep for a day. If that's alright with you."

Lucy watched him settle on the couch. "It's alright with me."

He felt Jesse's eyes on him when he lifted his shirt to inspect the bruises on his ribs. They were still there, and still pretty gruesome. He took his phone and snapped a pic.

"Really?" Jesse said. "Are you seriously taking a selfie on black satin sheets, looking like you were in a BDSM scene?"

"If this was a BDSM scene, it went badly. Or maybe really well? It's for my socials. The official story is I rescued my sister's dog out of my burning house, none of which was in any way my fault. I'll get my job back in a few months, and rake in tons of sympathy."

"You are the absolute worst."

"I practice."

Lucy made his post and watched as the hearts and comments rolled in, while Jesse shifted uncomfortably.

"For heaven's sake, come over here," Lucy said.

Jesse gasped dramatically. "And there was only one bed."

"Well?"

Jesse came over, sat on the edge of the bed, and reclined awkwardly. He was being ridiculous; they'd shared beds before. Lucy turned to face him. It hurt his ribs like a bitch.

"Do you need anything?" Jesse asked.

You. Don't go. He didn't let the thought pass his lips, and didn't even allow it fully into his mind, in case Jesse should catch on. "I'm good."

"Lucy, what are you going to do with new formula for the pills?"

"Give it to Ciceline," he said. "I'm in the dark about all of that stuff, just useless, but she'll know how to handle it."

Jesse gave him a little frown of disapproval and opened his mouth, probably to say something like 'Why do you say things like that?' because Jesse always tried to convince him that he was good at math and science, when he clearly wasn't.

"You should call Stella," Lucy said, before Jesse could get started. "Let her know you're staying for a bit, right?"

"Oh," Jesse said. "Yeah, true."

He dialed, while Lucy waited, drifting into that comfortable half-sleep that always came after something bad had happened, but he was in a safe place. And there was nowhere safer than Mia's.

He heard Jesse's call go to voicemail, and felt his gnawing anxiety. "Uhh, hey Stella," Jesse said. "I'm staying with Lucy for a little while longer. Just wanted to let you know. Call me when you get a sec."

He hung up and turned to Lucy.

"She's probably just on the phone," Lucy said.

"Yeah," Jesse said. "I'll try again later."

But that little frown had turned to apprehension. Lucy wasn't the only one who shared a connection with Jesse; Stella did, too, and if Jesse's intuition was telling him something was wrong, then it probably was.

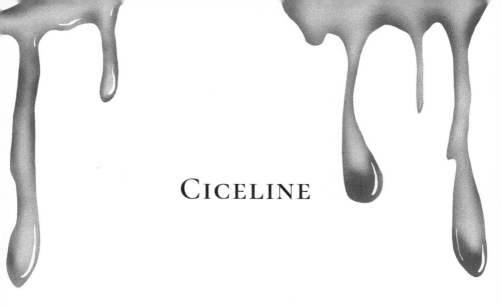

CICELINE

Ciceline had no sooner sat at the table and taken her first sip of tea when Stella's phone rang. She tried not to listen in as she ran her fingers through Lucy's fur, grateful beyond measure for the chance to do that again. He smelled of smoke and oil, and burrs clustered around his ears and feet. She plucked them off one by one and placed them into a napkin. She wished that dogs could be vampires. She would pick him over any human.

"Hey, Shep," Stella said. A perplexed frown creased her brow. "Are you in your car?"

A man's voice answered, clipped and dark, and Ciceline tuned in. She knew that tone. She couldn't make out the words, but the frown on Stella's face faded, and something like complete blankness replaced it. In the silence that followed, Stella's phone beeped with another incoming call, which she ignored.

"Wait, what?" Stella held up her hand like he was in the room with her. "You took my phone? You are a dick. I've called you that to your face a million times. The same way you always call me a pain in your ass?"

All bosses were alike. Ciceline was not about to sit here and watch Stella have an argument with hers, so she stood up, gently putting Lucy on the floor, and took her teacup to the sink.

"Jesse was doing rounds," Stella said, her voice a little frantic now, a little shaky. "He didn't steal anything, he took a fecal sample kit, which we all do, all day. I've seen receptionists take antibiotics straight out of the cabinet to take home, so I don't even want to hear this—"

Even with the water running, Ciceline heard the guy cut her off, and her own anger boiled up: men and their loud voices.

"Did you even check your cameras?"

He said something about her dog.

"The dog has been here for all of fifteen minutes. Anyway, what kind of vet doesn't allow dogs? You just saw me in the lab; you really waited until you were in your car so that you wouldn't have to say any of this to my face? What is wrong with you?"

Once again, the guy got mouthy; there was a tone that went right up Ciceline's back.

Michaela Westchurch was standing in the kitchen doorway, leaning on her cane, staring at Stella as if she already knew what was up.

"Next week?" Stella said, no longer fighting to hold back her tears. "Where are we supposed to go? Jesse is sick and you're throwing us out?"

The cup slipped out of Ciceline's fingers and, yes, this was rude of her, but she turned to Stella and gestured for the phone. Stella handed it to her, too shocked to do anything else.

Shep continued his rant, something about a deposit and having to clean up whatever mess the dog was making.

"The dog is mine," Ciceline said. "Hi, my name is Ciceline Taran, I'm a lawyer, you can google me. What's this about?"

He didn't speak at first; the hum of his car filled the silence, with tinny, talk radio low in the background.

"None of your business," he finally said. "I don't care if you're a lawyer. I'm well within my rights to fire both of them. New York State law—"

"Please don't quote law to me, it's the one thing that's guaranteed to get on my nerves. We won't be suing you for wrongful termination."

"Then why are we having this conversation?" Shep asked. "I have a meeting in ten minutes."

"Good, because I was just about to set up an online fundraiser for Jesse, since he's battling a life-threatening disease and his asshole boss fired him and his sister and threw them out of their house. You think he and Stella are popular in town? Google my brother Lucian Callahan, Jesse's best friend, with his million-plus followers. I'm not talking about a court of law, Shep."

He sputtered for a few seconds. "I'll sue you for libel."

Oh, how she loved when people threatened to sue her. She let a sweet smile seep into her voice. "I hope you do."

He didn't respond, other than to just breathe at her, like his heart was going too fast. Ciceline loved this reaction most of all, the speechless panic, impotent anger.

"Have a good meeting," she said, and ended the call.

Stella sank into the chair and wept into her hands.

Michaela stood in the doorway, tapping her fingers on her cane. "When do we need to be out of here?"

"A week," Stella said. "He's saying we broke our contract, and that Jesse was stealing supplies."

Ciceline picked up the mug she had dropped and rinsed it aggressively. *God.* This is why she'd pursued law in the first place. Nothing galled her like injustice.

"If Finn comes home," Michaela said, "we'll be gone, and there's no way to tell him."

"We'll find him before the end of the week," Stella said. "I know we will."

"Okay," Michaela said. "Yes. It's alright. We'll work it out. We always do."

Stella straightened up and wiped her face with a napkin. "The next vet is three towns over, maybe they'll hire us. We can take out the money we put away to buy the practice and use it for rent in the meantime."

"Yes," Michaela said. "First thing tomorrow, we'll start packing." She shuffled out of the kitchen, back toward the stairs.

Ciceline sat at the table across from Stella. "Hey. I owe you."

"Huh?" Stella said. "For what?"

"You helped my brother. You drove us to the hospital. You found my dog."

"I didn't—"

"I'm in a position to do something for you. If you'll let me, I can handle this."

Stella reached across the table and put her hand over Ciceline's. Her nails were bitten down, cuticles dry and peeling. Warm tingles raced up Ciceline's fingers.

"I'm serious about the fundraiser," Ciceline said.

"Thank you. It's not really about the money, but thank you."

"I know that. I was also serious about ruining him. If you're down for that."

Stella smiled. It gave her a look that Ciceline hadn't imagined on her before, a little predatory. She liked it a bit too much.

STELLA
OCTOBER 30TH

S tella had lost her job nearly a week ago, and it still hit her like a blow to the chest when she thought of it: his audacity, her own anger, the loss. She grieved for it along with everything else. And now, today, she would lose her home. They'd be out of here tonight, before Shep came back and had to look any of them in the eye. Stella had found them an apartment thirty minutes west. It was small; someone would have to sleep on the sofa. It helped to think of it as a temporary stopover, like a hotel on a road trip. Mom had gone over there to fill the fridge and stock up on paper plates and bathroom stuff.

Jesse had come home to pack. Finn had not.

She and Jesse sat in Finn's room, packing up the last of his stuff. His privacy was a non-issue now; they'd searched his room for clues since his disappearance and found nothing, no pills, no blood, not even a stick of incense. Just his clothes, books, comics, and a few hundred dollars of cash in the drawer. That worried her. If Finn had planned on leaving home, he would have taken it. Jesse thumbed through one of the Batman comics they'd found stored in a bin under Finn's bed, the same ones he'd had since childhood. Again, Stella saw him as kid; a bored . . . no, a lonely little boy asking for her attention.

"He'll come back," Jesse said. He plucked at the shoulder of his shirt. "He has to finish my tattoo. Or maybe I just want to believe that, I don't know." He put the book back, closed the lid, and placed the bin on top of the others.

"Wait a minute," Stella said. She shifted the boxes around until she found what she was looking for and pulled the top off, ripping her nail to the quick in her rush. "His sketchbooks. There was a phone number, I snuck into his room and saw it on his bed. I planned to come back and look again, but that was the night you went off with Lucy."

She dug through the bin, the dry, tattered papers catching on the over-washed skin of her fingers as she flipped through them. Jesse got on the floor and searched with her.

"It was a picture of a woman," Stella said. "Damn it, all these books look alike."

"Here." Jesse held up the sketch she'd seen that night, with the phone number scrawled at the bottom in unfamiliar handwriting.

Stella grabbed her phone and dialed.

'We're sorry, the number you have reached is not in service or has been temporarily disconnected. No further information is available.'

She ended the call, deflated and relieved at the same time. What would she have said? They sat on the floor, staring blankly at the sketch.

"Hey, actually." Jesse took a picture of the drawing. "Just in case."

The movers were due at three. It was 2:30. The angle of the sun into Finn's room was a weight on her chest.

"I got that interview next week," Jesse said. "She called me back."

Ah, the interview that Stella had turned down, at a veterinary emergency hospital three towns over. Jesse had offered it to her first, but she had declined. It didn't feel right to move on so quickly. Maybe she was being unrealistic, but going to work for a new vet after investing so much time and energy into this place, considering it her home, and then having it yanked away? She couldn't process it yet. The fundraiser was going better than she had expected but it wouldn't sustain them forever. A few months' rent at the most. They would have to manage the rest without Finn's or Mom's contributions. Mom had to give up her nice, relaxing job at the boutique; the drive was too long for her. It didn't seem likely that she'd find something that good again.

"Congratulations," she said. "Do you think you'll get it?"

"Maybe," Jesse said. "The vet there knows about—" He tilted his head to the side, frowning, and held up a hand for silence. His hearing had improved, and a little shiver crept up Stella's back.

"There's a key in the door," he said. "Mom should still be at the apartment."

"Finn," Stella whispered.

They got to their feet and hurried downstairs. Her heart thumped, but not with excitement or hope. Sweat prickled in her palms. This wasn't Finn. It wasn't anything good. They were on the middle of the staircase when someone shoved the door open with a grunt.

Jenny Treece stood in the doorway, with two cardboard boxes stacked in her arms. She froze, staring like a dummy with her mouth open and her cheeks pink. "Oh," she said in a small voice. "I didn't see any cars outside so I thought . . . "

"Yeah, they're parked in the back, where we always park," Stella said. "So you thought what? That we wouldn't be around to bother you anymore? What are you doing here?"

Treece put the boxes down inside — *inside!* — and planted her fists on her hips. "I'm moving in."

"We're still here," Stella said. "Get out."

Treece flapped her hands at her sides, trying to look annoyed and put-out, but coming across flustered. "Honestly, what's it going to harm if I leave a few things inside while you're moving the last of your stuff out?"

"Which box is your crown in?" Stella asked. Jesse glanced at her but said nothing, keeping behind her. "Your crown, remember? The one that I was supposed to fix for you?"

"Come on, you guys were stealing supplies, don't even try to blame that on me. None of this is on me. Shep offered me the position, how could I say no?"

"Shep offered you the position after you went through my phone and showed him my texts and told him that Jesse was stealing."

"Excuse me?" Jesse asked. "She gave him your phone?"

"You left it at work!" Treece said. "Unlocked! What was I supposed to do?"

"How about not look at it and hand it back to me?"

"Get out," Jesse said. His voice was strange; a dark, quiet sound that she had never heard from him before, but she didn't dare look away from her stare-down on Treece.

"Well, my name happens to be on the lease, starting at midnight." Treece said.

"Get. Out." Jesse hissed.

Treece's eyes widened until the whites were visible, and then Stella did turn around. Jesse's eyes were darker than normal. His lips were red, his skin shone with a flush that hadn't been there moments ago. She fought the urge to flee from him, to tell Treece to take her boxes and run. Her brother was an actual vampire and he appeared to be hangry.

Treece didn't need to be told again. She huffed and rolled her eyes, but Stella could see the disbelieving fear. Later, Treece would convince herself that she hadn't seen anything unusual, just some bitter guy being a jerk, but the way she hustled out the door, forgetting her boxes, said it all.

Behind her, Jesse sank onto the stairs and dropped his head into his hands.

"You okay?" she asked.

"Yeah," he said, muffled. "That was pretty awful of me, though."

"It actually wasn't, Jesse. It's okay to be angry."

He lifted his head, staring into the middle distance. "I think I'm going to go . . . to a place."

Stella studied his eyes. "You seem extra wonky. I could drive you?"

"No Stella, you have to stay here and move." His words slurred together. He shook his head and spoke more clearly: "I have an app."

"Someone can pick you up?"

"Yes," Jesse said. "They'll have a few extra pills."

"What's it like, Jesse?" she asked. "The whole needing blood thing."

"It's doable." He twisted his hands together in his lap. "Worse for me because I'm sick. I need it. I'd be dead without it. It starts to hurt."

Stella looked away. Thinking of those first few days after finding out about his sickness still put a knot in her guts. There was still a chance that she or Finn would get it, too. Maybe Finn was already a vampire?

"Ciceline put me down as her reserve or whatever it's called."

Jesse snapped to attention. "She what now?"

"She had to." Stella came back up the stairs and sat a few below Jesse. She'd been meaning to dust the railing. It was Treece's problem now. "The night I followed Finn, Carnelian told her to just let me get myself into trouble, and she said no, that I was her reserve, so I needed protection. She probably saved me."

He looked relieved and weirdly guilty. "That's pretty huge," he said. "You're only allowed one per generation."

"Oh," Stella said. "Wow. I didn't realize. That's . . . I'm grateful. I just don't know if I—" Someone knocked on the kitchen door and Stella jumped up to answer it. "That'll be Bottle."

When she opened the door, Bottle threw her arms around both of them, squeezing too tight, and announced, "Guess what? I put in my two weeks' notice."

Jesse pulled back. "You what?"

"Because of us?" Stella asked.

"Sort of." She let them both go. "I mean, that was the final straw. Who wants to work for a dick like Shep? This whole practice will fall apart without us. I've been thinking about it for a while. I'm going back to school."

"Oh, Bottle," Stella said, hugging her again. Something ugly and hurtful squirmed in her chest. It felt like jealousy, though she couldn't imagine why. "That's wonderful."

"Once I'm a vet, maybe we'll work together again at your new place."

"We'd love that," Jesse said.

Stella remained silent. The words wouldn't form yet, even the thought refused to manifest. All she knew was when she looked around the corner, she was not ready to work again; not anywhere, not right now. The thought of starting over somewhere else made her tingle with nausea.

"Jesse," Bottle said, "are you okay? You're looking like you did the day you got sick."

"Actually, I was going to head out to the doctor, and then to see a friend," Jesse said.

"Date with Jared?" Bottle asked. She must have realized her mistake, because she backed off. "Sorry, I should mind my business."

Jesse chuckled. "Jared's been ghosting me. Weird story."

"Wow," Bottle said. "How one-hundred-percent shitty of him."

"He never found out I was sick," Jesse said. "It's not like he bailed because of it. I'm going to spend the night with my best friend."

Bottle nudged him. "Finally, the foxy cellist. Go get it, Jesse."

"There will be no getting." He hugged Bottle and congratulated her, gave Stella a kiss on the cheek, and grabbed his keys from the table.

"At least take your overnight bag," Stella said. "You look like a guy who lost his job and got evicted."

"And dumped," Bottle added.

"Very nice." He went to the door in his worn jeans and black hoodie, but he did grab his bag before he left.

Then, Jesse was gone, and Stella had to face her last day in her home.

JESSE

J esse asked the driver to make a quick stop at the tattoo parlor before heading down to BLOOD. It was a different driver this time, a woman who handed him four pills without a word.

"I'll be really fast," Jesse said, as she parked the car behind the parlor.

The pills started to kick in as he got to the door, enough so that he could feel his fingers again, and the panic receded with the numbness. Maybe Lucy's father was right, and a new formula would work better, keeping his symptoms at bay longer. Or, if not, he would come to terms with the flares, and it wouldn't cause such anxiety anymore. Maybe one day he would get used to the idea that he was going to live.

Finn's boss, a thin, goateed man with sparse, long hair, was tattooing someone's back. He turned when Jesse entered, and the whir of the needle died down.

"I don't know where the fuck your brother is," he said. "He didn't show up for work. I had to cancel his appointments, it's bad for business." He wiped some blood from his client's back. The tattoo was a pink octopus from shoulder to shoulder. The lines weren't clean, and the details were muddy. Finn was already miles ahead of this guy.

"Uhh, sorry," Jesse said. "We're all looking for him, it's not like . . ." Getting defensive was the wrong approach here. Jesse took a breath and reset. "We're trying to find anyone who knows anything, so I was wondering if you've seen this woman around."

He clicked into his photos, pulled up the one of the girl in the sketchbook, and held it up to Jesse's boss, who snatched it out of his hand and removed one of his gloves.

"Yeah, that's Finn's girlfriend, Bettina. What, he never introduced you?"

"No," Jesse said. "Can you tell me anything about her?"

"Not much to tell," he said. "She's a model, she's very goth. They've been going out for a few months I guess, but I haven't seen her around in a while. I figured she went off on a photo shoot or something. She was always yammering about her shoots when he was working on her tats. He was forever touching them up, she kept saying they were fading and I figured she was just into him, because she was here even when he wasn't working on her. It was like I should have been paying her, she was here so much."

"Do you know her last name?" he asked. "Or how long ago she stopped showing up?"

"Clarke," he said. "Bettina Clarke. Google her, you'll see. She stopped coming in a few weeks ago I guess, I don't know." He bent over his client and the needle vibrated to life again. The person on the table flinched when he dove back in. "Come on, man," he said. "Hold still."

His own skin prickled with the memory of Finn's needle. Finn was way more gentle than this guy. He worked with care, when sketching, painting, and creating pieces. No wonder business was down without him.

"Did Finn ever mention wanting to leave?" Jesse asked. "Did he talk about . . ." *About me? About my sickness?* "Did he seem depressed or anything?"

"You know Finn," the boss said. "He keeps everything to himself."

"Yeah," Jesse said, though he couldn't agree, at this point, that he knew Finn at all. "Hey, let me know if he calls or anything, okay? Can I leave you my number?"

"Sure, man. I hope he comes back. He's got talent."

Jesse wrote his number on the back of one of the tattoo parlor's business cards, about 90% sure that it would be swept off the counter and into the trash, but what else could he do? He left Finn's boss to his squirming client and went back to the car.

"Thanks," he told the driver. "I seriously owe you. Umm, could you take me to BLOOD?" He still felt ridiculous asking that.

"Sure thing," the driver said. "And you don't owe me anything; it's already paid for."

"Lucy?"

"Yup."

Well, shit. He had never felt beholden to Lucy before.

As the car pulled away, Jesse took Finn's boss's suggestion and googled Bettina Clarke. The first thing that came up was her professional page, from her agency; she stared boldly from a hazy vignette, her dark makeup creating a striking contrast with the muted framing. Professional pages didn't offer much information, so he clicked on the next result: her social media. Her bio read, "The queenliest dead." The first row of pictures were all of her: at a club, in fishnets, with horns, holding a black and white parasol. One of them showed her smiling over her shoulder, without makeup, her hair down, exactly as Finn had drawn her in his sketchbook.

He scrolled to the next row and his stomach clenched. There was Finn, behind her, his head resting on her shoulder, her long-nailed fingers pressed against his cheek. Finn was smiling enough to show his dimples, which Jesse hadn't seen in probably over a year. The caption was "My forever."

The rest of the feed was pretty much the same, with pictures of Finn throughout, going back even past six months, to almost a year. Finn had known this woman for at least nine months, and had never once mentioned her.

The understanding gnawed at him, that Finn had an entire life that had nothing to do with them, an existence so far removed from his family that none of them had even guessed.

If he had managed to hide this from them, what other secrets was he keeping?

LUCIAN

Dreary, weak sunshine filtered in through the filmy loft window. Lucy pulled the hood of his sweater over his head and turned over on the bed.

"Lucy, come here," Ciceline called from the loft's kitchenette.

Lucy looked up, but once again, she was talking to the damn dog. She crouched down and fed it some ham from her sandwich. Lucy took out his phone and started scrolling. He'd checked Instagram three times within the last hour and no one had posted anything new. He checked the fundraiser. Sluggish today.

"You're so annoying when you're like this," Ciceline said.

"You're annoying."

"I'm going to the party tonight, loser."

"Have fun getting killed," Lucy mumbled from under his hoodie.

"I will."

If Lucy could pull his hood further over his head, he would. The way the dusky light slanted in through the fan window reminded him of his home in the woods. His house must be a blackened husk. Most of his stuff that had monetary value was locked away in a safe in Romania, but his favorite new clothes, books, things he had collected over the years, and worst of all, his cello — if they weren't burnt to ash, they were smoke-damaged beyond repair. The desire to sit out on his back porch, burning citronella and watching the night herons flock to the creek, was almost an ache.

"No one is going to get killed," Ciceline said, because she obviously wasn't ready to leave him alone. "This is on Yvette now. If they still have an issue, it's her they'll go after."

"Yeah, and she can't negotiate for shit."

"But I can, and we have the formula for the pills, so now we have leverage."

True, but that leverage was dangerous, because once Via Nova, or anyone, for that matter, found out they had it, they would become targets. And once they gave it up, they would have nothing to bargain with in the future.

"Lucy, come on, you haven't left this loft in days. They're not going to hit BLOOD. They know better. Mia wouldn't stand for it."

Little Mia. She just wanted to play music, dance, drink her Slutty Bloody Marys and Pumpkin Spice Chai Whatevers, wear long cardigans, and run her business. Yvette never bothered sending her into the field anymore. If only he could be enough of a loose cannon that they didn't trust him to work. Back in the late nineties, another group of insurgents splitting off from Carnelian had tried to burn down BLOOD. Mia's payback had been cataclysmic, so many dead vampires, bodies had turned up for years: floating in rivers, rotting in carparks, pieces of them found by dogs, one of them strung up in a haunted house. Points for creativity? She and Raven had seemed like easy targets, and successful enough to make an example of.

Oops.

In a way, Cice was . . . he didn't want to say right, but maybe not wrong. Via Nova wouldn't go near Mia. He still wasn't going to the party.

"I want you to come out tonight," Ciceline whined. "Don't be a square. I'm not staying in on my birthday."

Of course Lucy remembered that today was her birthday, or at least he remembered now.

His phone vibrated and a message obscured his camera app.

JESSE:

Hey guess where I am

LUCIAN

Are you here?

JESSE:

I took Carnelian express to espresso extra come down

LUCIAN

Be there in a minute :)

Lucy got up too fast — those delicate cartilages between the ribs yelled at him for it — and flipped his hood back.

"Oh, you'll get out of bed for Jesse," Ciceline said. She was leaning against the counter, scrolling on her phone while she ate her sandwich. "Tell him hi for me. And to tell Stella I said hi."

Oh, so it was like that, was it? "Why not message her and get her number?"

"I already have her number." Ciceline called Dog Lucy over to his crate. "I'm going out to buy decent clothes for tonight. I'll see you later." She grabbed her purse and was out the door.

"Be careful," he called out, after she was gone.

He dragged himself into the bathroom and finger-combed his hair in the mirror. It was a disaster. He had nothing nice to change into, so the black hoodie would have to do. The dullness in his eyes, dark circles, the pallor — well, Jesse had seen way worse and never judged.

He pinned his hair up in a bun on his way out and threw on some lipstick; might as well look like a fancy corpse.

"Be good, Dog Lucy," he said as he left, locking the door behind him.

Down through the club he went, and they were doing it up big in the main room. A giant LED skeleton hung from the center of the ceiling, wearing a black and red harness and holding a five-foot-long riding crop. In the elevated DJ booth, Archer was running a sound check comprised of ghostly "boo" noises and evil laughs. Archer sucked as a DJ. They really needed to hire more help.

"Buttercup," Archer's voice boomed. "Lose the morbs. We'd better see you tonight, you morose bitch."

A few cleaners turned his way. Lucy waved over his shoulder and kept walking. *As if.* Dinner and a movie in the loft with Jesse was all he wanted. Jesse hadn't yet officially broken it off with Jared, so movies and being sad together while listening to the thumping beats and shouting masses from downstairs would be as far as it went.

Outside, an icy rain pelted down, not quite sleet, but getting there. The cold air played havoc with his lungs and made his entire chest hurt. Streetlights flickered on as he walked under them. The smell of baking muffins, coffee, and roasted peppers wafted out from Espres*So Extra*, and his stomach clenched in hunger. Okay, so maybe he hadn't eaten since yesterday. Maybe he hadn't left the loft since Jesse had left, and maybe he was acting a tiny bit morose, but he and his best friend had lost their homes in the span of a week, and he had been tossed into a creek to die, so maybe he was entitled to a few days of sulking.

The bell tinged as he opened the door, and Mia blew a kiss from behind the counter where she was steaming a drink at the machine. Jesse was already seated on the blue and teal sofa, luminous and looking like the cat who drank the cream, if the cat was a vampire and the cream was blood. He was beaming that devastating smile of his right at Lucy. It was his favorite one: dimpled, with sharp little canines showing, like he'd always been way more of a vampire than Lucy could ever hope to be.

Lucy took the seat next to him. "You look . . . really nice," he managed. "Have you guys moved into the new place yet?"

"Today was our last day at the house," Jesse said.

"How are you handling it?"

Jesse studied him with a critical eye. "I guess we're both feeling some type of way."

Mia planted a mug on the table in front of him and tapped it with her fingernail. "Come on. Try this one."

The drink was orange, with chili flakes on top. Great, now he and Jesse could both sit here in their discomfort while he tried to choke down this concoction.

"Just taste it," Mia said. "You look like hell and you're no fun when you're like this." She sat across from them and set her chin in her hands.

He lifted the cup and took a sip. The spice almost knocked him back in his seat, burning along his tongue and down his throat. Chili peppers, orange, tomato? Definitely salt. He kept drinking. It was there, that thick, metallic tang, but the other powerful flavors overrode it. Even the texture seemed silkier, less clumpy. His eyes and nose burned, but he wasn't on the floor gagging and he didn't want to throw it up.

"See?" Mia said, when he slammed the mug onto the table. "Not bad, right?"

"No." His voice was hoarse with the burn, but he felt like he'd just woken up from a deep nap. "Not bad at all. Pretty good."

"Who's the best?" Mia said.

"You are, Mistress."

"You're goddamn right."

"Wait," Jesse said. "Why didn't you give me one of these drinks the night I showed up at BLOOD? I could have avoided the whole Black Room thing."

"You think this is easy to get? It's not like we have it on tap at the club. Besides," she patted Jesse's hand. "Did we learn how to take care of ourself during a crisis in a safe, controlled environment?"

"Yeah. I guess I did."

"Exactly," Mia said. "And what do we say?"

"Thank you, Mistress?"

Mia turned to Lucy and gripped his arm. "Oh Buttercup, I love him. If anything bad ever happens to him, I'd destroy the entire planet."

"I'd destroy it first," Lucy said, and Jesse did that shy little laugh.

"Hey, you know what you both need?"

"Oh my god," Lucy said, "please don't."

"A party. I better see your goth-ed up asses over there tonight."

"All of my clothes burned, Mia."

"Not all of them, Buttercup. I bet I have something to fit your hot boyfriend, too."

"Party?" Jesse asked.

"It's just a Halloween dance thing," Lucy said. "Costumes, Thriller, Rave in The Grave . . . the usual kind of stuff."

Jesse smiled at him. "Are you going?"

"Yeah, of course. I was hoping we could go together or something."

"Or something," Jesse said, low and flirty. "Maybe we could both use a little distraction. Sounds like fun."

"Totally," Lucy said. "It's going to be awesome."

He was such a sucker.

STELLA

It was after ten by the time the movers unloaded the last of the boxes into the apartment and hauled the rest of it into storage. Stella and Mom had the most dismal of microwaved dinners at the kitchen counter, then sat together, quiet with exhaustion. It was real. They were in a new home. It was ill-fitting and dark.

Mom got up and put a few groceries into the fridge while Stella took the TV out of its box and propped it up against the wall, too tired to install it. Instead, she sat on the floor and sent the same text she'd sent five times today: "*Finn, please check in.*" She had gotten one reply earlier: "*I'm safe.*" It was bullshit. He hadn't sent it.

What if the cops knocked on the door of this apartment, and this was where they'd learn that Finn been found dead? Images invaded her mind: officers with their eyes downcast, *sorry for your loss*. She was stuck on that one moment, when he was little and she had made him cry. How many times had she ignored him, or favored her time with Jesse?

No. Change was one of her major triggers and she was spiraling down the vortex. She took a few deep breaths and meditated on her senses:

A blank wall with a bare light bulb screwed into it. A white front door that needed to be locked but which she was afraid to lock in case Finn found out where they were and came home but didn't have a key. The *plink!* of the faucet in the bathroom one room over. Mom putting drinks into the fridge. Traffic, because this apartment overlooked the main road on one side and a parking lot on the other. The windows to both bedrooms looked out over the dismal parking lot and the lights glared in. How was she ever going to sleep in a place like this? Stella went to the kitchen window and stared at the street below, basking in the misery, letting it soak into her pores. A black SUV was parked across the street, the same one she'd seen every half hour since coming here. She thought about going outside and talking to whoever was behind the wheel; it couldn't hurt to get to know their bodyguards, but what would she say? Was she supposed to acknowledge that they were vampires, or was that not quite the thing? What were the rules of engagement, what did etiquette and decorum demand in this world?

Mom came back into the living room. "I'm going to take a shower and go up — and to go to bed, honey."

Stella gave her a weak laugh. Yeah, no "up" here. "I'll be in later," she said. She and Mom would have to share a room. Jesse would take the smaller one right next to it, and if — when — Finn came home, he'd be sleeping on the couch until they could find a bigger place. Or maybe he would move out.

Mom grabbed her overnight bag and shuffled into the bathroom. The apartment was so bare, every sound bounced around the walls; the clinks and plonks of bathroom sundries going onto the rim of the sink, no counter in there; the shuffling of clothes coming out of the bag; the unmistakable sound of Mom crying.

Maybe she wanted to be alone, but something about the suddenness of it made Stella bolt up, asking, "Mom?" in a voice a little too high and frantic for her own ears.

"It's okay," Mom said. "I just realized that I left my robe at the house."

The house, like it was a place they'd go back to once this was over. Stella cast her mind's eye around its familiar walls, and there it was: Mom's pink robe on the bathroom hook. Her comfortable one, that had been washed so many times the color had faded beneath the arms and at the elbows. She couldn't bear the thought of Mom having to spend this dark, lonely night without it.

"I'm gonna go get it," she said.

"No, you don't have to."

"It's a thirty-minute drive." Treece might be there, but so what? Stella had a right to her possessions. It wasn't midnight yet.

"I don't think you should—"

"I'll be back in an hour, okay?" Stella said. Anything was better than sitting alone in this cramped space.

"Be careful," Mom said.

"Okay. I'll lock the door." She grabbed her keys and headed back out into the night.

It turned out there was something worse than staying in that cramped space, and it was driving the familiar road back to the place her heart wanted to be. The longing she felt as she drove along the river was the taste of honey that would poison the rest of her time at the apartment.

She didn't want to deal with anyone seeing her car, so she parked around the corner, out of sight on the side of the road, and walked the rest of the way.

The house was dark when she opened the door, and the scent of her autumn candles and Mom's coffee still lingered in the air. She flicked on the lights in the kitchen. Those salmon pink countertops that Jesse hated now looked so comforting. A ring of coffee stained the table, and a square of dust surrounded the spot where their toaster had sat on the counter. In the living room, the floor was spotless and shiny where their sofa had been.

Stella climbed the stairs, every creak and groan of the wood completely expected, and went into the bathroom, where Mom's pink robe hung on the hook.

She needed one more look at the bay before she left for good. One last night on the widow's walk. With the robe over her arm, she passed their bedrooms — Finn's still smelled of incense — and at the end of the hall was the door with cracked white paint and a latch on the inside. The hallway was haunted by ghosts of herself, walking nightly to this door. She unhooked the latch and the door groaned open.

Even in the dark she knew the bumps and scratches of each narrow step, how the wood was smooth in the centers, and that someone, decades ago, had painted them white but the paint had faded, leaving most of the original grain. At the top of the stairs was another door, similarly weathered. She pushed it open and stepped out onto the widow's walk. The way the moon reflected on the bay, the smell of salt water, the lapping of the waves as a boat went by in the distance, it all overwhelmed her. How was she supposed to leave this?

But Jesse was alive, and if the cosmic cost of that was losing their home, then Stella would gladly tread back down those beloved stairs, get into her car, and drive to the crappy apartment.

Headlights blinded her as they swung into the front driveway, and she hit the floor without thinking. Treece, probably, bringing her bathroom stuff, overnight bag, and whatever she'd need for the first few days. She would set up in this house just as Stella and her mom had set up in the apartment. She'd put her shampoo or whatever on the porcelain dishes in the bath.

The car door opened, but it wasn't Treece who stepped out.

It was Shep.

Stella crouched behind the open door. Why the hell was he hanging around the house? He didn't even go inside, he just stood there in front of the porch. Stella could make out his lanky silhouette from the streetlight across the way. He shifted from foot to foot, waiting for something.

Or someone.

Holy shit. Treece. Were they getting it on? That's what this was about? Shep was married. Oh, this was juicy and delicious.

Stella was still so pissed, even if she did nothing with this information, she needed to know. She needed to document it. She'd never have the nerve to tell anyone aside from Jesse and Mom, but wouldn't it be a good thing to have, just in case he kept coming after them? What if he tried to escalate his accusations of theft? She would have something on him.

Her breathing sped up, and her fingers shook as she hit the record button. He was too far away; her phone wouldn't catch anything aside from murmuring. Stella snaked her arm out between the railings of the widow's walk. There were bushes around the porch, overgrown with vines and underbrush. She closed her eyes and dropped the phone. If it made a noise when it landed, she didn't hear it.

When she opened her eyes, Shep had turned to peer into the bushes. He hissed, like he was trying to scare an animal away, and something actually scuttled; a cat or something. Then he went back to shifting from side to side, occasionally pacing. Stella settled back behind the door.

The flick of a lighter and smell of butane and cigarette smoke shocked her, and she crept forward to peek down again. What the hell? Shep had never smoked in all the time she'd known him. Somehow this was more sinister than anything he'd done so far.

More headlights swung around — here came Treece showing up for their little fling? — and Shep dropped the cigarette and ground it out with his heel. The car stopped and someone got out.

Okay, this was also not Treece. She didn't know this person. "You have it?" they asked.

She dared to creep forward and angle her head to get a better look, and she recognized his silhouette, too: the man who had met Finn under the bridge that night, and chased her and Ciceline. A chilly sweat broke out on the back of her neck.

"I have it, but I have to start charging more," Shep said. "I can't keep watering it down. I nearly lost a patient last time, and I don't have anyone left to blame."

Ketamine. Motherfucker.

"Well, that's no good," the other man said.

"Can't be helped. If I lose business because of this, you guys all lose out, too."

The other guy said something too low for Stella to hear.

Shit, what if her phone rang? Why hadn't she thought of that? What if Jesse called or texted? *Shit shit shit. Please, Jesse, please, don't call.*

"It's not greed," Shep said, a little louder.

That guy would kill her; he'd tried it once before. He was a vampire, they had ways of covering these things up. Hadn't Lucy's yard been littered with bodies that had not shown up on any news reports? Shep — this smoking, drug-dealing Shep — would he let this man kill her?

Couldn't they finish up and just go?

"Last one," Shep said.

The other guy murmured something about bad reactions and it being cut with something.

"This is veterinary-grade Ketamine," Shep said. Why was he so loud? "It's not made for humans. I could offer you Phenobarb."

Mumble mumble "look into it," something something "ask him next time."

"And once again," Shep said, "I want to warn you of the dangers of putting this in the hands of young people. If you're trying to wean them off opioids, there are safer ways."

The vampire laughed.

Oh, wow. Shep didn't know his customers were vampires.

A third set of headlights came into view, and this time they turned around back.

"That's my new tenant," Shep said. "Just take it and pay me through the app. Let me know about the Pheno. This shit is dangerous."

They wrapped up their little deal and hustled to their cars.

Treece had to have seen that, but she probably thought it was her and Jesse, hurrying out one last time.

The two cars pulled away as Treece's car door closed.

What if Treece was part of this?

There was a portico over the porch, held up by thick, white columns. Doable. Stella threw the bathrobe down and swung her legs over the railing, easing herself down until she stood on its peaked top. She flattened herself on her stomach and scooted her feet over the edge. It gave her that unpleasant, out-of-control swooping feeling as she inched lower, searching with her feet for the column. When she found it, she wrapped her legs around and slid a little more, squirming down until she was hanging by her hands. Then, one hand at a time, she let go of the overhang and gripped the column. The rest was a quick shimmy to the porch, where she grabbed the robe.

The worst part was rummaging through the bushes to retrieve her phone; it wasn't cold enough to get rid of all the critters yet, and the vines and juniper scratched her up. There it was, still recording. She clicked STOP and shoved it into her pocket as she bolted around the corner to her car. Treece had seen two people talking out here and would soon look out the front window to see what was up.

Stella threw herself into her car and pulled onto the road without even putting her seatbelt on. She didn't stop until she had cleared the first turn, and there she clicked herself in.

A thrill ran through her, tempting her to accept hope, and for the first time in months, she did. Everything was working itself out.

JESSE

J esse had to admit, he looked pretty sharp under the red lights by the mirror in BLOOD's bathroom. He had packed clean, normal clothes, but apparently that wasn't enough for Mia, who had searched her closet and found themed costumes for them. When he'd come out of the loft bathroom looking like a goth had raided James Cagney's wardrobe, Lucy had looked him over and said, "How dare you, get out."

"You get out," Jesse had replied. Lucy pulled the '20s look off a little too well. Jesse was pretty sure the jacket was actual 1920s vintage, maybe the suspenders, too. Well, Lucy himself was vintage.

Lucy now stood behind him, reapplying his glossy, dark lipstick and smoothing down his iron-straightened hair. Ciceline snapped a selfie at the next mirror. She was in pinstripes, too, with suspenders, and black combat boots.

Club bathrooms had that liminal space feeling, a bubble outside of the chaos. Out on the floor, Nine Inch Nails was on full blast, people shouting along with the lyrics and grinding all over each other. In here it was shared makeup, fixed straps, bobby pins, wardrobe adjustments — a place to breathe.

Lucy pulled a cheap cardboard mask with glued-on feathers over his eyes before they headed back out.

They squeezed through the crowd, down a dim hallway plastered with band posters and lined with people waiting to get in. Lucy took his hand. Jesse's face felt flushed, sweat trickled into his collar in the overbearing heat. They edged around tables where people sat drinking, some out of tall glasses, some out of each other. Mia was somewhere behind the bar, mixing up her magic. Along the back wall, velvet sofas were getting way too much use.

Lucy pulled Jesse to the dance floor, where the massive skeleton hanging from the rafters changed colors and gyrated in time with the music. The DJ was remixing some darkwave song.

Jesse felt more in control than he had on his first night, when the lack of blood had made him vulnerable. He knew his way around a club; he'd always been the one to drag Lucy out dancing in college. All that time, thinking that Lucian was some shy, straight-edge kid who'd never seen a rave in his life, when in fact he had spent almost a decade playing in a band at a fetish club.

They pushed their way up to the stage, where the DJ's booth hung high above. If there was a ladder, it had been drawn up. Lucy leaned over and shouted, "Wait here, okay?"

Jesse gave him a thumbs-up as people jostled and crowded around him. Lucy disappeared to the wing of the stage, only to reappear a few seconds later, scaling the scaffolding stage right. He was quick and light as he clambered up hand over hand. How had Jesse missed this over-the-top strength? You only saw what you looked for, or maybe Lucy had kept it hidden from him. It made sense now, how he'd laid waste to the men who had attacked him, but he had to still be in pain, climbing around like that.

Once atop the scaffolding, he pulled his legs up onto the lighting rig. More than a few eyes turned his way. Jesse's stomach was in his throat as he watched Lucy swing from those delicate structures. A fall from that height might still kill him. Lucy hung down from his knees, lifted his mask, and waved to Jesse.

Ciceline bustled up to Jesse's side. "Pure thirsty dumbass energy right there."

Soon the entire dance floor was watching, all of them invested in this little venture. The DJ looked out, flaring his hands in a 'WTF, man?' gesture. Jesse's vision had grown sharp over the last few weeks: it was Archer DJing up there. He watched Lucy's progress as the club-goers urged him on, hands planted on his hips.

They cheered when Lucy got to the booth and banged triumphantly on the side. Hanging on to the top with one hand, he pulled a piece of paper from his vest pocket and plastered it up against the glass for Archer to see. All that for a song request?

All but a few people lost interest as he made his way back across the rigging and down the scaffolding, hopping to the floor from about five feet up and bounding over to Jesse.

"Whatever song you picked had better be worth all that," Jesse said.

"It is." His eyes were bright behind the mask as he took Jesse's hands and pulled him to the center of the floor.

The darkwave remix ended, and Archer took the mic. "Uhh, so this is non-traditional for our Halloween event, but we had a request so intense, it was hard to say no."

Jesse knew before the first note that it was going to be "Yeah!" but hearing it sent a thrill down his legs anyway.

They danced under the flashing skeleton, the crowd grinding around them, giddy with the change of pace. They danced without touching; Lucy kept his hands to himself, of course. But he moved stiffly. He was still dealing with his injuries, probably set back by his antics up there, but Jesse hadn't seen him smile like this in weeks.

That settled it. He'd have to be gross about it and break up with Jared via text. When the song ended, and Archer switched it back up to Halloween mode, he gave Lucy's hands a squeeze and said, "Don't go anywhere, okay? There's something I have to do."

Lucy's smile remained friendly and open. "Do whatever you need to do. I'll be waiting."

Jesse didn't go far — just to the edge of the dance floor — before taking out his phone. He had to scroll down past all the texts about Finn in order to get to the last one from Jared, and when he did, he paused.

'We need to talk?' No, awful. *'When can I see you?'* Too flirty.

He settled on, "Hey Jared could we have lunch sometime soon? I think we've been sort of ignoring each other lately and we should probably settle this." He hit send with a cold feeling in his chest; there was no way to misinterpret that. He hated breaking up.

The feeling of eyes on his back sent a little shiver along his skin. Jesse was suddenly back in the Black Room, with the dawning horror of certainty creeping up on him.

He turned, and there stood Jared on a balcony, phone in his hand, staring down at him. Jesse's heart stuttered. His breath came up short. He waved Jared down anyway.

The club turned claustrophobic again as he pushed through the crowd. There was no way he could do this inside, surrounded by strangers in this sweaty, sticky room. This time he went out through the front door, past the bouncers and the line of waiting goths. The chill of the night cooled the sweat on him. He waited by the ropes until Jared caught up with him and, without a word, followed him to the alley between the club and the next building over.

Under the dim yellow lights from the street, they stood apart, neither meeting the other's eyes until Jesse spoke.

"Jared, listen, I know it's been—"

"I'm breaking up with you," Jared said.

Even though Jesse had been trying to break up with him for weeks, this still stung. "Oh. Yes. I agree."

Jared said, "Before I say anything else, explain that phone call."

Jesse frowned. "What?"

"The day I called and you were . . . indisposed?"

He cast around in his mind for their last phone conversation and *oh there it was*, the humiliation of Jared thinking he was trying to phone-bone with him when, in fact, he had been crawling out of his skin.

"I was — am — sick," Jesse said. "That's what I've been trying to tell you. For a while it wasn't looking good. I'm in a medical trial."

Jared waved his hand. "Stop it. I know about the vampire stuff, I'm already a reserve so you don't have to give me that nonsense. When were you going to tell me?"

Jesse stood there blinking in the dank light, like he'd just been slapped. "I haven't been one for that long. I really was sick. Whose—"

"Okay, maybe so, but you had to have known about vampires at least six months prior. Carnelian's rules."

Jesse took a step back. "I didn't. I was dying. I didn't get six months to think it over, I got twenty minutes. When were you going to tell me? While we're at it."

"I was going to reserve you right away once I became a vampire. I wasn't even going to make you wait, Via Nova doesn't require the whole 'know them five years, wait six months' thing. But you were already on someone else's list." His eyes softened and he slumped a little. "You've always been in love with someone else. I knew that from the beginning and I chased you anyway. So, let me back up to that. I knew who you were before we met, because Finn is dating one of the models I shoot."

"Bettina Clarke," Jesse said.

"We hung out at a club, like BLOOD only classier. Neither of us has been changed yet. Finn is Bettina's reserve."

All this mess with Finn, over a vampire girlfriend? There had to be more to the story. "How did you even know about me?"

"I saw a picture of you on Finn's phone. I started following your socials, found out where you ate breakfast before work, and went there to try to pick you up."

Jesse leaned back against the cold brick wall. "Finn has pictures of me on his phone?" was all he could come up with.

"Yes," Jared said. "Finn is okay. I know you've been worried."

The strength drained from his legs. "You should have led with that."

Jared took his hands. "No. I told it in the exact right order. I'm glad we fell in love, even though it was just for a little while. I hope we can stay friends."

Gratitude cracked Jesse open; tears burned in the corners of his eyes. Finn was alive. Jared had made it easy for both of them to walk away. It was over. Lucy was waiting inside for him. He had lost his job and his home, but he had forever to start again.

Jared reeled him in for a hug, no heat behind it.

Jesse rewound the conversation and pulled back. "Wait, did you say Via Nova?"

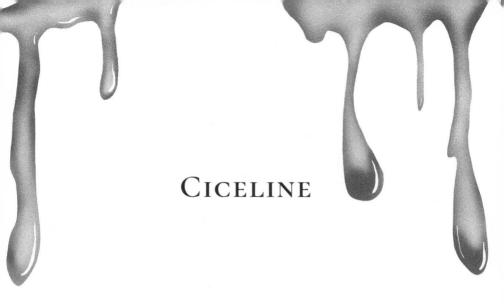

CICELINE

"Trust me," Ciceline told Lucy, "They're breaking up out there."

"Stop it," Lucy said. "No matter what happens, I'm okay with it."

The music slunk on with its low, grinding beats as they made their way off the floor. "I'm going to grab a drink," Ciceline said, leaving Lucy to wander around and find something to do until Jesse came back.

Mia hooked her by the arm before she got to the bar and pulled her aside. She leaned in close and said, "Jesse's ex is a Via Nova reserve."

Ciceline drew back. "What?"

"Yeah, I eavesdropped on them outside. I've seen him around a lot, which is fine, loads of people come through here, I don't mind Via Nova coming in as long as they don't start shit. Jesse was clueless about Jared, and Jared seemed pretty clueless himself. Jesse's brother is Finn, right? Because he said that Finn is a reserve, too. He's alive. I just thought you should know."

"Huh, how about that. Thanks, Mia. Can you turn the emergency exit alarm off for a sec? I want to go out the fire escape, take a quick peek at the guy."

Mia took her phone and fidgeted with the alarms. "You have thirty seconds."

Ciceline bounded up the stairs to the second balcony, shouldering past clusters of people, spilling a few drinks on the way. Most of them were too drunk to notice or care. She barged through the door onto the fire escape and pushed it closed behind her. No alarms went off and she had a few seconds to spare.

Jared was there, in the alley below her. She pulled her suspenders down and unbuttoned her shirt to the chilly night air; it soothed her skin after the cloying heat of the club. So, Jared was with Via Nova and he had used Jesse's brother to get close to him. *Gross.* Poor Jesse. He still didn't get how deep this went.

She leaned down against the grating to see Jared better as he ignited his vape and started pacing. His phone rang.

"Yes, be right over," he said.

He could lead her right to Via Nova, where she would finally play her ace: the new pill formula. She could broker for peace between the factions.

Of course, Jesse would find Lucy and tell him this whole thing. Ciceline had to follow Jared as soon as he left, before Lucy came out and got his silly ass involved. He wasn't in any condition to be doing missions tonight. He barely even held his own on the dance floor a few minutes ago, and that ridiculous climb up the scaffolding hadn't done him any favors.

Jared hung up and continued his nervous vape-pacing. Ciceline texted Lucy:

CICE:

I'm going to buzz off so you can use the loft for whatever nefarious and or sexy purposes you have in mind

LUCY:

You assume too much

CICE:

I really don't :) Try to remember how to use it.

LUCY:

Cice D: Why do I hang out with you??

CICE:

Because I'm the last relic of the parts of your old life you found bearable and we're unhealthily codependent?

LUCY:

WOW

CICE:

Because we're forced to murder people together & we share the same psychological damage that no one else could possibly understand?

LUCY:

Dark???

CICE:

Because the last person you loved was a controlling dickwhistle & therefore you're afraid to get close to anyone else and it's made you antisocial and unable to relate to other ppl

LUCY:

OK, ouch.

Jared put his vape pen away and walked down the alley. Time to go.

CICE:

OK bb vampire, have a fun sexy time. Pls take dog lucy out to pee. See you later.

She climbed down and crept after Jared. Her phone vibrated.

LUCY:

Something is going on u need to tell me what it is I'm coming outside

She didn't answer. Jared crossed the street behind the club and went to the parking lot.

LUCY:

Cice tell me. You're up to something.

Ciceline kept her eyes on Jared as she got to her car. Jesse would have told Lucy by now and he was probably on his way out.

Yvette sucked at negotiation and mediation, but Ciceline excelled at it, and this time she was stepping up whether Yvette liked it or not. She would make a deal for Finn and come to terms with them on everything else: Carnelian would share their oh-so-top secret recipe for the pills, and Via Nova would agree to not set up any politicians in their favor.

She should have been in charge of Carnelian anyway; the whole "heir to the throne" thing was so 1800s. By morning, everything would be settled.

She started her car and followed Jared down the road.

JESSE

n his way back into the club, Jesse shot off a text to Stella:

JESSEBESS:

> Just spoke to Jared he saw Finn at a club he said he was okay. Finn is going out with some model that's the girl in the pic that's how jared knows him. Going to follow up. Tell mom Finn is ok and I'll see if I can get him to come home.

If only it were that easy. No need to alert Stella to whatever vampire nonsense was going down.

He had to find Ciceline.

Mia found him first, linking her arm through his and pulling him past the dance floor, close to the front entrance where it was a little quieter. The door stood open, letting cool air flow in. "Ciceline is following your ex," she said.

"Shit," Jesse said. "I think he's involved in something bad. He knows where my brother is and they're both in this other group called Via Nova. I don't know how much you know about them but—"

She eased her grip on his arm. "I know about Via Nova. Don't you think you ought to tell Lucy?"

"Why?" Jesse pulled away from her. "So they can hurt him again? Finn is my brother. If anyone is going to try to get him out of this mess, it should be me."

"Lucy's going to go anyway," Mia said. "I would. Ciceline probably left already."

"Well, shit!" Jesse could not believe these reckless fools. Having such long lives had taken its toll on their self-preservation skills.

Lucy stalked up to them, anxiety written all over his face even behind his ridiculous mask. "Why is everyone keeping something from me? What's going on?"

"Jesse's ex and brother are both with Via Nova," Mia said. "Ciceline went out to get a look at the ex and didn't come back in." She turned to Jesse. "You have to be direct when he's like this."

"Why the hell would she—" Lucy turned away, grabbing his phone and texting angrily. "Where?"

"I don't know," Jesse said. "I just left him outside."

"Do you think it's a set up?" Lucy asked.

"Also don't know. Jared isn't a vampire yet. Or at least that's what he told me."

"Do you believe him?"

"When I met him in the Black Room that night, I . . ." He cringed. There was no other way to explain it. "I drank from him, and I don't know how much of a difference it makes, but it definitely worked."

"Ah," Lucy said. "You would probably have noticed a difference. Drinking from other vampires doesn't quite . . ."

"Hit the spot," Jesse finished.

"Yes. If I ask you to please stay here and not get involved, will you listen, or will you tell me to go fuck myself?"

"Absolutely go fuck yourself," Jesse said. "Because if this is a set up—"

"Then they have your brother and my sister, so I guess we're both going to go after them."

"This is not what I had planned for tonight," Jesse said.

Lucy's eyes softened as he took Jesse's hands. "What was your plan?"

"Vampire sex."

"Darling, that's not really a specific thing."

"We were going to invent it."

Mia watched them go back and forth over the rim of her light-up cup. "It most certainly is a specific thing," she said. "I'd hate to see this end in death instead of sex, but oh well, that's what happens when dumb meets ass. You should at least let me put a locator app on your phone, in case anyone comes looking, so I can send them to die with you."

"Doesn't Carnelian's app come with one?" Lucy asked.

"Sure," Mia said, "they'd be able to find you just fine. I wouldn't."

Lucy turned to her. "Huge favor. Dog Lucy, in the loft. Can you take him for walkies and make sure he gets fed and there's water in his crate?"

"Gosh, you are such a bother, Lucian."

"I'll make it up to you."

"Take the goddamn app, okay? That'll be a start."

"I think that's a great idea," Jesse said.

"It won't work if we lose service," Lucy said, "but sure." He handed over his phone, fidgeting and bouncing on his toes, as Mia downloaded the app onto it.

This could end tonight. Jesse could bring Finn home. Ciceline might even be in contact with them already, smoothing things over.

Something tingled at the base of his neck. *No, that's not right; none of this is right.* But what else could he do?

"Be careful," Mia said, handing Lucy his phone. "Come back here when you're done rescuing or whatever."

Lucy kissed her cheek. "Thank you."

To Jesse's surprise, Mia yanked him to her and kissed him, too.

As they walked to the exit, Lucy took Jesse's hand instead of linking their arms like he usually did.

There was always a feeling that struck when you left a club, especially on a chilly night. The sticky heat evaporated on your skin once you stepped outside, shivery-cold. The door closed behind you, leaving your ears ringing. It was like exiting a different planet and emerging in a place where normal rules applied again.

Lucy tugged on his hand when they got to the alley. "Hey, Jesse?"

Jesse stopped and turned to him.

Lucy took a step closer. "Would it be weird if—"

"It would not be weird," Jesse said, "I mean, yes, it would be weird, but that's okay."

"The timing isn't great."

"When is it ever?" He pulled Lucy's cheap mask off, setting it into his hair. Lucy gripped his suspenders and pulled him forward and wasn't that a nice surprise. Jesse had to lean down a few inches to meet his lips, just as he had always imagined. Lucy's lips were slick with cherry lip gloss, and now his were, too. The rubber band on Lucy's mask snapped, leaving it dangling from his hair. How was their first kiss happening in a dank alley behind a fetish club? Jesse put both hands on his waist, pulling him up close.

Lucy broke away first. "Oh my god. If we don't stop now, we never will."

"I hate that you're right."

They both backed off. Jesse straightened his suspenders and Lucy plucked the mask out of his hair and dropped it to the ground.

"I've been wanting to do that for so long," Lucy said.

"Pretty sure my thirst predates your thirst by fifteen years."

"Try a decade," Lucy said.

"We could have been having sex these last five years? I genuinely hate you."

Lucy shrugged, sheepish. "Sorry."

"Is this going to be a daring rescue?" Jesse asked. "Because if it is, I'm glad we did that. It adds to the overall ambiance."

Jesse started down the alley toward the parking lot, but Lucy pulled him back. He would not deny Lucy one more kiss before going — he could probably not deny him anything at this point.

Lucy gripped Jesse's hands and brought them up to his face, pressing a fervent kiss against his knuckles. His eyes were closed, brow creased like he was in pain.

"Lucy?"

Lucy only shook his head and squeezed Jesse's hands, pressing his forehead against them.Jesse's heart leapt into his throat. This felt like goodbye. *Let's stay here*, he wanted to say. *Let's go to the loft and forget everything until tomorrow. Ciceline will handle it, and Finn will be okay.*

"Are you alright?" was what he asked instead.

"Yes, of course." When Lucy looked back up, he was smiling. "Just had a moment. After all this waiting."

"Me too."

Lucy took them to Jesse's car, and Jesse dug his keys out of his pocket. Maybe Lucy didn't feel up to driving. They got in and Jesse started the car, turned on the heat, and put his hand on the gearshift. Lucy covered Jesse's hand with his own.

"Ride or die, huh?" Jesse said.

"How about just ride?"

Jesse put the car in drive and pulled out of the parking lot. "Oh, shit. How are we supposed to know where to go?"

Lucy leaned his head back against the headrest and closed his eyes. "Just go where I say. I'll try to tell you where to turn before we're right on top of it, but this method can get a little hairy, so be careful."

"Err, okay." He sat there at the parking lot's exit, grateful that no one was behind him.

"Okay, east," Lucy said.

"Which way is east?"

Lucy opened his eyes. "Left?"

Oh, this was not going to be frustrating or dangerous at all.

STELLA

OCTOBER 31ST

By the time Stella got out of the shower, it was past midnight. Her phone had a message from Jesse:

JESSEBESS:

> Just spoke to Jared he saw Finn at a club he said he was okay. Finn is going out with some model that's the girl in the pic that's how Jared knows him. Going to follow up. Tell mom Finn is ok and I'll see if I can get him to come home.

"Mom!" she called out. "Finn is alright!" She knew to always lead with the good news, especially when shouting from room to room. Her chest still clenched when she thought of the night Mom had called out, "Your father just fell in the kitchen." That had been before they knew how sick he was, before her life split into two chapters. Raising your voice was reserved for only the best or worst news, and you never buried the lede.

Mom's door opened and she peered out, her hand pressed over her heart. "How do you know?" she asked as she came into the kitchen.

"Jesse texted." Her voice sounded breathless and too high. She held the phone out to her.

Mom released a breath that sounded like she'd been holding it for days, but she also quirked an eyebrow. That always meant, *I'm not convinced*. "How in the world did Jared find Finn at a club?" she asked. "Why is Finn even at a club in the first place after all of this? It doesn't make sense."

It did if you were talking about the world of vampires, which was probably pretty cliquey. Did that mean that Jared was a vampire? Stella didn't know, and she didn't care. Well, she cared a little, but this could only be good news, and she wanted to bask in it for a minute before giving her suspicions the mic. Yes, Jesse's "everything is okay" tone was bullshit, but he was on his way to get Finn, so that had to be good.

"Seriously, Stella, how is Finn going to steal Jesse's medical trial pills, run away from home, and then go out to a club where Jesse's boyfriend could see him?"

"Well . . ."

"I'm calling Jesse." She shuffled in her pink slippers back into her bedroom.

Stella went to the window and leaned on the sill, staring out. No, it didn't make sense. Even when she stuck the "vampire" bit into the puzzle, it still didn't fit, but who could she ask? Mom was going to call Jesse, but of course he couldn't tell her anything. Ciceline might tell Stella something, though.

She scrolled back to the texts she'd received earlier from Ciceline. The first was a picture: a selfie in a club bathroom. She was dressed like a 1920s mobster with a purple boa and black lipstick.

STELLA:

Are you all at a party without me??

CICELINE:

Yes but not a safe one for you quite yet. If you're not too busy tomorrow, maybe come here? There's a place called EspresSo Extra. We can discuss your invitation to next year's Halloween party if you want ;)

Stella had replied with, *That sounds great, text me the location*, even though it made her spine tingle and her palms sweat. They really were going to sit at a café and talk about turning her into a vampire. She could not get her brain around it. No, she couldn't get her conscience around it. Where did these blood pills come from? There was always someone making a profit, and always someone being exploited. Even with the risk of her getting sick, these things needed to be addressed before she could consider it.

She clicked on Ciceline's number. It went right to voicemail.

"Jesse just said they were going to the club to look for him," Mom said, coming out from her room. "Lucian's with him. He didn't tell me anything else."

"He's driving; you know how careful he is."

Mom pulled a chair up to the table and sat down, tapping her fingers on the cheap fiberboard. She looked so tired. Stella had to look away, so she went to the window again, that miserable view. The road was deserted now, with only one streetlamp, and an all-night convenience store across the street offering any light. No headlights, no cars.

No cars.

Not even the black SUV. Stella leaned on the sill, tilting her head to see around the corner. Maybe they were parked down the road?

The SUV wasn't always around; it came and went, casing the neighborhood. If she had to guess, she figured she'd seen it maybe once every half hour. She looked at the clock; it was 1:12 AM. She would probably see it turning the corner again in a few minutes, and parking outside the apartment building.

Any minute now.

CICELINE

Ciceline followed Jared along the Southern State. Jared would have to be pretty slick to notice; it wasn't unusual for the same car to be up your ass the whole way. She hated driving this long, especially at night, but the dark highway was useful for exactly this kind of cloak and dagger bull-shittery.

Jared drove like an asshole, speeding in the HOV lane, too fast on even the most sphincter-clenching parts of the ride. If it wasn't for Finn Westchurch being involved in this, she'd turn right back around and forget it all.

An hour into the ride, it hit Ciceline where he was going. East, all the way. The hair on her arms stood on end so hard her skin ached. Jared, a Via Nova reserve, was heading toward the little cluster of blue colonial buildings in Montauk — Carnelian headquarters. She drove on with the radio off. Her phone pinged a few more times, but she ignored it. Of course Lucy was following her, and he probably knew where, too, with his annoying little intuitions.

Ninety minutes later, they came to the point where the Montauk Highway split into two roads. It joined up again after a few miles, so you could go right or left and still get there. Jared turned right onto Old Montauk Highway. Ciceline slowed down until he was out of sight and went left, giving him some time to get there first. After the two roads rejoined, it was only another few minutes to headquarters.

She parked her car in the woods before she got to the entrance.

The chill had turned bitter, and the wind ripped through her low-cut blouse when she got out. She hoped some shit was not about to go down while she was dressed like the bees knees. She checked her phone: almost midnight, and no service.

Up ahead, on a gravel walkway, Jared parked his car in front of Carnelian's main building. Quaint lamps lit the flaking blue paint and highlighted the leafless vines that grew beside the windows. Jared went to the door. When his headlights faded off, Ciceline crept a few steps further, keeping to the shadows. He turned back once, and she slipped behind a cluster of low-lying bushes. He clicked his key and locked his car. A bunch of camel crickets came sproinking out at her, landing on her legs and in her hair. She batted them away and hung back, waiting for Jared to enter.

It took a lot to creep her out. She usually considered herself to be the most intimidating thing in any situation, but watching him go into that well-known office gave her a shiver. Nothing about this was good. It was time to retreat, regroup, and call for backup. She turned to go back to her car.

A sword in her face stopped her. Behind the sword stood a man, backlit by a walkway lamp, recognizable only by a halo of short red hair. He was small, with thin shoulders. A bigger guy lurked behind. A bodyguard or something?

"Nice to see you again, Ciceline," he said, with a vague hint of deep south.

"Christ," Ciceline groaned. "The evil twin."

"Mia's the evil twin!" he barked. "Just another Carnelian drone." His voice sounded different to what she remembered; rougher, a little false. He sounded like a man in the middle of a Snap, but he was too young.

"She doesn't work for them anymore," Ciceline said, her own voice measured and calm.

"She supplies them with blood," Raven said, shoving the point of the sword in her face.

Swords, Jesus Christ. Better than a gun, anyway.

"Can we go inside and talk about this?" Ciceline said. "It's a little cold out here and I'm in this ridiculous costume." She forced a smile: *Haha, silly, harmless me.*

Raven jerked his chin toward the office building.

Ciceline walked with the sword to her back. "Can we let the guy go? Jared? He seems pretty clueless."

"He's not a prisoner," Raven said. "He chose to be here. He wants to help his boyfriend escape Carnelian."

"His boyfriend? Wow, they broke up like an hour ago."

"Either way, he can stay or go. I don't care. Get inside." He had the nerve to poke Ciceline with the tip of the blade.

"Watch the threads," she said. "This jacket is vintage."

Raven and the bigger guy stayed at her back as she approached the door. She could possibly disarm him, but what would be the point? She was here to mediate, to succeed where Yvette had failed.

The windows were intact; the door hadn't been forced. They had to have hacked security, which was bad for Carnelian all around.

Whoever was on duty that day had gone home hours ago. The wooden floorboards creaked beneath her combat boots, but Raven walked silently behind her.

Ciceline pushed open the door to Yvette's office. There were eight more men in there, and she only recognized one: huge guy, eye patch, with pink, shiny scars under his jaw and cheek. The guy who had tried to kill Lucian. Fucking vampires, they never stayed dead when you wanted them to.

Illuminated by the overhead light and the 1940s lamp, behind her desk with the red-sand hourglass on it, sat Yvette, looking put-together with her hair in a twist, beige suit, nails sharp and glossy.

All of Ciceline's witty and thoughtful repartee dried up. She'd thought about unseating and even killing Yvette, but seeing her there, small and scared, took her breath away.

Jared was seated at another chair, fingers twisted into knots in his lap, leg bouncing.

Raven closed the door behind them. "Have a seat."

"I think I'll stand." She couldn't look at Yvette, so instead she stared over her shoulder, and, *oh*, that's why Raven's sword looked familiar. It was the one from above the desk. Only one of them remained on the wall mount. How symbolic.

Eyepatch stared at her, so she stared back.

"You should see the other guy," he said. His voice was a rasp, probably because bits of his throat were missing.

The Other Guy still had both eyes and his entire face, but it would be foolish to goad him.

She turned to Raven. It was time to begin negotiations. "You're the leader of Via Nova?"

"I'm just following orders I believe in."

"Like leaving a body by the river and calling attention to all of us?"

"That one wasn't an order."

"Okay," Ciceline said. Jared's bouncing leg made the floor creak and it was starting to get on her nerves. "You should go."

He didn't answer.

"Carnelian must fall," Raven said.

"It has," Yvette said. "You've won."

Ciceline carefully did not react.

"No." Raven's voice was soft. "It's time to cut the head off the snake." He tensed his arm.

"Okay, now hang on," Ciceline said. "You don't have to do any of this, Raven, I have something you want, you don't have to—"

Raven swung the sword.

Ciceline had never seen it down from mount before tonight, but it was heavy and real. A live blade. Sharp enough to remove

Yvette's head from her shoulders in one swing. Her blood splashed on Ciceline's face, burning hot. All over Jared, too; he leapt back from his chair, knocking it over as blood splattered his body.

Yvette's head landed on the desk and — *Yvette's head landed on the desk* — her eyes twitched because the blood inside was still trying to fix the damage.

She knew, staring at those twitching eyes, that for all her wishing and scheming, all she wanted was Yvette out of power; not dead.

"Oh, fuck," Ciceline whispered. "Fuck!" It sounded helpless coming out of her mouth. She wanted Yvette to get back up and fix this. But Yvette's face was turning gray . . . no, that was just a trick of Ciceline's eyes, because everything was turning gray. The blood, the table, the wall, the light . . . all fading.

Ciceline sank down on the two-seater. Breathed. She'd definitely seen heads hit tables before, at least twice, just not the head of the woman who had gotten her out of a prison and given her a home, and the only family she'd ever known.

Jared was fainting in the corner, the rest of the guards weren't reacting, and Raven was watching her.

He stuck the blade under Ciceline's chin and lifted it. "Any more snakes?"

Yvette's blood dripped down her cheeks; Ciceline itched to swipe it away. She could handle this. She would succeed where everyone else failed.

"I have the new formula for the pills. It's yours."

LUCIAN

As familiar as Lucy was with the roads from Blood to home, they got turned around a few times, because of course they did. Jesse drove, shoulders and back tight, taking sudden turns whenever Lucy called out a direction.

Lucy wiped his palms on his trousers.

"You're freaking out," Jesse said. "How bad do you think this is?"

Death was hanging around again. "Bad enough for me to drop you off somewhere."

"Like hell," Jesse replied.

After about half an hour, Jesse suggested going east, and it was like a path opening in front of him. Why was Jesse so good at handling him?

"Getting closer," Lucy said, and then had to go back three seconds in time to figure out if he'd spoken out loud, because the thought hadn't even entered his mind yet.

"Okay," Jesse said. "Just let me know."

An itch tickled at the back of his throat, but not the kind that signified any oncoming hack attack from having to shout over the club music. He coughed, and Jesse glanced at him the way people did when they knew him well enough: at his shoulders, to see if they were rising when he breathed. He felt cared for, yet irritated.

"There's water in the back," Jesse said. "Can you grab one for me too?"

There Jesse went, handling him again. It was deft, he had to admit. Lucy wiggled out of his seatbelt and leaned over the seat to get two bottles of water from a half-empty crate. Next to it was a cardboard box filled with bags of different kinds of chips. Trust Jesse to drive around with water and snacks. He opened the bottle for Jesse and handed it to him, then his own.

The first cold sip eased his throat. On the second sip, he choked. It didn't go down wrong, it just got stuck, a painful spasm slicing through his neck. He tried to cough but couldn't draw in any air.

"Inhaler's in the glove compartment," Jesse said without taking his eyes off the road.

Jesse always had an extra one for him in his car. Lucy reached for it, but pain jerked him backwards. He wasn't okay. For no discernible reason, he was dying. Sitting here in the car with Jesse, unable to inhale, dizzy with panic, too-bright lights flashing in his eyes and a screeching ringing in his ears: this was death. His body pitched forward with loss of equilibrium, and the lights blinked out to nothingness.

It was over as quickly as it started. Jesse gripped his knee, his voice frantic as he called his name. There was no place to pull over.

"I'm alright." He was about a thousand miles away from alright, but he wasn't dead. Someone was, though. The specter of death enveloped him, tears stung his eyes and burned his throat, like mourning for someone he didn't even know was gone. He did not cry, though he wanted to. He sucked in a breath, took a sip of water, and said "I'm alright" once more.

"What was that?" Jesse asked.

"A really bad vibe."

"That was way more than a vibe."

"Yes. It's over now. I'm fine." Jesse's hand was still on his knee, which was comforting, but—— "Two hands on the wheel, please, or we'll both be dead."

Jesse exhaled a shaky breath and took the wheel in both hands.

As they approached a rest area off the parkway, it hit him where they were going.

Lucy took his phone out, opened his app, and clicked the panic alarm. The only response was an ellipsis that kept reloading. Carnelian would never let that happen. He dialed the international number, got an automated message about how important his call was to them, and hung up.

"Shit," Lucy said. "Pull over."

Jesse whipped the car into the parking lot of the rest stop. "Here?"

"No. I have to keep going, but I want you to call Stella and get a ride home."

"First, Stella is an hour away. Second — as established — go fuck yourself."

"Jesse, please, they'll kill you. Think of your mother. Don't do that to her." God, why was he like this? Why couldn't he just listen?

"Don't even come at me with that guilt bullshit. If they have Finn and they kill you, they'll come after me next anyway."

"They won't. I mean, they won't kill me. Probably. But even if they did—"

"Forget it, Lucy, I'm not leaving you. Call for backup, get Carnelian."

"I tried. Carnelian is gone, Jesse. There is no help. No one's coming. It's just me."

"What do you mean, they're gone?"

How could he explain it when he didn't know? "I can get there from here, I don't need your help anymore. I do this kind of thing alone."

"Bullshit."

"My mother was right, you're only going to hold me back. Get out of the car."

Jesse turned in the seat and stared at him. Lucy had raised his voice.

He had raised his voice to Jesse.

In the entire time he'd known Jesse, not once had they fought about anything. Small disagreements, teasing arguments, but they'd never been angry with each other. It hurt all the way through. How did people function like this? How did they live through anything with these feelings battering at them all the time, making them weak?

"You're gonna leave me in a rest area in the middle of the night, like a sitting duck, knowing that some cult took my brother. Wow, Lucy."

"Hate me if you need to." The words burned coming out of his throat.

Jesse grabbed his arm, almost yanking him across the console. "No," he said through gritted teeth.

He stared at the dark road ahead and pulled his arm back. Nothing had ever been as exhausting as fighting with Jesse.

"How close are we to the place?" Jesse asked.

"Close."

"What if I call the cops? It might make them back off or be too afraid to make a move."

"They'll send one cop, maybe two, and they'll be killed."

"There has to be someone—"

"I think they targeted your brother because of me."

"Well, you're wrong. His girlfriend got him involved. You don't know the whole story."

"When uprisings like this happen, people die."

"What choice do we have?"

Lucy dug his knuckles into his eyes to relieve the rising headache. It didn't help. "The choice to not die. What part of that are you not understanding? I can handle this. I'm an assassin, Jesse. Has that not sunk in yet?"

Jesse didn't answer; he sat gripping the wheel, not moving. If Lucy wanted him out, he'd have to literally shove him out the door, and he couldn't. He couldn't put his hands on Jesse in a way that would hurt him. He dug deep, looked for the ability, and didn't find it. Maybe he could trick him into getting out.

Lucy let out a sigh of resignation. "If you're not going to get out, can you promise to stay in the car when I go in there? I know the way from here, let's switch seats so I can drive."

Jesse arched an eyebrow. "Sure, whatever." He climbed into the backseat. *Goddamnit.* Lucy scooted over to the driver's seat.

Jesse swatted the back of his head. "Nice try, asshole. Drive."

Teeth locked together, hands too tight on the wheel, and foot too heavy on the gas, Lucy drove.

CICELINE

Yvette's head was turned toward her, blank eyes fixed on her face. Raven's blade jabbed the underside of Ciceline's chin. The rhythmic ringing in her ears faded and she found herself thankful that it had obscured the sound of Yvette's body hitting the floor, and her blood gushing out onto the rug. Raven's soldiers kept quiet; only the hum of the lights filled the silence.

"I don't care about the pills," Raven said. "And I have no use for negotiations."

Shit. Keep him talking. She was good at this; she could walk out of here alive. "So why all this? Carnelian is gone, you might as well tell me. If Via Nova doesn't want access to the pills, then what?"

"To change whoever we—" Raven clamped his mouth shut, hand tightening on the sword. Ciceline shrank back. "We raided the factory; we know how to make the pills now. And we're free from Carnelian's rules."

Well, fuck. "Free to leave drained bodies all over the island?" Ciceline asked. "That was you, wasn't it, putting every other vampire in danger? You're already all over the news."

"It wouldn't be a problem," Raven said. "If you had allowed

Via Nova to put legal protection in place. Someone to watch our backs and keep our secrets."

"Russel Busquet, right," Ciceline said. "The one who killed those kids."

No one spoke. Something in the room changed when she dropped that name.

Raven scoffed, breaking the silence. "Junkies."

She softened her tone. "Raven, come on, since when do you care about that? Addiction isn't a moral failing."

"Speaking of Lucian," Raven said. "When you said that Carnelian was gone? Clearly it's not, since the heir is still alive."

Panic squeezed her chest and constricted her throat. "Lucian's got nothing to do with this, Raven. You know him; he hates Carnelian. All he's ever wanted was to play his music and be left alone."

"For now," Raven said. "Back then, that's all I wanted, too. People change. What about fifty years from now? We just want to talk to him."

"You couldn't just ask him to come? He would have. Lucian was your friend."

"He was Mia's friend."

"No. Lucian thought the world of you."

This was going to come to violence; she'd have to kill Raven. How would she get through the rest of these assholes in the room?

"I thought he'd get here first," Raven said. "But since it's you, you're going to call him."

"There's no reception here," Ciceline said. "And even if there was—"

Raven pressed the blade closer to her neck. She grabbed it, slicing her palm and fingers, and jerked it to the side. Pulling Raven off balance, she stuck the point into the wall next to her head. "Stop touching me with that thing. I'm not calling Lucian."

Raven lunged, gripping Ciceline's suspenders to haul her up

against the wall. He moved fast, like his sister. "You'll call him when you see who we have in the dungeon."

In the corner, where he'd fallen off his chair, Jared roused from his faint, looked around in a daze, and started to cry.

"Knock that shit off," Eyepatch sneered. "You signed up for this."

"No," Jared said. "Nothing like this. You were supposed to change us without restrictions, that's all."

Raven dropped Ciceline to the floor, forcing her to struggle for balance. "Time to go. You too, Jared."

Jared wept harder, and Ciceline pitied him, getting his naive ass tangled up in this mess. He got his wobbly legs under him and staggered toward the door by Ciceline's side.

Raven shoved her, glancing back at Eyepatch, but Eyepatch stayed put and someone else followed instead, some douchebag with long, black hair in a braid. Raven yanked the sword out of the wall on his way out.

Ciceline took one last look — Yvette was still dead, that was real — and walked out into the night. She shivered, wrapping her arms around her middle. Her teeth chattered. It wasn't teeth-chattering cold, but she was outside of her body, still in the office with Yvette's blue eyes staring at her. She hadn't dissociated from shock in decades. It sucked worse than she remembered.

Jared slipped his jacket off and draped it over her shoulders. She looked at him in surprise. He shrugged, put his head down, and kept walking.

She had been planning on saving him anyway, but shit, now she really had to.

She and Jared walked in front, Raven's sword and Braid Douche's gun at their backs. A path cut through the woods behind the complex, and Ciceline had already guessed where they were going, and who was in there. Raven moved silently, like his feet didn't touch the ground. Ciceline's feet felt heavy, her body cumbersome and clumsy. She kept tripping over branches in the dark, and the shivering would not quit.

They came to a clearing in the woods, a trench with two steep hills on either side, and there it was: the entrance to an old silo dug into a hill. Carnelian had buried most of it, so only the circular, steel doorway remained visible from the front. They'd used it as a prison ages ago and then a disposal site for incinerated bodies. It had to be layered in ashes. If Via Nova had been here for a few days, probably actual bodies too.

Raven and Braid Douche corralled them toward the entrance of the silo.

"Call Lucian," Raven said.

"There's still no reception, hello."

"I have wi-fi calling," Jared piped up. "I have a really great plan."

Oh, fuck this guy. "There's no wi-fi here either," Ciceline said. "And anyway, I'd just tell him it's a trap and not to come without backup."

"That will make him get here faster," Raven said.

"If we get out of this ditch, we might have—" Jared began.

A flash of moonlight glinted off Raven's blade and he swung it in their direction.

Ciceline wanted to throw Jared down and dodge out of the way, but her feet were stuck in place. She panted like a wild animal.

Braid Douche doubled over, clutching his middle.

Raven flicked the blood from the sword. "Run."

The two of them stood there, gaping at him.

"What are you waiting for?" Raven said. "Go, before they come searching."

Jared grabbed her hand. "Come on!"

Ciceline stood her ground and found her voice. "Is Finn Westchurch in there?"

"Yes," Raven said. "I'm letting him out now." He took the key from his pocket and went to the door.

"How many more?" Ciceline asked.

"A few. I don't know."

She pulled her hand free of Jared's. "You should go."

"Where? I can't run off into the woods by myself! They'll chase me, they'll . . . Raven, please, you said this would be safe, you told me—"

"Go up that hill over the silo," Ciceline said. "Beyond it is the road. There has to be a cell tower or wi-fi close to here. Call 911 and tell them you got lost. And then, Jared, get on a plane and leave the country until this is over."

"Come with me," he begged. "There's coyotes, deer ticks, there's the East End killer, please."

"I am the East End killer," Raven said. "Someone will come to check soon; you need to be gone by then. Go!"

Jared jumped at the order, turned, and tried to scramble up the hill. Ciceline took pity and gave him a leg up. He clambered over to the top of the silo entrance and ran off without looking back.

Raven pulled the silo door open, and the stench hit first.

"You're keeping them in here? Jesus Christ, Raven!"

"It was the safest place," he said. "Via Nova wants Lucian. You should never have killed Russel Busquet. I'm sorry. My fight isn't with you or Lucian, just Yvette. I got my revenge and I'm done."

"Revenge? For what? And Lucy and I were supposed to be, what, collateral damage? Thank you, shithead!"

"I asked for a reserve," Raven said. "Yvette denied it, she said the new policy didn't allow for more useless people."

Ciceline rubbed her temples, where an ache started to throb, traveling into her throat and down her chest. Yvette and her terrible decisions.

"Mia cut me off. I had no one. I tried to do it myself," Raven continued, his voice as choked as hers felt. "I tried, but I messed it up. There was no one to help me. She didn't make it." He covered his face and wept. "I watched her die."

How easily it could have gone the same way with Jesse. It

nearly had. Wouldn't Lucy have burned Carnelian to the ground too? "Why didn't you just come to me? I could have—"

The pop of a pistol made her jump. She turned, ready to throw herself into the silo and close the heavy door behind her, but Raven fell forward into the dark opening.

Braid Douche was on his hands and knees, taking aim again, one hand over his bloody midsection. *Goddamn it.* Her shock over Yvette had made her sloppy. She hadn't even checked to make sure he was dead.

Another gunshot and this time something splashed onto her chest, a pinpoint of ice, not hot like blood should feel.

Braid Douche got one leg under him, crouching.

Ciceline yanked Raven inside the door and dragged it shut. It was so heavy. Why was this door so heavy? Raven had opened it with ease. Her arm was so weak. She tried to grab at her arm with her other hand, but it dangled at her side, useless.

The ice in her chest turned burning hot, a poker under her clavicle, and now it wasn't just her arms that were weak, but her legs too. She shoved with her shoulder until the door closed.

Another gunshot echoed as it bounced off the metal outside. Ciceline used what little strength she had left to drag Raven by the arm as she stumbled down a pitch-black hallway. She went as far as she could go. The gunfire stopped.

Ciceline slid down the wall with Raven beside her.

Something hissed in the darkness, a dragging sound, then the darkness overtook everything.

JESSE

J esse fought with himself as they pulled up to the cluster of free-standing business suites. Lucy was right, he didn't belong here. He wasn't some kind of badass fighter, and he would get in the way; but he couldn't bring himself to leave.

The buildings were blue — cute and rustic and unassuming. Nothing like the sprawling, art deco structure of the clinic or the gothic buildings he'd imagined when thinking of Carnelian's offices.

"I'll ask you one more time to drive away," Lucy said.

"What part of 'go fuck yourself' do you not understand?"

"Will you at least promise to do exactly as I say once we're inside? Without question?"

"I guess I can give you that," Jesse said. Guilt ate him up, but dropping Lucy off here and then leaving without him didn't bear thinking about.

They parked and got out. Gravel crunched under their feet as they went up the walkway to where Ciceline's car sat idling with its engine still running and the door open.

"This is bad," Jesse said.

"Yes." Lucy reached in, rustled around for something, and

pulled a few objects out. They glinted in the lamplight. She had left behind her weapons, which Jesse had to assume she wouldn't have done if she'd gone in there willingly. Lucy tucked the blades into various places in his ridiculous Halloween costume. "Can you handle knives?"

Jesse's voice shook. "I'm awesome with a scalpel."

Lucy pressed a switchblade into his hand and a stiletto into the other. "I need you to get out of this alive, okay? No matter what else happens."

"Well, same," Jesse said. "Don't you have any guns?"

"If you carry a gun, someone will eventually use it on you. Just do as I say."

"Within reason."

Lucy pressed a kiss to his temple, harder than necessary. "If we were within reason, you wouldn't be here with me."

"Do you have a plan?"

"I'm sticking knives in my sock garters, do I look like I have a plan?"

He was lying. Jesse didn't know how to ask what he was lying about, and anyway, there wasn't enough time. Lucy stalked onward, head forward, purposeful. He always glided here and there, as if he didn't quite touch the ground, but this was the walk of a hit man, and it was nothing like they portrayed in movies.

The door swung open when Lucy pushed on it, revealing a room that looked like a reception area to a car insurance office: plain rug, plastic chairs, a wooden desk with a closed laptop on it.

The tang of fresh blood seeped in from the next room, and a raspy voice called, "Come on in, Lucian."

Lucy reached back and took Jesse's hand, leading the way as they entered.

The man who had called Lucy in wore an eyepatch, and a sunken scar marked his neck, like someone had taken a bite. It took a second for Jesse to place him: at the creek, his body pinning Lucy under the water.

Blood drenched the carpet, so much that Jesse didn't crave it;

his reaction was pure human. He fought down the urge to be sick. A pair of stockinged legs with expensive heels on the feet stuck out from behind a desk. The rest was a blur: a stack of papers, a lamp, an hourglass, a woman's blond head. Yvette's blue eyes stared at them.

Jesse was maybe — probably — about to check out, just opt for unconsciousness, but then Lucy stumbled against the door-frame and it jostled him back to his senses. He put his hand on Lucy's shoulder.

There were six other people; their faces blended together. They had guns. Florescent lights glared above, making everything appear waxy and washed out, except the vivid stained-glass window behind the desk.

"Come in please, Carnelian," the guy with the eyepatch said.

"Don't call me that." Lucy's voice barely cracked above a whisper.

"That's how your laws work, right? The heir?" Eyepatch bowed with his arm folded across his middle.

"Where is Ciceline?"

"Out back being killed. In fact . . ." He nodded to one his guards. "Go make sure the job's done, and check on the others."

The man pushed past them as he left.

"Alright, yes," Lucy said. The strength had come back into his voice; it was clipped and businesslike. Jesse had rarely heard him use this tone. "Carnelian is mine, and when I'm dead, there's no one else. It will fall apart. What do you need me to do?"

"I love the way you and your sister think you can negotiate. You didn't even ask my name or try to create a rapport." He heaved himself onto the desk and Jesse had to look away as his weight jostled Yvette's head.

"Are you the one I'm negotiating with?" Lucy asked. "Are you the leader of Via Nova? Then, what's your name?"

He dipped his head. "Brett Busquet. I never reached my son's level of fame."

Jesse's clutched Lucy's shoulder, but willed the rest of his body to remain perfectly still.

"I see," Lucy said. "Well, your son was a murdering piece of shit, so definitely not sorry."

"Just following the orders of your mother, right?"

"That's right."

"Can you tell me how he died?" Brett patted the table beside him, like he wanted Lucy to go to him, lay his head on the desk next to his dead mother's and accept his fate.

"You have another man here," Lucy said. "Finn Westchurch."

A charitable smile twisted Busquet's face. "Let him go?"

"And Jesse."

"No," Jesse said.

Lucy ignored him. "Let the Westchurches go and I'll do whatever you want. I'll tell you everything. You can kill me at the end, and Carnelian will be done."

"You'll tell me anyway," Busquet said. "I can see the fear in your eyes."

The laugh that came out of Lucy was cold. "Not unless you do as I ask. And I'll take a few of you with me. You know that." He pointed out one of the men hovering close to Busquet. "You first, I think."

The guard flinched and took a step backwards.

"Lucy!" Jesse shook him by the shoulder and finally Lucy turned to face him. The anguish in his eyes made it real.

"Please go," Lucy said. "You promised you'd do as I asked. You don't have to be here for this." He turned back to the others. "Let him go and I won't fight. You have my word."

"Lucian, no. No!"

Busquet nodded, and one of the guards came toward him. Jesse tried to dodge, but the guy was quick and grabbed him by the arm.

"Get him out of here," Lucy ordered, "then come right back in and lock the doors. If you try to leave with him, I'll come outside and cut your tongue out. Jesse, get in the car."

"No!" It was the only word that would come out of his mouth.

"Drive away. Go home."

Jesse hooked his fingers around Lucy's arm, but was dragged away like a child. Lucy turned to him. The last thing Jesse saw was his tear-streaked face before the guard pulled him through the reception room and shoved him outside. The slamming door nearly clipped his nose and he fell back a step. The understanding that Lucy was going to die scooped out his innards and hollowed out his chest. This couldn't be happening.

Lucy had told him to go. When had Jesse ever not done as he was told, especially in a dangerous situation? He barely ever crossed the street outside of the crosswalk. The rational thing to do was what he had originally thought: Get help. Call the authorities. That was real life, that was the rule, it was normal. But "normal" wouldn't save Lucy and it probably wouldn't save him, either.

He beat on the door. He kicked it, screamed through it. It was all useless.

The windows. Those stained-glass atrocities he'd seen from the inside, if he could break one, it might distract them, give Lucy a chance.

He sprinted around the side of the building, listening for any noise from inside: screaming, crying, gunshots, anything.

The light from the lamps that lined the gravel walkway didn't reach him but there had to be a rock or something, anything he could use to smash the glass. His breath came loud and hard; he was running out of time. His fist, then. It would heal. If he lived.

He drew his arm back to drive it through the window, but dragging footsteps sounded from the path leading into the woods. Jesse froze.

Can't help if you're dead.

He fell back, seeking out shelter. His only option was a copse of low-lying bushes, so he dodged behind them and crouched down.

The footsteps stopped. Jesse fought the urge to shut his eyes and block it all out. When they picked up again, they scraped on the gravel, and a harsh, heavy gasping accompanied them.

The shadow crept up to his hiding spot. Jesse waited.

LUCIAN

They were still going to kill Jesse.

The question was, what was Lucian willing to do in order to save him?

Jesse screamed through the door outside. Lucy blocked him out.

Three guns were pointed at him, but no one had fired, so it wasn't to be the firing squad for his crimes.

Busquet Senior sat on the desk, tapping his fingers in Yvette's blood. Lucian could not recall ever seeing her bleed. She must have, at some point. She'd lost two fingers, although he couldn't remember when or how that had happened.

Busquet was doing an awful lot of sitting, wasn't he? Lucian had twisted Busquet's leg during their fight, snapping a ligament or two.

"My son," Busquet said. "It was a blade to his throat? That's what they said on the news."

"Yes."

"Did he know? Did he have time to cry out?"

"No. We tricked him into thinking I was going to be one of his victims. He died doing what he loved, anyway."

His mother's blank eyes regarded him. If he focused, he could imagine them moving.

The question was—

"Did you know you were there to kill him when you showed up?"

"Yes."

"Did you know who he was?"

"No."

Busquet stood, stiff on that leg, and took the remaining sword down from the board. Ah, so just like his mother, then. Who had the other sword? Were they trying to use it on Ciceline?

"What was the last thing my son did?" Busquet asked, moving closer. Tears slipped down his cheeks, but his eyes remained otherwise blank and impassive.

Images came unbidden, jumbled. Lucy's thoughts spiraled, he couldn't concentrate. Out of the hundreds he had killed, he was supposed to remember this one? Time had gone stretchy and nebulous, like a dream.

The question was—

Busquet yanked him toward the desk. Oh yes, now he remembered: Russel Busquet, the most recent one, only a few days ago. Or weeks?

"He grabbed me by the hair." *His eyes were blue and looked like he was already dead.*

"And then?"

Three other men hovered around them, out of reach.

"And then I pierced his jugular with a trocar, and he died."

Busquet placed the sword on the desk next to Yvette's head and ran his finger along the blade. "Relax," he said, even though Lucy hadn't made a move. "You're not going to die tonight. I've given this a lot of thought since our last meeting."

Good. Torturers were the easiest to disarm. Their blood was up, they took their time, and they made mistakes.

"How far do you think your friend will get before we pick him up again?" Busquet said.

Lucy didn't answer. Jesse hadn't even left; Lucy had felt the shift in him. Jesse wouldn't abandon him, damn it, no matter how much he begged.

"I've been thinking about what you love," Busquet went on. "At first, I thought, nothing, right? How could someone who has murdered since childhood be anything but dead inside? But that was shortsighted of me. Of course you love. We all kill, and we all love. Your sister is already dead."

No, Ciceline would never stand for being murdered. He clung to that belief.

"And Jesse Westchurch. I thought it was just him, but it's all of them, isn't it? The Westchurches. You love them all."

Busquet was saving them up for him. Lucy was supposed to watch. Tormentors were his favorite.

"Did you drink my son's blood?"

Ugh, did he ever. "Yes, and it was disgusting."

Busquet threw the hourglass against the wall. It shattered, scattering chunks of red sand on the carpet. Forgetting his caution, he clutched Lucy by the throat and shook him so hard his head snapped back. "Do you think this is funny?" he raged.

No, of course he didn't, and he'd done nothing to indicate that he thought it was funny. He couldn't say so while being shaken.

"Tell me in English, you bastard!"

"What language was that?" someone asked.

Busquet stopped shaking Lucy, shoved him hard against the wall, and spat, "Romanian." He lunged again, grabbing Lucy's face, studying his eyes. "Oh for fuck's sake, you Snapped. Feels less righteous like this. But it is gratifying to know that I broke you first." Busquet hooked him by the back of the neck and pushed him down onto the desk.

Snapped? Had he? He felt very calm. Was this what it was supposed to feel like? He had expected to at least notice it; this was nothing like he had imagined. Perhaps Busquet was mistaken. Lucy kept silent. Yvette's blood caked into his hair.

The question was—

"What else do you love?" Busquet bent over him, leaning all his weight on his neck. "What else?"

Someone came to his side and pinned his left arm to the table. His right hand was still free. His face was turned toward Yvette's head.

"Music," Busquet hissed in his ear.

Someone else took over holding his neck, freeing up Busquet's hands so he could swing the blade.

The question was, what was he willing to do?

The only thing you're good at, Yvette said.

Which was absurd, how could she say anything? Ah, maybe hearing the dead was part of the whole "Snapping" ordeal.

Three things Lucy had learned decades ago in America: His mold allergy extended to shrooms (spiked pizza? Who could you trust?) new music was as good as the oldies and sometimes better, and Jackie Chan was a superhero of imagination. Everything was a potential weapon: sand, chairs, a ladder, a bicycle.

That would be the 90s . . . the second 90s, the one with the internet. How had he lived long enough to see a thing like the internet? Could that be real? Losing track of the centuries like this should have been alarming, but he felt so rational. This was a Snap, getting the years confused? He could handle it.

The nineties. Jackie Chan. Improvised weapons.

Busquet raised the sword.

The question was—

The door slammed open and everyone jumped, even Busquet. It wasn't Jesse, thank god. It was the guard Busquet had sent outside after whoever was supposed to kill Ciceline. He panted hard, the left side of his shirt was streaked with blood. "We have a big problem at the silo."

Lucy reached out with his free hand and touched his mother's cold cheek, the elegant twist of hair at the back of her head.

'The problem probably had bleach-blond hair and a law degree. Lucian shivered a little — was that hope he felt? — but an open door also meant that Jesse could get back in, so this would have to be fast. The others clustered around him, within reach. The man at the door had a gun, too far away to disarm. If anyone got him tonight, it was going to be that guy.

The one holding his arm down scooted around to the front of the desk, putting them almost face to face. His eyes were wide, whites showing above the irises. He trembled so hard the corner of his mouth twitched. Lucy smiled at him.

Yvette kept staring, urging him to do the one thing he was good at.

Busquet swore through gritted teeth.

Everything was a weapon.

Everything.

The question was—

Lucian dug his fingers into his mother's hair.

The answer was:

Whatever it takes.

JESSE

J esse crouched behind the bushes and peered through the
branches at the two guards standing outside the building, a
big guy and a smaller, bloody one.

"I've got you," the bigger guy said, as he dragged the
bloodied man alongside him, setting him down under the stained-
glass window. "Hold this gun. Take my phone, call for backup."
He left the bloody man and edged around to the front door.

The bloody man's hand curled against his chest. In the other
hand he held the phone, his thumb texting slowly, slipping off the
screen. The gun had fallen beside him. He stopped texting, then
dropped the phone, too.

I'm really doing this. This is my life now.

Jesse crept along behind the shrubs. The phone lay on the
ground, face-up, its screen dimming. The next time Jesse moved,
he'd be out in the open until he got through the front door.

He heard the door open, and he ran, leaving his back exposed,
waiting for a gunshot, for the thud of a bullet in his spine. It never
came. He made it to the building and pressed himself against it,
his breathing too loud, his heartbeat shaking his entire chest.

The door to the reception room stood open and he inched
along the wall until he was next to it. Jesse had a switchblade in

one hand, a stiletto in the other. When he eased his fingers apart, the weapons had left handle-shaped grooves in his palms. Which would be better? The stiletto: ribs were hard to get through, much easier to go between them.

Jesse had never opened a switchblade in his life, but he pressed the button on the side and the knife popped out. If the stiletto didn't go in, he could try with this.

The man had his back to Jesse as he stood in the doorway to the office.

Jesse ran, lunged, and jammed the stiletto between the man's ribs. His own strength shocked him; his arm had never moved that fast or hard before. The guy didn't fall down dead like in the movies. He turned around. His gun fell at their feet, out of Jesse's reach. The knife in his back didn't seem to bother him much, and his hand shot out toward Jesse's face. Jesse dodged backwards.

A shout echoed from inside. It didn't sound like Lucy, but he couldn't be sure. The *pop!pop!* of a gun came from beyond the door. The guy looked away, distracted. Jesse flicked his hand out, grabbed the handle of the stiletto, and yanked it out. The man turned again and dove for Jesse, bellowing, and slashing with a blade of his own that he'd pulled from his coat.

More gunfire sounded from inside. Jesse's legs felt like hot water, his chest was hollow but for a terrified heartbeat rattling around in it. Lucy might be dead. Jesse was about to die. The dry air burned his lungs as he backed up, afraid to turn his back.

The man stumbled. Jesse took the opening, sticking the stiletto into the front of his chest this time. When he jerked it back out, blood shot from the hole in his shirt. The guy still kept coming at him. Fuck, he hated vampires. Then red bubbled from his mouth and he fell to his knees, dropping face-down in the doorway.

Jesse gave it three seconds, waiting for him to get up. He got closer and stuck him in the back again. The body jerked, but didn't move or try to fight him off.

The body.

He had killed a man.

He skirted around him — *the body* — convinced a hand was going to shoot out and grab his ankle. It didn't move, so he pushed the door.

His throat closed up, light poured into his pupils, his legs went numb. An unsteady drip-drip was the only sound. The fluorescents made everything smeary; it was too much to fit into his eyes. Blood slicked every surface, even the ceiling. Bodies sprawled on the floor, with open, sightless eyes. That was someone's hand beside the overturned desk. Everyone had to be dead.

Everyone except for the person crouched in the corner, blood-soaked, gripping a broadsword in one hand and a gun in the other.

The man Jesse had kissed in an alley an hour ago was gone. A stranger had taken his place, his hair matted with blood, his face nothing more than eyes in a red mask. He spoke, but Jesse couldn't understand the words; maybe it was the ringing in his ears.

The draining adrenaline, and the amount and locations of the blood blackened his vision. Jesse fell back against the wall and slid down, head throbbing, nauseous to the soles of his feet. He counted to ten, waiting for the oxygen to return to his brain, until he was sure he could get his legs under him without falling.

Lucy needed him.

He dragged himself to his feet. He had to step through the blood squelching in the carpet. Jesse forced his lips to move, his throat to work. "How much of this blood is yours?"

Lucy looked at himself, wincing, and peeled away half of his ruined shirt. Beneath it, a jagged slice cut across the side of his ribs, hard to tell if it was from a bullet or a knife. On top of whatever else was going on with him, he needed blood.

"I have the pills in my car," Jesse said.

Lucy spoke again, in sounds that Jesse couldn't understand until he realized it was Romanian.

"Lucy, it's me," Jesse said.

"Jesse?" He blinked like he was just waking up. "Jesse?"

It wasn't the repetition of his name that set his nerves on edge. Lucy sounded different, and Jesse couldn't put his finger on what it was.

"I told you to go," Lucy said.

It was the accent. Jesse had heard it slip out a few times over the years, vaguely, and had always figured maybe Lucy had been talking to his father recently and picked it up from him, but this was impossible to miss.

Blood seeped into Jesse's dress pants as he kneeled before Lucy and pried the hilt of the sword out of his hand. "What did I tell you about sending me away?"

Lucy stood up, one hand on the wall like he needed it to hold himself upright. He took in a deep breath, let it out, and said, "Hai să mergem."

Jesse's Romanian wasn't perfect, but he understood "Let's go."

With a sudden burst of energy, Lucy pushed past him and started ransacking bodies for weapons. He'd retrieved three more guns before Jesse had even taken a step, and the sword, too. He nudged Jesse behind him and fired the gun — *pop!pop!pop!* — into the bodies, before crouching beside a headless one: Brett Busquet. Jesse recognized him by the size of his remains. Lucy fished around in his pockets, and the body rocked with the movement. Jesse had to look away.

He made it to the door, almost tripping over the man he had killed, *the body*, and he leaned in the doorway, bracing his hands on his knees as he tried to get the blood flow back to his head. Everything buzzed. He couldn't feel his fingers.

The jingling of keys roused him, and there was Lucian, on his way to the front door with a keyring in his sword-hand. He handed it over to Jesse without a word and stalked ahead like a shark cutting through water.

Jesse followed him outside, stopping at the car to fetch the pills. He shook a few free and shoved the bottle into his jacket pocket. Lucy was already ahead of him, but he stumbled on the gravel and caught himself on a nearby tree, panting.

"Here," Jesse said, pushing a handful of pills into his hand.

Lucy nodded his thanks before dry swallowing them and pressing on. The gravel path gave way to brush and leaves as they left behind the lights of the complex.

Lucian was leaving him, becoming someone he didn't know. Jesse jogged to catch up and hooked him by the arm. Lucy turned, consternation barely visible beneath the mask of blood.

"I don't care what you did back there." Jesse said. "I care about how we're going to get Finn and Ciceline back from wherever they are, and I can't do that with a stranger."

Lucy reached out to cup Jesse's face with his hand. The bloody hand print he left stung and itched at Jesse's skin. "Dragul meu, I'm right here," he said.

He wasn't, and Jesse didn't know how to get him back. He shivered as a sick feeling crept over his skin; he had never felt so alone. They pressed on, following a path through the woods that was barely discernible in the moonlight. The path narrowed, with steep slopes on either side, until they came to a hill littered with white rocks and debris. A door stood out in the center of the darkness, metal and concrete. He took out his phone and turned on the flashlight. Lucy whipped around and snatched it, covering the light.

Jesse had told Stella he would bring Finn home, but there was a chance he'd go into this dungeon and find his brother's corpse.

Lucian opened the door and stopped at the entrance, both arms braced against the sides of the doorway. He dragged in a breath and called out, "Ciceline!" Then he pitched himself forward into the dark. Jesse hurried after him.

Jesse wasn't ten steps into the tunnel when something barreled into him — a big, panting thing that made him cry out and fall back, slamming into the wall. A tangle of arms and legs told him it was human shaped at least.

"Help us. Please help us!"

Jesse didn't need a light to recognize him. "Finn?"

"Jesse? Jesse, thank god, I'm so sorry, it's all my fault."

Jesse wrapped his arms around Finn's shoulders and squeezed him tight. He had spent days imagining, in the parts of his mind he didn't like to access, that the next time he saw Finn, he would be identifying his body. Finn was here, alive, crying on his shoulder, and suddenly Jesse pictured him as a child, the way he used to cling when Jesse picked him up, pudgy little arms around his neck.

"It's okay. We're getting out, we're going home."

Finn didn't let go. "There are more people in here, two who came in a while ago and they're hurt pretty bad. I can't see what's wrong with them, there's a lot of blood."

Lucy had already disappeared into the hallway. It was endless, as far as Jesse knew; he might as well be on another planet. Then he heard Lucy call out again: "Ciceline!"

"Shit," Finn said. "There's another one, I don't know who's who. I want to go home."

"We will. Let's get them first." He turned on his light again. The tunnel was straight, and his little circle of light illuminated rusted walls, and the silhouette of Lucian up ahead.

Behind them, the door creaked. Jesse knew what the sound meant before he even turned to see. He had forgotten to tell Lucy about the bloody man outside the office, the one who had called for backup.

He sprinted back toward the door. It clicked shut, and a bolt slid into place.

"Oh, no," Finn whispered. "No, no."

Jesse's mind echoed that sentiment, though it refused to leave his mouth. His mind was empty. His lungs were empty. He braced his useless hands on the door like he could push it open, but it was a waste of precious energy. He just didn't have the strength; even Lucy wouldn't be able to open it. They would have to sit here and wait for someone to figure out where they were, but how would anyone know?

Mia. Mia had made them install that app. There was no reception here, not in a silo with walls this thick, but she would spot their trail, at least. With Ciceline hurt, the best course of action was probably to sit tight and wait for rescue.

And if it didn't come?

He dropped his forehead against the cement. This wasn't fair, to die like this, so ridiculously. It wasn't fair.

No.

He had beaten death once; it was unacceptable to die in a godforsaken underground prison. He'd eaten enough shit tonight, this week, this month, this entire year. Maybe his entire life. No more. It was not okay for him to die here. This was a underground silo, there had to be options, and he was going to find them.

"It's okay," Jesse told Finn. "There's got to be another way out. We'll deal with it. Let's help Ciceline first." His voice sounded oddly calm and rational for someone who just got surprise-locked in a prison.

First: Follow Lucy. He tugged on Finn's hand and kept his phone light on. The hallway curved left, and around that corner a body lay on its side, facing away from him. The hair wasn't white, though.

A few feet away, Lucian knelt in a puddle of dirty water, hovering over Ciceline by the light of his own phone, pressing his jacket hard over her chest. He was muttering something over and over, and Jesse knew enough Romanian to understand this phrase. He had heard it before.

Please don't leave me.

STELLA

S tella waited two hours, but the car didn't come back. She
tried Jesse's phone; he didn't answer. Mom had gone back
to bed, but there was no way she was getting any sleep
either. Stella looked at Ciceline's text again — *There's a place
called EspresSo Extra* — and called the location up on her map.
She googled it, checking for businesses in the area, a place where
she could wait, a bodega that opened at dawn or something.
There wasn't much. There was, however, a likely-sounding nightclub across the street from it called "BLOOD." Just like that, in all
caps. That had to be where the Halloween party had been. What
did they do there, walk around the dance floor drinking blood?

Her legs itched to move, so she got up and checked outside
again. Still no black SUV. Maybe she just kept missing it?

Her best clothes were packed in a box somewhere. She
searched and found a nice pair of black jeans, a sweater with a gold
heart surrounded by bats, and low-heeled black boots. If she was
going there, she might as well fit in.

It wouldn't be too out of line for her to text Jesse at this hour
for an update. By now, he should expect it.

STELLA:

> Jessebess, if you're up please tell me how
> everything is going.

She got a reply two seconds later:

> Message not sent. Try again?

She tried again.

> Message not sent.

Maybe he had no service. The island had dead zones.

"Is that Jesse?" Mom asked, as she came from her room and headed to the kitchenette.

"No." Stella rubbed at her forehead, trying to quell the dawning of the thought. It wouldn't go away. "No, actually . . . I'm thinking about calling the cops." Saying it out loud placed the dread firmly in the center of her chest, where it wouldn't budge. Jesse and Finn were dead. All that remained was finding out.

Anxiety lies, her logical brain reminded her.

Yes, but sometimes it told the truth.

Mom came over and gripped her by both arms. "Before you do that, Stella, make sure that calling the cops won't put Jesse in any danger with those blood pills of his. He needs them. Do not make him lose those pills."

"I know, I just — what?" She felt her jaw drop and the word draw out. It would have been funny, if the blood hadn't rushed from her head. She sat down hard on the cheap folding chair.

"Stop it," Mom said. "I knew long before you did. Hell, I knew before Jesse. What boggles my mind is how anyone can look into Lucian's eyes and not see that he's a hundred years old. People really know how to kid themselves, don't they? He thinks he's got everyone fooled, like it's a trick of the light when you see all the years in him. I hated him when I first saw him; that man's eyes are a graveyard. But he was always so good to my children, wasn't he? Then Jesse had to go and fall his silly ass in love. Lucian saved my son's life. If blood is what keeps them alive, I have to accept that. Jesse would never hurt an innocent person. He doesn't have it in him."

Stella wiped her eyes on her sleeve. "I think he would have eventually told you."

"I know that."

"There's a lot going on with that world right now. That's how Lucy got hurt that night. There's another faction or something. Jesse kept it from me for the same reason."

"That's why the car kept driving by here?"

"Yes. Lucy and Ciceline sent protection, but I haven't seen them out there in about two hours, and that's unusual."

"I can't reach Jesse," Mom said. "Do you have any clue where they went?"

Stella fiddled with her phone. "I was going to meet Ciceline today."

"You should go." Mom took Stella's hand and squeezed. "If you think you need to call the police, I won't stop you; I don't know the rules of this game. Just make sure you don't get Jesse's pills taken away."

Stella went to the window and looked out again. She started back. There was a car out there now, but it wasn't the black SUV with tinted windows. This was a gray van. The driver had the window rolled down, and was looking up at her. She waved. He didn't wave back.

She backed away from the window and picked up her purse and car keys, jingling them in her palm. "Mom, I think you should get dressed. We shouldn't stay here." How in the world was she supposed to tell her mom that they probably should go out the fire escape, too?

"Where are we going?"

"I know of a place. It might get a little weird."

Mom looked resigned and unsurprised. "I can handle weird."

CICELINE

The need for blood ate her up. Her insides were hot and shriveled, a dry shell. She had only felt this kind of hunger once before, in another dungeon.

If she had kissed that rando in the street when she was ten years old, she would not be bleeding to death in a silo. But she wouldn't have lived past that year, actually, and possibly not even through that night. Dying at eleven would have been a tragedy, but even a century and a half wasn't enough. She was still too young.

Four lifetimes ago, some man in the street had offered her money and food in exchange for a kiss. It might not even have been bad, but she didn't want to. It was her choice. He did it anyway, and that was when she cut him, her dagger across his lips. She was in prison that night.

She saw in her mind, as clearly as yesterday, Tata, who had rescued her from hard labor. He was Roma, like her. All he asked was that she care for his and his wife's ailing child whenever they were away. Oh yes, and a small donation of her blood, monthly. Just a tiny cut to the wrist, an amount she wouldn't miss. His name was Doctor Latari, he had a laboratory in the cellar, and he needed samples to find a cure for his son's illness. Nothing sinister.

And Yvette . . . cold, distant Yvette, waiting for her child to die. Ciceline hadn't understood back then how she could be so cruel, but the years had taught her the harsh reality: don't get attached to anyone who isn't going to make it. It was only practical.

Imagine Yvette being the first to die, out of all of them. Imagine herself, about to be the second.

"Don't leave me, sora mea," Lucy cried, as his tears soaked her hair. As he called her "my sister," Ciceline realized he had Snapped; she heard it in his voice as it faded in and out in time with her heart. It brought her back to the first time Tata had Snapped, as Lucian lay dying.

That night, she'd heard Tata and Yvette fighting downstairs in the sitting room. She'd left her bed and crept to the top of the stairs as they screamed at each other.

"We have to do it now," Tata cried.

"He won't make it," Yvette snapped. "He'll die in agony instead of passing in peace, and I can't bear that responsibility. My son will die, but I refuse to be the one that kills him."

"He might not." His voice had sounded so strange to her, so hollow.

"And if he lives?" Yvette countered. "Then we've done the most immoral thing we can do. We will be ostracized, no one will align themselves with us ever again, and what have we done to him? Condemned him to decades of childhood."

'Decades of childhood' had made it click, finally, that she lived with vampires. Tata's laboratory, the blood donations, the vials of tinctures, dark red by candlelight — it all made sense.

The next morning, she couldn't find Tata. "It's for his own good," Yvette had told her. "His grief broke him."

He wasn't gone: she heard his footsteps in the attic. Now that she knew the secret, she could save the boy who had become her brother. She had climbed to the rooftop under the full moon, to the attic window, which had been barred to keep Tata inside. They had used bedsheets to tie her tightly to the bars and he had reached out of the window with a dampened cloth, which he pressed over her nose and mouth, so she could sleep through the worst of the pain.

The next time she opened her eyes, the sun was rising, and Tata wasn't at the window anymore. Yvette was. Ciceline had raged at her. She broke the window, spit, threw glass in her face, pulled on the bars. Yvette had watched impassively. Ciceline hadn't understood her back then, but she did now. How else could you function, knowing your child was dying? And that the only thing that might save him, might also make his death a thousand times more gruesome?

In the end, the guards had come. Ciceline was chained in a carriage, driven far away, and thrown into the dungeon. That was when the hunger started, nothing but a vast field of dark red, aching need.

There were others down there with her, human and vampire. The humans were mostly children, too small to offer much, and she had fought so hard not to rip their little throats out when the older vampires offered her tiny amounts of their blood to keep her alive.

The vampires in the corner, though, they had wailed for it, animals now, too far gone to be saved.

A few days later, another body had been dropped into the prison — a small, dying child, too sick to give them blood. He was the salt water that would quench them briefly but sicken them forever. She had changed him herself, away from the others, and tried to quiet him as he cried, "Don't leave me, sora mea."

Ciceline had turned him into another mouth to feed in the dungeon, and so she had come up with their escape plan: attack en masse the next time someone was thrown in with them.

Only a handful of them made it out.

If she was to die now, maybe it was only fitting that it

happened in another one of Carnelian's dungeons, with her brother.

There was another voice, though, and she couldn't make sense of it as she faded in and out. Someone pushed Lucy away from her with urgent hands, and then prodded around her chest. It hurt; she tried to shove the hands away. The voice murmured words too low for her to hear, or maybe the dull buzz in her ears was drowning out his voice. Her heart strained against her ribs. It felt like a feeble little bird crushed in a tight fist.

Then the pain came, clean and sharp. She would have screamed if she had the breath for it. The pressure rushed out of her chest and she took a short, gurgling breath that was nonetheless the best air she'd ever had.

"Sorry, sorry," the voice said. "Fuck. I've only ever done that on a dog before."

Ah, it was Jesse poking holes in her now. It would be nice to thank him later, but his little field medicine trick wouldn't keep her alive for long. The blood would just fill back up. She felt it trickling out of the exit wound, too. Her cells tried to repair themselves, but without fresh blood, it wouldn't happen fast enough. She hoped Jesse would take care of Lucy. Maybe Stella would take care of Dog Lucy, too.

"This would work better if I had some goddamn tape," Jesse said.

Why wasn't he getting them out of this dungeon, anyway? This was a shitty rescue. Still, how rude would it be to die after all the effort he was putting in to saving her? The least she could do was try.

STELLA

One car — not the gray one — stayed on their tail, too
close. Stella sweated the entire long drive, and Mom
remained silent, clutching her phone, ready to dial
911. The radio was off, and the only sound was the satnav calling
out directions. The car followed them to the parking lot behind
the nightclub called BLOOD. It was just after three AM.

The café was across the street, but they had to get through the
alley first, and it was still dark. The other car idled a few spaces
down. No one got out.

The knot in her stomach tightened as she stepped into the
chilly, wet night. They would not find Ciceline here. They
wouldn't find anyone. Her brothers were gone. After all of this,
after Lucian saving Jesse, after Jesse finding Finn, they were all
dead. Or they would simply disappear, and she'd never hear from
any of them again.

Her throat constricted. No, this was more catastrophic
thinking.

"Ready?" Mom asked.

Alright then, through the alley it was. As they made their way
through the parking lot, the door of the other car opened and a
man stepped out. He made no move toward them; he just

watched as they hurried toward the alley. They passed a railing surrounding some cement steps that led to a lower level of the club, and the man got on his phone, keeping his eyes on them.

Drunken party-goers still hung around the alley, leaning against the bricks and making out behind trash bins. Stella had been through scenes like this, just never with her mother by her side. The smell of blood was overwhelming here. Jesse had gone to this party? He had the pills, but did he also drink actual blood? *Gross.* She pushed the thought out of her mind.

They got to the front of the club, where a bouncer stood behind the ropes, in front of the closed door. There were still a handful of people, all costumed up, milling around outside. He turned them all away, waving his hand and repeating, "Move along, party's over. Everyone go home."

Stella came up to the side of the velvet rope and said, "Excuse me?"

"Move along," he told her, without even glancing her way. "Party's over."

"I'm looking for someone."

"Who isn't?" he asked. "Move along."

"I'm looking for Lucian Callahan and Ciceline Taran," Stella tried.

"Again," he said, "who isn't?"

"My name is Stella Westchurch."

The bouncer turned to them. "Westchurch, huh?" He looked at Michaela. "Jesse your son?"

"That's right," she said. "And we were followed."

The bouncer looked around as he left his post, clicking the rope closed behind him. "Alright, see that little cafe across the way? It's closed now, but the owners live in the apartment above. Go wait by that door while call them. I'll watch you until you're inside."

There were only a few cars on the road as they crossed the street to the dark café. The bouncer got on his phone, and watched them until a slight, blond young man came from the back of the building to unlock the door. He was wearing pajamas with pink dinosaurs on them, his hair was damp, and a ring of mascara was smeared under his eyes, like he hadn't finished washing it off.

"Please, come in," he said.

A bell tinged, the lights came on, and a red-haired woman behind the counter looked up from her phone with a smile.

Stella smiled back, but something itched at the back of her neck. The woman was small, with sharp red nails, her smile a few millimeters too wide. She was dressed in black, strappy gear, and fully made-up.

"Stella Fivestar," the woman called. "And . . . Mom Westchurch?"

"Michaela," Mom said. "And you are?"

"Mia." Her smile faded. "Oh, shit. That means Jesse didn't come back."

The man in pajamas sighed and took out his phone, scrolling through messages. "Nope," he said. "Nothing from Lucy."

"Do you know where they went?" Stella asked.

The man's hand landed on her arm, gentle as a butterfly, but she still jumped a mile. "Why don't you sit down? I'll get you two some coffee and something to eat." His voice was as soft as his touch. "Croissants?"

"Yes, thank you." They took a seat on a blue and teal sofa up against the wall.

Mia came over and sat on a plush chair across from her, sliding her phone across the table to show them a map on the screen. "So last night Lucian let me put a tracker on his phone for once, before he went off chasing Ciceline, who went off chasing the guy Jesse used to go out with. This is their trail. I can't tell you much more unless you can prove to me that you know what's at the heart of this."

Stella looked around the café. They were alone, the four of them, but she glanced toward the man taking a croissant out of a toaster oven. He brought it, with a cup of coffee, to the table.

"This is my business partner, Archer," Mia said. "Anything you say to me, you can say in front of him."

She still whispered it: "Vampires. Actual ones."

Mia laughed and clapped her hands. "Shout it! Vampires! Around here, most people just think it means you're a goth with a fetish."

Archer looked to Stella's Mom. "Sorry you got dragged into all of this."

"I can handle myself," Mom said. "I just want my kids safe."

Stella enlarged the map on Mia's phone. "It looks like his trail goes dead in Montauk, and then it doesn't pick up again."

"Yes," Mia said. "And that area is Carnelian's offices."

"But why wouldn't they call anyone to say what was up?" Archer asked. He took out his phone and clicked a few times.

Stella picked at the croissant, her stomach too twisted up to eat anything, and forget about coffee when she was already this keyed up.

"It could be that they're working out some details," Mia said. "Or maybe changing your other brother or something, or brokering for Jesse's ex. These things can get complicated, and Carnelian sometimes asks you to turn off your phone if they're doing legal shit."

She tried to feel relief. Her therapist told her to allow positive feelings in, that they weren't going to change the future and that it was irrational to think that she would be punished for them. But relief wouldn't come.

"I'm just getting a bad feeling," she said. "I know how that sounds."

Mia held up a hand. "If you think something is off, we should go check it out."

"You're coming with me?"

"Duh," Mia said. "If some shit really is going down, I'm the one you want there."

Archer shoved his phone back into his pocket. "Carnelian's app is down." To Stella and Michaela he said, "That never happens. Whoever did it would have to get past a lot of people to take out the mainframe, and I'm not talking about hacking. Or at least, not computer hacking. More like sword hacking." He made a swinging motion with his hand. "Killing people, is what I'm getting at."

"I got that part," Stella said.

"Alright." Mia slapped the table. There was a glint in her eye, too mischievous for this situation. "We have to stop at BLOOD and get someone to cover the café. We'll take some weapons, I guess. There's no telling how many people Via Nova has, if it's them. Since Lucy and Jesse disappeared around the main offices, that's where we'll go first. If nothing turns up, then we'll circle back and check the clinic. Good?"

"Good," Archer said.

"Mrs. Westchurch," Mia said, "you're staying here and that's final. Sorry, no moms allowed. Stella Fivestar: If you're anything like your brother, you won't stay put. I know you have your own car and you've already seen the exit where they got off, so short of locking you up in one of our really swanky and completely clean and inspected dungeons, I guess you're coming, too."

"Yes, of course I'm coming."

"See?" she said. "Just like your brother. Brave of heart, dumb of ass. Let it be known that I told you not to. Archer? Can you attest to that?"

"I swear on my immortal soul," he said.

Stella was sure that these two were probably very nice people when they weren't talking about weapons and dungeons. Had her brother really hung out with them? But there was no other way to navigate this mess. She opened her purse to pay for the coffee and croissant, neither of which she had touched.

Mia put her hand over Stella's. "Lucy's been talking about you all for ages; Westchurches don't pay here. Now come on, we need to stop at BLOOD. Michaela, you too; let's not leave you alone in the cafe."

Stella pulled her hand away. "If you try to lock me in, I'll fight."

"Not gonna lie, that would be hilarious," Mia said. "But this is the real world. If we're going to do this, I need you to trust me. No matter what we see. No matter what I do, alright? If your brothers are alive, and Lucy and Cice are alive, I'll do what I can to make sure everyone stays that way, but you have to stay out of the way and let me do whatever it takes. Promise me?"

Stella didn't hesitate. "Yes."

Archer followed when they left and locked the door behind them.

The club was as she had expected. She'd been out dancing at similar places with the Jenns. This one was kind of middle ground: with a giant skeleton in a harness hanging from the ceiling, it probably got pretty sexy in here, but it read more like a dance hall than a full-on BDSM sex club. A few janitors were sweeping black and orange confetti off the floor, while another scrubbed aggressively at a spot on the sofa.

"Jack," Mia said, "there's a dog in the loft. Can you feed him, play with him a little, and make sure he doesn't shit on the floor?" She tossed a key to the sofa-scrubber. He caught it one-handed and gave her half a salute.

They got into an old, shuddery elevator. The room they descended to was gaudy as hell. A small stage stood at the head of it, and a woman dressed in black was reciting poetry into a mic to literally no one. Mom hung back in the shadows, curiously quiet.

"Helen," Mia called. "Sorry to interrupt your rehearsal. Can you help out a friend, and then open the café for a while? We have a situation."

Helen The Poet alighted from the stage, one hand held aloft as if an invisible suitor helped her down. She glided over to them. "Oh my goodness," she said to Stella, "you're very beautiful. Are you a patron of the arts?" She held out her hand as if she wanted Stella to kiss it.

Stella shook her hand instead. "I'm a vet. But I go to the symphony sometimes, so I guess that counts."

"Oh, you must know Lucienne?" She pronounced it with a vivid, overly-French flair.

"Helen, this is Stella," Mia said. "She's Lucy's boyfriend's sister."

Helen gasped. "How wonderful. I love your energy."

"You're very kind," Stella said. "I enjoyed your poem."

Helen smiled. Her teeth were stark white against the black of her lipstick, and the canines had been capped with sharp, realistic fangs. It looked painful; how did she not scrape her bottom gums all the time?

Mom emerged from the shadows behind them, tentative, with her hand pressed to her chest. "Oh my goodness," she said. "Michelle?"

Helen stepped closer for a better look. "Mickey Whitley?"

Stella moved out of the way as her mom and Helen embraced, laughing. She held onto one of the high-backed chairs to stay on her feet. What in god's name?

"Bikini Girl #3!" Helen said, holding Michaela at arms' length. "Look at you, still so beautiful!"

"Oh, pshht, look at yourself. You haven't aged a single day."

Helen — Michelle? — shrugged. "Well, you know, I'm a vampire now."

"Good for you," Mom said earnestly. "I'm glad you found what you were looking for."

"Do you remember being on the set for the video, where we met that guy?" Helen asked. "Dancing Guy #6, right? He was so hot."

Stella's chest clenched. She knew this part.

Mom took Helen's hands. "His name was James Westchurch."

Helen looked from Mom to Stella, and back. "Oh Mickey, I knew you could do it; you were soulmates, I sensed it. How is he?"

"He passed a few years ago," Mom said, with the same poise and calm she always employed when saying it.

"Oh no," Helen said. "I'm so terribly sorry. That is so unfair, I wish I would have . . ." She glanced at Stella again before continuing. "But you must have had such a beautiful life together."

"Yes," Mom said. "We sure did."

"Wait, Lucian's boyfriend is your son?" Helen asked breathlessly. "Such beautiful serendipity. Lucian will take exquisite care of him, so don't worry."

"Alrighty," Mia said, "this is really neat and I'm glad you guys are okay with the time you're about to spend together, but we have to hustle."

Archer handed Helen a set of keys. "Take Mrs. Westchurch to the apartment, and then please open the café if we're not back by 8:00. Rein it in for the normal people, okay? Red lipstick, please. We'll be back soon. Got some bitches to cut."

Helen folded her hand over his. "Archer, you're so beautiful when you're dangerous. Thank you for entrusting your business to me." Helen kissed Archer on the cheek, then Mia, and then, naturally, Stella. "Don't worry. I treasure Michaela and I won't let anything bad happen."

"Mom," Stella said, "are you gonna be okay?"

Mom hugged her and said, "As long as you're careful, I'm alright."

"I will be," Stella said.

Helen took Mom's arm and walked her out of the room, chatting about how much catching up they had to do.

"Okay," Mia said. "We'll take my van because I've got some first aid stuff in there and a shit ton of rad weapons. Let's go turn some innards into outtards."

LUCIAN

L ucy had no concept of how long Finn was gone; he counted time on Ciceline's slow breaths. Thirty. Finally, Finn emerged from the dark hallway with a roll of tape in his hands.

"Where the hell did you . . ." Jesse began. "You know what, never mind, thank you." He took a deep breath, wiped his forehead with his sleeve, and taped over the hole he'd made in Ciceline's chest.

A sheen of sweat covered Jesse's face, yet Lucy was freezing. The dull whooshing in his head almost drowned out the rest of the surrounding sounds: dripping water, a distant, rhythmic human/animal cry, Ciceline's sporadic, wet gurgle. His vision was a too-bright circle surrounded by a blackened periphery.

Finally, Jesse said, "Okay," and sat back on his heels. "That will take the pressure off for now, but it's not going to last." He took off his suit jacket and placed it over Ciceline. Finn hovered somewhere behind Jesse, asking if there was anything else he could do.

Yes, there was.

"Finn," Jesse asked, "You haven't been changed yet, right? I think you've been a giver in the past? Are you okay doing it now?"

"Yeah, of course," Finn said. "I know how to do it." He sat beside Ciceline, nicking his wrist and pressing it to her mouth.

She couldn't swallow. It gurgled in her throat, a terrible, shuddering sound. All Lucy could do was squeeze her arm, willing her to live.

"She'll need more later," Jesse said. "Maybe you should save some. The other person?"

"I only saw him in by my phone light, but I don't think he made it. It looked bad." Finn shined his light down the hall, illuminating the body lying in a puddle.

Lucy followed as Jesse walked over and gently turned him onto his back. His face was unmarked, save for blood from his nose and lips. His eyes were open.

"Raven," Lucy said. He had played the piano so beautifully.

"Damn it," Jesse whispered. "I'm sorry. I know you were friends. Hey. Are you still with me?"

Lucy struggled to make the word "yes" come out of his mouth, but it kept getting stuck. He settled for a nod.

"Good," Jesse said. "We need to get out of here. Do you know a way?"

A way out of the dungeon? No, death lurked in every corner. The creatures would come out. Again, the words refused to leave his throat.

"Wait," Jesse said. "The packing tape, the noises? I know what this is."

Yes: it was Carnelian's dungeon, where Outcasts waited to die.

"Lucy, you told me that there were underground pill factories. This has to be one of them. Loads of underground tunnels, they would have room for it."

"Yeah," Finn said. "There were boxes where I found the tape, maybe they're shipping something out of here."

"People who work here probably aren't walking through the front every day. Okay." Jesse scrubbed a bloody hand over his eyes, leaned over Ciceline and took Lucy's chin in his hand. "I'm going to go look."

Panic ripped through him. Lucy gripped Jesse's wrist. "The creatures in the corner."

"You said that to me the day you changed me. Are there other prisoners? Vampires?"

"Yes. Jesse—"

"There's no other way," Jesse said. "You took the keys from Busquet, right? Maybe one of them will unlock another door."

They had fallen on the floor next to him. They jangled when he picked them up and handed them to Jesse. Jesse wrapped both hands around Lucy's, holding them tight. "Stay with Ciceline. If you need anything, or if she starts to make that gurgling noise, yell for me. Okay?"

Don't let them out.

"I won't," Jesse answered aloud. He reached into the pocket of his coat, which lay over Ciceline, took something out, and pushed it into Lucy's hand. It was the bottle of pills, about twenty left. "Ciceline can't swallow them yet, but you can." He pressed his forehead to their joined hands once before getting up. Then he and Finn left. Lucy followed their bobbing circle of light with his eyes until it disappeared around the corner.

The other children in the dungeon, where were they?

No, that wasn't now, that was the past. Time jumbled around him.

The human child who had helped him after Ciceline had changed him . . . that child, offering his wrist, his name was Stefan. The other vampire children had other human children to feed them, all thrown into the dungeon together, but Stefan was his. He had kept Lucy alive. The sharpness of Stefan's blood filled the ache in his stomach, he felt so strong after drinking, it was so good. He loved Stefan for that. He would have stayed with him forever.

One of the vampire children, completely feral by then, had broken its chains before their escape and crawled out of the corner, wailing for blood. Ciceline and the others were waiting for the trap door to open, too far away to help, when the vampire grabbed Stefan, so small and fragile. It pierced Stefan's neck and his blood sprayed into Lucy's mouth with so much more force than the trickle from his wrist.

He had been drinking that. Battening on it. How was he different from this monster?

They made their escape soon after, and Yvette started the war that had won her control of Carnelian, but killed all the leftover vampire children, except Ciceline and himself. He remembered their names, even if no one else did. Edward: hung by Carnelian. Jonathan and Sarlota: beheaded.

After the war, Yvette had taken him and Ciceline along as she disposed of their bodies, back to the dungeon. How stiff they all were as Yvette rolled them in. Lucian had bitten his lips bloody when they thudded against the stone floor. Yvette had no use for his tears. "It's over," she told them. "We won." But it didn't feel like a victory when Ciceline poured the kerosene into the trap-door, and he struck the match and let it drop.

Their charred flesh rose with the smoke, choking him; the bubbling and crackling of their bones and blood lingered in his ears.

But that had already happened. This wasn't that dungeon, and he wasn't a child anymore. He had to stay with Ciceline and keep her alive, but the flames crept up on him even now, eating away at the years in between, lapping at his ankles. They would burn him up too if he let them. He raced the fires, scrambling away from them.

If he kept running, he could hold on a little longer, maybe even climb back up to the present, and everything would be fine, perfectly fine.

He had done it before.

JESSE

Their footsteps echoed down the metal hallway, too loud for Jesse's comfort.

Once they were out of earshot of Lucy and Ciceline, Finn said, "I took your pills."

"I know."

"You could have died."

Yes, damn it, he could have. Almost collapsing during surgery, stumbling into BLOOD, picking apart his pills and discovering that he had been eating ashes . . .

"Yes," Jesse said. "I'm angry." It hurt to say so, he cringed away from it, his heart a painful little lump in his chest. He hated so much to tell people they had wronged him, and Finn was already so distant; this would drive him further away. "It wasn't okay and we need to square with that so you can finish my tattoo. But let's get out of here first."

"They took my girlfriend," Finn said, tears welling in his eyes. "Bettina, she works with Jared. I only went out with them a few times, but by then I knew it was real; the vampire thing, it wasn't a joke."

"Jared told me a little," Jesse said.

"I should have told you. I thought she was ghosting me, but

then the messages started." He stopped, wiping his face on his dirty sleeve. "I don't know if she's still alive. They sent me a box of her hair, videos of her crying, screaming."

"If she's alive, we'll find her."

"They told me to get the pills, bring them to someone at this time and location, and we'll release her. Except they didn't. Then Via Nova said I was a liability. I didn't know if they were going to kill me too or—"

Jesse grabbed him, pulling him into a hug.

"I think she's dead," Finn cried into his shoulder. "She's dead and I almost killed you."

"Don't borrow grief," Jesse said. "Let's get out of here, then we'll figure out what to do, alright?"

Finn pulled away, wiping his eyes. "Yeah, okay."

They pressed on and came to a long, decrepit walkway suspended over a chasm. The drop looked endless, but the echoing '*plink!*' of water far below proved otherwise. When Jesse stepped onto the bridge, it rattled beneath the weight. He had to hold the phone in one hand to light the way. His other hand was slick with sweat against the grit of the rusted railing as he crossed. It shuddered with each step.

There wasn't much of a platform to stand on when Jesse reached the circular door. A rhythmic churning noise came from beyond it, and when he put his hand against the cold metal, it was vibrating. He was only aware of Finn's approach by the sound of his footsteps. He handed the phone to Finn while he sorted through the keys on the ring.

It was the third key that slid in and turned. Jesse pushed down on the metal bar, and the door groaned open to a florescent-lit room with metal grates for floors and chain-link fences to the ceiling. Boxes torn apart and crushed littered the area, surrounded by empty pill bottles. A man with greasy, limp hair obscuring his face scrabbled around on hands and knees, digging his fingers into the holes in the gratings, like he was looking for something. He was the first one Jesse saw, but there were more, some wandering in circles, some lying on the ground, and they all jerked their heads up at once.

All movement stopped, while the rattling of machines in the distance continued. The crawling man looked past Jesse and fixed his eyes on Finn. His pupils dilated as he said, "Giver."

At that, the energy shifted and all the prisoners rushed the door.

Jesse slammed it shut and keyed the lock until it clicked. Bodies thudded up against it, their desperate howls drowning out the churning of the machines.

"Help me," a voice called from the other side of the door. "Please, I'm dying."

"Are we helping them?" Finn whispered.

"Lucy said not to. I think they'd kill you by accident."

Hand shaking as he cast his light all around the room, Jesse searched for anything that might signify an exit: a vent, a ladder up, anything. They crossed the bridge back and rounded another corner, where a hallway branched off from the one that had gotten them here. They'd missed this one.

Before Jesse could cast his light down the hall, something lunged at them. They fell back, tripping over themselves, scrambling away until they both hit the wall. Jesse dropped his phone, but not before it flashed on a human face with sunken eyes and bared teeth.

It — she — stopped, as if she'd been jerked backwards. She cried out in pain, a more human sound.

Jesse picked up his phone. The glass had shattered, but the light still worked. He shined it on the woman. Chains pinned her to the wall. Actual clunky chains, with manacles around her wrists, hooked into the cement behind her. Her black hair was short, with patchy curls crusted to her scalp.

"Please," she begged. "Water. Blood. Please, I'm dying."

Finn rushed to her, his hands on her face, at her wrists, trying to tug the chains from the wall. "Bettina, it's me, I'm here."

"Finn—" Jesse began, but before he could finish, another

vampire surged up from the dark beside her, grabbing Finn's ankle. Finn leapt back, and the girl sprung at him, snapping her jaws. Jesse caught him as he stumbled away.

They were awake now — wet sounds, gurgling, nonsense syllables. Jesse gripped the keys in his palm until he felt the cold bite of metal into his skin.

"We can't release you," Jesse said. "Just hold on a little while, and we'll be right back."

The girl sunk down to the ground and wept. "Finn," she cried, "is there water? You can leave me, but please, let me have water."

Jesse's own throat burned for it; his tongue felt like paper, and the reminder only made it worse. He had bottles in the car.

"Jesse, I can't leave her," Finn said. "I'll stay here."

"I can't let you do that."

"Then I'm taking her," Finn said.

Lucy had said not to . . . but Lucy was also clearly in some traumatic headspace, probably severe PTSD, paranoia, hyper-vigilance.

"You wouldn't leave Lucy."

Well, shit. "But we don't even have a key, Finn."

Bettina jerked her head up. "It's the small silver one that looks like a handcuff key."

"Oh," Jesse said. "Right." He held his hands out and approached her slowly, like he did when trying to handle a fractious cat. Her eyes gleamed, tracking Jesse's movements, glancing occasionally at Finn. "We'll get you down from the wall and take you with us, but I'm leaving the cuffs on. That's the deal."

"Yes," Bettina said. "Whatever you say."

"I've got pills. When we get back to the entrance, you can have some." It hurt his stomach to offer them. He needed the pills. They were his.

Jesse had to get too close to Bettina's face when unlocking the manacles. She smelled of mold and sweat, and she cried out when her arms fell free from the wall. Finn hurried over, lifting her gingerly away from the other prisoners as they wailed for freedom. Jesse fought the urge to shove her away from Finn's neck.

"Are you hurt?" Finn asked her.

"Everything hurts," she said. "But you have to leave the chains on me. I don't want to hurt you. But it's hard." She shut her eyes, turning her head to the side.

The other prisoners moaned and babbled as they left them behind.

Ciceline needed more blood, but now she would have to share it with Bettina, too. Soon, he and Lucy would run out of pills. None of them could last much longer in here. Jesse's legs wobbled and his eyes burned. The packing room seemed like their only option, but with Lucy and Ciceline injured, and Finn so fragile and mortal, he didn't like their chances.

When they got back, Ciceline was still breathing. Lucy sat beside her, one leg tucked under the other, the sword propped against the curve of the wall. When he saw them, he leapt up.

"Lucy, wait—" Jesse said, but Lucy grabbed Bettina and yanked her away. She cried out as he dragged her by the chains, a gun already in his hand.

"Hey!" Finn yelled. "Lucian!"

Lucy wrapped her chains around the rusted railing and turned to them, pointing a finger and rattling off something in Romanian too fast for Jesse to understand, though he caught the words 'danger' and 'kill.' He snatched the keys from Jesse's hand.

Jesse stepped between him and Finn. "This is Finn's girl-friend. He couldn't leave her behind any more than you could leave me."

Lucy hesitated. He turned to look at Bettina She sprung at him, catching him off guard, driving her shoulder into his ribs. He staggered back into Jesse's arms, and though the logical part of Jesse's brain knew that she was blood-addled, maybe dying, his lizard-brain wanted to snap her in half.

Fresh blood soaked Lucy's shirt. Jesse pulled him back and had to knock his legs out from under him to get him to lie down.

Lucy sucked in a breath when Jesse peeled the shirt away to check again. In the dim light he could see the blood welling up again, no sign of stopping.

"Damn it, Lucy," he muttered, reaching into the pocket of the coat over Ciceline for the pills, rattling them at him. "Why didn't you take these? I left them here for you."

"Ciceline," he said.

"No. We're gonna be out before she can even swallow them." He shook four pills into his hand and helped Lucy sit up. Watching him dry-swallow them made his throat ache.

Finn approached Bettina and unwrapped the suspenders from his wrist. Jesse didn't like the look of that red, raw cut, and he hated watching Bettina wrap her lips over it and drink. She groaned, a deep, longing sound that Jesse felt down to his bones. Finn could help him too, couldn't he?

Finn staggered to his feet and Jesse really didn't like the look of that. He helped Finn re-wrap the bandages, then went back to Lucy and Ciceline.

Ciceline opened her eyes once and said, "Sandu?" before closing them again. That rattle was back in her lungs. Or rather, one lung. He'd have to release the pressure in her chest again. Should he do it now, while his phone light still worked, or would that make it worse?

He sat down beside Lucy and asked, "How are you holding up?" but Lucy only nodded, eyes closed. "Okay," Jesse said. "So, I have to tell you. I found a way out."

Lucy opened his eyes.

"But you're not going to like it."

STELLA

Mia's ride turned out to be a fully armored but otherwise nondescript, white van, stocked to bursting with cheesy looking weapons: swords with rings on them, butterfly knives, long-handled axes, a rainbow katana.

"Do you think we're going to need these?" Stella asked.

"I hope not," Mia said, with a look that suggested maybe she hoped so.

"There's medical and vampire stuff under the floor, too," Archer said. "We use the van for blood deliveries; there's one bag left in the freezer."

Mia added, "I've got cookies in my backpack if anyone wants them."

The two fist-bumped before they all piled into the van with Stella in the second row, where there were no windows.

"Is it always like this?" Stella asked as they pulled out of the parking lot. "Fighting, people disappearing, murders?"

"Nah," Mia said. "You came at a bad time. Sorry. Probably every generation or two there's some kind of drama, but mostly we're extremely chill."

"That's what you all do?" Stella asked. "Just stay young forever and party?"

"It's not forever. Sometimes it's just a regular lifespan or shorter. Lots of vampires don't make it past 30, because they die in an accident, or don't drink enough blood to take care of themselves, or they can't handle living that long. That's why good times are important."

"Party to save a life," Stella said, with a small laugh.

"I think that has a real crucial place in the world. You don't live this long without cultivating little pleasures and delights or whatever."

Stella tried to recall her own small pleasures: Swimming in the ocean, the widow's walk on the old house, the holidays, a night out with her girlfriends, or a night in alone.

"You never know," Mia said. "Maybe one night some lonely soul comes into BLOOD and suddenly they've found their people. Or maybe life got to be too much, but then they came into EspresSo Extra and that one perfect cup of coffee had everything making sense again."

"I guess that's true," Stella said. "Not that I ever wanted to, or felt . . ."

"Suicidal?" Archer piped up. "It's okay to say the word. Been there, got the meds, backed off the cliff."

"You never know the thing that might make someone hang around an extra day," Mia said. "I hate Carnelian because they think you have to work for your right to exist, that you have to contribute something major. You're a vet, right?"

"Yes," Stella said. "Or, I was."

"I'll bet you've saved a kitty that belonged to someone who couldn't see their way forward without their best friend. How many human lives have you saved, too? It all matters."

Tears welled up and Stella didn't bother wiping them away, long past being ashamed of her feelings.

Mia went on softly, glancing at her in the rearview, "You do what you have to do to get by, especially if you're going to stick around for a few hundred years. Hey, hand me my backpack? I could use a cookie."

They continued east in the HOV lane. Buildings got shorter and more spaced out, and Stella felt the transition to eastern Long Island in her bones, better than any sign could tell her. Then the buildings were replaced by trees lining the roads as they drove past the Pine Barrens. Mia ate all the cookies herself; Stella's stomach couldn't bear the idea of food. The sun began to rise over Sunrise Highway. Stella had been awake all night, and found herself dozing off in spite of her anxiety. She assumed that Mia and Archer had also been awake all night, but maybe they were used to that.

Stella woke when she felt the hills and turns of the Old Montauk Highway. She blinked in the early morning light, rubbing her eyes as Mia turned left onto a private drive. A heavy mist from the ocean hung low to the ground. The dirt path gave way to a hidden, lamppost-lined gravel road. Her phone pinged, telling her that she was out of range.

"Stop," Stella said. "That's Jesse's car. Let me out." She yanked on the door handle, but it was locked.

"Hold up," Mia said. "That's Ciceline's car too. Let's not go rushing in. I'll check it out first."

Stella took three deep breaths and pressed her palm to her forehead. She tried her panic protocol — what did she smell, feel, taste, see, and hear? — but it was only the smell of the inside of a stale van, the feeling of nausea, the taste of rising bile, the sight of Jesse's empty car, and the sound of Mia getting out.

"Archer, stay with her?" Mia asked.

"I will," Archer said. "Be careful."

Mia went around the back to grab a weapon. When she crossed to the front, she had one of those long-handled double axes. She hefted it easily, though it must have been heavy.

First Mia checked the cars, rifling around in the seats. Then she approached the blue buildings looming up ahead. The door to one of them was open, and the light streaming out had a reddish cast to it. Stella wiped her palms on her pants. Mia pushed the door with the axe and disappeared inside.

"She'll be alright," Archer said. Stella jumped at the sound of his voice. "Mia's a little intense, but she's not faking it. She can fight, and she doesn't feel fear like normal people."

"Maybe she should."

While they waited, she scooted into the front seat to get a better look around. There were five buildings, though the signs for all of them were printed too small and were too far away to read. Lampposts circled the complex and lined the walkway, which wound through the buildings. Trees towered close, claustrophobic; not a lot of space around here except to the left of and past the building Mia was in, where they cleared out into a path. Stella traced it with her eyes.

"Archer, look," she said. "There's a footprint or something?"

They both peered out the window. Some of the gravel had been scraped away in a long line, and beyond it, another line.

"Stay here," Archer said.

Stella got out after him. He gave her a look but said nothing, and together they followed the marks. They found another footprint, and that same dragging line, like someone had limped away. Burgundy streaks colored bits of the white gravel at intervals.

"This is blood," she said.

Archer crouched down, pick up a rock, and licked it. "Yup. Someone made it into the woods."

Mia came out of the building and closed the door behind her.

"Anything?" Archer asked.

"Uhh, yeah, a bunch of dead bodies."

Stella's legs almost gave out.

"Not your brothers, or Lucy, or Ciceline," Mia said. "Sorry, I should have led with that." She put her hand on Archer's arm. "But Yvette."

Archer fell back a step. "Wow, no way."

"Yeah. It's a really heavy scene. We should check the other buildings."

"Actually," Archer said, pointing toward the path, "Stella is on to something."

"The silo?" Mia asked.

"Maybe," Archer said. "They used to use it as a prison, but it's been closed for ages."

"Bet you it's not anymore," Mia said. "The rest of the gravel around here is undisturbed, right? We should follow the blood."

"Let's take the van," Archer said. "Just drive through if it's overgrown."

"Good idea," Mia said. "Also, in case there are people with guns."

They crowded back in, with Stella squeezing into the front this time. The van plowed through the path, parting the low mist, and steep hills rose to either side as they pushed deeper into the woods. The way forward narrowed. There would be no turning around from this point, only backing up if they had to get out fast.

A man came through the path, holding his hand out in a "stop" gesture. He wore jeans and a flannel shirt, and had a buzz cut.

"Hmm," Mia said. "Carnelian or Via Nova? Or regular cop? Jeez, I hope not. That would be messy."

He gestured for her to roll down the window. Instead, she got on the speaker and said, "Hi! My name is Mia."

His hand fell slowly, and Stella watched the color drain from his face.

JESSE

"The way out is through the factory," Jesse said. "But there are people in there."

"They'll kill you," Lucy said. "You need me to . . ."

He gazed down at Ciceline and spoke in a language that Jesse recognized as Romani. She answered with a weak murmur.

Jesse sat back on his heels. "Someone has to try. We all need blood; we'll die without it." He turned back to Ciceline. "And you won't make it much longer without help."

She rolled her eyes in his direction. "Lucy . . . with you."

Lucy replied, but Ciceline put her bloody hand over his mouth. "Go."

Finn laid a hand on Jesse's shoulder. "I'll stay with both of them."

Behind them, Bettina gurgled out a moan. Jesse locked eyes with Finn, a warning to keep his distance from her. Her hands were chained behind her back, but her mouth was free, and she made a clicking noise with her tongue, dry and thirsty.

"Alright," Jesse said. "It shouldn't take too long. Me and you, Lucy, we get in, go through, and find the door. The key must be on this ring if that guy took it from Yvette, right? We get out the factory door, circle back to the front, unbolt the door, and we get to my car."

Lucy took Ciceline's hands and spoke again to her before pulling himself to his feet. Finn gripped Jesse in a hug before he left.

He and Lucy made their way down the dark hallway, lit again by Jesse's phone, which was now on 15%.

"Heads up," Jesse said. "There are some chained up vampires ahead. They're noisy and lunge-y."

Lucy replied with a short nod. He kept his right arm wrapped around his ribs, but his left was free, and he gripped the gun as Jesse lead the way. The chained-up Outcasts groaned and babbled as they passed by, too weak to do much else.

The machines thrummed and thumped as they crossed the rusted metal bridge. Jesse could smell blood, mixed with the acrid, powdery scent of the pills. He'd missed that smell when he opened the door earlier, but now it twisted in his gut, the need for it growing stronger.

They got to the door and Jesse fumbled with the key, his hands clumsy with tremors. When he managed to fit it in, a body hit the other side of the door. Lucy pushed Jesse behind him, gripping the gun tighter.

"Help me," the person behind the door cried out.

"We will," Jesse said. "But you have to let us through."

The replying laugh was high-pitched and frenzied. "Right! It's not just me in here! Good luck with that!"

Lucy pulled the keys free and pushed the door. It squealed open and the man with the shaggy, oily hair stood before them, grinning, eyes narrowed into slits. Maybe he was going to say something, but his neck was in Lucy's hand before the words came out. A cluster of Outcasts closed in.

Lucy's arms seemed to work fine now as he lifted the man off the ground with one hand and raised the gun with the other.

"Whoever leads us out the quickest," Jesse said, "gets blood the quickest, got it?"

The shaggy man gasped and wheezed in Lucy's grasp, clutching at his fingers, kicking frantically. Slowly, with a deliberate show of strength, Lucy let him down.

"Lucy," the shaggy man croaked, but Lucy cut him off with a glare.

The machines churned on from below. The entrance had to be down there, where the workers came in. Lucy pushed the man ahead of them, toward a staircase that circled the chain-link. Torn up boxes littered the stairs, empty pill bottles rattled against the metal as they made their way down, 'By Our Grace' on the labels. The body of a young vampire lay crumpled in the corner of the first landing.

Some grace.

The Outcasts followed them down the stairs. There were about ten of them who were able to walk. The others got left behind on the floor. They were all blown pupils and dry, gaping mouths as they licked their lips and plucked at their bloody clothes. The scent of decay wafted down, mingled with that of the pills, and beneath that: real, liquid blood. It didn't smell fresh, but still, through his revulsion, Jesse's stomach cramped. These starving vampires . . . he was starting to understand their point. Another hour and this could be him.

A hand landed on the back of Jesse's neck and he turned to push it off. Teeth flashed, too close to his face. He leapt away, but Lucy was quicker, whipping around to shove the bitey vampire away. It was the shaggy man. He flew backwards and hit the railing with a crack, shuddering the entire staircase as he nearly toppled over.

Jesse and Lucy stood back-to-back on the landing as the vampires closed in. Lucy raised the gun again.

"Stop," Jesse said. His voice shook as it echoed off the metal. "I know you're hungry. I know you're dying. We'll all die if we don't get out of here. Lucy and I are the only ones who can help. Grunt if you understood that."

No one grunted, but he got a few returning murmurs, and

they all stood down. The shaggy man got to his feet and peered at him from under lowered lids, a little more lucid than before.

Jesse breathed out. "Let's move on."

Lucy didn't lower the gun again as he moved them along. The rhythmic thudding of the machines overwhelmed any other sound as they approached the top of the stairs, where another blast door stood open. Lucy hooked Jesse by the arm so they could go in together.

Blood had congealed around drains in the floor, and shredded, empty blood bags lay scattered around them. The noise was deafening in here; centrifuges lined one wall, all of them off-balance, spinning empty vials and banging against the cement. The other wall was stacked with freezers, their glass shattered, trays all over the floor beneath them. He looked around at the starving creatures, and the weight of realization struck: Carnelian wasn't spending their millions on this. These people weren't paid in money, and they hadn't wasted away over a day or two. They were kept like this on purpose.

Again, Lucy took Jesse's arm, nodding toward the other side of the room: the door. They made their way, and the vampires followed. At the door, Lucy put the keys in Jesse's hands and stood at his back, holding the gun. Jesse tried key after key, his palms growing slick, fingers shaking, until the last key on the ring clicked in and turned. He wanted to cry with relief, but Lucy pulled the door open and shoved him out, then lurched through the door himself.

The vampires rushed to follow, but Jesse slammed the door shut, sick with his own betrayal. He had tricked them, and now they were wailing on the other side of the door, desperate for food and freedom. Fresh morning air rushed into Jesse's lungs, stinging on the way down.

"We promised we'd help them," he muttered. "Shit."

Lucy swept his arm out toward the woods while looking pointedly at Jesse. They couldn't have blood-addled vampires roaming around, nor did they have time for them.

A voice from beyond the closed door said, "Let me out, Lucy!" It was the shaggy man again. He laughed bitterly. "No, Lucy never would. Jesse Westchurch!"

The blood rushed from Jesse's head, and he turned to Lucy, who looked as flummoxed as he felt.

"I know it's you, Jesse Westchurch," the voice said. "I've seen you."

Lucy tugged on his arm, but Jesse pulled away. "Who are you?" he asked.

"My name is Oliver," the man replied, and Jesse didn't think he was imagining that tone: sly, animal cunning. "But Ciceline calls me Seattle. Via Nova didn't lock me up. Yvette did, for saving Stella's life. You owe me. *You owe me! Let me out.*"

"Shit," Jesse muttered. "Can't we just—"

"No," Lucy said.

"Don't leave me!" Oliver shouted. "Lucian! I'm Ciceline's friend! Lucy, please!"

"We'll come back for you," Jesse said. "We won't leave you."

The shaggy man — Oliver — kept pounding on the door. His voice rose in hysteria as Jesse and Lucy walked away, but Jesse could not make out any further words. It was too easy to see himself in Oliver's place, left alone, shrieking for blood.

They took a few more steps before Lucy fell against his side, breathing hard.

"What do you need?" Jesse asked. "I mean aside from pills. Anything I can give you?"

Lucy shook his head and took another step. Then another.

"I can carry you," Jesse said.

Lucy giggled, high-pitched and hysterical, and pressed onward. The hills were steep enough that at one point, Jesse wrapped his arm around Lucy's waist and lifted him for a few steps. His hand came away sticky with blood.

The crested a hill, where the first rays of sunrise crept through the mist, and Jesse stopped to catch his breath. Exhaustion and hunger dragged him down, but they couldn't quit now. They had to get down the hill, follow the path back to his car, and drive back to the silo. Get Finn, Ciceline, and Bettina into the car. And then get them . . . where? If Carnelian was really done, the clinic would be compromised too. To BLOOD? Maybe Mia could help, but BLOOD was hours away.

The silo's front door was just beyond the hill. Jesse took a step.

Lucy hooked his suspenders, yanked him back, and clamped a filthy hand over his mouth. Jesse knew better than to resist or ask why, allowing himself to be drawn down to the ground. Lucy flattened himself out, wincing as he lay down, and nodded over the hill.

Jesse peered over. Of course they weren't alone. In the time they'd been locked in, backup had arrived.

"Shoot them," he hissed to Lucy.

Lucy held up the gun.

"Empty?" Jesse said. "The whole time?" Lucy nodded. "Well, shit. Now what?" He looked over the hill, counted about ten armed people milling around, and took in Lucy's state. There was no way. Despair closed in. To come this far only to lose.

They could walk the other way until they got service; Mia's number was likely in Lucy's phone.

"Okay," Jesse whispered. "Hand me your—"

The blast of a horn made him leap out of his skin. His nerves were so jangled he almost cried out. What in the world?

Then came a voice over what sounded like some kind of PA, the hint of deep south unmistakable once you heard it: "Y'all better run."

STELLA

"How many people do you have up there guarding the silo?" Mia asked over the PA. "Tell them I'm coming." The man shouted something back, but Stella couldn't make it out. Mia started rolling the van forward before he was out of the way, giggling as she accelerated, making him have to haul ass. "Look at him go!"

Archer said, "Toot the horn and make him jump."

Mia did — more of a blast than a toot — and the man did more than jump. He leapt, scrambling up the incline to the side. Mia and Archer doubled over laughing.

The entrance to the silo was nestled into the dead end of the valley, a heavy door of metal and cement. A group of people stood in front of it, gesturing in confusion, arguing. Mia got on the PA again. "Y'all better run."

Some of them did, climbing the hill or over the top of the silo. One of them pulled a gun and fired. Stella shrieked and ducked down, but the bullet pinged off the windshield, cracking it. The van thudded over something, front and back tires, and there was a shout. Stella clamped her hands over her mouth.

Mia shrugged. "He should have moved."

"He really should have," Archer agreed. "I would have."

From the hill, another gunshot fired; this one bounced off the side of the van.

"Okay," Mia said, "this is pissing me off. I'm going to grab a weapon, cut someone's hand off, and send them back as a warning."

"They're shooting at us from the hills," Stella reminded her. "You can't dodge bullets."

"I'll be fine. My Buttercup is in there and I'm angry."

"Your Buttercup?"

"Lucy." Mia turned to Archer. "Bubbles, stay with Stella, would you?"

"Sure thing. Oh, hey, why don't I cover you if you're getting out?"

"Great idea," she said, and they fist-bumped again. Archer climbed over the seats and into the back. It took him forever to find whatever he was looking for while Stella's nerves ratcheted up another notch. Jesse and Finn were alive, they were dead, both possibilities existed beyond that door.

"I like this new one," Archer said, squirming into the front seat with an actual bow and a handful of short arrows. Two feathers were purple, and one was gold.

"Wow," Mia said. "Those are so pretty."

Archer rolled down the window and braced the bow up against the frame. "Thanks. I wanted the ones with the gold cock."

Mia snorted.

"Now hush," Archer said, and let an arrow fly. Someone screamed.

"Archer?" Stella said.

"It's so rad when you can pick your own name." He nocked another arrow. "And this one," he whispered, "is going in your eye."

More screams, and returning gunfire had them crouching in the seats.

"They don't have a lot to hide behind up there," Archer said.

"They have to peek out to shoot. Why don't you go, and I'll keep them scattered? It looks like they're running."

Not all of them. A lone man remained at the silo door, frantically trying different keys.

Mia leapt over the rows of seats into the back, took something from a hook, and went out the back doors. When she appeared in front of the van, she was holding a rainbow katana. The man at the silo turned and aimed a gun. Stella barely saw Mia move, and then she was in front of him, swinging the blade. He screamed and doubled over, folding his hand into his chest. No, not his hand. That dark smear that had hit the hillside was his hand, still holding the gun.

Mia gestured with the katana as she spoke, pointing it up the hill.

Archer leaned out the window and yelled, "Hey Mia, ask him if he needs a hand!"

Mia turned. "Oh my god, Archer, I asked you to stop saying that."

"You did?"

"Yes! It's played out."

"No it's not, it's still funny." He turned to Stella. "It's still funny, right?"

"Can we get in there?" Stella asked.

"Oh, yeah. Mia? Is it safe to take Stella out?"

"We're not taking her out!"

"I mean out of the van?"

"Oh." Mia watched the man try to climb the hill with one hand. She took pity and gave him a boost up that sent him flying. "Yes, but go around the left side, because most of them scattered to the right."

"Got that?" Archer asked.

Stella breathed in, held it for three seconds, and breathed out. "Yes."

He took her hand and helped her out of the van. Mia headed

toward the silo but stopped when two figures came ambling down the hill.

Stella's heart thudded so hard it felt like her ribs would shatter. One of those figures was Jesse, steadying some other person who was covered in blood. She rushed forward, but Mia was faster, getting to the bottom of the hill as Jesse and the bloody wraith stumbled down. Jesse couldn't hold onto the other person — her mind filled in the blanks, that had to be Lucy — and Lucy stumbled and pitched forward. Mia caught him before he hit the ground.

"Such a drama queen," Mia said, lifting Lucy easily and handing him over to Archer. "Get him to the van and get him some pills. He'll live. Save the real blood in case there's someone worse off in that silo."

"There is," Jesse said. He looked godawful, legs like water, lips pale.

Stella got to him, hands automatically assessing for injuries until he gently pushed her aside, turning his face away from her, squeezing his eyes shut. Of course. He probably needed blood, and she was too close. Stella stepped back, not out of fear, but out of respect for his space.

"Finn is in the silo," he said, his words slow and thick. "And Ciceline is hurt." He swallowed dryly, his tongue clicking at the back of his throat, and turned to Mia. "It's pretty bad. Can you help?"

JESSE

With Lucy safely in the van, Jesse followed Mia as she hustled to the silo door, with Stella close behind.

"What happened to Ciceline?" Mia asked.

Jesse fought to get his brain into gear, his mouth to work. "Hard to see. Shot? Pneumothorax, I used the trocar. She needs blood." Just saying the word brought on a fierce pang of hunger. He could smell it everywhere, ached for it. His veins and arteries felt gummed up, his heart worked overtime. "Finn is with her, and his girlfriend."

"Mia's got supplies in the van," Stella said.

"Good, because . . ." Jesse swallowed again and tried to speak, but the words wouldn't come.

They entered the silo by the light of Stella's phone, and Jesse led them down the rusted hallway. Before the circle of light reached the alcove, he heard the noise. It wasn't Ciceline's breathing, he couldn't discern that at all. It was something softer than that, a sound he associated with the Black Room. It twisted his stomach into a knot, but this time not with hunger. They rounded the corner and Stella swung her phone light around.

Jesse's eyes adjusted and Finn came into focus, sprawled out on the floor, arms splayed like he'd been pulled away. Bettina leaned over him, one arm stretched and twisted behind her, still attached to the chain, her face buried in his neck.

Jesse grabbed her. She shrieked as he yanked her off of Finn and threw her. Her body hit the railing and he heard something crack.

In the dim light he could barely make out Finn's features, and there was no way to tell how bad it was. When he put his fingers to Finn's neck he found a wet mess of skin, and yes, a pulse, but his heart would empty him out if Jesse didn't stop the bleeding. If she'd gotten to a major artery, blood would be hitting the ceiling, and it wasn't. Unless his blood pressure had already plummeted? The skin flapped open, as it would with a dog bite. Finn's hands came up, swatting at him in a panic as he tried to speak, but choked.

Stella got on her knees beside him, her hands frantically covering Jesse's to try and stop the blood. Her voice was calm. "Finn, we're here, it's okay."

Jesse couldn't think beyond his panic. Unless they had come here in an ambulance with EMTs, all they would do was watch Finn and Ciceline die, then they'd watch Lucy lose his mind completely, and hey, maybe Jesse would join him.

"Shit," Mia said. "Let me think. We could—"

"Change him," Jesse said. "We could do that, right?"

Mia took a steadying breath. "Yes. We could do that, but we would need . . ."

Finn reached up to put his hands over Jesse's and Stella's.

"Then what are we waiting for?" Jesse asked. "Change him!"

Before I turn into a monster myself.

STELLA

"Alright," Mia said. "Jesse, you carry Ciceline so you don't eat your brother. I'll carry Finn and send Archer back for the girl. Stella, keep the pressure on his neck and don't worry about anything else."

"Got it," Stella said, perfectly calm.

Jesse rose, stumbling under Ciceline's weight. Stella got to her feet, fingers pressed to the flapping skin of Finn's neck as Mia lifted him. His pulse thrummed like a plucked guitar string. They turned to go, and her phone light moved down the hall, illuminating another body. Stella couldn't make out any features.

"Oh," Mia said in a small voice, as she caught sight of it. Then she shook her head and burst back to activity, rushing them to the door, where the brightness of morning burned Stella's eyes again.

Archer hovered over Lucy on the second seat, opening a supply kit. "Fuck," he said when he saw them.

"He can wait," Mia snapped. "There's a girl inside, go get her while I try to get real blood into Ciceline and save this kid." She placed Finn in the back of the van and rifled around in a compartment, pushing aside frozen gel packs until she came up with a bag of blood.

Jesse eased Ciceline down beside Finn and grabbed Archer's

sleeve. "There are people locked up in in there; dangerous, starving."

"We'll deal with them later," Archer said, and sprinted back into the silo.

"What do we do?" Stella asked.

Mia stared at Ciceline, looking as if someone had slapped her. "I'm not sure. We don't have enough to save everyone." She cradled Ciceline's head, bringing the bag to her mouth. Ciceline's eyelids flickered and her tongue slipped between her blue lips. "Fucking Carnelian," she whispered.

Stella looked away, focusing on Finn instead. He gripped her wrist in one hand, Jesse's in the other. His eyes pleaded with them. Stella knew what hypovolemic shock looked like. She knew what death looked like.

Archer returned, carrying Bettina, her wrists in chains, another chain wrapped around her mouth. The spirals of hair were missing, but Finn's charcoal sketch had done justice to the rest of her features. He put her in the front seat and came back around.

"Mia," Archer said, "the clinic?"

Mia didn't look up from Ciceline. "Probably infiltrated, we can't take the chance."

"Then once we're in range," Archer said, "we'll call Carnelian South and have them meet us at BLOOD."

"It's a long ride," Mia said. "It'll be too late."

"Not for Finn." Archer climbed into the van. "Finn? We can save you, but I need your consent. Do you want to live for a really long time? Blink once for yes, twice for no."

Finn's eyes rolled as he tried to focus. He squeezed Stella's wrist, looking from her to Jesse.

Say yes, she thought. *Say yes say yes say yes.*

Finn turned his eyes to Archer and gave one long blink.

"Awesome," Archer said. "Jesse, keep your fingers on that wound and don't vamp out. You know how bad this'll be and I don't have time to get fancy." He reached up and sliced his wrist

on the butterfly knife that hung behind him, flinching and hissing
in a breath. His lips were pressed together, eyes cast down, all
business.

Stella recalled his words from earlier. *Been there. Backed off the
cliff.* Her heart ached.

"Great," Mia said. "One down, but we still have two dying
vampires. Bettina, if she's even alive. Lucy will make it to
BLOOD. Ciceline won't."

Stella leaned over Ciceline, studying her face. She wasn't
breathing, her skin had gone gray. She touched her cold cheek,
stroked a lock of white hair from her forehead. Her wrist was so
close to Ciceline's lips.

"Use mine," Stella said. "And change me."

Mia snatched her arm, nodding.

Jesse looked at her without moving his hands from Finn. "It's
not what you wanted."

No, perhaps not, but she wanted even less to watch someone
die. Hadn't that been one of her fears? Centuries filled with loss
and grief? Here was a way to avoid it, at least this once. Ciceline
would see another day; how could she deny her that?

Her pain, her terror, her sleepless nights — these didn't come
from sadness, they came from love.

"You'll die and come back to life," Jesse said. "It hurts."

"I understand." Jesse had done it, though not in a moving
van. She could do it, too. She was glad they were going back to
BLOOD, that's where Mom was.

Mia nicked Stella's wrist and said, "You're tall."

Stella frowned at her.

"You might have enough blood left over for Finn's girl, if she's
alive up there. But that's not my main priority. Here." She jerked
Stella's wrist toward Ciceline. "Once Ciceline is back in the game,
I'll change you. Jesse, take some pills from the glove compartment. Archer, have someone meet us at BLOOD. Ciceline will
still need help if she makes it."

If. This could be for nothing.

"After the change," Jesse told her. "It's not bad."

"Right," Stella said.

Ciceline's cold lips touched her skin, a pull from inside, drawing out, vertigo.

What would she do with all of this extra time?

Mia bowed her head over Ciceline, pushing the soaked fabric of her shirt aside and peeling a piece of tape away from a perfectly circular hole in her chest.

"How do you do it?" Stella asked.

Mia flicked her eyes up at her. "Do what?"

The colors and shapes of the world blurred around her. "How do you fill hundreds of years?"

Mia shrugged and went back to her work. "However you want."

JESSE

B LOOD had a basement, which housed not only supplies, but a set of private rooms: ten-by-ten spaces with red-painted walls, velvet fainting couches, and floor lamps with black lace lampshades. They took Stella and Finn to a room together, and Ciceline to a separate one.

"I patched Lucy up a little and got him some blood," Archer said, sagging against the wall outside of Ciceline's room. "Physically he'll be fine, but he's not . . ." He glanced over at Jesse. "He's in a weird place. Anyway, Carnelian South can spare one medic for Ciceline. She'll be here in thirty minutes."

"Just one?" Mia asked. "Ciceline needs more help than I'm qualified to give."

Archer lifted his hands helplessly.

"But she'll live?" Jesse asked.

"Yes," Mia said. "Thanks to your sister. It'll be rough, though."

"Bettina?"

"Alive. I'm sure she'll extend her most profound apologies when her skull heals."

"Lucy tried to warn me."

"Don't blame yourself for saving her. Imagine how Finn would feel if you hadn't."

Mia took him by the arm and led him out of the hallway and upstairs to the poetry room. Lucy sat on a high-backed chair, staring into the middle distance.

Thank you, Jesse.

"You don't have to thank me," Jesse said out loud.

"Are you two talking telepathically?" Mia asked. "Because that freaks me out. People shouldn't be able to do that. Lucy? How about it, huh? English, maybe?"

Lucy held his hands out: *Sorry.*

Mia sighed. "Whatever. Archer, I need you to direct the medic downstairs when she gets here." She pointed to Lucy. "You, Bloodbath. Go take a shower, you look like post-prom Carrie."

Lucy pushed himself off the chair, but didn't leave. He reached out to Mia.

She backed up a step. "What?"

Archer held out his hand.

"Stop it. What are you doing? Do as I say."

Lucy gestured with his fingers: *Come over here.*

"Knock it off," Mia said. "Raven made a choice. Shit happens. I'm not going anywhere near you, covered in blood like that. Whose blood is it? Is it Raven's?"

Lucy shook his head.

Mia looked to Jesse. "What happened? How did he die? Did you see anything?"

"I didn't, I'm sorry. Ciceline might know more."

"Was Raven working for Via Nova?" she asked.

No one answered.

"Why?"

"Mia," Archer said. "Who knows?"

She ran to them, collapsed in their arms, and wept. They held her tight, Lucy squeezing around her shoulders with one arm, the other hanging useless at his side.

As useless as Jesse felt. This was not his scene.

He went out through the Black Room, as he had the first night, to the alley. Cold air filled his aching lungs, and the roar of cars on the street made his head throb. He dug out his phone and dialed Mom.

She picked up on the first ring. "Jesse?"

"We've got Finn. He's alright."

"What happened?" she asked, her voice choked with tears.

"It's a long story. I'll tell you when we get home, but right now we're at this place . . . We're with Lucy and Ciceline. Their mom died."

Then Jesse was crying into the phone. Ciceline had told him that vampires rarely changed their parents, because it was natural for them to die first. He slid down the brick wall to sit on the cold ground. He didn't have any tissues to wipe his face, so he used his sleeve like a little kid.

"Alright, honey," Mom said.

"Lucy's not okay. I think he needs . . . I don't know what. A lot of time."

"Which he has," Mom said. "Right?"

Jesse's tears stopped like turning off a faucet. She had always known, hadn't she? "Yes. Lots of time."

"Stella and Finn?"

Was this even his to tell? "I think you'll have to talk to them."

"Well then, everything is gonna be fine, isn't it, Jesse?"

"Yeah. I know you were waiting and there wasn't any service where we were."

"I know, baby. I'm right across the street at the café. Do you want me to come to you?"

"How did you . . . No, it's better if I go there, it's chaos over here."

Footsteps approached from the end of the alley, and someone peered around the building. Black curls once again made him think 'Lucy!' but once again, it wasn't.

"Mom, I have to go, Lucy's dad is here."

"Come on across when you're done," she said. "I love you, Jesse."

The tears came once again. "I love you too, Mom. I'll be there in a few."

He hung up and got to his feet as Lucian's father approached, walking with his shoulders hunched, wringing his hands.

"Doctor Latari?" Jesse said. "You got out of the clinic?"

"Security was down and there were many available cars in the garage. My children?"

"They're alive. Ciceline was injured, but Mia says she'll recover. Lucian . . . He's inside. Yvette is dead. I'm sorry, I don't know if you were still close, and I probably should have let one of them tell you that, but Lucy isn't handling it well."

"Finally Snapped, did he? About time. Oh, no no no, don't be sad. That's over a century of pain he's carrying around, he'll shed it now. I'm sure he'll be wonderful once he's on the other side of it, if you're willing to wait." He offered Jesse a hand-kerchief.

Jesse wiped his eyes. "I've waited this long, what's another year or two? I really am sorry about Yvette. I only met her once and I hated her, but still."

"Yes, well . . ." Doctor Latari paused for a moment. "We haven't been together since Sandu was a child. She locked me in the attic to stop me changing him as he was dying, so you know, naturally we split after that."

"Oh." What else could he say to that? "So that's it? Carnelian is finished now?"

"Not yet," Doctor Latari said. "Carnelian is international." He tapped his bottom lip. "They will need a new leader for the Eastern division, though, to bring it into modern times if it's to survive at all."

"Someone like you?"

"Me? No, never me. I'm not made for that work, and neither is Lucian, before you ask. No, someone tough, but honest, who can keep our way of life secure and protect our secrecy, but also get us what we need to live. The old way and the new way must meet, and we haven't figured out how yet. We need someone who understands that keeping vampires as servants or locking them in factories isn't quite the thing. I hate to cut this short, Jesse, but I'm eager to see my children."

"Of course," Jesse said.

Doctor Latari walked past him but turned when he got to the door. "I'm sure Lucian will want to see you before . . . whatever he decides. He's never spoken to me about anyone else the way he spoke about you. I hope that makes this more bearable."

Jesse nodded, unable to speak.

Doctor Latari disappeared into the club.

LUCIAN

The smoke breathed down his neck, but Lucy ran, and clawed, and climbed. It was hard to concentrate on the real world with that going on in his head, but he would do it for as long as it took. Yes, this time felt different — the flames were hotter, faster, singeing his seams — but he could do it.

Tata had come up to the loft while Lucy stood under the hot water of the shower, scalding himself clean. He'd helped him bandage the gash in his side, brought him pills, and explained what should happen next. Lucy was terrible at making plans even in the best of times; always better to have someone else tell him what to do, especially because he couldn't quite clock what year it was. Time kept bouncing around on him.

Now Tata paced the hallway outside the room where Ciceline was recovering, whispering on the phone in Romanian. Lucy tuned it out. Ciceline needed his attention.

She was awake on the narrow bed, holding his hand. She didn't have the strength to wipe her tears, so he used the sleeve of his shirt.

She spoke in Romani, "Let me take care of you like you did for me."

No, he couldn't put that on her. She'd spent her life caring for him.

"Then please don't take too long," she said.

He laughed. As if he had any control over it. The urge to let go was strong.

"It's hard, Lucy," she said. "Don't be discouraged when you backslide after a good month."

Yes, he knew this; he'd seen it many times.

He leaned to kiss her cheek. Ciceline tried to sit up, but paled with the pain and collapsed back down on the bed. Would she never learn? He told her to rest, by now unable to rewire his brain to the present, to English, but Romani was her language, too. He checked her bandages and tucked her back in.

Outside in the dark narrow hallway, Tata gave Lucy a nod of acknowledgment, and Lucy went on his way, up the stairs to the main floor.

Mia and Archer stood by the bar, whispering, Mia with her hands flailing around, Archer with his in his pockets, subdued. Seeing them vaulted him back into the 90s. Mia had reset to her usual facade of dark, manic cheer. He'd always seen it for what it was, but now he truly understood it, because he had done the same for so long. *I'm fine. This is fine. Everything is fine.*

They saw him coming and Mia rushed to embrace him, but stopped short when she got close enough, her arms still out.

"Wait, is this for real?" she asked. "You're honestly standing right here losing your mind? What's it like?"

He held his hands out. Impossible to describe.

"Oh Lucy, don't go," she said. "Stay here; we can take care of you. Come back down to the private rooms, we have restraints. Non-leather ones for vegans."

No one could shock a laugh out of him like Mia.

Archer came up behind her. "Lucy, are you really . . ? But you look fine. Mia's right, you should stay."

He closed his eyes and breathed through the longing. The flames were rising, he needed to wrap this up.

Mia reached up and hooked him by the back of the neck. He leaned down, and she kissed his forehead, whispering "Goodbye, Buttercup."

He didn't wipe her lipstick off. He wanted to take it with him.

"Don't say that, Mia," Archer said, pulling him into a hug. "'Goodbye,' jeez. See you on the other side, right? You'll remember us?"

"Desigur." Of course, but there was no guarantee. Some people completely reset after a bad Snap. It was rare, but it happened.

Jesse, Jesse, *Jesse*, he felt him enter the room from the outside before he saw him standing in the doorway.

Jesse — 2007, a tiny college dorm, a shy smile, amber eyes watching his fingers as he played a popular song from the radio to seem more youthful.

No. Jesse was a grown man, with a few days' worth of stubble, and grief in his eyes.

Mia and Archer released him and retreated down the hallway, leaving him alone with Jesse in the cavernous room. He wanted to run to him, but his legs were weak with dread. This was going to be the hardest. They met halfway, under the skeleton, and Jesse reeled him into a careful embrace, mindful of the bandages under his shirt.

"You're leaving," Jesse said.

Lucy nodded against his shoulder.

"Where?"

"România."

Jesse pulled away, searching his eyes. Lucy tried to convey what was in his mind, how tightly he was holding on, how fast the fire was eating its way up now, but he would stay, if Jesse asked him to. He could climb back up. His will was strong enough.

"Tell me to be alright and I will," he said, and it came out in English.

Jesse shook his head. "I'll miss you."

I'll miss you too. Even when I can't remember you, I'll miss you.

"I'll wait for you," Jesse said. "But you have to promise me you'll get help when you come home."

He would promise Jesse anything; this was the least of it, the easiest thing. "Îți promit."

Jesse brushed his hair back. "English too mainstream for you?"

Only Jesse could make him laugh with absolute joy at a time like this.

"What's another year, year and a half?" Jesse asked. "But after that, I'm coming to get you. Don't make me do that."

Never. If he came back at all, he would never keep Jesse waiting again.

"Can I kiss you goodbye? Are you in a place where you can say yes or no?"

Lucy answered by linking his fingers behind Jesse's neck and kissing him first. He could stay, Jesse could make this better . . . but his father cleared his throat from the hallway. He wouldn't have interrupted if he didn't have a schedule. Carnelian Romania hadn't fallen, and the jets were still flying.

"La revedere, dragul meu," Lucy said.

Jesse laughed, a fractured little sound. "How dare you."

Once more he took Jesse's hands and kissed them, but he didn't risk looking up again to meet his eyes, because if he did, he would start fighting to stay, clambering back up, and the fires would chase him, maybe for years, until he went down unwillingly.

Tata came and led him away to the car he had stolen when he escaped the clinic. Whose it was, Lucy didn't know or care. JFK was the closest airport with private jet service. The ride made him feel sick; the prospect of ten hours in the air was even worse.

At the airport, Tata took care of the paperwork, and Lucy had nothing left to take with him on the jet. It had all burned, and soon, he would burn with it.

"Romania is doing excellent things with Athanasia Disorder," Tata said, as they walked through a private terminal. He spoke in Romanian, which was easier to understand. Lucy hadn't even noticed how he'd been struggling with parsing English until he didn't have to anymore. "It's so much better than in America, less barbaric. The first few weeks won't be easy, but soon you'll be clear for a more autonomous arrangement, where you can walk the halls, and there is plenty to do at the facility. There's even a pool and a spa, and of course you'll be allowed to play music, should you retain that skill. I wish I could have stayed in Romania, but your mother, well, no matter, my dear. I'll check myself in with you. Once it's established that you're no longer a danger to yourself or anyone else, and I'm stable enough, you can stay with me until you're yourself again."

What if he never was? What if he just didn't come back? A pool, a spa, the best care? Lucy didn't want any of that. He wanted to stay on the island. He wanted Jesse back, and Ciceline, his creek with the night herons, sunrises from his rowboat, the smell of the ocean on warm days. He wanted to go home and power-wash his deck, but of course, his deck had burned with the rest of the house. He wanted one of Mia's disgusting drinks. Would anyone make him a drink like that over there? No, he would be forced to drink fresh blood, forced to eat, handled like an object.

They entered the jetway. Three security guards waited for him at the door of the jet, two men and one woman, with guns and batons and tasers hanging from their belts. He could take them all in the span of thirty seconds.

"Easy," his father said, with a gentle hand on his arm. Lucy wasn't sure if he was talking to him or to the guards.

One guard approached him with restraints, cuffs that went up to the elbows, the kind of thing you'd see in one of BLOOD's private rooms. "We don't want any incidents to happen mid-flight," he said in Romanian. "Do you consent to this?"

"I can get out of those."

The man took a step back. The woman came forward. "Sedation?"

Lucy turned to his father. "Won't that make it worse?"

"Yes, for a short time when you wake up. I think it will be safer, but it's up to you."

He couldn't hold on for another ten hours. And then what? What if it got really bad and he managed to get into the cockpit in his confusion? He approached the group of guards, arms out, palms up. The flames rose, relentless. Time to let go. "I consent to everything. Get it over with before I change my mind."

The years burned through him, scorched his thoughts, incinerating them before they had a chance to make sense, leaving behind nothing more than a blanket of ash.

CICELINE
APRIL 12TH

The first thing Ciceline had done the moment she'd gotten out of the bed in Mia's dungeon that November morning was call the mostly defunct Carnelian cleaners. There were only a few left, but she had them clear the bodies from the office, rip up the rugs, incinerate every bit of physical evidence, and scrub everything with active-oxygen-based disinfectants. The second thing she'd done as executor of Yvette's will — which she had drawn up — was to sell the entire lot for ten million.

A month later, Ciceline bid it all farewell. The broken stained glass, the antique desk, the kitschy hourglass of red sand, and the two broadswords — she had them destroyed.

Now she parked outside the new site and surveyed it from her car: white office buildings, newly-planted cherry trees showing the first of their spring greens.

Yvette was gone. After more than half a millennium of life, she was dead. Ciceline sat with it for a moment, wondering if she could have gone through with it, if it came to that. If she could have killed the woman who had raised her. It was probably better that she never had to find out. She didn't miss Yvette, and didn't feel bad for not missing her.

Dog Lucy bounced around in his harness beside her.

"You need to pee?"

He yipped in response. Ciceline unhooked him from the seat-belt and took him out, where he christened the new parking lot.

Another car pulled up next to her silver hybrid; the man inside waved and got out.

Turned out his real name was Oliver and he had a Master's in business administration. She didn't like the name Oliver — he would always be Seattle to her — but she did like him. She handed him the keyring. "Do you feel ready for this?"

"So ready," he said. "You can rely on me."

"So, what do you have?"

He bounced on his toes as he retrieved a booklet of papers from his satchel, which he wore crossed over his chest like a true nerd. "Tons of applications. Primarily, everyone who rents a block will be a vampire. So far, I'm looking at a blood lab — duh — a law office, a walk-in clinic, real estate, a few medical specialists, and, as you requested, a psychiatrist along with a few psychologists and counselors who can share the space. And your office, naturally."

"I'll need to interview the psychiatrist myself. Can we set up a meeting?"

"Absolutely." He took out his phone and scrolled through his calendar app.

"How old is she?"

"Just over a hundred. She was in Europe during World War two. She's Roma, like you. Specializes in PTSD and trauma." Seattle stared at her, waiting.

"Sounds good. I'm free next Thursday."

"I'll set it up."

"Thank you, Seattle. Listen, I have tons to do today, so can you—"

"Actually, one question," he said. "Jesse Westchurch. How is he?"

"He's fine. Seriously, you were probably the least scary thing in the silo. Promise me you'll make an appointment with this psychiatrist."

"It's on my calendar."

"Not for me," she said.

"Oh. Of course."

She held out her hand. He had to juggle his papers, satchel, and keys to shake her hand.

"This is going to work, right?" he asked.

Ciceline lifted her good shoulder. The other one still ached when she moved her clavicle. "I hope so. We'll see."

She put Dog Lucy back into his seat, buckled him in, and made her way west.

The new offices weren't far from BLOOD; about forty-five minutes. She pulled into the parking lot behind the club, unbuckled Lucy, and took him out. A bit of cold rain pelted down on her spring parka. She pulled the hood up and lifted Lucy as she crossed the street to EspresSo Extra. He didn't like to get his paws wet. The bell tinged as she entered.

Archer took orders behind the counter while Mia ran the espresso machine. The line of people went to the back of the seating area. "We'll need more cinnamon," Mia said to a woman in the kitchen, before spotting her. "Oh, Ciceline! Give us a second, alright?"

"I'll wait." She took a seat on the teal-striped sofa, pulled Dog Lucy up beside her, and watched customers come and go until Mia and Archer were able to go on break. The new workers were vampires. She could always tell. After about ten minutes, Mia pulled up a seat across from her.

Archer served her coffee and a chocolate scone before taking a seat. "Wow," he said. "I'm loving your 'Welcome to My Lair' hair."

Ciceline reached up to comb her fingers through her dark curls. She hadn't felt like bleaching or straightening it in a few months. "Thanks."

"How's Lucy?" Mia asked.

"Busy." No need to tell them that he had, for a few weeks, stopped speaking entirely and could do nothing but play the cello. That he'd played so much he'd worn down his calluses and the skin beneath, bloodying the strings. He was on the other side of that now. "Our father doesn't want to sell his estate, so Lucy came up with a themed B&B. They're getting it set up, zoning and all of that. The plan is to do vampire weekends, complete with legit blood drives. Some of the blood will actually be donated, too."

"I love that idea," Mia said. "Archer!" She punched his arm hard enough to make him wince. "That's such a great idea, legitimate blood drives? Ciceline, could we do that? We could reduce the prices of our blood drinks and bring in hundreds more clients."

"It's doable," Ciceline said, "but one thing at a time. Raven."

Mia folded her hands and looked down.

"I pulled a lot of strings for this, because no matter what he did before, Raven saved my life, and probably Lucy's too. He'll be listed among the victims. He had a legal identity, so there's no way to keep him anonymous, but he won't be blamed for the murder. Russel Busquet is responsible for the murders on the west coast, and we're pinning the Long Island one on Brett Busquet. It won't be connected to you."

Mia put her hands over Ciceline's. "Thank you. Raven didn't do anything that the rest of us haven't done. I know times have changed, but we've all taken lives. He just did it for a different reason."

Carnelian had always justified Ciceline's kills to her: murderers, cult leaders, abusers. She couldn't decide how much that mattered now. She sipped her coffee while Mia processed.

"I wish he would have come to us," Mia said. "How did we let it go this far?"

"Don't put that on yourself," Ciceline said. "It doesn't matter how badly you fell out; Raven made a choice."

Mia drummed her long nails on the reclaimed wood and said nothing.

"Well," Ciceline said, rising as she scooped Lucy up, "I have another appointment; sorry I can't stay."

"You'll tell us if you need anything," Mia said. "When Lucy comes back, send him over. I still have some of his stuff in the loft."

"I will." Ciceline turned in the door. "Oh, I almost forgot: Carnelian isn't doing deals anymore. Whatever contracts you were under to remain in their service, or whatever you owed, is null and void. You're free."

"Ciceline." Mia's voice was an astonished whisper. Archer said nothing, his hands clasped over his mouth.

"Happy Easter, or whatever," Ciceline said with a wave, and left them gaping at her in the doorway.

The two-hour drive back east in the rain made her neck and shoulders ache, her eyes burn, and her hands cramp. She forced the fear down. Only good news today.

The Westchurches had not wished to meet her in their temporary home. Stella hated it; it was cramped, dark, and uncomfortable. They'd agreed on an unfussy, dog-friendly coffee shop, with rustic wood floors and a mural of greenery on the wall.

They were already there when she arrived. Jesse stood outside, under the overhang, chewing on his cuticles. He looked better than the last time she'd seen him, when he'd been in the beginning of a relapse. It would continue to happen, though hopefully future recurrences would be less severe when the new pills started to come out. Right now, he just looked like a man pining for his tragically absent lover.

"He's fine," Ciceline said, as Jesse opened his mouth to ask. "He talks about you constantly." Well, he had played "Unchained Melody" on his cello for a week straight, anyway. Jesse didn't need to hear from her that Lucy had spent February convinced that Jesse had died during the change, and everything after it was a dream. That was done now, and if Lucy ever wanted to tell him, that was his business.

"Can I call him?" Jesse asked.

Ciceline reached in her purse and pulled out Lucy's phone. "Sorry. He still has some rough days here and there. I have to make sure he can get his life back when he's ready." She'd taken over his accounts, posting pictures now and then to make it look like he was on sabbatical and helping their father.

"Let's go in," she said. "You're about to have a terrific day."

He tilted his head, but she only smiled mysteriously.

The Westchurches were seated in a corner, with Finn and Bettina sharing the bench, hands linked on top of the table. They had matching tattoos of tiny vines around their ring-fingers. Bit of a shock that they'd gotten to the other side of Via Nova together, but then again, sometimes trauma brought people closer. Mrs. Westchurch was sipping at a cup of tea or coffee.

Stella rose first, with her arms out, to give her a kiss and a hug, and a kiss for Dog Lucy too. Finn and Bettina stood awkwardly, unsure how to greet her. They settled for handshakes. Bettina kept her eyes downcast. Weird dynamic, with Ciceline being the head of the syndicate that Via Nova had tried to take down, yet the Westchurches went on like none of it mattered. Families were wild. A bit callous maybe, but it wasn't their mother who was beheaded.

Ciceline pulled up a chair, set Lucy on her lap and her briefcase on the floor, and took out her papers. "First of all, how is everyone?"

Murmurings of 'fine' and 'good, thanks,' though Jesse remained quiet.

"Mrs. Westchurch? I have your contracts ready to sign."

She held up her hand. "Not yet. I'm taking my whole year to think it over, thank you."

Stella got that little worried crease between her brows: anything could happen in a year. Ciceline had never seen a family change a parent, because Carnelian always talked everyone out of it.

"That's okay," Ciceline said. "The clinic is at capacity right now anyway, and they're not entirely back in the game yet, but I'll make sure that they will be by the time you decide. In the mean-time, let's get down to the real business."

"Okay, out with it," Stella said.

Oh, this was going to be fun. "My meeting with Doctor Shepherd went as expected."

Stella dropped her gaze. "That's alright."

"As *I* expected," Ciceline corrected. "Your recording was great leverage. He'll sell, and at a ridiculously good price. He's retiring. With no need to buy ketamine anymore, and no one to hawk it to, maybe he'll even stay out of trouble. The house and the practice are yours. You can rent it to Treece, or you can give her the boot."

Stella took her hand and said, "Thank you, Cice."

Jesse and Mrs. Westchurch looked positively stoked, but Stella didn't look as thrilled as Ciceline had imagined she would when she had practiced this scene in her head. Hadn't she wanted that house more than anything?

"Can we chat outside?" Stella asked.

What the hell? They went outside, Lucy on the leash at her heels.

"Is everything okay?" Ciceline asked.

"Yes." Stella said. "I'm grateful. But my plans have changed a bit. I've really loved being a vet, but I don't think I can go back to it."

"Okay. What will you do?"

She blew out through her lips and rolled her eyes, like she was about to drop the most absurd news Ciceline had ever heard. "I got accepted into med school."

"Stella, you're brilliant." Ciceline said. But . . . "Which school?" How far away was it, and how long would Stella be gone? Who would she meet there?

Stella smiled at the ground as her cheeks flushed. Ciceline felt her face grow warm, too.

"Stony Brook."

Thank god.

"I was trying to figure out how I could stay somewhere close," Stella said. "It'll cost extra, but . . ."

"Well, no, obviously you can stay at mine."

Stella took both of her hands. "I wasn't angling for that, I swear."

Which was hilarious: Stella couldn't angle to save her life. "I know."

"But I accept. School will take up most of my day, so I won't be hanging around you."

"I like you hanging around me."

Stella grinned and stepped closer.

Ciceline had to take a breath before speaking again. "I'm not home a lot during the day either. But I'm home at night. I'll help you study, or whatever."

"'Or whatever,'" Stella said.

I haven't done this in a long time, I'm going to mess this up, I'll find a way to self-sabotage, you'll get tired of me, I'm not as good as you think I am. You saved my life and I don't deserve you.

The words crowded into her head, shouting her down. She shoved them away because fuck the brain weasels. Stella was waiting, searching her eyes, hopeful.

"Draga mea," Ciceline said, because it worked for Lucy. "We have all the time in the world."

Apparently, it worked for her, too, because Stella leaned in and kissed her, a feather-light brush of her lips. Ciceline had forgotten how that feeling tingled up her back and down her arms.

She couldn't wait to relearn it.

JESSE

OCTOBER 27TH

Three crows bathed in the fountain at the dog park, splashing until their feathers gleamed. Jesse buttoned his jacket and pulled his scarf tighter; the creeping fog dampened the already chilled air. Dogs chased tennis balls thrown by owners who had no idea that a vampire sat among them; that a vampire chatted with them at the grocery store, stood in line behind them at the deli, treated their pets, performed surgeries, and cried with them when it was time to say goodbye.

He'd had two flares, one in December, and another in March. Both were likely due to stress, inability to sleep and heal, and not enough time to take in the blood he relied on in raw form. The relapses were terrible, but bearable. Any pain was bearable if he could see his way to the other side of it.

Barney the pug came bounding up to him and pawed at his pants, and Jesse bent down to pet him. Ms. Skeltin — his client now — was not far behind.

"Doctor Jesse!" she said, leaning down to hug him. "You're looking so much better than last I saw you."

Yeah, that day. He'd had to go running out on his appointments again. The flares liked to sneak up on him. "Thanks. Feeling a lot better, too."

"How is Doctor Stella? I miss her."

"I miss her, too. She's still around on weekends, still taking patients. You should come in and say hello; she'll be at the office Saturday morning."

"I definitely will," she said. "I don't miss Doctor Shep at all. I'm dead set on not going to Treece, even though she's like, two blocks over from me now."

Jesse.

"A friend of mine checked out her new place and said it sucked," she said.

Jesse.

He felt Lucy, could almost smell him. Roses and black pepper.

Jesse said, "I feel bad about the whole thing, honestly."

"Well, I don't."

The bare, spindled branches of a cherry tree traced lines in the fog beyond the fountain, yellow leaves decaying in a circle around the trunk. He looked at Ms. Skeltin, blinked, and looked back to the tree. Lucy stood beside it, in dark trousers and a black hoodie with Espres*So Extra!* splashed across the front in red lettering. His curls were smooth and tied back, shorter than last time he saw him. He leaned against the tree, hands in his pockets. Jesse gave him a small, secret smile.

Ms. Skeltin looked over her shoulder at the source of Jesse's distraction. "Oh my gosh, I didn't mean to keep you from your friend, I'm so sorry! Is that Lu-shen?"

"Lucian, yes," Jesse said, and waved him over.

Not exactly what he'd had in mind for their reunion, but the joy of seeing him again up close overwhelmed everything else. He sucked the tears back. No need to get Ms. Skeltin all worked up.

She shook Lucy's hand before Jesse could even say hello to him. "I'm Marcie, Doctor Jesse takes care of my Barney now that Doctor Stella is gone. I follow your socials, you are so cute in person. I'm dying to go to Transylvania on one of those tours, and

I also just love your playing, I keep hoping you'll make a CD. Do you think you ever will?"

"Maybe one day," Lucy said.

Jesse hadn't heard his voice in a year. He had an accent now; slight, but present.

She glanced back and forth between them. "Oh, of course. I won't keep you. Come along, Barney. Lu-shen, such a pleasure to finally meet you. Doctor Jesse." She reached across Lucy to hug Jesse again. "Take care of yourself. Love to Doctor Stella." She hooked a leash onto Barney's collar and led him away.

Jesse scooted over on the bench and Lucy sat beside him, tucking one leg under and turning to him. Jesse did the same.

"You look beautiful," Jesse told him.

"So do you."

They snickered at each other.

"I was planning on running into your arms when I saw you again," Jesse said.

"That's so mainstream."

"Tell me everything," Jesse said.

"I'm alright." Lucy took his hand and linked their fingers together. "Ciceline got the offices up and running. She hired a psychiatrist all the way from the west coast. I'm going to see her next week."

"That's the best news I've heard in a long time."

"After the first few months in Romania, I got out of the clinic and went to work. I helped my father get his business off the ground. I've never done anything like that before and actually succeeded; it was fun. Ciceline gave advice, but honestly, I did a lot of it myself. I never thought I could do that."

"I did."

"Thank you for that," Lucy said. "For believing in me."

"Duh," Jesse said. "And your job with the orchestra?"

"Oh, yes." He tapped his fingers against the bench, looking away. "I retired."

"Wow, Lucy. That's pretty huge."

Lucy waved his hand. "It's okay; the touring was a lot. I can travel any time I want to, and it would be nice to actually see the places I go to, instead of rehearsing all day and crashing in a hotel." Still, there was something wistful in his voice.

"What will you do now?"

"Ah," Lucy sighed. "I haven't decided yet, but I have some ideas. I can play in a different orchestra. There are others in New York. Ones that don't travel as much."

"That's quite a step down. You'll lose your position as principal, won't you? Are you okay with that?"

He lifted one elegant shoulder. "I think so. I could also teach. I might enjoy that. I've never taught anyone before."

"Private classes?" Jesse asked.

"Well, a college, maybe."

A dreadful feeling coiled tight in Jesse's stomach. He hadn't cheated death to continue settling for unsatisfactory situations; he was tired of letting go of what he wanted in the name of selflessness, and he wanted Lucy. He opened his mouth to say so.

"Five Towns, or Stony Brook, maybe," Lucy said.

Right here on the island. Jesse let go of the breath he'd been holding.

Lucy reached up and cupped his cheek. "Dragul meu. Why would I leave again? I want to be where you are." His hand froze. "Is it alright if I still call you that? Or is it weird now?"

From the way a shock of desire bolted up his entire chest? "It's okay," Jesse choked out. "Totally okay."

"Good. Now you."

"Oh, check it out." Jesse rolled up his sleeve to show Lucy the crow tattoo on his shoulder. Finn had completed it over the summer, and it had been peaceful between them in ways he hadn't expected.

"Wow," Lucy said. He had the absolute nerve to look shy. "You look really good with ink. Finn told you it will fade, right?"

"Yeah, but that's okay. It's probably safer to let them disappear, right? For the next . . . life or whatever."

"That's right. All tattoos are temporary for us."

"I'm okay with that. Oh, and I hired someone new, so I can afford to take some vacation days now and then, and I have more time to, you know, actually live my life. Do you want to walk and talk? There's a coffee shop?"

"Let's."

They held hands as they walked.

"Have you heard from Jared?" Lucy asked.

"We keep in touch." Ciceline had worked up contracts for some of the people who'd been baited by Via Nova. Some had run as far from that world as they could get, never to speak of it again. Jared had taken the change. "He's alright."

"I'm glad."

"Oh, and I got a cat."

"What's its name?"

"Lucy," Jesse said, and it was worth it to watch Lucy nearly break his neck turning to glare at him. Jesse laughed. "His name is Pumpkin Spice. He's an orange tabby."

"Ah. Well, I'd like to meet him."

"Yeah, because you know, my mom went back to the boutique and she's renting the apartment above it. Finn moved in with Bettina, and with Stella staying with Ciceline a few days out of the week, it's just me and Pumpkin most of the time."

"I'll be right over," Lucy said.

They left the park, their steps in sync.

"I went to see your house," Jesse said. "It looks like it could be rebuilt, though it'll take forever. If you're looking to teach, you probably don't want to be too far away. You can stay with me. We lived together once before and it worked out."

Lucy walked with his head down. "I — yes. I would love to take you up on that."

"But? You're out of Carnelian now, right? You can do what you want."

"I will keep helping my father, and Ciceline asked me to advise her on policies. But yes, I'm out for good. I just don't know what to do with myself if someone doesn't tell me. I've never known anything else, and I'm afraid of literally everything. Being a vampire doesn't solve your whole life."

"Life isn't a thing to be solved," Jesse said. "It's a thing to be lived."

"Wow, Jesse, that's so deep. You should put that on a bumper sticker."

"Shut up." Jesse shoulder-checked him. "Tell you what. Let's go out to BLOOD this weekend. We'll just chill and make ridiculous requests from Archer."

"Archer's not DJing anymore," Lucy said. "They hired someone else."

"Thank god. After, we'll go to the loft and get whatever you need, and come back to mine. On Monday you can make some calls while I do rounds in the afternoon. It's just a start, Lucy, you don't have to do everything at once. And you don't have to do it alone."

Lucy leaned against him. "I like that idea. I'm not in a big rush. You only live once, for a really long time."

The fog burned off as they walked. The crows flew south overhead, silent, silhouetted against the afternoon sky. Jesse would not be separated from the shapes the sun made on the grass as it danced through the bare branches, would not be separated from the scent of the river on the breeze, the smell of the earth. Or from Lucy, walking beside him in the autumn sun. Jesse was only 34, and he had all the time in the world.

ACKNOWLEDGMENTS

It takes a team to write a book, and I have a big, amazing team. Thank you to Rachel Pollock and Crystal Schubert, my forever critique partners, and everyone at Red-Eyed Frog. Big thanks to my sensitivity readers, developmental readers, and fact and language checkers: Marissa Eller, Hannah Mugford, Emily Sexton, Raluca Tunison, Roxana Arama, and Ashley Stapleton Ellis.

My trusted beta readers, Kris S, Rena Soutar, Mary, Tanja, and Lena, thank you.

Shout-outs to my league of maternal cousins: Meg, Spence and Tasha, and Chrissie and Timmy, who are like sisters and brothers to me, and all the kids, who are like nieces and nephews. To The Bitches Of Eastwick and the TOTK meme chat, to Jeremy for hanging with me since high school, and to Kim for nights of ice cream, movies, and talking until 1 AM even on work nights about everything in the universe. And to my work-friends, for being so encouraging.

Such a tremendous thank you to my past agents, Caitlin McDonald and Emmy Nordstrom Higdon, for making me a better writer. I learned so much from both of you. Caitlin, your continued support has been immeasurably valuable. Thanks also to my past agent-sibs. You are all amazing!

All writers owe their gratitude to Victoria Strauss of Writer Beware. Thank you for looking out for us.

Huge thank you to my amazing cover artist WeirdUndead for bringing the cover to life, to Kota for being a fabulous editor and all-rounder, and everyone at Inked In Gray. You all make publishing so much fun!

Finally, none of you would be holding this book in your hands right now if it weren't for my wonderful editor and friend, Lauren Davila. Lauren, you are this book's hero. A million hearts to you!

About Jules Devito

Jules Devito was born in Queens, NY, and raised on eastern Long Island, where she still lives with her son, her Mom, two rescue Salukis, and some fish. Previous publications include "Little Red Riding Hood: Redux," and "The Tiny Book of Tiny Stories." Her work has been featured on Joseph Gordon-Levitt's HitRECord On TV. She is also a massage therapist, a dancer, a lapsed martial artist, occasionally an avian rehabber, a prolific fanfic writer, and a total beach goth.

Thank you from Inked in Gray Press

Thank you so much for reading Carnelian by Jules Devito! We hope you enjoyed it! We'd love for you to leave a review on any retail and review platforms such as Inked in Gray Press website, Bookshop.org, IndieStoryGeek, Goodreads, or Amazon.com

If you enjoyed Carnelian, we invite you to sign up to our spam-free newsletter where we share new releases, giveaways, and other bookish surprises. You can sign up here.

Printed in the USA
CPSIA information can be obtained
at www.ICGtesting.com
LVHW090719270924
792085LV00001B/5